A Lady's Rules for Seaside Romance

THE HARP & THISTLE
BOOK 3

ARDEN CONROY

DRAGONBLADE PUBLISHING, INC.

ARE YOU SIGNED UP FOR DRAGONBLADE'S BLOG?

You'll get the latest news and information on exclusive giveaways, exclusive excerpts, coming releases, sales, free books, cover reveals and more.

Check out our complete list of authors, too!

No spam, no junk. That's a promise!

Sign Up Here

www.dragonbladepublishing.com

Dearest Reader;

Thank you for your support of a small press. At Dragonblade Publishing, we strive to bring you the highest quality Historical Romance from some of the best authors in the business. Without your support, there is no 'us', so we sincerely hope you adore these stories and find some new favorite authors along the way.

Happy Reading!

CEO, Dragonblade Publishing

Chapter One

London, May 1899

THERE ARE TWO situations in which an unexpected, urgent letter is not only most unwelcome, but draws an additional essence of doom. Anytime past midnight, and in the midst of guests. The more guests present and more elevated the event, the more wrenching of the gut when the mysterious note is shoved beneath one's nose for examination posthaste.

Fortunately, this moment was neither past midnight nor amidst guests, because the sense of doom in the moment soared so high, it went above the London fog.

It was early afternoon, before The Harp & Thistle opened. Night didn't yet darken the windows of the famed London pub, and outside, the sun darted between gray clouds while people passed by going about their business. The employees of the pub, meanwhile, prepped and cleaned for opening.

Victor McNab scowled at the letter pressed between the extravagant footman's white-gloved fingers. The young footman's face was expertly blank as he waited with utmost patience. Victor ripped the letter out of the man's hand and shoved it into a trouser pocket without a glance. The footman didn't flinch, but the corners of his mouth turned down ever so slightly.

"I will not be joining you," Victor said in a low growl, knowing he would be expected to. "It can wait, and you may share my response with them."

The footman swallowed and twitched as if ready to argue, which would have been utterly foolish. Victor may have been in a plain, woolen waistcoat and trousers, his black hair and beard may have needed a good trimming to be in fashion, and his white, linen shirt could have used a pressing. He was rough inside and out and, by all appearances and surroundings, squarely working-class. Most thought he was. But this footman would have known the truth. And thus would have also known how offensive that slight twitch could be perceived.

As if coming to that same conclusion, the footman briefly bowed without comment then left.

Through the window, Victor watched the glossy, black carriage depart. There was, quite literally, only one reason a footman would dare step into his pub. However, Victor didn't have time to dwell on that reason, nor a desire to deal with it, either.

The sound of clinking glasses pulled Victor to his present task and he hitched back around the bar and over to the inventory book still laid open. He drew a finger down the page to where he kept track of the different types of glassware. Rocks glasses and pint glasses were their most used, but they also had a few wineglasses for the rare wine order, and a mix of others as well.

The wineglasses were mostly used by his brothers' wives. And the Dowager Marchioness of Litchfield. Or, as Victor had known her for countless years, Anne Winthrop.

"All right, I think I got them all." The interrupting voice nearly made Victor jump. Victor turned to look at his employee Dev Keer. Keer, a wisp of a man with a thin mustache, was looking down at a small pad of paper in his hand. He sniffed and pushed his spectacles back up his nose. "I counted eighty-two pint glasses, seventy-six rocks glasses, forty shot glasses, twelve wineglasses, twelve juice glasses, and thirteen pitchers."

Victor nodded slowly while his employee recited his findings. "The pint glasses and rocks glasses need to be at one hundred. How did we lose seven pitchers?"

Keer shrugged after writing on his notepad, then stuck the pencil behind his ear.

"Regardless, you know where the replacements are. They must be washed first."

Keer gave a grunt of agreement. "Who was that nob?"

Victor closed the inventory book. Though the majority of their patrons were regular Londoners, they were known to attract a few men from the nobility who occasionally preferred a less refined environment in which to imbibe. Or to place wagers on fights, especially when his brother Dantes used to be in the ring. "What nob?"

"The man who was just here."

"That was a footman."

"Ah." Keer stood there, waiting.

Victor's jaw tightened. For many years, the pub had been run solely by Victor and his brothers, Dantes and Ollie. It had been ten years now since the pub had been rebuilt and his brothers married. Because of these marriages, both men had pulled back from their responsibilities at the pub. Victor, of course, had had to hire other people to fill in the gaps. He didn't like having people outside the family work beside him, partly because he had to show them patience he wouldn't normally give to his brothers, but it had been a necessity. Especially since every year, the pub had been attracting more and more patrons.

Keer had worked for Victor almost two years now. There were three other men who worked full-time for Victor as well, and a few other men and women who were part-time, but Keer was the one Victor trusted most. He never complained, was always on time, and rarely needed days off. Keer learned quickly and took care as if the pub were his own. But most of all, like Victor, he used to work on the docks, which meant the man worked his arse off and wouldn't turn his nose up at a task, no matter how mundane or dirty. Victor heard nothing but good things when he asked around about Keer as well. But Keer was also not in a place to be nosy about Victor's personal life.

"It's none of your concern what he wants," Victor said darkly.

Keer didn't get the hint. "Aren't you curious what the note says? It seemed pretty important, delivered by a man as fancy as a peacock."

"No."

Keer inhaled from his nose, realizing belatedly he was overstepping. "Ah. Um, before I go back in the storeroom, there's something I wanted to talk to you about."

Victor glanced around the dark-wood-paneled room. They had two hours until opening, but the tables still needed to be wiped down one more time, and the floor needed to be mopped. A few lightbulbs needed to be replaced, and one glass lamp shade had been shattered the night before by a drunk fisherman telling a wild story about a mermaid. In his mind, Victor started listing the tasks that were being put off by a talkative employee.

"I've worked here for almost two years now," Keer said, bobbing on the balls of his feet.

Victor's attention snapped to the man.

"And, well, I wanted to discuss, um..." Keer fidgeted and scratched behind his ear. "Well, I would like a raise."

"A raise."

"Yes. I think I deserve it."

Victor stared at the man, who then responded with an awkward chuckle. Menacing stares were something both Victor and Dantes excelled in. Dantes terrified anyone who looked at him, mostly because of the deep scar slashed over his entire face, but he had a wildness about him as well. Victor, well, terrified people by simply existing. His voice was dark, his mood was dark, his expression naturally menacing. And he was more quiet than not. This put people off of him. Sometimes he used it to his advantage.

"Bold of you to ask for a raise before the two-year mark." Victor crossed his arms.

Keer scratched his jaw. "Is that a no?"

Victor's eye twitched. Patience. "I will consider it, and we will discuss it at a later date."

Relief spread over Keer's face and he retreated to the store-room to replace the lost glassware.

The front door to the pub opened. The blissful silence was suddenly punctured by the shrieks of two eight-year-old boys, the loud giggle of a two-year-old girl, and the overlapping chatter and laughter of Victor's brothers, their wives, Anne, and Anne's daughter, Lady Mary.

The twins, Theodore and Simon, immediately scrambled up two barstools and knit their little hands together patiently. As everyone else situated themselves—including setting down numerous boxes and bags—Victor went around the bar and stopped opposite his nephews. His niece, Lily, was still too young to sit atop the barstools and instead settled into Dantes's arms.

Victor placed his hands on the bartop. "What'll it be, lads?"

"Apple juice!" The boys grinned in unison. The twins were a funny pair. They looked exactly alike with their mother's red hair and their father's green eyes. But Theodore was the picture of prim, with his hair neat and his clothing crisp. Nothing ever seemed out of place with him. Simon, meanwhile, was the rascal of the two. Victor would often see flashes of Ollie in the boy when Ollie had been that age. Rambunctious, a bit of a mess, and always doing everything possible to make people laugh.

"No apple juice." Victor gave them a stern look. "One must ensure one drinks enough plain water each day. I can always tell when I haven't had enough water, I feel sluggish. There is something about juice that isn't quite as healthy as plain, old water."

The boys looked at each other then sighed when Victor gave them glasses of water.

"You know." Ollie came to stand behind his sons and frowned. "Most uncles at least try to be fun."

As Victor eyed his youngest brother, he poured pretzels into a bowl—a relatively healthy snack, all things considered—and the boys perked up when he pushed it toward them. Lily screeched,

"Pwetzels!" and Dantes grabbed a handful for the dark-haired girl.

Victor raised a sardonic eyebrow at Ollie, and Ollie rolled his eyes.

The children now occupied, Victor went back around to the patron side of the bar to greet everyone. They were all talking at once, per usual, but he somehow managed to figure out they had stopped by two modistes—the House of Worth and Madame Claudette—to pick up their dresses for the upcoming summer season.

Victor's attention went to Anne. He turned to face her fully and ignored everyone else, despite their ear-splitting volume.

"Guess what we did today?" Anne beamed up at him, causing his heart to skip a beat. Victor glanced over to Mary, who was gently bouncing from foot to foot. Mary had some resemblance to Anne but took strongly after her father, Bernard, who had been tall and lanky, with dark-brown hair. Anne, meanwhile, was blonde, blue-eyed, and shorter than her daughter.

Victor looked between them but couldn't guess what else they had done. However, he did note that behind Anne's excitement lay something else. Sadness, perhaps? "I don't know. What did you do today?"

Mary was the one who spoke up. "I was measured today!"

Victor crossed his arms. "For?"

Mary, he just now realized, was carrying a magazine. "My debut next year! Silly Uncle Victor. Look at this one." Mary showed him the cover of *Le Moniteur de la Mode* and flipped to a page inside. She then turned it so Victor could see better. It was an illustration of a model wearing a cream-colored dress with a long train and elaborate trim. There were bows, beads, and sequins over nearly every inch, like stars in the night sky. It even had pleats on the hem.

He couldn't even begin to guess how much something like that would cost. "That's very nice."

Mary laughed, glanced once more at the dress with awe, and then hugged the magazine tightly.

"But you don't debut until next year," Victor said. "Why were you measured today?"

Anne spoke. "Oh, it's a nearly year-long process and you have to get in as early as possible before their appointments are all filled. She will still need to go in for several fittings, not just for her presentation dress, but for several other dresses for the season."

Victor furrowed his brow. "But what if she grows?" The first time he'd met Mary, she'd been a small child, and he had watched her grow up through the awkward, gangly years to become the elegant young lady she was today.

Anne exchanged a giggle with Mary. "Victor, she's done growing. But just in case, the fittings will be able to address that."

"Oh." This revelation that Mary was done growing forever lifted an odd feeling with him, almost like nausea. He distracted himself by recalling the note in his pocket. "Actually, Anne, do you have a minute?"

Mary's eyes darted between them until they settled on Anne. "Mama, will you…?"

"Soon," Anne replied in a low voice. "Don't worry. Go show your Aunts Vivian and Evelyn your pretty dress again."

Seemingly satisfied, Mary practically skipped over to the women and they immediately flipped through the pages while huddled together.

Without saying anything, Victor began walking toward the back office while Anne followed. He shut the door behind them and went to sit on the edge of his desk. His lips pressed tightly as he tried to figure out what to say next.

But often, with him, words didn't come. Thus, he pulled the unopened letter out of his pocket and handed it to Anne.

Anne studied his face, her own pinched with the same concern he felt, and she gently took the envelope and observed it. "This is from the Duke of Invermark," she said after a long moment, her voice quieter than usual.

Victor didn't respond. He didn't need to.

Finally, she looked up at him again, now paled. "When is the last time you spoke to them?"

Victor sniffed. "Back when Ollie and Evelyn got into that trouble. You recall that?"

Anne blinked rapidly. "You haven't talked to them in almost ten years?"

"No. And before that, the last time I spoke to them was when I'd been sixteen."

Anne glanced down at the envelope. "Do your brothers know you received this?"

"No. A footman delivered it not long before you all arrived."

Anne turned it over. "You haven't opened it yet." She met his eyes again and he swallowed. "You're nervous to."

Again, he kept quiet, as she had figured it out on her own.

"Do you want me to open it?"

Victor held his hand out and she gave him back the envelope. "No, but..." He paused as he looked down at his calligraphed name on the front of the envelope.

Anne put a gloved hand on his forearm. He stared at it. "When Bernard died, you were there for me." She stammered a bit. "He and I had been separated for a year by that point, and we held no affection for each other. But we had two young children. It was difficult, as you know."

Her eyes held his as he recalled that time. With their families enmeshed through the marriage of Vivian and Dantes, Victor and Anne were family in a roundabout way. But it was more than that. Victor and Anne were friends as well. And when Bernard Winthrop, the former Marquess of Litchfield, had been killed after a drunken horse race at some country house in Kent, it had been hardly a thought for Victor to be there for Anne and help her navigate the sudden life change. Vivian was Winthrop's sister, and had done her best to help Anne, but she'd had her own emotions to face with her brother's death, and a young marriage to worry about as well. Regardless, Anne had seemed to prefer Victor's companionship during that time, thus they had quickly became good friends. It wasn't long before Anne had insisted he quit calling her "Lady Litchfield," as she thought the formality no longer necessary between them, but also because it made her think of her dead husband.

"You were solidified as my dearest friend from then on." Anne gave him a small smile that caused his heart to pick up its pace. She was a pretty woman, with her golden hair and clear, pale-blue eyes. Those eyes always belied the emotion she felt, no matter how much she tried to cover it up, but she usually wore her explosive emotions on her sleeve. But those eyes could hypnotize a man. Even now, Victor still could not fathom what in the blazes that cad husband of hers had been thinking. How could Winthrop have wanted more than what he'd already had? How could the idiot not see how lucky he had been?

Victor nodded in acknowledgment and ripped open the envelope. After taking a deep breath, he pulled out a piece of paper and read the single sentence written upon it.

It's the duke. You must come, posthaste.

Victor swore, then showed Anne the letter.

She read it. "Are you going to go?"

"I have no choice." He was rather sure what the visit would entail.

"Are you going to tell your brothers?"

Victor gave this some thought as he placed the letter back in the envelope. He looked at the closed door. "No. Not yet."

"When are you going to go?"

"As soon as you all leave. You will keep this to yourself, though, yes?"

Her brow furrowed. "Of course. Why don't you come by for dinner tonight? You can tell me what happens."

Victor nodded. It was fairly normal for him to dine with Anne and Mary, and Anne's son, Freddy—the current Marquess of Litchfield, though it was difficult for Victor to think of him that way—when he was home from school. He dined at Anne's house once a week. At the very least. But he had a horrible feeling that tonight, he would need her friendship in a dire way.

Chapter Two

"WHAT DID UNCLE Victor say, Mama? Did you ask him?"

Anne smiled at her daughter as they entered their home. Bernard had always hated their London residence because it was just outside of Mayfair by a few houses, thus they technically didn't have a Mayfair residence. But Anne loved it. It was bright and airy, with pastel-colored rooms and matching pastel furniture, more to her liking than the severe colors in fashion like red and black. Several footmen rushed past carrying boxes and bags to give to the maids to put away. The boxes and bags contained their wardrobe for the upcoming summer holiday in Brighton. Ever since Anne had married, she had spent every summer in Brighton, as it was where Bernard's family would go on holiday. His grandmother, the late dowager duchess, had had a beautiful home there she had passed on to Vivian.

But this would be Anne's last summer in Brighton, at least until her daughter married. Next year, with her daughter out, they would summer at one of the Duke of Chalworth's country residences so they could entertain for his granddaughter Mary's benefit. "I didn't have a chance to talk to him about that, dear. He had something else going on, and it wasn't a good time for that."

"Oh." Mary looked down, seemingly disappointed.

"There's plenty of time, though, don't you fret." Anne tried to sound positive. Her daughter wanted to ask Victor for a favor related to her debut next year. But now, with whatever was going on with the Duke of Invermark, she wasn't sure it was a good time to ask.

"What did he need to talk to you about?" Mary tried asking in a barely interested tone.

But, of course, Anne knew her daughter and knew how inquisitive she really was.

Anne directed Mary into one of the sitting rooms and rang for tea. "He will be coming by for dinner later. If he is up to it, he can tell you."

Mary pouted a bit in evident disappointment but didn't argue.

It was time to redirect. "Are you looking forward to the seaside?"

Mary clasped her hands together and shifted in her pastel-blue-cushioned chair. "Oh, yes! I am so excited. You promised you would allow me to attend balls there, remember?"

Anne sighed. "I remember."

"The full ball, that is. You've allowed me to attend the early parts of balls for the past two years. But this year, you promised I can stay the *entire time*."

At that moment, Lina, a maid who unfortunately strongly resembled a mouse, brought in their tea and began setting everything out for them. Anne had, in fact, promised this to Mary. The balls in Brighton were much smaller than the London balls and would be a good way for the young woman to get used to everything a ball entailed.

The maid left.

"I did promise that." Anne poured tea for her daughter and then herself. "Do you think you can manage your excitement for a few more weeks?"

Mary took a sip of her tea. "I think so. Though barely."

Anne chuckled. She recalled, with fondness, the sheer excitement an upcoming debut brought forth.

"And the pier!" Mary set her teacup down. "Promenading on the pier, going to the beach, the aquarium, the Royal Pavilion, shopping on Queen's Road—"

"More shopping?"

Mary looked up through her lashes. "Perhaps?"

Anne laughed. "We shall see when we get there." Anne was glad her daughter was looking forward to their holiday. "I know you are eager for next year, and I want you to enjoy your first year out, but we don't need to buy up *all* the fripperies in England."

Mary smiled. "Were you excited for your debut, too?"

"Of course. All women are to some degree."

"What was your debut like?"

Anne straightened and forced a smile on her face. "Very lovely. I recall the nerves I felt at the Queen Charlotte's Ball. It almost felt like a dream when it was my turn to approach Queen Victoria and the large birthday cake beside her, and curtsy. It felt as if someone else were controlling my body. Can you believe you will be curtsying to the same queen your old Mama once did?"

Mary laughed. "You're not so old." A funny look crossed Mary's face as she began to fuss with a glove button. "Is that where you met Papa?"

Anne took a sip of tea to buy time. Ever since her husband had died, they hadn't spoken of him often and the questions of how Anne and Bernard had met had been few and far between. It was only recently that her daughter had begun to notice young gentlemen and giggle over the idea of romance. It had taken longer than Anne had expected for Mary to ask about her meeting Bernard, but she'd also known it would come someday.

Anne recalled meeting her future husband for the first time clear as day. Bernard had been guffawing with a group of other young men, all of them holding some kind of a drink in their hands. The young marquess had been taking a sip from his glass when Anne had happened to be led past him by her mother. She'd glanced his way. He'd spotted her, stilled, and watched her like a hawk. At the time, it had made her feel special. "Yes. I met him at one of the balls, though not the Queen Charlotte's Ball."

Mary waited for a long beat before saying, "And? Then what happened?"

"Why, we married and had you and Freddy, of course!" Anne said brightly.

Mary opened her mouth as if she wanted to ask more questions about it—Anne knew by now her daughter had likely heard about Bernard's behavior that had led to the separation—but went an entirely different direction. "Do you think I'll find someone, Mama?"

Anne swallowed the lump in her throat and leaned toward her daughter, sandwiching Mary's hand between her own hands. "Of course you will," Anne said with seriousness. She could feel the tears forming in her eyes and hoped Mary didn't notice. "No need to rush it, though. You're only seventeen. It's quite all right to be out for a few years."

Her sweet daughter marrying. The thought, in truth, terrified Anne. But it was what people did, and there was nothing she could do to stop the inevitable from running at her at full speed.

Mary gently pulled her hand away and grabbed a small finger sandwich. She took a thoughtful bite and swallowed. "Freddy should be home soon, yes?"

"Yes!" Anne was grateful for the change in subject, even if her daughter likely hadn't done so intentionally. "Two weeks, then we will be leaving for Brighton soon after that."

"I do enjoy those train rides." Mary made a noise of excitement. "I love flying through the countryside, in those train cars with actual tables you can sit at and eat a meal with silverware and plates."

"It is very nice."

"Will Grandad be there?"

Anne nodded. "Grandad, your Aunt Vivian and Uncle Dantes, Uncle Ollie and Aunt Evelyn, and of course all of their children. The same as every year."

Mary took another thoughtful bite of her finger sandwich. "Do you dance at balls, Mama?"

Anne blinked. "Mary, that's quite a nosy question."

But Mary only stared back with wide, innocent eyes.

"Of course I don't dance at balls. I'm a widow."

Mary's eyebrows furrowed. "I didn't realize that meant you could never dance again."

Anne set her teacup down. Why was this conversation making her so nervous? "I suppose technically, now that so much time has passed, I could. But I'm not really that interested in it, to be honest."

Mary took in a breath. "Why wouldn't you want to dance?"

Anne cleared her throat. "Mary, dear, I'm not a young lady like you."

"Well, you aren't an old one, either. What if you marry again—will you dance then?"

Her cheeks were feeling hot. Anne gently pressed her hands against them. "Marry again? Oh, that, I doubt very much."

Mary shifted in her seat in a way that looked like she was settling in. Anne braced herself because her daughter did this right before beginning a long discussion about something. Anne didn't understand where this line of questioning was coming from, either. Neither Mary nor Freddy had ever asked if she would marry again. But maybe, because it had been so long, it made sense they would start to wonder. "Mama, you should try to find a dashing gentleman this summer."

"Oh, dear, I don't think so." This conversation was making Anne uncomfortable. Why was her daughter encouraging this?

"Why not? You don't dance anymore. You hardly go to any parties. You barely socialize with anyone outside of the family."

Anne opened her mouth to deny this but promptly shut it closed. It was true. A widow was required to mourn for two years, perhaps four, at most. But in that time, maybe Anne had gotten too used to the isolation. Though she had been going to balls the past few years, she'd never really participated in them, other than watching from the side.

"I don't know about that," Anne finally said, her voice wary.

She poured more tea into both of their cups, needing to do something.

"Well…" Mary lifted her teacup and her eyes lit up. "What if you treat this summer as your own debut?"

"Mary." Anne placed her palms on her lap, trying to will patience. "I think it's very nice you are worried about me so much, but I really don't want to do that. I'm quite happy being on my own and being a mother to you and Freddy. I don't need to be married, or be a wife. I'm rather content with the way things are. Being your mama is all I want."

Mary gave a little pout.

"I know the idea of balls and dancing and romance is exciting to you, but I'm forty years old, dear. I was married once already. None of that appeals to me in the least anymore."

Mary let out a long, dramatic sigh. "I think it's splendid for someone to fancy you. Do you not wish for that excitement, hoping to see the gentleman you fancy while out for a promenade? Or look around the crowd at a ball hoping you will get a glimpse of him, and he of you while you sparkle?"

Anne narrowed her eyes. "You speak about this as if you've experienced it yourself."

Mary took a hasty sip of tea, but her pinked cheeks belied her true feelings. "Surely not."

"Hmm." Anne studied her daughter and it was quite clear the young woman was trying to feign innocence. Mary was always chaperoned by either Anne, one of the aunts, or the governess. Then again, the young lady was almost of age. It wasn't completely out of the question that she may have admired a young gentleman or two from afar during rides through Hyde Park or when she'd been allowed to attend the first hour or two of a ball during moments of social mingling.

Anne made a hasty decision. "Mary, my dear, I think it's time we have an honest discussion about men."

Mary's eyes went wide and she hastily set her cup back down on its saucer. "You make it sound dreadful."

"That's because it is," Anne said. She ran her hands over her skirt. "The most important thing you need to know about men is, nine times out of ten, they are not to be trusted."

Mary blinked several times. "What does that mean?"

How was Anne supposed to explain this without squashing her daughter's hopes and romantic heart? "What I mean is, some men will do anything to tempt you into getting into trouble if it benefits them. Others will do sneaky things that would upset you if you ever found out. They're also larger and stronger and can quite easily hurt you."

There was a flicker of pain in Mary's eyes. "Surely, they can't all be bad?"

"No, of course not." Anne thought about Freddy and that familiar sense of worry for his future churned in her stomach. "But you have to be careful. Very, very careful. They are good at hiding the darkness in their hearts." Anne sighed to herself. Mary wouldn't ask outright, but Anne knew she was likely thinking of her uncles, the McNabs. All of them were good men. But even *they* had their own sordid pasts. Dantes and Ollie both had been forthcoming about their wild pasts to their wives, so she respected them for that. And they doted on their wives now, at least.

Oddly, Victor had been quiet regarding his own past. Dantes and Ollie would both openly admit to their past scoundrel behaviors, but Victor had never mentioned anything like that—ever. In fact, Anne had never known him to have a woman in his life. She assumed he had kept that all secret for reasons known only to him. And she also assumed he would never marry like his brothers had, either.

Though she supposed that wasn't so surprising. Victor was a private person, often closed off, and didn't talk much about his past in general, though over the years, he had provided her with snippets of it. She knew he had spent his first years of life wealthy because his father, who had been banished from his noble family, had founded a railway. Then when Victor had been ten years of age, both of his parents had died and the brothers had ended up living on the streets of Whitechapel, where their mother had been from. Even though their grandparents, who had disowned their son, had eventually taken them in several years later, Victor never had returned to the life he had been born into. He seemed to embrace the working-class side of London, and from the age of sixteen on had been completely on his own, working on the docks and odd jobs here and there until the brothers had started The Harp & Thistle. Anne had never asked but always assumed the brothers had been disinherited, like their father had been.

Victor didn't partake in society events like his brothers did thanks to their wives. And he had, on numerous occasions, expressed he had absolutely no desire to, either.

To Anne's relief, Mary seemed to lose interest in the conversation and went on to more lighthearted subjects, such as a new puppy her friend Lady Tabitha had received for her birthday. Anne listened with interest, but her mind was still on the subject of men.

All Anne knew was that she didn't want Mary to end up with someone like her father. But how did a mother explain that to her daughter?

Chapter Three

WHEN VICTOR ARRIVED at the Duke of Invermark's townhome in Mayfair, he was ushered in immediately. The stout, bald butler led him quickly through the home instead of right into the receiving room. As they hurried, Victor thought he heard weeping. It was quiet, and muffled, but in the silence of the house, he could still hear it.

Victor stopped. "Is someone crying?"

The butler paused, too, and his mouth opened a bit, as if unsure what to say. But the man was saved from making that decision when double doors up ahead flew open. "Is that Victor?" a woman's shaky voice called out.

Victor and the butler made eye contact, and the stoic man gave Victor a small nod, indicating he was allowed to go to that room.

Victor blew out a breath and headed to the room, his feet feeling like leaded weights.

The Duchess of Invermark was inside the room waiting for him. She clutched a handkerchief close to her person, and her eyes were red. It had been years since he had last seen her, and her eighty-some years were showing. As long as he had known her, she had never been thin. But she had lost considerable weight since he had seen her last, and the fullness in her face that had always given her a youthful look had lessened.

"Victor, you came." She smiled through her tears.

"What's happened? I received your note and came as soon as I was able to."

The duchess opened her mouth to respond. But instead, she began to wail.

Victor took a hesitant step forward. "Marjory."

She sniffed. "Your grandfather. He's dying!" The wailing turned up.

Victor felt the blood drain from his face and he took a few stumbling steps before collapsing into a nearby chair. He'd suspected that was the reason for the visit. He and his grandparents had no relationship and otherwise would have had no reason for him to visit. But he was not prepared for this day to come. "How sick is he?"

Marjory sniffed and dabbed at her eyes. "He's not sick."

Oh, blast. The duke was already dead! Victor's heart rate shot up alarmingly and he slouched further into his chair.

Marjory set a fist on her hip. "I said he is *not* sick!"

But Victor hardly heard her. All he could think about was his pub. The Harp & Thistle. What was he going to do with it?

"Victor!" Marjory shouted the word and stomped a foot.

Victor's thoughts immediately cut off, but he still couldn't form words.

The door opened. "Marjory, are you crying *again?*" A man's voice came through the door.

Victor's grandfather, the Duke of Invermark, sauntered in. Victor could hardly believe his eyes and jumped up to his feet. "What is the meaning of this?!" The duke was not dying. He was not sick, nor already dead. In fact, there seemed to be nothing wrong.

His grandmother had given him the fright of his life.

Victor was next in line to the dukedom, as his father had been dead since his childhood. Once the Duke of Invermark passed, Victor would become the duke himself.

It was as ominous as it sounded.

Victor didn't know anything about being a duke. He was a pub owner—he worked on the docks. He'd grown up in Whitechapel. Well, for part of his life anyway.

Eventually, he'd made the decision to leave the aristocracy behind for good and embrace his working-class roots.

And ever since then, he had been in deep denial about the fact that one day he would have to take over the dukedom. Whether he wanted to or not.

He had been sure today was that day and had nearly expired from it. But his grandfather, though in his nineties, looked as healthy as one could be.

The Duke of Invermark took his wife's hands in his. "We talked about this," he said in a warning voice.

"I know." She sniffed again and dabbed at her eyes. She then cleared her throat. "Now would be a good time, don't you think?"

The duke looked over at Victor, who was still standing. "You're right. Give us a moment?" the duke said. His duchess nodded and hurried out of the room, shutting the door behind her.

"Thank you for coming," the duke said. Unlike Marjory, Fergus looked the same as Victor remembered except with a slightly more aged face. Fergus had been gray as long as Victor could remember. He also had a head of hair and a beard that was the envy of many men. He was built how Victor imagined their ancient highlander ancestors had been built. Tall, wide-shouldered, large torso, strong arms and legs. Fergus's wild, green eyes, the McNab green Victor and all his brothers had inherited, were as bright and lively as ever.

Nothing seemed wrong at all.

"Why have I been summoned?" Victor asked while forcing a bored expression. Finally, his heart was beginning to calm.

Fergus lifted his bushy, gray eyebrows and meandered over to a large portrait above the fireplace of the duke and duchess and their son. It had been painted when Victor's father had been a boy. And he saw far too much of himself in that child.

He looked back at his grandfather.

"Have I ever told you how our line of McNabs came to be?"

Victor bit the inside of his cheek. Had he been summoned here for a blasted history lesson? "I don't recall."

Fergus put his full attention on his grandson. "One thousand years ago, our direct ancestor—let's say our twentieth or so great-grandfather—was returning to shore after war. Probably a battle with those blasted Campbells."

"You tried to get Ollie to marry a Campbell woman." Victor couldn't resist pointing this out.

Naturally, Fergus denied this and closed his eyes briefly for effect. "I would never do such a thing."

Victor rubbed his temple. "Get on with the story."

"As I was saying, our ancestor was returning from battle. There were many men pulling the boats and whatever else they had ashore. They were unloading their injured, their dead, what have you. As they were doing so, our grandfather noticed a woman on a rocky outcrop. She was the most beautiful woman he had ever seen in his life. Curiously, she paid no mind to the filthy, hungry men. She was watching over the water, as if men returning from battle had no interest to her. Oddly, none of the other men seemed to notice her much, either, which he thought was strange. Eventually, her interest in the sea waned and she looked over at our grandfather and they made eye contact. She smiled at him and he fell in love immediately. But he couldn't do anything about it at the time. He forced himself to return to his task, to help his clan."

Fergus was on about some fairy tale. The man loved to tell stories, from what Victor remembered. But this was the first one he recalled where their family had been woven into it.

"That night," Fergus continued, "our grandfather asked if anyone knew who she was. Unfortunately for him, no one did. Night after night, day after day, he went to the rocky outcrop, hoping to see her again. But he didn't."

Fergus stopped and watched Victor expectantly.

Victor lowered his eyelids, and in the most unaffected voice he could muster, said, "And then what happened?"

"Eventually, he gave up. But one year to the day later, he took one last hopeless chance and returned to the rocky outcrop."

"Let me guess—she was there." *Christ, get to the point!*

"Ah." Fergus held up a finger and mischief glinted in his green eyes. "When he arrived, he scrambled across the rocks and became startled when a seal leapt out of the water, landing in front of him."

Victor frowned. *A seal?*

"The seal lounged, as seals do."

"Of course."

"But then—" Fergus squinted, one eye more squinted than the other, and he shook his finger at Victor. "Then the seal took its skin off like a coat, flung it to the side, and out came the beautiful woman!"

Victor wrinkled his nose.

"They married and had ten children, all of whom lived to see one hundred years."

This was a waste of time. "Fergus, I didn't come here for fairy tales."

"Och." Fergus crossed his arms.

However, despite the fact that Victor knew he could leave, he couldn't help but poke at his grandfather and his ridiculous story. "How did that even work? Was she nude or did she have clothing on beneath her seal coat?"

Fergus turned his eyes up to the ceiling and tapped his chin.

"And then, what, he brings this nude woman home with him to his clan and they all cheer and that's it? They wouldn't find it suspicious, think she was an enemy, or anything like that?"

"Well, those details have been lost to time."

Victor sighed. "I should go." And he took a few steps.

Despite his age, Fergus was able to scramble faster than Victor and stand in front of him to block him. "I haven't finished yet, laddie. They had a happy marriage, or so the story says. But the day their youngest child turned seventeen, she was called back to the sea and left her husband and life behind."

"That's a terrible ending."

"The ending isn't the point, Victor. The point is every single one of their children had a selkie for a mother. A creature with magical blood."

Victor stepped to the side and again began walking to the door. "What in the blazes is a selkie?" He called over his shoulder as he began to pull the door open, but Fergus's huge, meaty hand slammed it shut.

"A selkie is a woman who can shapeshift into a seal when she wears her seal skin. A woman with magic. My point, Victor, is that we descend from a magical creature."

Victor checked his pocket watch. He would be expected at Anne's soon. "Fantastic story. May I go now?"

"No." Fergus then extended an inviting hand to a nearby chair.

With a sigh, Victor went over to it and sat. Fergus took a seat in another chair. "I asked you to come here to let you know I'm dying."

Victor clenched a fist but otherwise didn't show his distress outwardly. "You look and seem perfectly fine to me. Aside from your seal story."

"I know." Fergus looked out into the room with an empty gaze. "The fact remains that I am over ninety years. But alas, unlike our twentieth great-grandfather's half-magical children, I will not reach one hundred. But most in our line do live exceptionally long lives."

Victor felt darkness roll over him. "Except my father, right?"

Fergus's eyes immediately snapped to Victor. "Generation after generation, we have an abnormal number of centenarians. But we are *not* immortal." His voice sharpened. "Your father chose to abandon his responsibilities, take up with a woman from a low class, and then die from one of his insipid locomotives."

Thirty years had passed since Victor had *abandoned his responsibilities* as well and run away from his grandparents—this house—at sixteen years of age. A big reason behind his decision to leave had been arguments regarding his father and comments about his mother.

Victor rubbed a hand over his face. Defending his parents for the thousandth time would not solve anything and he would rather just leave instead.

"All right, fine, you're dying," Victor redirected. "But you said you're not sick." Victor was trying to figure out what in the blazes was the point his grandfather was trying to make. "Just because you're over ninety doesn't mean you're about to die. You could still have several years left, and for my sake, I sincerely hope you do."

Fergus sunk back into his seat and knit his fingers together. "I am fit as a fiddle, aye. Feel as healthy as can be. But I will be dying this summer and I know that as fact."

Victor leaned forward, concerned. "You aren't planning to—"

"Och, no." Fergus waved a hand, but there was a long pause as he weighed what to say next. "There was a point to my selkie story. While we may be one thousand years out from it, magic remains in our blood, though it has lessened over time."

Victor lifted an eyebrow and thought about Dantes's lifelong bad luck. Or good luck, depending on how you looked at it. And Ollie had once commented a few years ago about being able to talk to ghosts. At the time, Victor had suggested Ollie visit a doctor. But could that have been... No, that was ridiculous. Victor waved that thought away. Selkies weren't real, and the McNabs didn't have magical blood. Victor certainly didn't.

Fergus leaned forward and said in a low whisper, "I can predict my death."

Of course, Victor didn't believe this for a moment, but he decided to humor the old man anyway. "And how do you know you're going to die this summer?"

"A feeling." Fergus tapped his head.

"Right." With a sigh, Victor slapped his palms down to the arms of his chair. "I should go."

"You are missing the key piece here, Victor." The elderly duke rose at the same time. "I *know* I will die in the next few months. I am giving you fair warning, something other heirs do not get the benefit of."

"You're not going to die this summer."

"Aye, but I am, whether or not Marjory or I—or you—like it." Fergus began leading him to the door but then went a bit off to the side to a table. There was a thick stack of paper atop it, tied neatly with twine. Fergus took it and handed it to Victor.

"What is this?" Victor asked as he took it.

"Everything about the dukedom you'll need to know. The properties, the servants at each property, tenants, financials, etcetera."

A flush of heat hit Victor. But, no, the duke dying this year was preposterous. Victor gave his grandfather one last look over. Yes, the man was old. But he was still spry, though a bit creakier than he had been his younger days. He could hear just fine, see just fine, and still had the bulking form typical of the McNab men. If Fergus lived another ten years, Victor wouldn't be surprised in the least.

But he did remain the heir, whether he liked it or not.

"Any chance someone else could take over instead?" Victor asked. "Someone far more suitable than myself? I think we both would agree of my brothers, I am the least suited for the position."

Fergus let out a grumbling noise as he looked over his grandson. "In truth, I can't imagine you rubbing elbows with aristocrats. Perhaps you should find a way to make yourself more suitable, then."

Victor lifted an eyebrow as he hefted the mass of papers in his arm. "And how do you suppose I do that?"

"I haven't the faintest idea. The one good thing about knowing you're going to be dead soon is you find you stop caring about things that don't matter. And, frankly, I could care less what happens to the dukedom once I'm gone. If you make a fool of yourself, it has no effect on me."

As there was nothing more to say on the subject, and he desperately wanted to leave, Victor moved to the door.

"Ah, just one last thing," Fergus said. "Do you think…?" The elderly man was, for the first time Victor had ever seen, at a loss for words. Fergus cleared his throat. "Could we have been better grandparents?"

"Yes," Victor replied.

Fergus nodded, considering this. "Dantes came back around. And Oliver never left us once we brought you boys in. Could we have done something to get you to come home before now?"

Victor stared back unblinking, feeling darkness trying to overtake him. "That depends. I know you were upset with my father when he married my mother. They had us. Didn't you wonder what happened to us after he died? After *she* died?"

"Victor, laddie, your mother was a laudanum addict from the slums. And Irish, at that. Look at where we are right now." Fergus glanced around the opulent room. "She didn't belong here. And do you think she'd wanted anything to do with us?"

Victor scowled, remembering the times he hadn't eaten for days in order to feed his younger brothers. The violence they'd witnessed. The never-ending peril and worry as he, a child himself, had taken care of two small, orphaned children. "You didn't answer the question. Ollie was a toddler!"

There was no emotion in Fergus's eyes. The man did not seem affected by this at all. And his answering shrug solidified that.

"Then, no," Victor said in a dangerous voice. "You couldn't have done anything to bring me back."

"Fair enough, then." Fergus opened the door but didn't pass through it to walk Victor out. "Good luck, then, laddie."

Victor walked out of the room without responding. And he didn't look back as he walked out the door.

Chapter Four

ANNE PACED IN her parlor, feeling unusually nervous while awaiting Victor's arrival. She walked back and forth across the floor while peering out the window and fidgeting her hands, as if this could somehow calm her nerves.

He should be here soon. Any moment now. He was always punctual, arriving at the exact same time for every single dinner they'd had together now all these years.

Victor had been having the occasional dinner with her and the children for nearly ten years now. It was something she had suggested they start after his brother Ollie had married Evelyn—which had left Victor the only unmarried brother in their family. She'd known he didn't have any other family, aside from a few people with whom he wanted no contact, and would be seeing his brothers much less. Although she had to admit it had been a bit improper for her, a married woman, to invite an unwed man without her husband present, separated though she and the marquess had been. But to her, it hadn't seemed so bad, as they were related through marriage in a roundabout way thanks to Vivian and Dantes. Plus, Anne had thought Victor could use the company. At first, he'd seemed a bit uncomfortable, especially around the children, but he'd kept coming back anyway. And after some time, it had become normal.

Anne briefly paused in her pacing as her mind went back to

that time in her life, when her dinners with Victor had begun.

Her separation from Bernard had begun not long after his and Vivian's grandmother had died. The older woman had left her entire fortune to Vivian when it had been expected to go to Bernard. When that had happened, something in him seemed to change.

Bernard had never been a good husband—he'd succumbed to every temptation within reach of an aristocratic man—and he'd treated her horribly. But when his sister, Vivian, had received the fortune, Bernard had turned into a monster.

He'd hidden it well enough to outsiders. The queen, for example, had been completely charmed by him until the very end and had wept at his funeral. But there was an exact moment Anne could pinpoint that had changed their marriage permanently, and ended any last bit of affection she'd held for him.

They—or, it turned out, just Anne—had cut back on spending to improve their dire finances from his scoundrel habits. Anne had gone to a millinery with Vivian and there had been a pale-blue hat with a bow-shaped adornment Anne had fallen utterly in love with. It had matched her pale eyes and gone well with her fair features. She'd felt stunning in it during a time in her life where she'd had very little self-confidence.

As it had turned out, Vivian had secretly bought the hat for Anne. Anne had, of course, been furious at first. But Anne had decided to wear it once, hoping her husband would see how pretty she'd looked in it. Maybe he would remember the young lady he had chosen to marry. Maybe he would stay home with her instead of leaving for the evening like he always had. It had been silly of her to think a hat could change a man, but she'd been desperate.

He'd come home that day, drunk as usual, and seen the hat. Anne, who hadn't wished to lie, had told the truth about where it had come from when he had asked. Something in Bernard had seemed to crack. His rich sister, the sister who had a fortune he thought was owed to *him*, had bought the hat for Anne.

They'd been near his desk and in a fit of rage, he'd shoved the contents of the desk to the floor. Then he'd shoved Anne and she'd fallen to the ground.

Of course, the children had heard the commotion and come running in with the governess. Freddy and Mary had seen Anne sprawled out on the floor with Bernard looming over her, red-faced with anger. The children had both been quite young at the time. And while Mary had been too stunned to react, Freddy, the brave boy, had stepped in front of Anne to defend her. And Bernard had responded by slapping him across the face.

A child. *His* child.

Bernard had fled, and once she had calmed the children down—Freddy had been far more level than she had expected—Anne had immediately gone to the only person who could help her: the Duke of Chalworth.

At first, he'd seemed to not want anything to do with the situation. It was not unusual for a man to mistreat his wife in such a way, and it could have been argued Anne had been lucky it hadn't been worse. That was, until she told him, "Bernard likely will not live long enough to inherit the dukedom. His body will succumb to alcohol or idiocy before that. Your son slapped the next Duke of Chalworth. He *will* do it again. It *will* get worse. And only *you* can do anything about it."

With the threat his son had imposed on his small grandson, the duke had seemed to come to terms with reality. In an unprecedented move, the duke had forced his son out of the familial home, cut his funds down to a paltry weekly amount, and told the scoundrel to fix himself if he wanted anything back. Bernard couldn't even see his own children without the duke there, and this was a country where children went with their father during separations. They *never* stayed with their mother.

Not so long after, Bernard had succumbed to both the alcohol and the idiocy. He never had attempted to see his children after the first few months.

"Mama." Mary's voice pulled Anne back to the present.

"What are you doing?"

Anne blinked a few times, remembering with relief that it was 1899 and not 1889. "What do you mean by that?"

Mary grinned as if she knew a secret. "You are pacing. Why do you always pace before Uncle Victor comes for dinner?"

Anne lifted her chin. "I do not."

"Oh?"

"I'm merely impatient because I'm quite curious about an errand he had to run today." She knew he'd been summoned to see his grandfather, the Duke of Invermark. She had been so blasted curious about what that meant. Victor despised his grandparents, and they showed an equal interest in him. The duke must have been quite ill if he'd been reaching out.

"There he is!" Mary jumped with excitement and pointed at a dark figure who walked by the window. "Hurrah! Uncle Victor is here!" Mary immediately ran out into the hallway, leaving Anne behind without a thought.

Anne's heart raced. It was a silly thing, always doing this when she saw Victor. Of course, she did secretly think he was an attractive man—anyone could see that. He was tall, with broad shoulders, and she knew he often had to move and lift heavy objects at the pub. Often, she caught herself watching when he did. Beneath his clothing, he was probably quite muscular. And his thick, black hair and beard led her to wonder about…

Anne pressed a hand to one cheek and pushed the thought away. What was she doing, thinking such things! She reeled herself back to propriety. No, she didn't mind looking at Victor. But she wouldn't *dare* act on it. He was her dearest friend in the whole world, and the children adored him. After everything Bernard had done, Victor was a positive male influence in the children's lives. If she pursued anything, which she wouldn't, eventually, it would have to end, as she saw no future with *any* man. She had already learned once the kind of a hold a man could have over a woman. She would never let herself get into such a vulnerable position ever again.

The butler, Harris, opened the front door and Mary immediately began making excitable conversation. Victor, of course, remained silent, but Anne knew well enough he was listening to every word her daughter uttered.

Anne appeared in the hallway and Victor's attention immediately went to her. He gave her that intense stare she never could get used to. Maybe it was the piercing, green eyes. She shook away the spine-tingling feeling it caused.

Anne began to approach them as Harris took a stack of paper from under Victor's arm. It was tied together with twine. What was that for? "How do you greet guests, Mary? Is it by badgering them with a breathless string of questions and stories?"

Victor held Anne's gaze for several beats longer before returning his attention to Mary.

Mary gave him a hasty curtsy. "Sorry, Uncle Victor. How is the weather?"

Though Victor didn't laugh or smile—he never really did— amusement danced in his eyes. "The weather? Why, Lady Mary, don't you have more interesting conversation, such as the dress you had picked out earlier?"

Naturally, Mary returned to her rapid discussion about visiting the two modistes, and her debut next year. It would be all she would talk about for weeks. If not months.

Anne smiled and shook her head with amusement. "Mary, dear, why don't you go look at your fashion magazines for a bit while I visit with Victor? I'll let you know when it's time to join us."

"Oh, all right, Mama!" Mary immediately rushed up the stairs to her bedroom, where Anne knew magazines from Paris were spread all over her bed.

Anne motioned for Victor to follow and they went into the parlor. "As you can see, she is very excited. It's all she wants to talk about."

"I imagine such an event is exciting for a young lady."

Anne went to sit in a chair, and Victor followed into another.

"It is." She paused. "She's been begging me to ask you something. I'm not sure how you will feel about it."

Victor's brow furrowed ever so slightly. "Yes?"

Anne began to fidget and kept her eyes averted. "She wants to know if you will attend her coming out ball next year for the season, one that I will be hosting. She wanted you to be her chaperone, since Bernard isn't here, but I told her *no* because you're an unmarried man. As an alternate, she *may* have asked that you be the one to propose a toast at the dinner. I did say I wasn't sure how you would feel about that, though, and suggested Dantes instead, since he's truly her uncle by marriage and the one in your family fully immersed into the ton and—"

"Anne." Victor leaned toward her, looking quite serious. "Take a deep breath."

Anne's widened eyes lifted to his and she did as he suggested.

"One more, for good luck."

She gave him a small smile but took another deep breath. It did help, and her voice calmed. "You really only need to say a few quick words, show your face for a bit, let her see that you were there. I know you wouldn't want to be around something like that for long. But it would mean a lot to her."

Victor bowed his head. "I would be quite pleased to do that for your daughter, unless *you* would prefer someone else? Someone a bit more refined?"

"No! No, of course not." She knew he was likely referring to her father or the Duke of Chalworth. However, her parents were often on the Continent and would never interrupt their never-ending holidays for their daughter or granddaughter. And while the duke would be happy to give a speech about his granddaughter, Mary was quite insistent on it being Victor. "You're not unrefined, Victor. Oh, Mary will be so pleased to hear you will be there and do that for her."

But the happiness of this was short-lived, and worry set upon her brow.

Victor leaned forward again, clasping his hands together.

"Something else is on your mind."

He knew her so well. "Mary has been asking me about my debut. And about Bernard."

Victor stilled. "Has she?"

Anne pressed her lips together tightly and nodded. A footman, David, appeared with a glass of whiskey for Victor and a glass of wine for Anne.

After thanking the man, the pair took thoughtful sips. Victor spoke first. "What do your children know about everything that happened?" He paused. "Forgive me. That's none of my business."

This was a topic they had never really breeched before. Victor had known Bernard for a long time, as Bernard used to be a regular at their pub. The McNabs were all quite familiar with Bernard and his habits, thus it wasn't something she and Victor had ever really talked about. He already knew most of it. Admittedly, it wasn't really something she *wanted* to talk about, either. But with Mary's debut looming, it was a subject that could no longer be avoided. Especially with her dearest friend.

"Don't be silly, Victor," Anne said with reassurance. "You, of all people, should know you can ask me about anything." She set her wineglass to the side. "Well, I told her the truth about my own excitement about my debut. About meeting her father, and all of that." She forced a smile.

Victor waited a beat, studying her face. "There is something about it you are grappling with."

So perceptive. "Yes." Anne recalled the hat story, which she had never told Victor about. "The children once saw what Bernard was capable of. But they were otherwise ignorant to his behaviors. To them, he was simply a very busy marquess. Of course, you and I both know his absence wasn't for important reasons. He was at brothels, or gambling, or drinking."

Anger flashed in Victor's eyes. "What do you mean, they once saw what he was capable of?"

But Anne waved him off. "It doesn't matter. It's long in the past."

"Anne." He said it on a whisper.

She looked away. "Anyway, I'm trying my best to be excited for Mary. Admittedly, her upcoming debut brings up feelings of dread, of worry. But I refuse to let my past color my daughter's future. I will be nothing but positive for her."

Victor nodded slowly.

"Marriage is a farce, Victor. Especially for women."

Victor's dark brows pulled together. "Marriage can be good, Anne. My brothers have been married to their wives for years now. I never thought either of them would ever be happy in such an arrangement. But they are." He leaned forward a bit. "You are close with Vivian and Evelyn. Have they ever expressed regret in marrying my brothers?"

"Of course not," she replied, a bit aghast at such a question. "I'm surprised at you, Victor. You've always been quite vocal about your dislike of marriage. On numerous occasions, you've said you would never want a wife or children."

"The responsibility of it does terrify me, yes." Victor rubbed at his chin, as if lost in thought. Anne forced herself to remain quiet and see what he said next. Had his visit with his grandfather changed his mind? Would he want a duchess at his side? Heirs?

Oh, the mere thought of having to go through pregnancy and labor again nearly made her shudder. Another reason Anne would never again be a wife.

"Though I can't recall the last time I've made that comment," Victor said slowly.

"What are you saying, you've changed your mind?" Anne tilted her head. "Are you saying you *want* to get married?"

"I…" Victor blinked several times at himself and then met her eye again. "No."

Something about this conversation was increasingly bizarre and Anne wanted nothing to do with it. *Time to move on.* "Enough about that. I have been on pins and needles waiting to hear about your visit with your grandfather. What was that stack of paper you brought with you?"

"Hell." Victor regarded his glass of whiskey, avoiding her eye.
Anne furrowed her brow. "'Hell'?"

"Business-related hell."

"Ah. So? Your grandfather, is everything all right? Is he ill?"

Victor let out a long sigh and glanced at the empty fireplace.
"The man is as healthy as one can be at his age."

"Oh. But that's good news, isn't it? I know you don't wish to
take his place."

"It *is* good news." But the way his gaze was vacant, to Anne,
it seemed as if he were unsure.

Anne waited for him to continue, but he didn't. Apparently,
she would need to fish it out. "What did he wish to talk to you
about, then?"

Victor put his attention squarely back on her and his stare
caused her heart to hitch. "He wanted to tell me I'm related to a
seal."

Anne laughed loudly, but, when she realized Victor was
serious, immediately recovered by clearing her throat. "Forgive
me. A seal?"

Victor suddenly rose up to his feet and went over to a window that looked out at the sidewalk and street beyond that. He
pressed a hand to the wall beside it and told her a ridiculous story
about being related to a magical creature called a 'selkie.' The
Duke of Invermark seemed to truly believe it, and that the
McNabs had magic in their blood. Which, of course, was
preposterous.

Finally, Victor said, "Fergus told me he will die this summer.
He's convinced of it, that he can predict or sense his death
because of the magic in our blood." He then scoffed.

Anne went to his side. She put a light hand on his arm and
tilted her head back to see him better. Victor's hand immediately
dropped from the wall and he stared down at her with intensity.

Anne lightly rubbed his arm for comfort, ignoring the hardness she felt under his sleeve. "It will be fine, Victor. No one can
predict their own death. I'm sure you still have plenty of time

before taking over the dukedom."

Victor merely stared back, silent.

Anne pulled her hand away from him. The moment felt too intimate in a way, and if someone walked in right now, she would be embarrassed.

Victor seemed to return to himself as well and he looked away from her. "Those papers I brought, it isn't business-related. Pub-wise, I mean. Though it does contain hell."

She lifted her eyebrows. "What is it, then?"

"It's everything I need related to the dukedom. Fergus said I should familiarize myself with it before it's too late."

"That isn't the worst idea. You haven't been a part of that world for a very long time."

Victor's throat moved on a swallow. "I know." Then his green gaze returned to hers. "It isn't merely about the responsibil-ities it entails. It's the people as well. I don't know anyone anymore." He rushed a hand through his dark hair. "I went to prep school at eight years of age, just like everyone else. But I left when my father died. My grandparents sent me back at sixteen, but I didn't last more than a few months. And that was it. I hardly remember any of those lads anymore. I don't care if I'm related to Fergus, or to a blasted seal—I'm not of your ilk."

"You mean, you're not a titled aristocrat."

"Yes."

"But that isn't the reality, Victor, no matter what your life has been for the last thirty or so years. Even now, I should technically call you 'Lord Victor' in any conversation."

Victor appeared to pale upon these words. "What do I do, Anne?" He whispered in a rare, vulnerable way. "How do I not fail at this? And how do I not fail the life I already built? How do I not fail both, when they are so at odds with each other?"

Anne pressed her lips together tightly as she stared up at him. His eyes pleaded back, needing her answer. Anne doubted his grandfather would die in just a few months, but he *did* need to start easing into his future. But how?

"What if you came to Brighton this year and stayed at Vivian's cottage? The last time you were there was…" She trailed off as an old, locked-away memory began to flail in her mind, as if trying to rip out of a bag. In a panic, she shoved it away. "It was the summer Dantes and Vivian married. It's far more informal there than London during the season. Once the queen leaves for the Isle of Wight for the summer, many titled aristocrats will be in Sussex until she returns to London in September. You could reconnect with people you know, or at least get used to what being in that life is life. I'm sure Vivian would be happy to throw a ball to give you an opportunity to reconnect with people."

Victor rubbed the back of his neck. "I can't leave the pub for a summer."

"Victor." She touched his arm again and his green eyes snapped to hers. "Forgive my forwardness, but you don't have a choice."

With unexpected haste, Victor pulled away from her and it caused a pang of hurt. "No. I'm sorry," he said in a stern voice. "But I can't do that. I won't be doing that."

Before Anne could respond, Harris came into the room and in his usual prim voice, announced dinner was ready to be served. She forced a smile. "Never mind all that, then. It was merely a suggestion." Though it would be nice for Victor to be with them at least one summer. Anne always missed him every year. *They* always missed him, she quickly corrected herself.

Chapter Five

BY THE TIME Victor had returned to The Harp & Thistle, the night crowd was at full force. He was a bit stunned, in truth, when he pushed through the front door and was slammed with a wall of ear-splitting noise. Overlapping loud conversations, the piano banging away a bright, twinkling tune. The place smelled of fish from the dock workers, sweat from the laborers, leather from the leatherworkers and cobblers. And of course, beer and whiskey. It seemed a bit early in the night for the place to be packed wall to wall, but every once in a while, they had a busier evening than usual.

His stomach twisted with panic as he realized, with his absence, they'd been severely understaffed. Victor swore under his breath and began shouldering his way through the crowd.

It was both a blessing and a curse that the pub had become so popular after it had nearly burned down back in 1889. Before then, it had been beat up and rough, the true definition of a hole-in-the-wall. But since the renovations, and Dantes's marriage to a duke's daughter, which had caused a stir amongst all of London, the place had become far more popular that it used to be.

Though he would never admit this out loud, Victor missed his brothers working by his side every night as they used to. He was glad they were happily married, and glad for Keer, whom he couldn't run the pub without, but it wasn't the same. He missed the way it used to be.

Thankfully, though, Dantes still worked at the pub a few nights a week, and this night was one of them. Victor quickly made his way across the pub to the back office to safely put away the stack of paper from Fergus, and came back out to the floor.

Dantes, Keer, and the new hire Benny O'Shea were behind the bar slinging pints and whiskey glasses. O'Shea, round-faced and round-bellied, huffed as he tried to keep up with the other men's pace. They didn't notice Victor, as they were far too busy with taking orders to notice anything else. Victor took a moment to watch them under anonymity. Dantes had been doing this for as long as Victor and had it down to a science. But he also didn't have patience for large crowds and Victor could see the signs of barely contained irritation in his brother's face. He scowled, was short with people, and between that and the deep scar that slashed over half of his face, only the regulars who knew him dared order from him.

Keer, thusly, had twice as many patrons at the moment. And so did O'Shea. O'Shea was stumbling about, glasses slipping out of his hands, liquid spilling over the edge, coin dropping to the floor. It reminded Victor of Ollie.

However, Keer slid down to help the stumbling man. Keer filled five whiskey glasses within seconds, which Victor had to admit was impressive. Keer then gave the new hire a quick shoulder squeeze and returned to his place behind the bar, where he continued taking orders, filling them, and taking coin at lightning speed.

Victor left his hidden spot and joined Dantes.

"Thank Christ. Where have you been?" Dantes asked while slamming the cash register shut.

"Anne's," was all Victor offered. He had debated telling his brothers about their grandfather's prediction and decided against it, as it made no sense to put that on them when it wouldn't happen. He also ignored the way his brother seemed to be pointedly staring at him.

"Anne's, you say?" Dantes said, clearly trying to get some sort of reaction.

Victor ignored him as a tan, plump, slightly drunk gentleman plopped onto a barstool that had just been vacated. "Billy." Victor gave the man a nod. Billy had been a regular of theirs since the beginning. "Pint?"

"Aye." Billy gave an answering nod as he pulled forward a young lad who looked about sixteen years. Freckles dotting his face, coupled with a cowlick on his short hair, gave him an innocent air. "Today was my boy Phillip's first day working with me at the docks!" Billy gave the scrawny boy a hard, but proud, pat on the back, causing the young man to lurch forward.

The corner of Victor's mouth twitched. He recalled his first days working on the docks after he'd left his grandparents'. Never had he felt so much pain in his life. "How are you feeling, Phillip?"

The young man winced. "It feels like every muscle in my body has ripped to shreds."

Victor nodded. "I remember that myself. Took about two weeks until it started to ease."

Phillip swallowed. "That long?"

Victor filled and shoved a pint to Billy, then filled a whiskey for Phillip. "On the house, lad. This will help." Victor looked him over. The boy's arms were stick-thin. "Wouldn't have more than one of these, if I were you."

"No, sir," Phillip replied with wide eyes. "Thank you."

Billy nudged his son and jutted his chin at Victor. "Mr. McNab here started at the docks at the same age as you. Now look at him, eh? Built like a bull." Billy snarled and flexed his muscles. Dantes laughed. "Rich as a king, too."

"I am not rich," Victor lied. He knew he stood to inherit a fortune. And even now, he hoarded money, in truth, but that was because he knew what it was like to be without.

It also was no one's business that he had money.

"Right, right," Billy replied. "Like I said, Phillip. Built like a bull, rich as a king, and has a pretty, golden-haired wife." Billy let out a sigh. "Ah, you should see the lass. She comes in often." Billy looked around. "Not here tonight. She has a bosom out to here, and hips out to here." Billy made exaggerated curves away from his body using his hands. "And a wee waist for grabbing."

Victor resisted the urge to snarl at Billy's crassly detailed description of Anne. "I'm not married."

Billy took a thoughtful sip of his pint and let out a noise of satisfaction. "What? Look, fine, deny your money, but why would you deny the wife?"

Victor glanced at Dantes, who had his arms crossed and a huge grin on his scarred face. Irritation flared. "Because I don't have one."

"Oh." Billy blinked a few times. "Well, then your special lady, I suppose."

Victor took in a deep breath for patience, but the irritation was climbing to fury. "I don't have a special lady, Billy."

Billy's face twisted with confusion. "Who in the blazes is that woman you're always making eyes at, then? The one who's always with your brothers' wives when they come in?"

Dantes howled and slammed a giant fist to the bartop. Victor gave him a death glare and Dantes retreated, laughing hysterically.

Victor bit the inside of his cheek. He absolutely did *not* make eyes at Anne.

"Phillip," Billy said to his son, who was hanging on to his father's every word. "You should see the women who come in here. Like that one over there." Billy pointed to some brunette woman nearby. She was all right, Victor supposed. "These beautiful women come up to Mr. McNab here, rest their pretty, round breasts on the bartop so they smush together like so." Billy demonstrated with his hands. "Then they flutter their eyelashes at him."

"They don't do that." Victor had moved on to another order but stayed in this area of the bar to make sure Billy didn't keep putting the wrong ideas into Phillip's head.

"Aye, they do. But Mr. McNab doesn't notice it, you see." Billy held up a finger of silence when Victor opened his mouth for another retort. "But the second this pretty, fair-haired lass comes in, he watches her every move. Constantly asks what she wants. Spends the whole evening talking to her."

Victor scowled. "That is a gross exaggeration."

But Billy ignored him. "For years now, he has been making those eyes at her that he keeps denying. And, apparently, has never done a thing about it." Billy narrowed his eyes at Victor. "Perhaps my son *shouldn't* look up to you."

Victor swore under his breath and went on with his evening, leaving Billy and Phillip to their own devices.

A few hours later, when the crowd started winding down, Dantes approached him. "You're all set for me being gone this summer?"

Victor was washing glasses and he handed a wet glass and dry rag over to his brother. Dantes took them automatically and helped dry. "Yes," Victor replied. "Two extra hands will be around, the same men as last year."

"Good." Dantes shifted as if uncomfortable and then cleared his throat. Victor could tell there was something on his brother's mind, but for whatever reason, he wasn't bringing it up without coaxing.

Victor shot him a look. "What's the matter?"

Dantes met his eye and then quickly looked away. "Vivian wants me to convince you to come to Brighton this year."

"No," Victor immediately said with sharpness. It was the same reply he gave every summer. However, this was the first time, as far as he knew, that Vivian had asked Dantes to try to convince Victor.

Dantes took another wet glass to dry off. "I think you should consider it."

"Why?"

Dantes lifted a shoulder, trying—and failing—to appear nonchalant. "You work yourself too hard. You've always done nothing but work, Victor. I get it, I really do. I know how important this place is to you. But there's more to life than work. And everyone would like you there, too."

Victor didn't respond and kept his focus on his own task. How would that even work, anyway? Leave Keer in charge while he was gone for three months? He couldn't leave this place in someone else's hands, especially for that long.

He looked down the bar at Keer, who was counting the register. How would the man fare? Victor brushed aside the thought. It didn't matter. It wouldn't happen.

For a few minutes, the brothers washed and dried in silence, and Victor thought the subject had dropped.

Unfortunately, it hadn't.

"You know, Winthrop's been dead for eight years now," Dantes said with a far-too airy tone.

Victor slammed a glass down and the air seemed to still. Even Keer seemed to freeze—Victor could see him out of the corner of his eye. But everyone soon resumed their activity.

Dantes looked down at the slammed glass, then back up at Victor. Mischief danced in his green eyes. "Did I touch a nerve?"

Victor took a deep breath and as he found he couldn't bring himself to verbally deny it, glared instead.

Dantes returned to his task. "Look, I know you used to say all the time you would never want a wife, you would never want a family, because you had already raised a family—me and Ollie when we were in Whitechapel—and you didn't want to do it again."

Victor clenched his jaw.

"But you know, Vivian pointed out you haven't said that since her brother died."

"Don't be daft," was all Victor offered. It annoyed him that earlier, he himself had made the same realization.

"I'm not. I'm being sensible." Dantes took another glass that Victor had handed over, dried it, and set it to the side to be put away with the rest. "You spend a lot of time with Anne, and with Mary and Freddy—when he's home, anyway."

Again, Victor kept silent.

The glasses were finished and Dantes crossed his arms and leaned against the counter. "Victor."

Victor gave his brother a bored look.

"Serious, just for a second. Brother to brother, this stays between us. I won't say a word to Vivian or Ollie."

Forcing the ire back down, Victor met his brother's eye and waited.

"Is there something going on between you and Anne?" Dantes asked this quietly so no one else could overhear.

Victor clenched his teeth so hard, he was sure they would shatter. "No." Why in the world would Dantes ask this?

Dantes frowned, which was irritating. "Do you *want* something to happen?"

Victor's immediate reaction was to deny this, because that was the truth. But this was a rare moment of Dantes showing genuine concern for Victor. Thus, he gave his brother the same consideration and briefly contemplated the question. Anne was beautiful—it would be idiotic to deny it. Everyone could see she was. Even Billy had mentioned it. And, fine, yes, she had very nice curves that he, once or twice, had allowed himself to admire for a fraction of a moment here and there, and he wasn't one who generally admired a woman's form.

He did enjoy being around Anne, and anytime he saw her, yes, it was the best part of his day. There was always a strange but pleasant sparkling feeling inside of him when he knew he would see her soon.

But this didn't mean he wanted any romantic ties to her. He had never desired romantic—or physical—ties with anyone before, woman or man. Why would that change with Anne?

Either way, Anne had expressed multiple times she would never remarry. Not that he wanted that, but he was quite happy with everything exactly the way it was. Being at the pub every day, his romance-free friendship with Anne, having the same exact day over and over. It would have sounded boring to his sixteen-year-old self, but now that he was in his forties and had molded his life into something he was pleased with, he didn't want *anything* to change.

He wanted his life to stay exactly the way it was, thank you very much.

If he even toyed with the idea of something happening with Anne, which he wouldn't, it would never be able to go anywhere because of her aversion to marriage. It would end the most important friendship he'd ever had in his life.

No, pursuing anything would do nothing except rip apart a life he was quite content with and did not want to change at *all*.

"Victor." Dantes chuckled. "You have been standing there for an entire minute thinking about that question. Any response you'd like to share?"

Victor came back to the present, realizing his major error. "Yes, you're idiotic. No, I don't want something to happen with Anne."

"All right," Dantes replied simply. "If for some reason you were, you know, on the fence about that. Unsure. This summer would be the perfect time to figure it out once and for all. Don't you think?"

Victor narrowed his eyes, but as usual kept quiet.

Dantes hesitated but seemed to realize Victor was letting him toy with the idea. "You'd see her every day. For three months. Maybe that would help clarify things?"

It wouldn't clarify anything, as there was nothing to clarify. But it would be nice to see everyone. Every summer, he was here in London while they were down there in Brighton. Sometimes, he felt a pang or two of envy knowing they lounged about, or whatever it was they did there, while he sweat.

"Anne suggested I go to Brighton this year as well," Victor admitted. Was the family conspiring, or was everyone simply tired of him isolating himself? When Dantes's eyebrows rose,

Victor hurried to the next thought. "Not because of your ridiculous assertions. But because she thinks it would be a good way for me to reconnect with the aristocracy."

Dantes frowned. "Why would you do that?"

"Because, very unfortunately, one day, I'll have to take Fergus's place."

"Ah. That is an excellent point. Yes." Dantes nodded vigorously. "You should absolutely go to Brighton this summer to, erm, 'reconnect with the aristocracy,' Lord Victor." He turned a hand in the air. "And, perhaps, accept the fact you have deep affections for a certain fair-haired lady as well?"

Victor took a dangerous step forward and Dantes jumped back with a laugh, in case a fist flew. "So should I tell Vivian it was this easy to convince you?" Dantes asked.

"No," Victor replied with a dark voice as he began walking to the end of the bar to get out from behind it. He needed the safety of his office. "You can tell her I will not, under any circumstance, go to Brighton this year or any other year."

Chapter Six

IT WAS MERE days until their departure for Brighton, and the house was a flurry of activity. Freddy would be home from boarding school any minute, and Anne had her lady's maid, Dutton, packing Anne's belongings for the trip while other servants prepared Mary's and Freddy's belongings as well.

While Dutton wrapped a white, cotton summer dress in tissue paper, her gray hair fighting to escape its tight knot, Anne looked over the dresses still draped across her bed and the furniture around her bedroom. It looked like a seamstress's studio had exploded and left dresses and underthings all over.

Many of the garments were brand new for the season, and Anne was always excited for new frocks. But there was one dress in particular she could not wait to wear. It was a silk and satin peach dress with two bodices. The day bodice had a lace panel with collar for daytime modesty. The evening bodice was the same shape but without the lace panel. And the skirt was a frothy confection of shimmering silk and tulle.

Anne picked up the evening bodice and held it up to herself in front of the mirror. "Oh, Dutton, I simply cannot wait to wear this one," she said with a sigh. It had taken a long time for her self-confidence to come back after her husband had passed. She felt far more secure now than she had before, but her self-assurance still could admittedly be lacking. Sometimes, like that blue hat all those years ago, something in particular made her feel magical when she wore it. Like no one else could outshine her. This dress made her feel that way.

Anne returned to her bedside and gently laid the bodice back where Dutton had originally put it. She ran light fingers over the cool silk of the peach skirt.

The door to her bedroom flew open and Mary came skipping in. Mary went directly for her mother, still standing near the peach dress. "Oh, Mama, I love that one." Mary lifted the skirt from the bed and held it up to Anne. "Doesn't Mama look pretty, Dutton?"

Dutton smiled over her shoulder at the girl. "Very pretty, indeed, Lady Mary."

Mary smiled at the skirt held against Anne for a moment longer and then put it back upon the bed. "I bet all of the men will be vying for your attention when you wear that."

Anne's eyebrows lifted high. *"Mary!"*

Mary laughed. "Silly Mama. Oh, how I wish this year were my debut!" The young woman spun in a circle. "I love the romance of balls. The anticipation of who will ask for a dance."

Anne frowned. "There won't be as many balls as you think. It's Brighton, not London."

"Have you decided if you will dance this year?"

"Of course not." Anne couldn't even remember the last time she had. It had been before her husband had passed. She would, of course, attend any and all events to which she received an invitation, but as a widow, she generally stayed off to the side with the other wallflowers. "I don't want to give anyone the wrong idea, anyway."

"What wrong idea?"

Anne studied her daughter for a moment. She didn't like broaching this subject with her children, but Mary was nearly an adult now. "I don't wish to ever remarry, and dancing with a gentleman might give him the idea that I might."

Mary opened her mouth but hesitated, as if unsure about her

response. Her mouth clamped closed for a moment and then she finally said, "Dancing doesn't mean anything, Mama. It's not like you're making your debut and are on the marriage mart. I think men can understand that well enough."

But Anne knew the true ways of men. A man would take a simple, unplanned glance from a pretty woman as an invitation to a tryst, even though that glance almost never meant the woman wanted such a thing. A widow, especially, must be wary, as her virtue was no longer something the ton viewed ought to be protected and such status caused men to release their meager restraints. And should a man ask for more, he would easily pretend to be a kind gentleman, only to turn into a monster after the wedding. Anne had seen countless men manipulate themselves into women's lives, only to turn into their true, ghastly selves once the woman couldn't go anywhere. If Anne accepted a man's invitation to dance after abstaining from it for so many years, they would most definitely take it as a show of interest for something more. And when it came to widows, *something more* more often than not meant covert affairs.

It wasn't even the widowers or bachelors she'd need to worry about. The married men would see her as an opportunity as well.

Mary, of course, wouldn't know any of this.

Mary mistook Anne's silence on the subject as an invitation to continue. "There's nothing wrong with befriending a handsome gentleman, Mama. You're friends with Uncle Victor, are you not?"

Anne suddenly felt very aware of herself. "Yes. What about it?"

"If you danced with Uncle Victor, it would hardly mean anything." Mary looked at Anne with large, dark, innocent eyes. "Right?"

Anne couldn't help but envision dancing with Victor. His large hand resting on her back, his other hand holding her own. She could almost feel his arm around her, his body's closeness, the heat that would radiate off of him, his deep voice as he spoke something private into her ear.

She had to resist a shiver.

Unfortunately, part of Anne's mind still occasionally succumbed to the idea of romance, and because Victor was the only unmarried man she saw frequently, her mind often put him as the subject of those fantasies. But those visions did not reflect any affection she held for him. Not only was there no romance or attraction between the two of them, Victor didn't know how to dance. Also, his life was the pub. The man had never married because he was already married to his pub.

Anne smiled at her daughter. "Victor doesn't know how to dance, Mary. And if he did, dancing with him would hardly mean anything. You know that."

Mary considered this and walked along the bed a few paces, ending at one of the corner bedposts. She began tracing the carved design with a finger. "I feel so badly for you, though, Mama."

Anne blinked. "Why?"

"Don't you get lonely? Don't you ever want that excitement again, the one you felt when you made your debut? The anticipation of a handsome gentleman putting his full attention on you and *only* you?"

Anne really didn't want to cloud her daughter's vision of the world. "It isn't the same once you're my age. And anyway, I've had enough sadness in my life. I don't wish to experience falling in love with someone, only to go through more heartbreak after that." Out of the corner of her eye, Anne could see Dutton studying her. However, she was too cowardly to look at the woman.

Mary stopped her tracing and slid her attention to Anne. There was a glitter of mischief in her eye. "You don't have to get married, Mama. You could just do it for sport, you know? Dancing and flirting, I mean."

Anne felt a strange squeeze of caution. "I don't think you should be thinking of that kind of thing."

Mary sighed and shook her head. "Is there something *wrong* with dancing and flirting?"

No, but she certainly didn't like hearing her daughter talk about it! Anne cleared her throat. "I suppose not."

Mary clapped her hands and made an excited squeal. "Good! Now, do you have any stationery?" But Mary didn't wait for an answer. She went over to Anne's vanity and began rifling through it, quickly finding what she was looking for. She held up paper and a fountain pen in triumph. "Aha! Now, Mama, come here."

Mary took a seat in the plush chair, looking far too old to Anne. But Anne set aside the motherly caution she felt about nearly everything and went to her daughter's side. Admittedly, she was rather curious about what was on her daughter's mind.

Anne watched as Mary wrote, in perfect script at the top of the page: *A Lady's Rules for Seaside Romance.*

Mary ended it with a flourish, then looked up at Anne, who was now beside her. "What rules would you put in place for yourself if you were to enjoy the company of a handsome gentleman just for the summer? Since you don't want anything permanent?"

Anne's mouth dropped open at her daughter's candidness. "This is highly inappropriate!"

Mary's eyebrows pulled together and her bottom lip stuck out in a pout, but she wasn't backing down.

Anne sighed. She could humor her daughter, at least. It wasn't like she was suggesting Anne casually go to bed with people. Mary's suggestion was quite innocent, really, having fun at the expense of her mother. Perhaps Anne could attempt to embrace that girlish part of herself this summer. It wasn't such a terrible idea, and like Mary said, it wasn't as if she were making a commitment.

"Fine." Anne gave in with a sigh. "Never chase a gentleman."

Mary nodded and wrote that rule down. "What else?"

Anne looked over at Dutton, who was watching them with interest but immediately returned to packing upon being caught.

Anne's attention returned to her daughter. "This is all rather silly."

"Oh, Mama, have a little fun with it." Mary smiled up to her, and there was another twinkle in her eye.

Anne let out another long sigh but was too embarrassed to say anything else.

Mary took it upon herself to begin writing. She read aloud as she wrote, "Never flirt first."

Anne inhaled through her nose.

As if knowing the shock her mother felt, Mary looked back up once again. "I'm hardly ten years old anymore. I do know what everything entails. I'm not suggesting *that!*"

Anne did make a point to not keep her children in the dark about what intimacy between married people entailed. She had explained flirting, courting, and what happened on the wedding night. Boys generally learned about all of this, but girls absolutely did not. However, Anne did not want Mary to experience the traumatizing shock that Anne, and most women, experienced. It was a difficult few conversations, but Mary knew the facts of it all.

Mary, to Anne's chagrin, wasn't embarrassed by those conversations. She'd also asked far too many questions for Anne's liking, some of which had made Anne blush.

But she was glad the young woman was not ignorant, at least.

Dutton's voice called out, "No funny business with the men. Don't give them that satisfaction." She then *hmphed.*

Mary giggled as Anne tore a look to her lady's maid. The woman just shrugged and went about her business.

"Do not put that one down, Mary," Anne warned.

"Oh, fine."

For a few more minutes, Anne and Mary added more rules. Rules that would protect Anne. And not long after the list was complete, Harris announced Freddy's arrival.

Mary jumped out of the chair, clearly thrilled her brother had returned.

"Mary, dear." Anne tried to calm the excitable girl. "Go greet your brother. I'll meet you down there in one minute."

"All right, Mama," Mary said as she rushed out of the room.

Anne lifted up the paper and read it to herself:

A Lady's Rules for Seaside Romance
Never chase a gentleman.
Never flirt first.
First and second conversations should be less than ten minutes.
Kissing is acceptable, but do not make the first move.

Anne frowned at that rule snuck in by Mary but kept reading.

No gentlemen with bad hygiene.
No gentlemen who only talk politics.
No gentlemen more than ten years older or younger.
No gentlemen who don't laugh.
No gamblers.

Anne could hear the excited chatter of her children carrying throughout the house. She was eager to join them but wanted to finish this rules business first. Something was missing. Anne lifted the pen and hovered it over the paper for a long moment until she realized the most important rule of all had been missed. She wrote it down:

Never fall in love.

With a nod of satisfaction, Anne folded the paper in half, then threw it randomly into one of the traveling trunks to promptly forget about as she rushed past Dutton and out of the room. Her darling boy was home.

Chapter Seven

Victor lifted his knuckles up to the door on St. James's Street, knocked twice, paused, then knocked twice again. A graceful elderly man in a butler's uniform answered. "Ah, Mr. McNab," Wilson the butler said with an air of distinction. "It has been a spell since we've seen you."

The butler stepped to the side to let Victor into the old, red-brick Georgian building. Victor nodded at the toughs who leaned against the wall farther down the hall. As they knew him and his purpose, they had no interest in him.

"Is he in?" Victor said to Wilson.

"Yes, he is. He's been expecting you."

"I know." Victor gave the butler a nod. "Some things have come up, so I've been a bit delayed."

After brief parting words, Victor left the butler behind and walked down the hall, the toughs eyeing him as a reminder they were there. He pushed through an ornate door in the back and emerged in a large room filled with men in top hats. There were a few tables around which many lounged or stood beside, but the large, round table in the middle held most of the room's attention. It was surrounded by a tight ring of men and a cloud of cigar and pipe smoke stretched over it.

Victor had once known many of the men, all of whom were nobs, and a few looked his way. He'd gone to boarding school with many of them when he'd been young. Now, they may as well have been strangers.

Victor leaned against a pillar at the edge of the room to watch, recognizing the energy that permeated the air. There was a tense game afoot. He didn't know what card game they were playing, nor did he care. He hated card games, for he couldn't be anonymous with them.

Something must have happened because the crowd of men began talking amongst each other excitedly.

One of the men on the outer edge noticed Victor then and, to Victor's irritation, began making his way over.

Like all the other nobs, he wore an expensive top hat over his blond hair. As was in fashion at the current time, he also had a neat, blond beard, and of course a bespoke suit. Round, wire-rimmed spectacles sat upon his nose, and he was eye to eye with Victor, something Victor was, frankly, not used to seeing outside of his family. Curious, Victor gave the man a quick study. He was of a similar build as well, though with less muscle tone. Was this how Victor would have looked if he'd spent his life lounging about instead of slinging shipping crates and pints?

"Mr. Felton Ashby." The bespectacled man held a hand out. Victor briefly hesitated before shaking it and introducing himself back. Whenever he'd come here, he'd never interacted with the nobs in attendance. This was a first.

"Do you play cards?" Mr. Ashby asked as he looked over Victor's mass-produced clothing.

"No, I'm here on personal business."

"Ah." Mr. Ashby bobbed on his feet. "There's some excitement occurring at the moment. You are about to witness the Earl of Harrington's youngest son's ruin."

Victor set his eyes upon the crowd but couldn't see the men in the game. The crowd was too thick.

"I was fortunate enough to get out of that game early," Mr. Ashby said. "I'm here merely for a lark, though, not to bring shame upon my family. Unlike that fellow, I'm not tempted in the least by the slim possibility of winning a fortune, though I wouldn't be upset to fill my pockets. A few drinks, good conversation—that's all I require, really."

Victor wasn't familiar with this man, so he gave him another quick study. He looked to be about thirty or so, thus they would have run in different circles. Victor gave the younger man a nod and said, "Many lives have been ruined here." He really wanted to get about his business, not chitchat with a nob, though he did seem agreeable enough.

Suddenly, there was a cacophony of noise. Men made swift movements forward and shouts rang out.

"And there it is," Mr. Ashby said with a laugh. "Poor old fool."

The Earl of Harrington's youngest son jumped up onto the table. The lad looked even younger than Ashby.

Mr. Ashby laughed. "The man has gone mad—look at him!"

Victor watched as the young man began shouting out a string of curse words, kicked about the contents of the table, then lunged at someone. "I'll kill you!" the earl's son shouted. "You've ruined me! I'll kill you for it!"

The sound of a door banging open caught Victor's attention and the toughs came bounding in, shoving their sleeves up to their elbows. They pushed their way through the crowd, which was now cheering on the fight.

"My word." Mr. Ashby chuckled. "They are out for blood, aren't they?"

Victor crossed his arms and watched with a furrowed brow. There was the sound of another door banging open, this time from the other side of the building. It caught Ashby's attention, and then he nudged Victor. "I've never seen him out here before."

"Who?" Victor asked, then he saw to whom Mr. Ashby was referring. A very large, irate Welshman came roaring into the room. "You mean Bron? Sorry, Bronwell?"

Mr. Ashby glanced back at Victor his mouth agape, but he

quickly slammed it shut.

The rough-and-tumble owner of the gaming hell rushed by and spotted Victor, tapped the side of his nose as they held each other's gazes, then tore into the crowd to get to the fight.

"Forgive me." Mr. Ashby put his full attention on Victor. He wasn't even trying to hide his curiosity now. "But who, exactly, are you?"

Of course, Victor wasn't going to satisfy the man's curiosity. He gave a small bow. "Good afternoon, Mr. Ashby." And Victor went about his business, ignoring the multiple fights that had now broken out, and went into Julian Bronwell's office.

Victor sat in one of the leather seats near Bron's desk and glanced about the room. A violin and its bow had been set on a small table beside a wingback chair and a few feet away from that was a music stand with sheet music on it.

He knew Bron to be a musical talent. Unfortunately, there wasn't much he could do with it.

The door leading to the office opened and closed. Bron walked in and rushed a hand through shoulder-length dark hair as his chest heaved with exertion. He then collapsed into his chair behind the desk. "Thanks for coming, and waiting. Had to go deal with that before I talked to you."

Victor nodded.

"Surprised to see you out there mingling with the nobs." Bron arched his dark eyebrows.

"He took it upon himself to approach me. An overly friendly gentleman. Wanted to know how I knew you."

Bron let out a breathy chuckle and then leaned back in his chair, knitting his fingers together behind his head. "What was the lad's name? He doesn't come here often enough for me to remember."

"Felton Ashby."

"Christ, what a name." Bron shook his head. He then opened a bottom desk drawer and pulled out two glasses and a bottle of whiskey. He poured them each a finger's worth without asking

Victor if he wanted one.

Victor took it, anyway.

"I'm assuming you're here for the horses?" Bron asked.

"Yes."

As Bron took a sip from his glass, he opened the slim top drawer of his desk, pulled out a thin booklet that he tossed to Victor, then pulled out a fountain pen. Victor took the pen once he'd opened the booklet.

"This came out last week, and I was surprised when you didn't show. You always show when it's put out. Thought you were dead." Bron ended this with another chuckle. "Couldn't imagine you not making wagers on the June races."

Victor unscrewed the cap of the pen. "Something unexpected came up, but I'm here now."

"What came up?"

Victor opened the booklet and eyed the page. All of the horse races that would occur in June all over England were listed in here, including the names of the horses in each race. Most people preferred to place wagers the day of the race in case the animal's odds changed, but Victor didn't need to do that. For each race, he took a minute to consider the names, then underlined the horse on which he wanted to place his wager.

"A visit with my grandfather," Victor finally said. He didn't need to explain what that meant. Victor and Bron had been friends for ages, meeting as young lads when they'd worked together on the docks. Bron knew the hellish future that awaited Victor.

Bron took a thoughtful sip of his drink. "Any news on that yet?"

"No, thankfully." Victor underlined another name.

"I'm surprised you visited him. I don't think you've ever done that, now that I think on it."

Victor flipped the page and underlined another name. "He wants me to prepare for the day I take his place. Gave me a stack of papers filled with…God knows what."

"You haven't looked at it?" Bron asked, doing a terrible job at masking his surprise. "Aren't you at least a bit curious what it all entails?"

Victor tapped the pen against his chin as he studied the names of another race. "Not really, no." He paused and looked up to meet his friend's eye. "But the future does loom ominously, doesn't it?"

"How did he seem when you saw him?"

"Still full of piss and vinegar. The man has several years left in him. I'm not going to worry about it now. I have enough to worry about without that."

Bron watched Victor flip through the booklet. "It wouldn't be a bad idea to be prepared. I bet it would take away some of the anxiousness it causes."

Victor paused. Anne had said something similar. So had Dantes. He looked up. "In truth, I'm not as concerned about the management of it."

"Oh?"

"I know there are competent people he relies on. Hopefully, they will be as loyal to me as they are to him. What I'm most concerned with is having to be around, well…" Victor looked at the door that led out to the gambling area. "Them."

"Why?" Of course, Bron came from a fully working-class family, whereas Victor came from a strange family that was half nobility, half working class. Bron hadn't the faintest idea what life in the nobility entailed, nor did he much care.

Victor didn't know what it entailed, either. Unfortunately, he *did* have to care. "One day, I'll be flung into that life. And I will have no choice but to be involved in it. I have to vote in Parliament. I have to ensure my estate is healthy for the people who rely on it, during a time where estates are bleeding dry. Farmers are leaving for more lucrative jobs, which means less income. I'll have to be around nobs on a frequent basis and the last thing I need to add to everything else I'll have to worry about is making an utter fool of myself. I was taught much of it as a boy, but that was so long ago."

"Bah." Bron waved a hand. "Who cares?"

"Because, unfortunately, I do have family that have embraced that life and I do not wish to reflect poorly on them." His thoughts went to Anne, but he shoved that aside. He'd meant Dantes and Ollie, not her. "I don't wish to speak the wrong way to someone and unintentionally offend them, and then have bloody gossip spread all over because I didn't shake their hand the right way or bow the right way, or call them by the correct title."

"You're right, that does sound like hell." Bron leaned back and spread his arms wide. "This is London's most exclusive gaming hell, and the wait list to become a member is five years long. But I've wanted you to be a member from day one. It could be a good way to start interacting with them. Of course, you'd get in right away."

"Thank you." Victor returned his attention to the booklet, underlining another name. "I doubt it, though. You know I don't care for card games."

"Well…" Bron leaned forward and lowered his voice. "That's not all we have here, you know."

Victor looked up and cocked an eyebrow when he found a wicked grin upon his friend's face.

"Women!" Bron shouted in his booming voice and flung his giant hands out to the side once more. "Courtesans, actresses, singers, gorgeous nob widows. We have them all, if you're so inclined."

Victor stilled. "Widows come here for entertainment?"

"That they do. Women have the same desires as men, but they have to hide it. Here, they can be as free about that as they wish." Bron held up two palms in a show of defense. "Now, you have to understand I won't name them."

"The Dowager Marchioness of Litchfield." Victor felt the darkness overtaking him at the thought of Anne coming here. Or anywhere like this place. Would she? Maybe not. Yet she seemed right at home at his pub, which was only marginally better than

Bron's. "You must tell me if she is one of those widows."

Bron held a look of shock for a moment before a wide grin spread over his face. "Is that the woman you're sweet on?"

Victor's knuckles began turning white around the fountain pen.

Bron noticed. "She is, isn't she? My, my." Bron leaned forward. "Such jealousy. I've never seen that on you before."

"Does she come here or not?" Victor asked through clenched teeth. What was the matter with him? What did he care if Anne was a widow who came here for companionship? It was nonsense for him to care. But in the moment, he didn't care about being sensical. Visions of Anne sneaking here under the shadows of night were haunting him.

Bron opened his mouth and let it hang there for a moment. "No." Then he added a grin at the end. "But that reaction told me everything I need to know about her."

Victor inhaled through his flared nose, decided it would be best not to respond, and returned to the booklet. There were only a few more races to go through.

"Her husband used to come here," Bron said, knowing this would reel Victor back into the conversation. "Couldn't stand the man."

"I'm not surprised he came here," Victor replied. "He went anywhere that would let him in."

Bron leaned back with a sigh of satisfaction. "Wish she would come in, though. You could let her know she's welcome to join." He lifted his eyebrows at this. "I could give her a personal tour."

Victor narrowed his eyes.

Bron laughed knowingly. "Ah, McNab, you can be easier to read than a two-story-high advertisement."

His task now complete, Victor screwed the cap of the pen back on. "Surely, I don't know what you mean."

"Have you considered getting her help?"

"For?"

"Easing back into being a nob. And all of that."

Victor studied his friend. Bron was one of the few people in the world who knew the full facts of Victor's life. He may have enjoyed pestering Victor, but they had been through much together and considering the years they'd partnered up for the horse races, Victor knew he could trust Bron beyond measure.

"You know my family goes to Brighton every summer," Victor said.

Bron nodded.

"I've been toying with the idea of going this year. I don't want to, mind. It doesn't appeal to me in the least and I have a business to run here that I don't like to be away from."

"Understandable."

"But my family really wishes me to go this year."

"Does your dowager marchioness want you to go?" Bron asked, all of the previous humor gone. He clearly knew this was time for serious input.

Victor inhaled deep. "Yes, she does."

"What, exactly, does your relationship entail?"

Victor looked elsewhere in the room in thought. "Nothing, other than friendship."

"Do you want it to be something else?"

His attention moved back to his friend. "I don't know," Victor admitted. "I've never cared about women in that regard before. You know how difficult it is to become successful when you come from nothing."

"I do."

"Marriage, family—women in general were too risky for my life. God forbid there be an unexpected pregnancy. I didn't want it. I knew it would be between them and my pub, and I wanted my pub. That was the only certainty I've had in my life."

Bron nodded. "I understand that as well." He paused. "I feel like you're about to say, 'but.'"

"I am," Victor admitted. "However, I don't know what the 'but' is."

"From what I'm hearing, and correct me if I'm wrong..."

Bron took another sip of his whiskey as he considered his next words. "You are happy to continue on with the bachelor life. You're quite content with your life as it is. Your daily routine, the success of the pub, the home you return to every night. But this dowager marchioness with whom you spend an inordinate amount of time is a temptation."

Victor hesitated. But if he were to talk through this with anyone, Bron would be the best person. He didn't know Anne personally. "Yes." It was the first time he had ever admitted this to anyone, much less himself.

"What, exactly, are your feelings for her? What, exactly, is this temptation? Is it purely physical? Or is there more to it?"

"I…I don't know."

"Do you wish to take her to bed? Become her husband? Fool around for years without the attachment of matrimony?"

Victor had thus far been so focused on ignoring these types of questions, he couldn't even fake an answer.

Thankfully, Bron understood. And he offered the same advice Dantes had. "Go to Brighton this year, then, and figure it out. Spend time with her. Maybe you won't like being around her on a daily basis. Maybe you'll accept what that jealousy you just showed over the mere *idea* of her being a patron here meant. Maybe you'll have a tryst and get bored immediately. Maybe you'll take the years of pining after her off your plate."

Victor was not the type to engage in trysts, but Bron didn't need to know that. But the appeal of having to worry about one less thing? Anne had taken up his thoughts for far too long. As long as Dantes and Vivian had been married—longer, rather. It was time for him to figure out what his feelings and attraction to Anne meant. And with everyone in his life suggesting he go to Brighton, perhaps that was a sign. Most likely, whatever he felt for Anne was nothing he couldn't move past with time. But at least he would know for certain.

Bron took the horse race booklet back from Victor and thumbed through it. "Are you done with this?"

"Yes. I've underlined all the horses that will likely win in June." Though he didn't *always* get it right, he mostly did.

Bron studied one of the pages. "I'll never understand how you know that. Will you ever share your secret?"

"It's no secret," Victor said. "I just know who will win, that's all."

"Right." Bron set the booklet down.

"And as usual," Victor added, "you keep a third of the winnings." Bron and Victor had set this up ages ago. Because Bron was well known as a gaming hell owner, it wouldn't be unusual for him to place wagers for clients who wish to remain anonymous. Victor had made a fortune on being able to predict with ninety-percent accuracy of horse race outcomes. Bron had to do all the legwork, but considering the riches it brought him, he had never complained and was more than happy with the arrangement.

They didn't bet on every single race, as it would catch too much attention. But Bron would pick one or two races, place the bet, and then they would win. Most of the times, Victor would then come here to the hell to collect the money, but sometimes, Bron would deposit it on Victor's behalf.

Victor rose up to his feet and the men shook hands before Victor departed. The family was leaving for Brighton tomorrow, so he had little time to prepare. He first needed to speak to Keer. Perhaps he would offer up that raise Keer had been asking for and hope he would be amenable to running the place for a few months.

The thought of letting someone else run The Harp & Thistle made him nervous. But then he thought of Anne. Her beauty, her friendship. By summer's end, she could be his, and he could be hers—if that was what he, and she, wanted. He could know what it felt like to have her hand in his, to be in his arms, to have his lips trailing along her neck.

Yes, he wanted her. It was ridiculous to deny it. But what he felt for her, he still couldn't bring himself to figure out how to describe.

Chapter Eight

Platform Six at Brighton Station swarmed with people disembarking from the express train from London. The station was noisy from the steam engines and whistles, as well as porters calling out to match up luggage with passengers—plus, the sheer amount of conversation from hundreds of people.

It was a trip that took less than two hours, and Anne was glad for the respite from activity. Freddy had returned from school the day before and she had not had a chance to spend significant time with him until the train ride. And once they arrived at Summerwood, Vivian's summer cottage, it would be quite busy once again as everyone settled in.

The Winthrops and McNabs had traveled together in the same train car and Freddy talked nearly the entire time. He admitted to some hijinks to Dantes and Ollie, who were greatly amused, though Freddy's grandfather the Duke of Chalworth made a few grumbling noises to gently make his thoughts on it known. None of it was too terrible, in Anne's opinion, typical childhood mischief like hiding harmless garden snakes in a friend's sock drawer.

Freddy had also talked endlessly about his new friend Ralph, and Anne was endlessly grateful her son had found this new friend.

In an odd way, Anne found peace in these stories. Freddy's

stories were only mildly naughty and showed that he was still a good lad, even as he grew up.

She would never admit this aloud, but she continued to look for signs he would grow up to be like his father. So far, though, he remained the good-natured, thoughtful boy he always had been. Very different from Bernard.

Anne led her children to the end of the platform to wait for everyone else. Vivian and Dantes were trailing behind with their small daughter, Lily, and the Duke of Chalworth. Far behind them, Ollie and Evelyn were doing their best to wrangle the twins. Valets and lady's maids—and Mary's governess, Miss Stewart—were somewhere in the crowd as well.

Freddy, who seemed to have grown an entire foot since last summer and was now as dark-haired and willowy as the rest of the natural-born Winthrops—seemed to be seeking something.

"Freddy, dear, what are you looking for?" Anne asked, looking in the same direction to see if she could figure it out.

"I told you Ralph comes to Brighton in the summer, yes?"

"Yes, darling, several times." Anne grinned. "I very much doubt he would be on the exact same train as us, though."

Freddy continued searching for another moment as Mary pointed to a few people and asked if they were Ralph, but he soon gave up, dropping his head a bit with disappointment.

"I'm sure if you ask your Aunt Vivian nicely, she would be happy to have Ralph and his family over for dinner sometime."

Freddy's face lit up. "That would be aces!"

Anne's eyebrows lifted at the new slang, but she kept her thoughts on that to herself. Slowly but surely, the family reconvened, though Ollie had to take his sons outside due to their boredom from being confined in a train car. They had had quite enough of traveling and made sure everyone on the platform knew it. Evelyn stayed back with the rest, still waiting for their luggage and the servants who'd traveled with them.

While the family talked amongst themselves, and Freddy began teasing Mary about her new frocks that she, of course, had talked about during the trip, Anne kept her eye out for her lady's maid, Dutton. Twice, her eyes played tricks on her when she thought she saw Victor walking toward them and her heart leapt in response. But the men she had mistaken for Victor were merely tall strangers and hardly even resembled him upon inspection.

That familiar feeling of regret she experienced each summer when Victor stayed behind settled in for the next few months. It never seemed to get better with each year.

Anne wondered what Victor would have been doing right now. Here, she could just barely sense the salty sea air, visions of summertime activities swirling in her mind with the scent. Meanwhile, Victor was in a smoggy, warm London, likely in his office hunched over some kind of paperwork. Though he always insisted it was where he was happiest. In fact, he probably did not even think about her—them—when they were gone.

She and Victor saw so much of each other the rest of the year, though. Did Victor ever miss her, even a little, when she was gone?

But Anne shook the thought away, embarrassed at herself. Of course he didn't miss her. Being separated from a good friend for a few months should be nothing at all.

At that moment, Anne spotted Dutton and Miss Stewart walking together. Anne waved high above her head to get Dutton's attention. Dutton's eyes landed on Anne's and she smiled in acknowledgment.

The younger Miss Stewart, clutching a book against her brown dress, didn't yet notice the family, as she was engrossed in conversation with someone else. Anne recognized the other servants who traveled with the rest of her family, but for a moment she didn't recognize the man beside Miss Stewart. Probably because she couldn't quite believe her eyes.

Mary and Freddy exchanged excitable whispers as Vivian and Dantes exchanged wide-eyed expressions of shock.

It took a moment for Anne to understand why, to believe her eyes.

It was Victor. In the flesh.

He wore light-gray trousers and a coat with a dark-blue waistcoat, and he carried a hat under his arm. Even with the travel, his black hair was neat and nothing about it was out of place. His thick, short black beard also looked as if it had been trimmed, which was nicely different.

As Anne took him in, Victor's attention left Miss Stewart and snapped to Anne. They were in a crowded place, but it felt as if they stood close, alone in an empty room. Anne felt her face get hot.

"Mama, Uncle Victor is here," Mary said at Anne's side.

Anne blinked in an attempt to recover. "Yes, I can see that."

"I thought you said he wasn't coming?"

"That's what he had said."

Dantes cupped a hand around his mouth. "Oi! Victor! What are you doing here?"

No one had known he was coming?

Freddy and Mary left Anne and hurried up to Victor but stopped themselves short from hugging him. It was something they used to do when much younger, but with age had stopped doing. Freddy gave a short bow and Mary gave a curtsy. Victor ruffled Freddy's hair, the faintest twitch at the corner of his mouth, and talked to the children for a moment, though Anne couldn't hear what they said. There was a warm glow in her heart as she watched the trio together.

Vivian appeared at Anne's side, holding Lily's hand while watching the scene as well. "He does adore the children so," Vivian said airily.

Anne wrinkled her nose. "They're hardly unlikable, Vivian. And they *are* his niece and nephew."

Vivian shot her a wide grin. "Technically, they are not."

Anne ignored the comment. "You didn't know he was coming, either."

Vivian shook her head while Lily made a fussing noise—soon, Dantes may need to bring her outside as well. "Dantes tried to convince him to, but Victor refused and was rather stubborn about it. Apparently, it became quite the heated discussion. I wonder why he changed his mind?"

"Indeed."

While Victor greeted Dantes and the Duke of Chalworth—they were closest to his approach—the women congregated along with Anne's children. Evelyn expressed concern at the unexpected arrival, Freddy had a bit of a frown on his face about the whole thing, but everyone else brushed it off. Though Anne wasn't worried, she did agree something was going on. Perhaps Victor had finally agreed with Anne that the summer would be a good way to test the waters of the aristocracy.

Victor shook hands with the duke and met eyes with Anne. He began walking in her direction but became accosted by the other women, who pelted him with questions. "I changed my mind," was the only explanation he gave to his unexpected arrival.

Anne's heart began to beat a bit faster, though, when Victor finally came to greet her. The rest of the family became distracted by the arrival of luggage and they all began to exit the station, Anne and Victor trailing behind.

Victor offered his arm to her, catching her off guard. This wasn't the first time he had done so, of course, but it wasn't a common habit of his, either. "I have to say…" Anne looked up to him as they walked. It was rather nice to be walking arm in arm with a gentleman, even if it was only Victor. "It took me a moment to realize you were you. I can't believe you decided to come visit. I heard your explanation, but I don't believe it for a minute."

He glanced down at her, and though he didn't smile, there was a glint in his eyes. "You don't believe I'm here because I changed my mind?"

"Of course not. You don't change your mind. Once you make a decision, that is it."

He held her gaze for a long moment then looked back up. "I gave some thought to your suggestion about coming this year and agreed it would be a good idea."

She gave him a triumphant grin. "You should listen to me more often."

He grunted, and she knew him well enough to know this was a sound of amused agreement.

"Why didn't you travel in the same car as us?"

"I didn't realize you all were going to be on this train," he said. "Then as I disembarked, I saw Dutton and Miss Stewart."

As the group emerged from the station and out into the sun, Anne had to shadow her eyes over the brim of her hat with a flattened hand. Victor secured his own hat back upon his head. "I'm quite glad you are here this year, Victor." Anne thought she felt his arm flex beneath her hand. "Are you planning on staying the entire summer?"

Victor looked down at her and as he stared at her with intensity, in a way that made something inside of her hitch. "I'm planning on staying the whole time, yes."

Anne tamped back the thrill this lifted within her and placed her attention up ahead, where Vivian pointed out a few carriages waiting for them.

Salty air swept past Anne's nose, and a gull cried overhead. "I heard Dantes tried to convince you to come this year, too, and you were quite against it. Word is there was a heated argument as well."

Victor stopped walking. "What else did he say about it?" His voice was low and tense.

Anne stammered. "N-Nothing, just that he couldn't change your mind."

His tension eased. Rather odd. "I was, admittedly, nervous about leaving the pub. But Keer has proven himself to be reliable and, I suppose, I feel comfortable enough with him to join you all this year. He was quite happy with the opportunity, thankfully."

They began walking again. "What are you hoping to accomplish while you are here?" she asked.

Up ahead, Vivian's footmen began loading up the numerous

traveling trunks across four carriages.

"Reacquaint myself with people I used to know as a boy, meet those I don't know at all."

"You could also reacquaint yourself with other things as well. Balls, horseback riding—things of that nature."

Victor frowned.

"You have had *some* exposure to all of that, though, right? I mean, you won't be a complete novice to everything."

"No, I wouldn't be, but I haven't been on a horse for many, many years, for example. I may as well be a novice."

"It will come back to you once you get into it again."

Victor's green eyes seemed brighter than usual. "Would you be willing to help me with that?"

Anne blinked. "What do you mean?"

"Horseback riding. There are stables at the house, correct?"

"Yes."

"Would you accompany me at the stables? Once I get the hang of it, we could go on rides together." His eyebrows lifted ever so slightly.

Something about this felt off, but Victor's face held no expression. She was reading too much into it. "That sounds lovely. I would like that." Anne smiled.

For the briefest moment—and Anne wasn't even sure she truly saw it—Victor glanced down at her mouth. The unexpected change in attention caused something in her to falter.

What a silly reaction. When someone smiled, others often looked at the smiling mouth. It was nothing more than that.

When the family finally arrived at Summerwood, there was the usual flurry of activity of exiting the carriage, luggage being unloaded and brought in, bedrooms being assigned. Everyone scattered. Anne joined her children up on the third floor, where their bedrooms and the nursery for the little ones awaited. Once Freddy and Mary were settled, Anne went down to the second floor and aimed for the bedroom she stayed in every year.

As she passed one room, though, Vivian rushed out of it.

"Anne! Over in here." Vivian waved her into the room.

Frowning, Anne doubled back and found Vivian and Dutton in this other bedroom.

Vivian clasped her hands together and brought them up to her chin. "I'm doing some redecorating and three of the bedrooms are unavailable this year. Would it be all right if you were in this one this summer?"

Anne looked around the bedroom. The wallpaper was cream with thin, blue stripes, and there was nautical-style art all over the room. Several large windows, with sheer, lace curtains, looked out at the sea. "Of course," Anne said. "It's a beautiful room."

"Oh, good. I'm glad you think so."

Anne walked an exploratory circle around the room. She opened a door and found a linen closet. Anne shut the door and found a large wardrobe down the wall. This room had far more storage space than the one she normally used.

As she reached the other door, though, she realized it had a lock. Curious, Anne twisted the lock then pulled the door open. But it wasn't a closet. All she found was another door behind it.

"What is this?" Anne looked over her shoulder at Vivian.

"Oh! Um…" Vivian wrung her hands.

Anne turned back to the mysterious door when she realized she heard voices on the other side. What in the world? She tried twisting the knob, but it was locked.

"I've been considering what you said." It was Victor's muffled voice. To whom was he talking?

"And?" Dantes replied.

"I don't know. I simply don't know how to go about it. I feel absolutely mad, though. It's madness, right? It must be. It can't feel like this."

Anne frowned and knocked on the door rapidly, then set her fists on her hips.

The door opened, revealing Victor. And, presumably, the bedroom he would be staying in for the next few months, right beside her own.

Chapter Nine

V ICTOR CLENCHED HIS teeth so hard, he was sure they would shatter. His brother had gone way out of line this time.

Anne stood frozen in their apparently shared doorway, staring up at him with giant eyes and flushed cheeks. She was clearly not pleased with this arrangement.

Not that he was happy about it, either. An unmarried man and unmarried woman—widow or not—should absolutely not have had connecting bedrooms! It was the height of impropriety, and both Dantes and Vivian would have been well aware of that.

He had to think quick on what to do. He didn't want to get so furious with his brother that Anne might take it personally. Nor did he want to direct his upset at Vivian, as she was the hostess and had clearly planned this the moment she'd realized he'd come.

Based on the veil of smugness on her face as she stood behind Anne, though, she was well aware of his inability to utter a negative word. He swore to himself internally at being outmaneuvered.

Victor looked back down to Anne and held her gaze. She stared back, her own jaw set tight. They came to a silent understanding, gave each other a slight nod, and closed their respective doors at the same time.

Immediately, he could hear Anne's high-pitched angry voice,

though it was muffled enough he couldn't pick up on much of what she said aside from, "What game are you playing here, exactly?"

Victor spun around and took three long strides over to Dantes, who wore an infuriatingly blank expression on his face. His hands were shoved into his trouser pockets, too. Dantes was far too relaxed for the moment, and it only made Victor's ire worse.

Victor stopped before Dantes and crossed his arms. "I'm not doing this."

Dantes grinned, the old, deep scar slicing into his face stretching with it. "You don't have a choice. The other bedrooms are already taken. The remaining empty bedrooms are being redecorated."

"You're lying," Victor said darkly, and he followed it with a scowl. They were both well into adulthood, but Victor still knew what would strike fear into his younger brother.

It worked. Finally, Dantes cleared his throat and rubbed at his nose. No trace of the smile remained. "Look, I know you're not happy about this—"

"No, I'm really not."

"—but a few minutes ago, we were discussing you and Anne again. And maybe this *is*, in fact, a good idea."

Victor sighed and pinched the bridge of his nose. "No, this is highly inappropriate. In every sense of the word."

"Such a rule follower," Dantes said. "Except when it suits you better not to be."

Victor knew he was referring to the years they'd lived in Whitechapel, which obviously had been a completely different situation. The decisions Victor had made as a boy regarding fighting or stealing or whatever else he'd had to do had been, quite literally, the difference between life and death.

This situation was not.

But he also knew, if Dantes had his mind made up on something and Vivian supported him on it, there was nothing he could do. With a sigh, Victor made his way over to his small traveling trunk to finish removing his items. Dantes had insisted on having a valet help with it, but Victor had refused. He had no valet of his own.

Dantes went to lean against the wall in a place within Victor's line of sight. He lowered his volume. "You just told me a moment ago you came this summer to determine if you wanted your friendship with Anne to become something more."

Victor didn't look up as he began pulling out the remaining button-up shirts and setting them atop his bed. "No, if you were listening, the main reason I came here was—as I've said numerous times already—to reacquaint myself with the aristocracy. I am confident Fergus still has many years left in him, but I do not wish to be thrust unprepared into that life, either." He took an armful of shirts and made his way over to a large armoire and pulled open a drawer. "In regard to Anne, you are correct. I don't know what affections I have for her and would like to figure that out."

"Right," Dantes said, though his voice sounded unsure. "Forgive me, but how do you not know how you feel about her?"

Victor lowered his eyelids. "How many months did it take you to accept you were in love with your wife?" He only realized how that sounded as the words left his lips.

A huge, mocking grin spread across Dantes's face as Victor shut the drawer a bit too hard. "I'm going to let you stew on that one for a minute, Victor."

"That is *not* what I meant," Victor said with a warning voice, but he did have to concentrate on ensuring he did not deny this too quickly. "Anne and I have been good friends for a long time now. I am fairly certain that is all it is, but since I am already here for the season, perhaps it's worth examining, since I never have before."

Dantes laughed and shook his head. Further denial would not help Victor's case, so he decided to let it lie.

There was a time, years ago and in the midst of a downpour, he had made a promise to Anne.

Admittedly, the conversation had been vague—few words were said between them—and then it had never been brought up again. But he had seen that look in her eye—she understood what he was implying.

At the time, she'd been separated from Winthrop. Then Winthrop had died and she'd had to go through the required two years of mourning. It could have been brought up after that, but it never had been. And now, nearly a decade had gone by.

And in that time, he had grown to care for her very much. But was it as a friend? Or something more?

That is what he needed to figure out.

It didn't help that Victor didn't understand women in matters of the heart, which was his own fault.

The difference between Dantes and Victor in this regard was Dantes had once been in love long before he'd met Vivian. Dantes had known what that felt like.

And Ollie had once been a self-proclaimed scoundrel. He'd known what attraction felt like.

Victor had never been in love. He was never a scoundrel.

He didn't know what love *or* attraction felt like. Maybe he would mix up the two and make an arse of himself.

What he did know was when women batted their eyelashes at him and leaned forward to expose their cleavage, it was to get free pints. He wasn't that daft.

"Victor?" Dantes's voice brought Victor back to the present issue at hand.

Victor placed his attention on his brother.

"So, you're going to examine this friendship you have with Anne, then, this summer?" Dantes ended this with that infuriating, knowing grin.

Victor turned away, afraid his face would give away how much of his mind the subject had been taking up as of late. "I need to finish unpacking. Get out."

⟫⟫⟫⟩⟨⟪⟪⟪

IT WAS LATE evening and the first day at Summerwood was coming to an end. Anne, exhausted, was up in her bedroom with Dutton, who was helping her ready for sleep.

As Dutton pulled the nightgown over Anne's head, Anne glanced at the locked door connecting to Victor's room. After the discovery of the connecting doors earlier, they had not yet had a chance to discuss the situation. Victor was, by far, the most practical of the McNab brothers, and she also trusted him explicitly. She didn't need to worry about him acting improperly.

It helped, too, that he was clearly as displeased with the situation as she was. More, in fact. The look on his face when he'd realized what that door led to! She had never seen him look so furious before.

Actually, he was so furious by it that she couldn't help but wonder—was it because of the door, or was it because *she* was behind the door?

Yes, it was a bit improper, but they weren't two eighteen-year-olds, either.

They had no scandalous past that would make the situation uncomfortable. And she was a widow, which allowed her far more freedoms than married women or even spinsters her age.

Still studying the locked door, she bit her bottom lip despite her attempts at brushing this all off.

Why Vivian had done this, she hadn't the faintest notion. But it shouldn't have been that big of a deal if the redecorating excuse was true. Maybe it hadn't been intentional—it had just so happened that Anne and Victor had these rooms because there was nowhere else to put them.

Now she felt a bit bad for going off on Vivian. She'd been so embarrassed by Victor's reaction, she'd taken it out on Vivian.

Promising herself to apologize in the morning, Anne crossed the room to her wash table to wash her face and brush her teeth for the night.

"Would you like the windows open, my lady?" Dutton said to Anne's reflection in the mirror.

"Yes, please. Thank you, Dutton."

The windows were quite large and opened outward with a turning handle. Dutton cranked one window open, and while Anne completed her tasks, moved down the line of widows.

Fresh, cool, salty air rushed in, billowing the lace curtains aside each window. The heat that had been captured quickly began to dissipate.

Anne climbed into bed, saying goodnight to Dutton, and the lady's maid snuffed out the lamps, enveloping the room in darkness.

After spending a minute or so shifting into comfort, Anne finally let out a sigh and clasped her hands over her stomach.

Ten minutes later, she was still wide awake.

Then it was fifteen minutes. Twenty.

There was a very faint noise and slight shake from footsteps in the adjacent bedroom. Anne's eyelids flew open. The only reason she could sense it was because the room was so still and quiet. Next door, Victor was puttering about, likely preparing for sleep as well.

Anne sat up and when she heard more footsteps, flung her legs over the edge of the bed and went over to her armoire, where her housecoat was.

After tying it on with a few quick movements, Anne tiptoed over to the door. She wanted to confront Victor, find out why it was *so terrible* for his bedroom to be next to hers.

As she stood at the door and quietly unlocked it, she could still hear him walking around.

Anne lifted a fist and her knuckles hovered at the door. For a moment, she hesitated. But then she forced herself to knock.

There was a pause before the footfalls went over to the door. And a moment later, the door flung open. Victor, backed by a fully lit room, did not look pleased to see her. And the severe shadows that framed his frown, due to her bedroom lacking any light, only made it worse.

After giving him a pleasant smile, Anne slid past him and began looking around his bedroom. While hers was nautical-themed, his was just another masculine room with dark-wood paneling and furniture. The bedding was dark green, as was the wallpaper.

"What do you think you are doing?" Victor asked in a dark voice, still at the door that was now behind her.

"Being nosy," Anne replied as she began meandering about the room. She noted a small traveling trunk set to the side. "Do you have a valet here?"

"No," he replied, still sounding irritated. "I don't have one and there are no extras sitting around. You can't be in here, Anne."

Anne, of course, had no intention of leaving just yet. She spotted the twine-tied stack of papers his grandfather had given him and went over to it.

"Have you looked through this yet?" she asked, not picking it up but noting it was still tied closed.

"It's not exactly on my list of immediate priorities."

An envelope sat neatly beside the paper stack. "What's this?" She picked it up.

Victor immediately appeared at her side and took it from her hand. "Correspondence for Keer. He will be updating me on business matters once a week unless something comes up. I wanted to let him know I've arrived, and to remind him of expectations while I'm away."

"I see." She let her hand drop to her side. "How do you like your room?"

"It's fine."

"It's a handsome room," Anne replied.

Victor pressed the envelope back down to where he had placed it before. It was this moment Anne realized Victor was still in his day clothing. "You're still dressed." Her eyebrows pulled together.

Victor stilled, causing her to look up to him. "What, exactly, were you expecting to find when you knocked upon my door?"

She felt her face redden. "Oh! I meant… I meant that you're still in your day clothes! I wanted to talk to you before you went to sleep."

"I am not the least bit tired," he replied. "Unless I leave the pub early, which doesn't happen often, I generally go to sleep after two in the morning and get up around the noon hour."

Anne realized she didn't even consider this as a problem he would have to face. "You're going to have to get accustomed to different sleep patterns."

"Yes." He crossed his arms and gave a single nod. "You said you wished to speak to me."

"Oh. I did say that, didn't I?" Anne licked her lips and realized with a bit of embarrassment that Victor watched her do it. It finally hit her, then, how truly inappropriate this situation was. She cleared her throat. "Why are you mad our bedrooms are connected?"

Victor dropped his arms to his side. "Are you serious?"

She gave a nervous chuckle. "No. I mean, yes. I mean—" She closed her eyes to slow herself. "Your ire is too much for the situation. Look, I know this is an odd arrangement, but it couldn't be helped."

"No?"

"Vivian said these were the only available rooms for you and me."

"And you believe her?"

Anne hesitated, then frowned at such a question. "Why else would she put us in connecting bedrooms?"

Victor looked her over before crossing the room to his windows. With his back to her, he began cranking them open just as Dutton had done in Anne's room. "You're right. Nothing else was available."

Again, Anne's eyebrows pulled together. Victor was acting rather odd about all of this, so she decided to go for humor. "I don't need to worry about you breaking into my bedroom to ravish me, do I?" She tacked a laugh onto the end.

Victor spun around, his face as white as snow. The man looked truly horrified by the mere suggestion. "Of course not!"

Surprised by his severe reaction, she placed a hand over her heart as if she could push back the humiliation that rose. "I was only jesting!"

Victor rubbed a hand over his jaw. "I'm exhausted. I should call it a night." Before she could protest or point out just minutes ago, he'd said he'd been wide awake, he began to gently nudge her to her back to the door by placing a light hand on her back.

"Tomorrow morning," she said while looking up at him, noting he *looked* wide awake, too. Was the closeness of their bedrooms too much for him, making him uncharacteristically shy with her? There was one way to find out. "I know something that will help you adjust to a new sleep schedule. It will include hours of rigorous activity and you'll be too exhausted to have trouble sleeping at night." Still trying to insert humor into the strange moment, she was actually referring to activity like horse riding and lawn games. Though she'd purposely said it the way she had to see how he would react.

He let out a groan of frustration as they finally arrived at the door and hastily reached for the doorknob, as if eager for her departure. Notably, he did not ask to which activity she was referring.

Goodness, she didn't even get an eyeroll from that one. "I often go to the stables first thing," she explained to, hopefully, cover up her failed joke. "I prefer it when the rest of the house is still asleep. Find me there?"

"I will," he replied in that dark, raspy voice of his. It seemed to spark something in her.

Anne stepped through her doorway and turned around. "Goodnight, Victor." She gave him a pleasant smile.

"Goodnight." Immediately, he shut his door and locked it.

As Anne did the same, she couldn't help but giggle to herself.

~~~~~~~~~~

Chapter Ten

</div>

AFTER A RESTLESS night, Victor found himself in the unfortunate situation of waking at the first morning light. With stubbornness that could have rivaled a mule's, he refused to get up at such an ungodly hour and kept his eyes shut tightly. However, as the sky became lighter, and sleep continued to evade him, he relented and sat up with a grumble, accepting his fate.

Victor washed for the day and dressed in his usual black suit with dark-gray paisley waistcoat and white, button-up shirt under that, then combed his black hair neatly. Though he had trimmed his beard the day before to look a bit more polished, he couldn't bring himself to trim his hair. It looked better a few inches longer than the really nearly-shorn styles most preferred these days, and thus he slicked it back as usual. As he inspected himself, he thought of his grandfather's full head of gray hair. Looking back over his shoulder to ensure no one else was in the room—not that there should have been—he leaned forward to inspect his hairline.

No grays. Yet.

Satisfied, he made his way downstairs to the dining room, where he was served a larger breakfast than he normally had. By himself, he consumed three eggs, two pieces of toast, four sausages, one cup of coffee, and one glass of water. The meal ended with a promise to himself to eat extra vegetables during
~~~~~~~~~~

the other meals.

Now finished, he debated what to do while everyone slept, but the butler, Keane, answered that easy enough. As a footman began clearing away his empty plates, Keane appeared. He was younger than Vivian and Dantes's butler back in London, Heaton, but he was mostly bald now except for a circular wisp of light-brown hair that reminded Victor of a medieval monk.

The butler gave a small bow. "I trust everything was to your satisfaction?"

As if he would complain about food he didn't pay for or cook himself. "Yes." Victor swiped at his mouth with a white, cloth napkin before the footman took it. "I usually don't eat this much in the morning, but I found I couldn't resist."

Keane smiled. "Thank you for the compliment. I'll be sure to pass it on."

After Victor rose from his chair, Keane escorted him out of the room. "I presume you are heading to the stables now? Lady Litchfield mentioned you were to go riding together."

Victor frowned at the man as they stopped in the hallway. "She's already awake?"

Keane gave one elegant nod. "You may get to the stables by heading out that way." The butler indicated down the hallway. "Would you like me to show you?"

Victor turned down the offer and went in the direction the butler had provided. He quickly found his way outside. The sky was now a dusty gray-blue and the grass damp with dew. The air felt cool in his lungs, and he could nearly taste the sea salt and grass.

The stables were easy enough to find, and as he began to approach them, a black blur shot across the fenced-in paddock. A woman atop the glossy, black horse wore a moss-green riding habit consisting of a short but masculine suit-like jacket with a sidesaddle skirt. Medium-green soutache looped around the edges of the jacket and skirt hem. Her blonde hair, in a low knot, was topped with a small, black top hat with a black bow on its side.

Anne, evidently unaware of Victor's approach, leaned forward with concentrated determination. She shouted out commands to the horse and the horse kicked up dried dirt as he went into a full gallop, admittedly striking a bit of fear in Victor's heart. With terror tinged in his mouth, he watched as, a moment later, the horse soared over a log fence as if it flew with wings.

Letting out a breath of relief, Victor arrived at the paddock fencing and rested his arms atop it to watch. At the same time, two stablehands came out of the stables and, without appearing to notice Victor, mirrored his stance.

Anne was attracting an audience, and Victor discovered he really didn't like it.

Anne and the glossy, black horse cantered around for a bit, but then the horse began galloping again, flying over the log fence as if it were nothing at all.

Victor was in utter awe. He had never seen her ride before, though he knew it was a favorite pastime of hers.

Now, he wished he knew how to ride. Then he could be in there with her while those two cads down the fence watched *them*, not *her*.

The men, both sporting tweed flatcaps, didn't take their eyes off Anne as she kept exercising her horse with expertise. The stablehands talked to each other in hushed tones, but Victor wasn't an idiot. He could tell by the low tone, low chuckles, and raised eyebrows they were talking about her in a lewd way. For decades, he'd had to overhear what men said about women behind their backs. At best, it was admiring women's bodies, at worst, crass fantasies. They often made those same eyebrow wiggles the stablehands were making right now.

Doing his best to ignore the swirling anger and jealousy, Victor cleared his throat loudly while giving the two men a deadly stare. When they spotted him, they jumped.

Both men swallowed, tipped their hats at Victor, then hurried back inside the stable without uttering a word, knowing they had been caught red-handed.

Anne and her horse flew over the low log jumping fence again and when they came to a stop, Anne finally noticed him.

The moment her eyes met his, his heart hitched.

"Victor!" she shouted with a grin, waving a hand above her head. As she directed her horse over in his direction, Victor found a latched gate and went through it.

The horse came to a stop at a respectable distance. Old, faint memories of being taught how to approach an unknown horse—never from the back, and always calmly—echoed in his mind from the distant past.

Victor slowly approached woman and beast. "That was quite incredible to watch, Anne," Victor said, and he meant it. He wasn't one to compliment, but he felt compelled to compliment her in the moment. "I had no idea you were such a talented horsewoman. I'm sorry I've never seen you before."

She shrugged one shoulder. "Thank you, Victor. It was nothing, though. Just a little bit of exercise."

"If you say so. May I help you down?" He reached up to her and she paused, her eyebrows rising, but then nodded in agreement. He clasped his hands around her waist and lifted her easily off the animal, then brought her down to the ground directly in front of him.

She looked up at him, her face flushed. Her gloved hands had braced against his shoulders. Realizing this herself, she pulled them back as if she had touched fire.

"Are you all right?" he asked with a frown.

Anne blinked up at him several times before taking a few steps back. She pulled off one of her tan gloves then pressed a hand to her cheek. "Yes. Riding is vigorous exercise." Her flush deepened, however. "Would you like to meet Onyx?" She turned away to pet the stallion's neck. "He's very gentlemanly and loves pets."

Victor hesitated but reached out to pet the horse, too. Onyx's ears flicked and he turned his big head a bit so his eye could see Victor and Anne.

She watched Victor for moment and then tore her gaze away. "Why don't you get acquainted with Onyx? I'll be right back."

Victor watched her drape the long side of her riding skirt over her left arm. He could just barely see the trouser-like part of her ensemble underneath the skirt as she walked away and disappeared into the stables.

"Tell me, Onyx," Victor said lowly. "How does an old man like me woo a pretty lady like her?"

Onyx pulled his top lip back as if laughing, then let out a snort. Victor scratched behind the horse's ear, which seemed to please the animal. Though Victor wasn't an expert on horses, it was clear to him Onyx was special. He looked strong but lean, and his coat, mane, and tail were all a healthy, glossy black.

As Victor began petting Onyx's neck, winning a few more happy snorts from the horse, Anne reemerged from the stables, leading a white horse with brown spots. Onyx let out a whinny and jumped a bit on his front hooves. When Anne stopped by Victor, the horse on her lead went up to nuzzle Onyx.

"This is Pancake." Anne gave the new horse a gentle pat on her side. "She's the mare you'll be on today."

Victor narrowed his eyes. "Pancake."

"Yes." Anne smiled. "Don't let Onyx fool you—he's a spirited horse and not for a beginner. Pancake is the horse Mary usually rides, as she is very sweet and docile. It is difficult to upset her."

Out of the corner of his eye, he spotted the stablehands peeking out around the door. They snickered and ducked back in when Victor scowled at them.

"To be clear," Victor said, still petting Onyx, "you want me riding a young lady's mare. Named Pancake."

Anne let out a squeak of a laugh, then cleared her throat. "Yes. She is also Onyx's sweetheart."

Victor's eyelids lowered along with the corners of his mouth.

"If you wish to learn how to ride, which is a requirement of the aristocracy, I suggest you start with a horse that doesn't give a fig about anything."

Pancake flicked her tail, as if agreeing.

"Onyx seems far more fitting for me," Victor replied.

Anne considered the black stallion. "There has been more than one time where he has reared up with no warning beforehand. I knew what to do in those situations. Would you?"

"No," he admitted. Unfortunately. As Pancake's giant, horsey nose went to Victor's ear to sniff him, he relented. "Very well. Pancake it is."

Anne let out a small laugh again and she led Pancake away from Onyx. As if understanding what this meant, Onyx meandered away and began nibbling at tufts of grass he was able to reach just beyond the fence line.

"To get used to being on a horse again, you'll climb up to your saddle and then I'll lead you around a few times."

Resisting a grumble at starting *this* basic, he followed direction without complaint, knowing Anne wouldn't change her mind about this.

Once Victor was settled, Anne began leading Pancake around the paddock. "It's important to always pay attention to your horse's mood," Anne began. Victor stared down at the top of her hat as she walked beside them, holding a long rope like a leash. "Their ears are the most telling. Ears to the side mean they're relaxed. Ears to the front, something has caught their attention, which means you should be on alert."

At the moment, Pancake's ears were to the side.

"If their ears are back or flat, they are angry or upset. Both are concerning, and you need to be extremely cautious. Prepare for anything to happen. They might kick, buck, rear, or bolt. And the sheer size of them means they can easily throw you to the ground. That was how Bernard was killed."

This comment caused Anne to become quiet. After leading Victor and Pancake around the paddock for a bit, Victor took the reins on his own. Anne told him how to use the reins, how to gently tap the horse with his heels. After about an hour of lessons, Victor found himself feeling more confident and refamiliarized with his old childhood lessons. Anne tested him a bit, making sure he knew how to stop the horse, increase speed, and lower speed.

"Would you like to try leaving the paddock for a bit?" Anne asked.

Victor looked out at the endless green that expanded beyond the paddock and felt a pull to it. He looked down at Anne, who had to shield her eyes in the now-bright morning sun in order to look up at him. He noted clouds were coming in, though, which would shield the sun and make the ride more pleasant. "I think I would like that."

"Excellent. Let me grab Onyx."

A few minutes later, the stablehands opened the gate and Victor followed Anne out to the field.

For the first few minutes, Victor was admittedly slightly nervous, but Pancake didn't seem bothered the least. Onyx appeared rather happy to be out there, snorting and whinnying with joy.

As Victor was mostly focused on his first ride, there wasn't much conversation. After about half an hour, they found themselves on a hilltop. They paused to give the horses a rest and were able to look out over the distant English Channel. Pancake's ears flicked and turned forward briefly but returned to the side.

Onyx, meanwhile, gnawed on grass.

"What do you all usually do in the summer?" Victor asked. "Do you generally stay at the house or go into town?"

Anne looked over at him. She was so elegant in her top hat and green habit. She shifted in her sidesaddle seat. "We go into town a few times, but we mostly stay around Summerwood or visit others. More people will be here in a few weeks once Queen Victoria leaves London. There's a ball coming up at Tanglebrush Manor, a small one. Then, once the queen leaves for Osborne House in a month or so, there's the masquerade at the Viscount Bell's. Lord and Lady Bell throw it every year."

"A masquerade? I believe you've mentioned it in passing a few times over the years."

Anne brightened. "Oh, yes! It's one of my favorite events of the season."

Personally, Victor didn't find the idea of a masquerade appealing and with all of the other events he would likely attend, decided that one, he would sit out. He didn't have a costume, anyway.

"I imagine you have to plan for that one ahead of time," he mused aloud.

There was a flicker of disappointment on her face. "Oh, yes, I suppose that means you won't be able to attend? Oh, bother that."

"That's all right. It doesn't appeal to me much, anyway. What are you going as this year?"

"A swan! Oh, Victor, I can't wait to show you it. It's so beautiful. The dress is covered in white feathers and my hat will look like a swan sits right atop my head."

There was a sudden gust of wind, which caused Pancake to lift her head from grazing. Her ears briefly went forward again.

"Smells like rain," Victor said and he noted Anne's face was pinched with worry. He then looked over his shoulder. Dark clouds fast approached.

Anne looked to see what he stared at. "Oh!" she shouted with alarm. "Where did that come from? We must head back before we get caught in that. Do you think you're comfortable going at a quicker pace?"

Victor wasn't sure, but he could see they would soon be in danger. Anne's shoulders were far too tense for those clouds to portend merely a little rain.

"Lead the way, and we'll follow," he replied, hoping he sounded sure of himself.

They began galloping toward Summerwood as humid, earthy air filled his lungs. As the dark clouds got closer, the wind became stronger. The scent of rain strengthened and a few drops landed on his face.

Alarm bells were ringing in his head and he observed Pancake's ears. They were back now but not flat, and she didn't seem tense otherwise. But Onyx's ears, Victor was alarmed to discover, *were* flat and the stallion started to jerk around erratically.

Anne's mouth was set tight and she leaned forward to say something to Onyx. Victor couldn't hear what she said but knew she was trying to comfort the animal.

But then, in the distance, a lightning bolt cut across the sky and an earth-shattering crack of thunder followed. Onyx bolted forward at a full gallop, then made a sharp turn right, sending Anne flying.

Chapter Eleven

I T FELT AS if Anne floated with the wind. Everything seemed to happen slowly as she was flung off Onyx's saddle, and the stallion's gallops echoed in her mind as he got farther away.

A boom of thunder shook the air.

And then, she was on the ground. It felt as she had been hit by a runaway carriage.

"Anne!" Victor's terrified voice shouted from somewhere.

Anne squeezed her eyes shut as she turned to her side and brought her knees up to her chest, desperately trying to catch her breath. The wind had been knocked out of her, and each breath she tried to take sounded like a wheeze.

A raindrop splashed on her cheek and she managed to open her eyes.

Victor dropped down beside her on all fours, his green eyes wild and frantic as he listened to her trying to catch her breath, the labor of it exacerbated by her panicking. The rush of fear Onyx had caused still bounced around in her like thousands of rubber balls.

"You're all right, calm down," Victor said in a strained voice. She stared up at his face as he quickly looked her over, presumably to make sure there truly was no sign of injury. His gaze went back to hers as more raindrops began to fall. That was one of the most terrifying moments she had ever experienced, but she felt better knowing Victor was here. She knew he wouldn't let anything happen to her. "Shh," he said gently as she wheezed again. "Close your eyes. Focus on your breathing."

Anne did as he'd said. And after a few tries, her mind finally regained control of her lungs. She took three deep, slow breaths, and then opened her eyes again, feeling far more like herself.

Victor hovered right over her, his hands pressed into the ground on either side of her shoulders. For a long moment, they stared at each other, and a strange sensation began swirling through her like smoke. A distant memory sparked of a thunderstorm like this one, of her being on the ground just like now, and Victor being there with her.

Something flashed in his eyes and he swallowed, then sat back to give her space.

"Does anything hurt?" he asked. The rain was now falling steadily, but he didn't seem to notice.

Anne mentally searched herself. "I don't know."

"Do you think you broke anything?"

"No. Help me up." As she tried to sit forward, he helped push her back up to sitting.

Rain was starting to trickle down her hair. "Where is my hat?" She looked around, frantic. As soon as she'd spotted it some distance away, she jumped up to her feet, but the blood rushed too quickly and she faltered.

A large, strong hand pressed into her middle back, the touch causing her heart to skip a beat.

"I'll get it." Victor was quite close and frowning down at her. He must have been rather irritated with her. When he let her go, she was overwhelmed by the strange sensation of cold emptiness.

The hat was a good twenty feet away. Victor grabbed it and returned to give it back to her. With a swallow, she secured it back on her wet hair.

"Which way did Onyx go?" Anne looked around but all she could see was rain and fog. Visibility had decreased significantly.

Horror struck her anew—she had lost Vivian's horse! Oh,

blast, how could she have done something so stupid? "We have to go find him!"

The rain became a downpour, deepening Victor's frown. He looked her over and then began shrugging out of his coat. "*We are going back home.*"

"But—"

"No *buts*, Anne. There's thunder. And we are in the middle of a field." He moved behind her and draped his jacket over her shoulders. It felt warm and dry, and she mumbled a *thank you*, though she felt bad. He rested his hands on her shoulders for a second, then pulled away. "We need to get back. We're going to be soaked to the bone in just minutes, and it's going to take a good amount of time to return."

Anne looked over at Pancake, who shook from head to tail, flinging water every direction. Victor did have a point.

"You're positive you're all right?" Victor, his hair now soaked, water dripping down his face, ambled over to Pancake.

Anne followed, clenching the coat around her tightly. The riding skirt was too wet and muddy now and had to be dragged. She must have looked ridiculous. "Yes, I'm fine, just a bit shaken up and a little sore."

Victor nodded and placed one foot in Pancake's stirrup, then threw his other leg over the saddle to take his seat. He looked down at Anne and held out his hand.

Anne stared at it and blinked. "We only have one horse now," she said stupidly.

"Yes, you're going to have to sit with me."

"It's not a sidesaddle."

"No, it's not. There isn't enough room for you to sit sidesaddle." He shoved his hand forward with impatience.

"I can't sit astride!"

"*Anne.*" Victor wasn't bothering to hide his ire now. "This is not exactly how I expected to spend my morning, and I would like to get back into warm, dry clothes. I am hazarding a guess you would, too."

She let out a huff of a breath and then, trying to hide her embarrassment, gathered up her green skirt—thankfully, this habit had trousers underneath—and climbed up to sit directly in front of Victor.

There was absolutely no room between them. Anne tried to move forward a tiny bit, to no avail. Her bottom was right up against his front. Her back pressed up against his chest.

This was the most inappropriate situation in which she had found herself in quite a long time, made worse by the building soreness from falling off Onyx.

And she couldn't help it. She started laughing. This was absurd!

Victor sighed, and Anne guessed he probably did not find this situation nearly as amusing as she did. "Do you want to hold the reins?"

"Yes," she choked out as she grabbed the leather reins, gently tapped her heels into Pancake's side, and Pancake began running through the rain. It wasn't a full gallop but would get them back much quicker than a trot.

Water pelted Anne's face and within minutes, any dry spots left on either of them were gone, and her body ached. She could feel the cold wetness of Victor's shirt through the jacket he had given her, but behind that, his chest was hard and warm. It struck her that he'd given his jacket to her without a thought. He hadn't even asked; he'd just draped it over her.

She tried telling herself it was merely something a good friend or a gentleman would do. And maybe it was. But something deep within made her seem more unsure about it than she would have expected.

Naturally, she waved that silly thought away. This was Victor, the most gentlemanly person she knew. Of course he would give his jacket up to her.

Pancake began running over rough terrain, causing Anne to bounce around in the saddle a bit. Victor made a pained noise, then his arm wrapped around her middle, pulling her closer and holding her tightly like a vise.

His arm was hot and solid against her softness.

She thanked her lucky stars for the loud wind and rain because she let out a gasp at the unexpected, extremely intimate movement. Victor was *holding* her. Tightly. Against his front.

Oh, dear, and she could feel *everything*.

Even his breath as it swept hotly over her neck.

Anne swallowed and tried to keep her concentration on Pancake, but her mind kept trailing off because Victor was not a touchy person.

Sometimes, he would walk arm in arm with her, but he usually didn't. He didn't hug, and he only shook hands if he had to. He'd probably pecked her on the cheek three times in their entire friendship.

But right now, he was holding her like a lover would. And he wasn't letting go, or loosening his grip. In fact, with each bolt of lightning and resounding boom of thunder, Anne would flinch and his hold on her would tighten, as if he were attempting to reassure her.

Her face heated as she jostled in the seat again against him. Victor's hand, which cupped around her side, twitched.

"Bit of a rough ride," she said, trying to sound bright, hoping it would lessen the awkwardness.

But Victor didn't respond.

Now she was curious. She forced herself to look up at him and found his jaw set tight, and redness on his cheekbones just behind and above his beard. He noticed her looking up at him, glanced at her, then quickly brought his eyes back up to face forward.

He cleared his throat. "It's a rough ride, and there's no chance I'm letting you fall off again." His voice was dark and husky as he said this.

For the briefest of moments, her body became confused by that voice, by the way he held her close. Desire began glow warm inside her.

Until she realized what was happening—then it came to a screeching halt.

Victor was only holding her like this so she wouldn't fall. Again. And his voice sounded like that because he was cold and wet and annoyed.

This was a giant sign that her openness to a seaside romance this summer was a good idea. Clearly, she had been without a gentleman's attention for far too long. For a minute there, she'd thought Victor had been attracted to her. What a ridiculous thought!

Soon the stables were in sight and she felt Victor's body relaxing. Which made her feel a bit wretched.

Pancake went into the stables and Victor held Anne until Pancake came to a complete stop. As she slid off the animal, she realized how rubbery her legs felt.

Victor followed down and placed a hand on her back again.

A pleasant feeling began to buzz throughout her body. Maybe she had hit her head and didn't realize it.

One of the stablehands appeared and Anne frantically told him what had happened with Onyx. The man was quite concerned for Anne's wellbeing and when he expressed his worry over her, she swore she could feel darkness clouding the air around Victor. But when she looked in that direction, Victor held a level face, watching the gap-toothed stablehand, unblinking. As if he hardly noticed the man at all.

"I have a feeling I know where he is." The stablehand spotted Victor, swallowed, then put his attention back on Anne. "I'll go get him now so he doesn't get too far." He then climbed atop Pancake and went out into the rain.

Anne found a nearby bench and collapsed into it, letting her head drop back against the wall, pulling Victor's jacket around her tightly. Though the thunder had weakened and all but disappeared, the rain was still coming down hard, pelting the side and roof of the stable loudly. Unfortunately, it was a good walk back to the house. Hopefully, the rain would let up soon, too.

Otherwise, they would be stuck here.

When she opened her eyes, she found Victor farther down the stables, his back to her. A tawny horse had its head out, and Victor was gently petting the animal.

Anne watched, enamored by the sight. Victor's hand, large and masculine and rough, gently pet the horse. His white shirt, soaked almost transparent, clung to every curve of his shoulder and bicep. It was the same hand and arm that had held her close just moments ago. She could still feel his arm around her, his hand gripping her side.

With a swallow, she allowed herself a study of the rest of him. Victor was a large man—all of the McNabs were—but she'd never really *studied* him before.

She felt her face flush at the thought. She had never really looked at him in this way before. Then again, it was a bit impossible to ignore it now. His white shirt and dark trousers clung to every inch of him. And she could practically see through the shirt, as if he didn't wear one at all. He had muscles all up and down his back, muscles she hadn't even known existed. She had seen him at work, the way he would carry heavy barrels on each shoulder as if they were mere pebbles, so she knew where they had come from.

Anne shifted in her seat and looked around to make sure no one saw what she was doing.

"It doesn't seem to be letting up yet." Victor let his hand drop from the horse and turned around to face her.

Anne opened her mouth to reply with an agreement but stilled as she set her eyes upon Victor's front. He was walking toward her, and what a sight he was for feminine eyes! The last time she'd let her late husband touch her had been before Freddy had been born. Now it felt like part of her was sputtering back to life.

She could see everything. The hardness of his chest, the ropes of muscle on his stomach and side.

The hair. Dear Lord, the hair. *That* was an unexpected discovery. And she was surprised to find herself not put off by it, but extremely intrigued.

She made a squeaking noise.

Victor hurried over to her, stopping directly in front of her. "What's wrong?" he asked, his voice hard with alarm.

She began to stammer but quickly recovered. "N-Nothing."

Blinking, Victor looked down at himself and swore out loud. "I need my jacket back," he said with haste.

"What?"

"My jacket." He looked her in the eye and there was a wildness there that caused her heart to hitch. She jumped up to her feet and shed the jacket.

Victor turned away, slid the jacket back on, and then turned back. "My apologies for that. I had no idea I stood before you in such a state." He seemed put out by whatever had just happened, so she decided to let it go. In truth, she wasn't even sure what to say herself.

"I, um…" Victor cleared his throat and rolled his neck. This seemed to get him back to normal. He looked down at her again, no hint of embarrassment anywhere. "I apologize for the unfortunate way we had to return."

She leaned back against the wall and crossed her arms. "What do you mean?"

"The rather, ah, close way we had to sit together."

"Oh. Right." She forced a shrug. "It's not a problem, Victor." *Not a problem that you held me like you would hold a lover, no, sir.* "We didn't have a choice."

Though he hesitated, he ultimately nodded in agreement, then went to the large opening of the stables to study the ongoing storm.

Anne had known Victor for long enough, and knew him well enough, to spot the sudden but minute tension that pulled his shoulders and back.

Something was on his mind.

"This rain, the mud. Summerwood." He paused but didn't

turn around. "It reminds me of something."

Immediately, dread twisted in her stomach.

When she didn't respond, Victor turned around and walked back over to her. "Do you know what I'm referring to?"

On a gulp, she shook her head.

Victor ran a hand through his soaked hair then licked his lips. He was nervous, she could tell. And she didn't like that one bit. "The summer Vivian and Dantes married. It was the only time I've ever been to Summerwood before this year."

He paused, waiting for a reaction from her.

She forced stillness.

"You ran after Winthrop and fell in the mud. Do you remember that?"

No response.

Victor sighed, and after briefly hesitating, sat next to Anne on the bench. He rested his elbows on his knees and leaned forward, as if considering what to say next. He angled his head to look back at her and her heart began racing. But it was with fear, not excitement or anticipation. *Please don't do this, Victor.*

"You had fallen in the mud," he began again. "And I helped you get up. We laughed about the state of your clothes—you were absolutely covered in mud. We had just made a promise to each other."

"I don't know what you're talking about."

He was quiet a long time. "You don't remember it? Or how I ended that conversation? Or do you deny it?"

Her heart felt like it was going to break through her ribs.

Of course she remembered it. She had spent years trying to forget it. They had never put to words what that promise was, but she had seen it in his eyes.

And he must have seen something in her eyes. Though what, she couldn't say.

But it had been the lowest time of her life up until that point. Bernard had not yet been deceased, but he'd been all but gone from their lives. Her marriage had failed. She'd been melancholy.

She had never felt so alone before.

And there had been her new friend pulling her out of the mud.

Whatever he'd seen in her eyes that day, he'd mistaken what it had meant.

And she had dreaded the day he would bring it up.

But she couldn't give him anything, if he wanted something. She could not promise herself to him, if that was what he wanted. She could not commit herself to him—she could not, would not, commit herself to anyone ever again.

"I have to go," Anne said, the panic in full force. She hurried out toward the house without a further word, without a further glance back, without answering his question. And she sobbed in the rain as she ran.

Chapter Twelve

May 1889

ANNE RUSHED INTO Vivian's receiving room, desperate for a moment alone. The entire day had been spent at the annual London flower show, then they'd come to Vivian's for dinner. Vivian's father, the Duke of Chalworth, had mentioned a photograph of Vivian and Bernard when they'd been younger. Anne had known it was in Vivian's receiving room and had offered to fetch it. She was so tired and needed a moment alone.

She found the silver-framed photograph immediately on the sideboard and looked down at it with a small smile. It wasn't a perfect portrait—in fact, it was so full of movement, it was blurry. Her husband was almost indecipherable as he cartwheeled across the picture. Vivian stood nearby, grasping at her stomach and laughing loudly.

It had been taken before Anne and Bernard had met, and he seemed far more carefree. She could not imagine him doing a cartwheel nowadays.

Anne's lip began to quiver, and her hand flew up to her mouth in an attempt to still it. She had to put the photograph down and collapse into a nearby chair. From a pocket, she revealed a handkerchief and began dabbing at her eyes, intent on not letting them redden or swell.

Recently, Bernard had come home in the middle of the afternoon unexpectedly, a strange new habit of his as of late. Usually, he did everything he could to stay away from the house, from her, from the children.

When he'd left again after being home for a short time, suspiciously changed into a new suit with refreshed cologne, he'd told her he'd been heading to Brooks's and would need the carriage for that. It was where he often spent his spare time, so this part wasn't strange to her.

But this time, Anne had run outside to watch Bernard and the carriage depart. She didn't know why she'd done it, really, as she had never done it before. But though her husband had never been the greatest spouse, these last few months—ever since he had lost his inheritance to his sister—his behavior had worsened an alarming amount. His drinking was nearly constant, his dislike toward her had become hatred, and she was bracing herself for him to escalate beyond cruel words into cruel touches.

As she had watched Bernard's carriage that day, though, something odd had happened.

One block away, it stopped, and her husband stepped out to jog up to a townhouse. Anne watched him knock upon a front door that belonged to Mr. and Mrs. Harrington. Mrs. Harrington was a woman so beautiful, Anne always felt small near her. One could almost feel the woman's presence when she entered a room. The way men stopped what they were doing to gawk at the woman seemed to change the air around everyone.

As Anne had gripped her doorframe, feeling the blood drain from her face, Bernard disappeared inside the townhome. She watched for fifteen minutes, hoping he would reemerge.

But he didn't.

The carriage, the visit to Brooks's—they had been a ruse. Bernard thought she was stupid, so easily fooled.

And she was, for a long time at least.

Holding back tears, Anne had then gone into his office, dug through everything, and found letters from Mrs. Harrington. She'd sat down and read through every single sordid word, words she wouldn't dare utter aloud herself. Simply reading them had caused her to blush.

After reading through them all, Anne had leaned over into a rubbish bin and vomited.

Bernard was a frequent visitor to brothels, so infidelity was not new behavior. She no longer let him touch her and the brothels kept his hands away from her. Though she hated the visits, they also gave her some measure of peace. Those women didn't care about her husband—he was a means to an end for them. Because of that, she saw it more as a relief than a burden, in an odd way.

But a full-blown liaison? With someone they knew? Someone they saw frequently at social events?

That was inconceivable. While Anne struggled at home alone, already distraught over their crumbling marriage, Bernard had begun to lay in Mrs. Harrington's bed, the pair laughing, fooling themselves into believing what they were doing was fine because they were simply married to the wrong people.

A few days after that, Anne had met with a solicitor and had brought the letters for proof of infidelity. That morning, Bernard had grabbed her chin threateningly, which she'd told the solicitor about as well.

She'd spilled everything about his mishandling of their money, the thousands of pounds of debt he had racked up.

And that morning, the morning of the flower show, she'd finally heard back from the solicitor. *"Unfortunately,"* the man had written, *"your evidence, your husband's behavior, is not enough for Parliament to grant a woman of the aristocracy a divorce from her husband."*

It was simple, short, straight to the point.

And thus, this would be her life. The spot in her heart that had once held hope for love and romance was now filled with fear and terror.

As Anne sat in the chair in Vivian's receiving room, the photograph of Bernard mocking her, a few sobs escaped to cut into the stilled air.

Unless Bernard was able to secure a divorce, as it was easier for men—though she'd given him no cause to pursue one—or he died prematurely, this would be her life.

The sobs turned into full-body shakes and the floodgates opened.

Followed by the door.

Anne flew to her feet, humiliated, and found herself face to face with a man she had never met before. He looked a bit similar to Vivian's friend Mr. Dantes McNab, with the same green eyes with that slight wildness to them. He had hair the color of ink, and stubble where a beard should have been, as if he hadn't shaved for a day or two. And he was quite tall, with huge shoulders and thick arms and thighs, but a narrow waist.

He also looked really crabby. And quite uncomfortable at the sight of her.

"Oh, goodness, I'm so sorry," Anne said with a hiccup. As she began dabbing at her eyes, she sniffed. "I made an excuse to come in here to gather myself, and everything hit me all at once."

The dark-haired man didn't say anything but continued watching her, unblinking.

Anne began sobbing again and when she was upset, some-times she lost control of her mouth. "My husband is having an affair with an acquaintance, after years and years of visiting brothels. He's drunk all the time and yells at everyone constant-ly—on the rare occasion where he's actually home. When he *is* home all he does is try to make me feel as horrid as possible." Realizing what she had divulged to a complete stranger, she cursed at herself, then apologized again for her vulgar language.

"Who is your husband?" he asked. His voice was deep and oddly calming.

"The Marquess of Litchfield." She paused. "Why did I tell you that? Why am I telling you anything? Oh, blast, I've lost my mind!"

"I won't tell a soul."

She looked up at him and could see in his eyes that he meant it. She felt very aware while being under that unusually sharp gaze of his. "Thank you."

He took a few hesitating steps toward her. "Would you like to escape?"

"'Escape'?"

"I have a hansom that should still be out front. You're welcome to use it to get home. Just tell the driver Victor offered it, if needed."

It took her a moment to understand what he was saying. She had some coin on her, but she was too distraught to think if she had enough for a hansom or not. He was offering to pay for her. This touched her more than she wanted to admit—this stranger was showing her more kindness in one small gesture than her husband had their entire marriage.

The door to the receiving room opened again and another man entered the room, his hands rubbing at his face. "What are they feeding those animals? That stench has burned into my nose for eternity." As he moved his hands away, he startled at the sight of Anne. "Oh. Sorry."

"This is Lady Litchfield," the man she assumed was Victor said. "She's using the hansom to go home."

The other man, much younger than Victor, frowned. "Why?"

Victor's eyes narrowed and his voice became a dark warning. "It's none of your business why."

The younger man gave Victor a strange look before turning to her. "I should warn you, the horse was rather...foul today for some reason."

Anne put a hand to her mouth before looking at Victor.

"It's true," Victor said, pulling his shoulders back and straightening his spine. "It was actually rather ghastly."

Anne couldn't help but start laughing, and Victor met her laughter with his own. She accepted the kind offer, thanked him, and handed over the photograph with instruction to give it to Vivian. As Anne slipped out the door, she overheard the younger man say, "Did you just laugh?"

Chapter Thirteen

June 1899

ANNE AWOKE WITH a gasp and immediately became consumed by the most wretched headache. Wincing from the pain, she pulled a nearby rope to ring the maid and fell back to her pillow with a groan, placing a hand over her forehead.

A forehead that felt like fire.

That would explain the vivid dream of when she'd first met Victor. It was awful how dreams amplified emotion. That feeling of hopelessness she had felt that day, the little beacon of light from Victor's kindness that had pushed through the fog—it all felt like she was back to that day, even though it had been an entire decade. Though why that old memory was the one that had become a fever dream, she hadn't the faintest idea.

Dutton knocked quietly before entering the room and appeared at Anne's bedside with a tray containing soup and water.

"How long have I been asleep?" Anne asked in a raspy voice.

"About four hours, my lady," Dutton replied, setting the tray on the nightstand.

Anne began shaking from chills, as if she still wore the rain-soaked clothing. "I can't believe I've succumbed to fever the first day of our summer holiday."

"You're lucky that's the worst that happened to you today," Dutton said with a pointed look. "Mr. Victor McNab told me everything that had happened."

Anne's eyebrows pulled together as she moved to sit up against pillows Dutton situated for her. "Why did he tell you about that?"

"He was worried you have an invisible injury. Merely a precaution, my lady, for me to watch out for." From under her arm, Dutton pulled out a little stand that she unfolded and bridged over Anne's lap. Dutton then put the tray upon it. Aside from the bowl of soup and a glass of water, there was a small crystal vase with a little daisy in it.

"How sweet." Anne touched the flower gently with one finger.

"Mr. McNab asked me to give that to you." Dutton avoided Anne's eye as she said this.

"He did?" Anne pulled her hand away from it but kept looking upon it. "Why?"

"To brighten your spirits, I imagine. Everyone was worried when you still slept hours after coming in from the rain. Is there anything else I can get for you?"

Anne recalled earlier that morning, when she and Victor had had to share the saddle. The way his arm had wrapped around her had turned her into a silly girl who'd then become brainless over his wet, clinging, transparent shirt. She should absolutely not be turning into a silly girl over Victor. Or any man, rather. She needed to rectify this at once. "Could you please have Lady Vivian come in here?"

Dutton gave a quick curtsy of acknowledgment and departed the room.

A few minutes later, Vivian entered, a deep frown on her face. She hastened to Anne's bedside. "Dutton asked me to come in and see you. Is everything all right?" Vivian didn't wait for a response before putting a hand to Anne's forehead. "You do have a fever."

Anne spooned some of the broth but let it fall back into the bowl. "Yes, I feel rather terrible. The chills are atrocious."

"I should fetch a physician, I think."

The last thing Anne wanted was more fuss over her. "Please, don't. I'll be fine."

Vivian lowered to the edge of the bed and eyed the daisy, but she didn't say anything about it. Likely, she assumed it was simply a decoration Dutton had put on the tray. "Victor told us what happened with the rain, and Onyx."

Anne's eyes went wide with panic. She had forgotten all about the horse! "Oh, Vivian, I am so sorry. He got away from me! The rain came out of nowhere. I know how sensitive he is and wouldn't have taken him out if I'd known we were going to get storms."

Vivian waved her off. "He's already back in the stable. There's a particular meadow he likes, and anytime he escapes, he always ends up there. They found him not long after you returned with Pancake. Don't fret."

Anne let out a breath of relief.

"I heard you had to share a saddle with Victor, though. *Astride.*" Mischief glittered in Vivian's eyes. "How was that?"

Anne swallowed and lied. "So humiliating, Vivian."

Vivian gave her a coy look. "'Humiliating'? Oh, I don't think that's what you felt."

Anne, suspecting this was an innuendo, narrowed her eyes at Vivian, who only laughed in response. Feigning disinterest, Anne began to stir her soup and forced boredom on her face and in her voice. "Did he say anything about that?" She was, admittedly, a bit curious about how Victor had perceived the moment. He'd definitely disliked it. But how much?

"Oh," Vivian said too brightly. "Just that you had to share the saddle and he had to hold you to keep you from falling off."

Anne stopped stirring, tilted her chin up, and closed her eyes. "Yes, that did, in fact, happen."

"And then he said once you were back at the stables, he could tell you were getting ill."

Anne's eyes flew open. She had not felt ill in the stables. "How?"

Vivian pursed her lips before saying, "Because you were staring at him." Then she smiled. "And you were red as you did so."

"I have a *fever*!" Anne was outraged by Vivian's insinuation.

"Normally, I would believe you—well, maybe—but we heard all about what happened when he came into the house afterward." Vivian looked Anne over and cocked an eyebrow. "You know, soaking wet?"

Anne let out an overly dramatic gasp. "What are you insinuating?! I-I should be insulted!"

"So, you *aren't* denying you were staring at him and blushing?"

Anne's mouth dropped open and she stammered. Vivian was reading far too much into this. All right, yes, Victor had looked nice in the wet shirt. It had been nothing more than appreciation of a fit male form. It was absolutely not an appreciation of Victor himself. She let go of the spoon and it clinked against the bowl. "I did have a purpose for requesting your visit and it wasn't to pester me."

"But it's so much fun." Vivian pouted.

Anne rolled her eyes. "I think you should throw a ball."

Vivian pulled back a bit, as if surprised by the suggestion. "A ball? When?"

"I think a week from now would be good. I'll be better by then. And not everyone will be in the area quite yet, so it won't be as crowded. Freddy mentioned his new friend's family summers nearby. I think it would be nice to invite them and get to know them."

"If you want that, I suppose I can throw a ball on short notice. As you said, not everyone is on holiday yet. And Father *has* been bothering me about throwing more social events on his behalf. But why a ball and not a dinner party? You never seem very interested in them."

For a moment, Anne debated if she should be honest about this. On one hand, it would be far easier if she lied and said she simply thought a ball would be good fun. But Vivian was right—it would be odd for Anne to say that. Vivian would see through it as clearly as glass. If Anne were honest, though, she could at least redirect Vivian away from Victor and quash whatever it was she thought was going on. Because it was clear Vivian had some incorrect ideas floating around in her head.

"It has been a rather long time since I've truly enjoyed a ball," Anne said. "I haven't danced since I went through mourning. Plus, I think this summer would be a good time to dip my toe back in the romantic waters."

Vivian's mouth become a perfect O.

"*Potentially.*" Anne gripped her bedding and said this a bit louder to make the point. "And I am not being serious about it. I only want to play around a bit. Some dancing here, flirtations with my fan there, you know. Nothing serious at all. Then, once summer is over, I'll leave that silly business here."

"I don't understand," Vivian admitted.

"I'm happy with my life now. But I haven't pursued male attention since I was a debutante. I don't know… Maybe it would be a bit fun to do so? I don't want to take it too seriously, though, which is why I thought being a bit silly over summer would be a good way to do that."

Vivian's eyebrows furrowed and she twisted her mouth.

Was she upset with Anne? Anne's late husband *was* Vivian's brother. And though the last few years of his life, they had not been on good terms—in fact, Vivian had cut him out of her life as well—Bernard was still her brother. And they'd been close growing up. A sense of dread flooded her. "Oh, dear, should I not be talking to you about this?"

Vivian's eyes softened. "That's not it." She paused and looked down at her hands. "I know my brother did not treat you well." Another pause. "I've never told you this before, but when I learned about his passing, I wasn't surprised at all. I figured one day everything would hit me, that he was gone. There were days where I was a bit sad, but I never sobbed over it. I don't think he ever would have gone back to who he used to be. I mean, if that accident had not happened. He would have only become worse, more erratic, more dangerous. I just wish things had been different. If anything, I felt regret that I could not have helped him more."

"Vivian, you did so much for us. For him. You already did plenty."

"Maybe." Vivian looped a loose piece of dark hair back around her ear. "I mourn who he used to be, I suppose."

Anne reached around the tray and placed her hand over Vivian's. "I know."

After a long moment, Vivian sighed and then straightened. A sad smile lifted her lips. "Very well. I think throwing a ball in a week's time is a brilliant idea." And then, she suddenly stood. "Though I probably should go begin the plans for that. Do you need anything?"

Anne shook her head. "I'm fine."

Vivian nodded and left the room.

Anne looked back down at her soup, but she had no appetite. There was a strange nervousness swirling around in her stomach that took away any hunger she may have had. Gently, she moved the tray and stand over to the other side of the bed and threw the blankets off, then began crossing to the other side of the room.

Briefly, she stopped as her eyes set upon the door that went to Victor's room. On a swallow, she made her way over to the door and pressed a hand to it, then listened.

There was no faint sound on the other side.

With a quick flick of a wrist, she ensured the door was locked before heading over to her vanity. It took searching a few drawers, but finally, she found what she was looking for.

She unfolded a piece of paper and reacquainted herself with it.

A Lady's Rules for Seaside Romance
Never chase a gentleman.

Never flirt first.

First and second conversations should be less than ten minutes.

Kissing is acceptable, but do not make the first move.

No gentlemen with bad hygiene.

No gentlemen who only talk politics.

No gentlemen more than ten years older or younger.

No gentlemen who don't laugh.

No gamblers.

Never fall in love.

Satisfied, Anne put it back in her drawer. She recalled briefly when Vivian had been seeking a husband years ago, she'd had a difficult time finding a gentleman who would make a good mate. So many of the men in their social class were scoundrels. For a brief moment, Anne felt a sense of hopelessness but then pushed that away. She wasn't seeking a husband. She was seeking someone who would happily walk arm-in-arm with her and make her stomach flutter with butterflies.

Then she would leave him behind—where he belonged.

Almost anyone could do for that purpose. In fact, a scoundrel might even be a bit of fun, so long as she was careful not to lead him to expect too much. It wasn't like she was ever going to marry anyone, or take the man seriously, either.

There was a slight breeze that came in through the windows and with it, voices from below. Anne went over to one window and looked down at the expansive, lush lawn. Everyone was outside right now and it appeared they were playing croquet.

Anne smiled to herself as she watched. She still felt horrid, though the chills had lessened, but she could manage to watch for a minute or so. It appeared to be a game of four with Mary, Freddy, Victor, and Ollie. Everyone else, save Vivian, watched from the side. Mary tapped her mallet against a red ball and the ball rolled over the grass and through a metal hoop. Freddy went next, and then Victor. Anne watched with interest, as she didn't think Victor had ever played the game before.

Victor swung the mallet a few times, as if testing his swing, and then finally made contact with a green ball.

It flew off at a severe angle.

While Ollie patted Victor on the back, Mary and Freddy clapped animatedly.

Anne covered her mouth to keep from letting out a laugh.

As Victor crossed over to where the green ball was, Ollie took his own swing. However, Anne didn't watch how Ollie did. Under the veil of secrecy—no one had any idea she was spying on them from her window—Anne let her eyes anchor on Victor. She watched him cross the lawn, now wearing a dry, dark suit, and he gently swung the mallet in time with his steps. Then he suddenly stopped about ten feet short of the green ball, turned around, and looked up directly at her standing in the window.

With a sharp inhale, Anne took several steps back to where she knew he couldn't see her. Her heart pounded hard in her chest and she covered her mouth with her hand. She wasn't doing anything wrong, so why did it feel as if she had been caught doing something quite naughty?

Chapter Fourteen

A LL WEEK, THE children had begged to promenade on the pier. And now that the ball was done being planned, the hostess of the summer house had finally relented to the begging of her daughter, niece, and nephews. Thus, the entirety of the McNabs and Winthrops were in town for the first time that season.

Victor was walking with Vivian, and the pair trailed behind everyone else as they meandered along the pier that jutted out into the sea. He didn't really understand what the point of a promenade on the pier was, but everyone else seemed eager for it, so he'd gone along.

As Vivian chatted with him about the ball tomorrow, most of Victor's attention was on Anne up ahead, Freddy and Mary on either side of her. Ollie, Evelyn, and Dantes buzzed around erratically like busy bees, chasing after their inquisitive young children.

After the fiasco with the horse-riding lesson, Anne had been ill for a few days. But ever since her recovery, she seemed to be keeping a distance from him. At meals, she avoided his eye, and during games, she'd rushed to partner with others before he could say anything.

It was becoming a bit frustrating. He wanted to put to rest— quickly—what his true feelings were for her, but he couldn't do that unless he interacted with her. It really shouldn't have been this difficult to figure out.

But every effort he made, she seemed to run off. Not always literally, but there just so happened to be an excuse every time.

Whenever he managed to talk to Anne, she would humor him for a minute or two, but something always pulled her from the conversation. Once, she'd stated Evelyn had been calling for her, but Victor hadn't heard anything. Another time, Freddy had passed by a window while they'd been outside and she'd claimed, "It seems as if he needs something." Thus, she'd rushed inside. Later, Victor had asked what the boy had needed and had received a quizzical look in response.

Then he thought about riding lessons. Anne couldn't say *no* to those, as the ongoing lessons had been her suggestion. She had agreed. However, upon his arrival, Freddy and Mary had been there, too. Not that he'd minded their presence, of course, but he couldn't very well accomplish his task with them there, either.

Anne's rather odd behavior should have put him off. Instead, it flamed his determination.

He would get to the bottom of why she was avoiding him, if it was the last thing he did. Though it was quite obviously rooted in that first disastrous riding lesson.

Christ, what a morning that had been. Between her nearly scaring him to death, then riding astride right against him?

Victor wasn't a man who thrived on touch or affection. It wasn't something he had had in his adult life, and he was just fine without it. But having Anne tucked safely against him, his arm wrapped around her tightly, her bottom flush against his front as Pancake had run over rough ground... He prided himself on control, but every pillar of it had faltered in that moment.

His idiotic brain had become hot mush during that twenty-minute ride, a sensation he had never experienced before.

Infuriatingly, Victor had to admit having a woman in his arms in such an intimate way *was* exceptionally pleasant. It had sent his heart racing while anticipation had gripped his stomach—a sense of excitement that something had been about to happen.

What he couldn't figure out—needed to figure out—was if it was because it had been Anne, or simply because it had been the first time he'd held a woman that way.

One thing he knew well, though, was Anne could drive a man to madness.

"Tomorrow should be fun, don't you think?" Vivian's voice jerked him back to the present.

Victor shook off the sudden change in his mental focus and looked at Vivian with a lifted eyebrow.

"The ball tomorrow, Victor." She tilted her head and mischief glinted in her eye. "I wonder, will you seek out a lady's attention?"

"Likely not," he said with a dark voice, hoping she wouldn't continue this subject.

Up ahead, the family went to stop at the rail along the pier. Victor watched Anne hold her hat as she tilted her head back to observe a pair of seagulls flying overhead. Vivian led him over to the rail as well, but there was some distance between them and everyone else. "I think you should, personally." Vivian rested her arms atop the fencing.

Victor put his full attention on his brother's wife. The slight rise in her voice caused him pause. "You think I should what?"

She looked out at the sea with a smile. "I think tomorrow would be a good way to get the rusty limbs moving. I bet Anne would be happy to dance with you a few times if you asked her to. Of course, there will be other ladies there you could ask, if you would like me to introduce you to them?" She looked up at him now.

Victor tried to hold her gaze as a normal person would, feeling oddly nervous under her scrutinization, as if she could see something he was trying to hide. "I don't think so."

"Then Anne would be happy to be your dancing partner. When you do take over the dukedom, you *will* have to partake in such activities. Best reacquaint yourself now before people watch too closely."

Victor kept quiet. Vivian was, of course, right and it was partly why he was in Brighton. Though he had learned how to dance some when he'd been younger, he hardly remembered how to anymore. He supposed it wouldn't be difficult to get back into it, however. How different could a waltz be these days? It would be more about remembering how to lead in an adult body, maybe observing anything new before daring to try it. And Anne had promised to help him reacquaint himself with the aristocracy and all that pertained to it, if he so wished.

"Has Anne told you about her plan for the summer?" There was that funny lilt in Vivian's voice again.

He frowned over to her. "What are you talking about?"

Vivian shrugged one shoulder. "She told me she would be looking for a male companion for the holiday. If you understand." She allowed a pause and looked him over. "You didn't know about that, did you? Oh, dear. I figure you would have—you two are so close. It didn't even occur to me that she would have kept that from you."

Victor froze, the stretched silence cut through by waves rolling ashore below. What exactly did that mean, Anne was looking for a male companion?

As Vivian lifted an eyebrow at his lack of response, he had to figure out how to properly respond, posthaste. On one hand, he didn't want to give away how much he disliked this bit of news. On the other hand, he didn't need Vivian to know the main reason he was here in Brighton was to figure out his true feelings for Anne. Not because of the looming dukedom.

"I see," was the best reply he could come up with.

Vivian let out a long sigh, but before she could respond, there was a commotion farther down the pier, where the family was.

Freddy was roughhousing with another young lad. The two young men pulled apart and were, quite obviously, glad to see each other, as their hair was messy, but both had enormous grins on their faces. The other lad had a mass of blond hair. Beyond him was a group of blonds walking toward him. The young man's family, Victor assumed.

"That must be Freddy's new friend," Vivian said.

"New friend?"

The pair began to approach the group. "Yes, Anne said Freddy made a new friend at school and they've been inseparable. They summer in Brighton, too, and he begged me to invite them to the ball tomorrow."

"Ah, yes. I did know about that. Did they accept the invite?"

"They did. Are you familiar with the Ashbys, by any chance? That's Freddy's friend's name, Ralph Ashby. I don't know much about them. I think the father was a third or fourth son of an earl."

Victor frowned to himself as they reached the family. Ashby. That name sounded quite familiar. But where had he heard it?

Vivian immediately went over to Anne right as the singular woman amongst the Ashby family approached, obviously the mother of the group. The two groups immediately became enmeshed. Freddy began to introduce his sister to the Ashby boys, and the young men all bowed to her. If Victor had to guess, Freddy's friend Ralph was the youngest of the family. Victor eyed each lad, aware that they all seemed enamored by whatever it was Mary was saying to them. Just an hour previous, the Winthrops and McNabs had left the aquarium and Mary seemed to be talking to the young men about fish tanks.

Then, as Victor continued studying the row of lads, his eyes landed on the eldest son right as he introduced himself to Mary. He wore a top hat over his blond head, and round spectacles perched atop his nose.

"Felton Ashby." The man gave the young lady a lower bow than those of his brothers. He took Mary's hand when she offered it and kissed the air above it. Mary of course was quite flattered to receive such attention from an adult. As the eldest Ashby rose back up to his full height, his gaze met Victor's and flashed with surprise.

For a moment, they held each other's stare. But then Ashby privately tipped his hat at Victor. Victor was definitely sure this was the same annoyingly chatty fellow he'd met at Bron's gaming hell.

Fantastic. Victor would be prisoner to the cad's incessant chatter for the entire season.

Ashby smartly didn't approach Victor in the moment. Men generally didn't discuss their socialization at gaming hells around women. Instead, Ashby went to his mother's side and was promptly introduced to Anne. Ashby took Anne's hand when she offered it, the same way he'd taken Mary's. Except this time, he actually kissed the top of her hand. *Not* the space above it.

Victor clenched his teeth.

And went to stand near Anne.

"Oh! Victor." Anne smiled up at him. "You remember Freddy has been talking about his new friend, Mr. Ralph Ashby? This is young Mr. Ashby's mother, and his oldest brother... Forgive me," she said to Ashby, her chin dipping down. "I'm learning so many names at once, I've already forgotten yours!"

Ashby grinned. "It's no bother, Lady Litchfield." Victor didn't like the way Ashby seemed to purr her title. "Mr. Felton Ashby. Charmed." Ashby then turned to reach out to Victor. Privately, Victor noted his was the first male hand Ashby had reached out to shake. Suspicion snaked through Victor. He held Ashby's gaze and squeezed the man's hand. Hard.

Ashby's smile briefly tensed from pain before he pulled his hand out of Victor's grasp and shook it at his side. "I'm sorry, and you are...?" Ashby darted his eyes between Victor and Anne in a questioning way.

Victor opened his mouth, but Anne spoke first. "This is my friend Mr. Victor McNab. His brother is married to Lady Vivian here..." Anne then introduced everyone in the family. When she mentioned she was a widow, Victor made sure to capture the minute movements of Ashby's reaction. Though there was no overt reaction upon the news that Anne was eligible, Victor could clearly see in the way Ashby's eyes briefly widened that tidbit of information had caught his attention.

The younger, bespectacled man had not been anything but friendly and pleasant to Victor in the now two times he had met him. And yet, something about him sent off warning bells. After raising his brothers in Whitechapel, plus decades of running a pub, Victor had learned to listen to those internal warnings. They were never wrong.

However, this was regarding Anne and, admittedly, Victor was biased in that regard. Those warning bells could simply have been the result of jealousy. He wasn't so foolish as to ignore that possibility, though he would never admit it aloud to anyone. Ashby had youth on his side. And, Victor supposed, women would likely find Ashby's countenance appealing. He wasn't glaringly ugly and seemed to have a pleasant look upon his face.

As Victor studied him, Ashby and his mother were trying their best to keep up with Anne's explanation of how the Winthrops and McNabs were woven together. And then, when Anne got to Ollie and his wife, then went to explain who Evelyn's baron father was, Ashby and his mother both started to look vacant in their gazes, as if overwhelmed by all this information at once, though the Ashby family was a full crew of young brothers on its own.

"I expect we will be spending a lot of time together," Anne said with a laugh, glancing over to her son and his friend, who were leaning over the railing to see who could spit the farthest. She frowned deeply at this behavior. Ashby went over to his youngest brother and said something in a low voice. Being the oldest brother himself, Victor didn't need to hear the man to know he was threatening the young lads to quit it. Or else.

Of course, it worked. Oldest brothers knew how to be quietly terrifying.

Ashby hovered nearby for a moment to ensure their rude behavior remained rectified, then said something to Mary, eliciting a laugh.

With nothing to say, Victor crossed his arms and spent the rest of the outing observing. And he didn't like how often Ashby seemed to appear at Anne's side.

Chapter Fifteen

ANNE WALKED ARM in arm with Freddy and Mary as they approached Summerwood's ballroom. Light, orchestral music floated in the air and blended with the hum of the crowd. French doors along one side of the large room were open to let the cool, sea air in. Moonlight danced along the watery horizon, as if it couldn't help but swing and sway to the string instruments.

As they greeted Vivian, Dantes, and the Duke of Chalworth, Anne recalled the children being young and sneaking around during dinner parties, watching the festivities from the stairway in their pajamas, as if Anne and Bernard couldn't see them. And she recalled all those times they'd begged to go to balls, too, but instead had had to stay home with the governess or nanny.

Though Freddy was still too young to attend the ball past the first few hours, this would be the first ball Mary would be allowed to attend in its entirety.

It was a major milestone and Mary had been vibrating with anticipation all day. Anne smiled to herself as her children let go to disappear into the crowd on their own, with the governess Miss Stewart trailing Mary. Anne already knew Freddy was seeking out Mr. Ralph Ashby, or one of his uncles if the youngest Mr. Ashby had not yet arrived.

Mary, meanwhile, shone in a dress of silver and blue change-able silk, and as she made her way around the room with Miss

Stewart, who wore a plain, brown gown, as one would expect of a governess, people took notice of the young woman. It was hard not to notice Mary—she was growing up to be quite the beauty. But it was hard for Anne to accept her little girl was nearly an adult now.

As a footman walked by, Anne lifted a glass of champagne from his tray and downed it quickly.

"I didn't realize your daughter was out, Lady Litchfield." A man's voice caused Anne to turn. It was Mr. Felton Ashby, the eldest of the Ashby sons. He looked quite handsome in a tuxedo and gold-rimmed spectacles.

Anne knew the Ashby father had passed some years back, and Mr. Felton Ashby was, in a way, the father figure for the boys. Freddy had told her the eldest Mr. Ashby had remained unmarried in order to help his mother, as Mr. Ralph Ashby had been only a tot when their father had passed from old age. But now, Mr. Ralph Ashby was fifteen years and didn't need the attention a young tot required. And the other brothers were, of course, older as well.

Anne couldn't help but admire the eldest Mr. Ashby for being so involved in his brothers' lives. It reminded her of Victor. And Victor had come out of that experience a responsible, good person. Surely, Mr. Ashby had, too—how could someone not? And would Mr. Ashby be seeking a bride now that his involvement with his brothers has lessened?

"She's not out." Anne smiled up at him. "Mary does not come out until next year. This is the first ball she's been allowed to attend in full, in fact. As you can imagine, she's quite excited."

"Yes, I imagine so." He looked down and held her gaze for a moment. "Forgive me, but I have a bit of an intrusive question I've been trying to answer for myself since we met yesterday."

Anne blinked at his forwardness. "Oh?"

Mr. Ashby let out a small laugh and looked a bit sheepish, with a slight blush rising on his cheek. "Ralph insists you are Lord Litchfield and Lady Mary's birth mother. But I insist that is an impossibility, and you must be their stepmother. Which is the truth?"

Anne frowned, trying to understand where Mr. Ashby's assumption had come from. "Why, because of their dark hair?" Both Freddy and Mary took after Bernard in that regard.

Mr. Ashby hesitated. "That, and you are far too young to have a daughter who is about to come out."

Unable to help herself, Anne lifted her eyebrows sky high. "How old do you think I am, Mr. Ashby?"

"About my age?" he replied with liquid ease.

"And how old are you?"

"Thirty-two."

Anne's mouth fell open a bit, but she shut it quickly. She was actually forty. And she noticed Mr. Ashby fit one of her rules: any gentleman she put her sights upon should not be more than ten years beyond her own age.

But she also wasn't a young, naive girl. This was an obvious attempt at flattery.

"Mr. Ashby," Anne said as he grabbed two passing champagnes and handed one to her, "is that your style of flirtation?"

He was taking a sip as she asked and coughed. He then cleared his throat. "Forgive me. Am I that transparent? I suppose yes. However, it *was* a genuine question I turned into a vehicle of flirtation." He grinned, and Anne noted his grin was quite attractive. Genuine, not forced. "I suppose I have been found out." He gave her a small bow, but there was an amused twinkle in his eye.

Anne gave him a skeptical look but softened it with a small smile. "No, I am not their stepmother, Mr. Ashby. Trust me, I was there when they were born."

Mr. Ashby chuckled and gave her a long look over that made her ears feel warm. As she didn't know what to do next, she put her attention back on the crowd and sipped her champagne. After a moment, she noticed Freddy and Mr. Ralph Ashby talking to Victor. She had never seen Victor at a ball before. And here he was, his beard and black hair trimmed neatly—more so than usual—all while wearing a rather nice tuxedo. Forget the surprise of him attending a ball. She had never seen him in a tuxedo before! And he was quite the sight.

Something inside of her leapt.

"May I ask another question, my lady?"

Anne watched Victor for a moment longer before forcing herself to look away. "Yes, Mr. Ashby?"

Mr. Ashby's gaze went from her to Victor. "May I inquire as to your relationship with Mr. McNab?" He paused. "I do not wish to insert myself into a preexisting romance."

Anne's face went red hot. "Oh! My late husband was Lady Vivian's brother. And Lady Vivian's husband is Mr. McNab's brother." She had explained this already to Mr. Ashby and his mother the previous day, but perhaps she had told them too much information at once.

Mr. Ashby took a sip of champagne and then said, "Ah, that's right. I tried following along yesterday when we were all introduced on the pier. So that is the extent of your familiarity with Mr. McNab?"

Anne swallowed. This was quite the question. Yet could she blame him for asking? This was all rather different than things had been when she'd been a debutante. It made sense to ask pointed questions of a widow before uncomfortable situations arose. "I would say Mr. McNab is one of my closest friends. But as to your question, if there is a preexisting romance, there most definitely is not." Nor would there be, but she didn't feel that would be worth including.

Mr. Ashby stared off for a moment and then he bowed. "Pertinent information for me to know, Lady Litchfield." When he stood straight again, he said, "May I be so bold as to ask for a dance later this evening?"

Anne felt an old ghost of girlish giddiness. "You may." She offered her hand.

Mr. Ashby pressed a kiss to the tops of her fingers. "I look forward to it." He let her hand go and took a few steps back without taking his gaze off of her. He bowed briefly again. "Until then," he said.

"Until then." She curtsied. She watched as he made his way through the crowd to where Victor, Freddy, and Mr. Ralph Ashby had been, but the gentlemen were no longer there. Mr. Ashby seemed to realize this too, as he then looked around the crowd. His attention seemed to land on something and he began going in a different direction. Anne bobbed her head to see, finally realizing it was Ollie, Evelyn, Mary, and Miss Stewart. Mr. Ashby approached them and though she couldn't hear what he said, Ollie and Mr. Ashby shaking hands told her he was greeting them all.

With nothing else to do, Anne began making her way around the ballroom to see who was in attendance that evening. She stopped and talked to many familiar faces. There was Lord and Lady Bell, with whom she spoke with for a good while about Freddy's schooling and Mary's upcoming debut. They had three children, all of whom had married in the last few years. Lord Bell was a viscount with a country estate not far from Summerwood and the families often interacted during the summer. Anne also crossed paths with the elderly Mr. Thornwood and Mr. Pratt, friends of her father's, and of course, the Duke of Chalworth's, hence their presence. Every year, they asked if her parents would be visiting, and every year she told them *no*. Ever since she'd married Bernard, her mother and father had taken a step back from her life.

Eventually, she made a full circle about the room and ended with her daughter and Miss Stewart.

"Have you seen any of your friends, dear?" Anne asked Mary, who continued to look about the room with utter awe. "I know you and Lady Cecile enjoy each other's company and I thought I saw here around here somewhere."

"Oh, yes! I saw her, Mama. Did you know she is getting her dresses for next season from Doucet? Her Mama took her straight to Paris for the fittings!"

"Oh my," Anne responded, knowing she should sound impressed but not so much that her daughter would be jealous. Though Anne knew well enough there was probably a little bit of that jealousy in there somewhere, no matter what she said. "How nice that you're able to easily drop in to your dressmakers. Imagine having to do all of that travel for dresses!"

Mary's eyes brightened at this. "You're right. That would be awful!" And then, looking past Anne, she said, "Oh, hello, Uncle Victor!"

Anne froze and swore she could feel his dark presence behind her like a shadow. "Lady Mary," Victor responded in his deep voice. He appeared at Anne's side but continued talking to Mary. "I saw you flitting about like an erratic butterfly."

Mary laughed. "It's the first ball Mama has allowed me to attend. I wish to speak to *everyone!*" Mary then looked at Anne, and there was something unsure in her eye. She wrung her fingers together. "Actually, Mama, I wanted to know something. If a gentleman asks me to dance, am I allowed to?"

Anne's eyes widened. "Absolutely not!"

Mary pouted as her shoulders fell. "Why not?"

"You haven't come out yet. You *know* you're not allowed to dance with a gentleman yet at events like this one."

Miss Stewart, remaining in the background, was biting her lip at this conversation. Her eyes went back and forth between Mary and Anne. "Actually, Lady Litchfield..." The governess stepped forward. "I should tell you that Lady Mary was already asked to dance by a gentleman."

Outraged, Anne did her best to level the rising emotion. "Who would dare ask a young woman who has not yet come out to dance? That is highly improper!"

Mary rushed her palms over her skirt and mumbled, "Freddy's friend's brother."

Anne felt a jolt of sick in her stomach as the thirty-two-year-old Mr. Felton Ashby came to mind. Though it wasn't unheard of for a young woman to have a much older husband—sometimes twice their age, if not more—Anne had been quite cautious when it came to men since her own experience. And in her opinion, a thirty-two-year-old had no business showing interest in a seventeen-year-old. But even the worst scoundrel wouldn't ask both a mother and her daughter to dance the same night. She was worrying far too much. "Which brother?"

"Mr. Lucas Ashby."

Relief flooded Anne. She let out a breath. "And how old is he?"

"I don't know, twenty, perhaps?" Mary looked at Miss Stewart, who nodded in agreement.

Anne's shoulders loosened. Though Mr. Lucas Ashby should still have known better. And likely did. "He is simply going to have to wait one more year to ask you, Mary."

"But, Mama!" Mary whined.

"No *buts*, dear." Anne made sure to hold her daughter's gaze. "You simply cannot dance this summer, with anyone, and *both* of you are well aware of this."

Mary let out a long sigh and rolled her eyes. "Yes, Mama."

"Now, don't make me regret allowing you to attend your aunt and uncle's ball tonight."

Mary's head dropped. "No, Mama."

"Good." Anne squeezed her daughter's arm. "Go find Lady Cecile again and giggle about dresses some more."

Mary and Miss Stewart gave departing curtsies and disappeared into the crowd.

Anne turned to Victor, who generally remained quiet when she had difficult discussions with her children in his presence. "Did I handle that well, do you think?" Anne wasn't sure. This wasn't a large ball. Rules about propriety were rather set in stone, but still, she felt badly.

Victor was staring down at her with his usual intensity. "I believe so, yes."

"I hate to be a spoilsport, she was looking forward so much to tonight. But it's a bit odd for him to be asking her to dance, don't you think? I'm surprised she even entertained the idea enough to complain when I said *no*."

Victor slowly nodded, taking a moment to consider something. "I'm not as familiar with those types of rules as you are, but I didn't get a good feeling from it."

"Nor I." Anne could feel the worry settling on her brow. In truth, it put her on alert. But she couldn't figure out why. Mr. Lucas Ashby was young, and maybe he'd been swept up in the atmosphere and taken a chance on asking her. Or, possibly, he'd made an incorrect assumption with her presence here. Mamas generally knew which young ladies were out, but it wouldn't surprise Anne if the sons were ignorant to it.

"In fact, if I may speak freely…" Victor trailed off but seemed to hesitate.

Anne tilted her head. "Of course you may speak freely, Victor."

"Forgive me, but something about it seems especially odd. I would go so far as to say *concerning*."

"I was thinking the exact same." Anne looked around the room. "I think I shall keep an eye on that Mr. Lucas Ashby."

Victor knit his hands behind his back. "That's a good idea. I might do so as well."

She looked up at him, a bit surprised by this. "Thank you."

He replied with a tight-lipped nod. Anne expected him to end this conversation and disappear into the crowd, but she was quite pleased when he stayed with her.

"Dantes and Ollie have spent the last hour introducing me to people."

"Oh? How did that go?"

He shrugged. "Well enough. I'm not one for idle chitchat, so it was a bit torturous in that way. But these are people I will have to get to know at some point."

"Did you like any of them?"

Victor was quiet for a long moment before a hint of humor

glimmered in his eyes. "In truth, no."

Anne laughed. "It's a formal occasion. Once you get to know people better over time, I'm sure you'll discover friendships are born."

"Perhaps."

At this moment, Anne decided to tell Victor about Mr. Felton Ashby. And why she did, she couldn't say. It didn't seem to be something of Victor's business, or something he would even care about. But it also felt strange not telling him, like breaking some sort of rule. "Mr. Felton Ashby has asked me to dance tonight."

Victor's full attention went down to her and a dark intensity began to build around him like a shadow. As her dearest friend, she knew well enough what that was—he was angry. But why would he care so intensely about this? "Why does he want to do that?"

Anne resisted the urge to stammer. Was it shock from his change in mood? Or perhaps she was offended by the question? "I don't know. It's merely one dance, Victor. Are you saying no one should want to dance with me?"

Victor's eyebrows pulled together. "No."

"He's only a few years younger than I, and his youngest brother is dear friends with Freddy. I think it would be strange for him not to ask, don't you?"

"No," he replied darkly.

Anne blinked. "Are you upset?"

Upon this question, something within Victor shifted, as if he'd rearranged something inside of him. There was a funny look on his face and then the intensity, the dark cloud, disappeared all at once until he exuded an air of vague boredom. "No. I'm not upset." He paused. "However, I do regret not asking you first."

Anne blinked in surprise. "I'm sorry. If you want, I can reserve a dance for you. I didn't know you would want to—"

"No matter." He searched her face for a brief moment. "I'm not prepared to be on a dance floor, anyway." And then he suddenly bowed low before rising back up to his full, rigid height.

"Enjoy your evening, Anne."

With that, he turned and left, leaving Anne blinking rapidly after him. A dreadful feeling squeezed her stomach, as if she had done something wrong, even though she knew she hadn't.

Chapter Sixteen

VICTOR RUSHED THROUGH the crowd to disappear at the edge of the room, his heart pounding hard as he did so. He had secretly been looking forward to the ball tonight—words he'd never expected to think to himself—and for the last few days, he had prepared himself for the best way to ask Anne for a dance.

Relieved to find respite, he leaned against the wall to catch his breath. He had spent hours debating how to handle this evening. It would be a good opportunity to get close to Anne, to understand if his attraction to her, his feelings for her, had any substance to them. He could finally discover if it was merely a symptom of loneliness, and she happened to be the closest woman in his life.

Victor knew social rules well enough to know one dance with her wouldn't be considered unusual with their ages and the way their families were enmeshed. Everyone here knew about the ties between the Winthrops and McNabs. They knew Anne was a widow and had been out of mourning for a number of years now.

But when she'd said that blasted Ashby had asked her to dance first, he'd turned into a coward. Another man asking Anne to dance was not something he'd been expecting, which he was now realizing had been utterly daft.

Of course, other men might ask her to dance.

They probably had before, too, while he'd been in London.

But she had told him before how much she disliked balls since Winthrop's passing. If a gentleman had asked her to dance previously, she likely would have turned him down. He had been banking on their friendship to get her to agree to a dance with him.

But now, she was apparently dancing again. And probably would have many suitors once the word spread.

Anne, no matter what his true feelings for her were, was a beautiful woman. She had money and a title. Her son, already a marquess, would be a duke someday. Her daughter would no doubt end up marrying someone of influence.

It shouldn't have surprised Victor for someone to show even a modicum of interest in Anne.

But still, he did not like it. Not in the least bit.

Victor took in a deep, slow breath as he watched the large room over the heads of the people around him. He was always in control, and he never let that control slip. Sometimes, plans didn't unfold as expected. It was that way with business, and it could be that way in his personal life, too. All he had to do was adjust to this new and unexpected obstacle. That should have been easy enough, shouldn't it have? He wasn't about to give up on Anne, or uncovering the depth of his affection for her, even though a man much younger than himself had shown obvious interest.

Pushing away from the wall, Victor then moved through the crowd invisibly. No one took notice of him, and he liked it that way. He was never quite sure how he did it, but it was a skill he'd developed when they'd been children living in Whitechapel. He had learned to move about without notice, without making sound, somehow blending in to the surroundings as if transparent. He'd used this skill as a boy to survive. Sometimes to steal food. Sometimes to steal money. Though he'd broken the law multiple times every day, he'd found he hadn't cared much then. Dantes and Ollie, who'd been a toddler at the time, had been fed and as safe as they could be in their circumstances. Most importantly, they'd been together and not split up amongst different orphanages.

Victor would have done anything for his brothers then. And still did.

Spotting his brothers and their wives hovering near the dance floor, Victor watched as Ollie leaned down to Evelyn to whisper something to her and she smiled up at him in response. Dantes had an arm around Vivian's waist as if he would never let go and wanted everyone to know it, too.

Pride bubbled in Victor's chest. His brothers, against all odds, had ended up with happy lives filled with love.

It was all he had ever wanted, what he had worked for his whole life. For Dantes, for Ollie, to be safe and happy.

A pause amongst the musicians caused Victor's attention to shift away from nostalgia and pride to his present issue at hand. The quiet meant the musicians were taking a break. Dancing was about to begin.

Victor hastily searched the room until his eyes found Anne. His attention anchored to her as if there were no one else around. She was talking to her children and, if he had to guess, reminding them that they weren't yet adults and must not act as such.

Freddy said something and left. Victor watched the boy weave through the crowd with a sulk on his face and hunch in his shoulders, until he left the ballroom. Now that dancing was beginning, he was no longer allowed to be present.

He put his attention back to Anne and Mary. Mary had a pout similar to Freddy's, but she no doubt knew arguing with Anne would have been futile. He had no idea what their disagreement was this time, but when he followed Mary's gaze he discovered she was watching the Ashby family. The mother of the gaggle of sons was deep in discussion with one of the other guests. Mr. Felton Ashby, the blasted idiot, was having a private conversation with two of his four brothers, one of whom was Freddy's friend Ralph. The youngest Ashby would also be leaving the ball now due to his age. But the other brother Victor wasn't yet familiar with. Based on the way Mary watched the trio, however, the unknown brother was likely Lucas Ashby, the one with whom she wished to dance despite Anne's protests.

Mary let out a dramatic sigh that he had heard himself far too often in these last few years. The corners of his mouth nearly hitched at this.

Victor left his spot and grabbed a glass of champagne for himself. Gentlemen he had met earlier, some viscount and the viscount's younger brother, came to talk to him, though he was only paying a fraction of his attention to them, but enough to have a respectable conversation about labor strikes. Victor, being a working-class man, would always be on the side of the workers. But he also knew that view would not be welcome amongst the people in attendance and thought it best to keep those opinions to himself, as he would one day have to spend significant time with them. He couldn't change anything by making enemies, either.

As he barely listened to their chatter about labor, his attention was pulled back to Anne like the magnet she seemed to be. Music was beginning to play again, which meant the first dance of the evening was about to begin.

Frustration ground at him. It should have been him getting that first dance with her. If only he hadn't been such a coward about it! Regret at his weakness gnawed at him.

But how would Anne have reacted if he *had* gotten the chance to ask? Would she have seen it as nothing more than a friendly gesture? Or would suspicion have started to poke at her mind?

The more important question was, which way did he *want* her to see it?

Victor continued his nearly obsessive watch of her. She was stunning tonight in a peach, satin dress. He wished he could tell her how beautiful she looked. But he wasn't a man who expressed himself with words very well.

Mr. Felton Ashby approached Anne and as he spoke to her, held out his palm in invitation. Victor downed his glass of champagne, excused himself to the viscount and the viscount's brother, left the ballroom, and ran upstairs. He had barely been able to withstand the first few hours of the ball. Now, it was simply intolerable.

The music was playing by the time he'd reached the second floor, and it echoed throughout the large, darkened home. His heart began to race faster, faster. He could watch Anne, watch Ashby, safely from up here.

Victor ran down the dim hallway, took a turn to another dim hallway, and eventually found himself at the end of it. The end wasn't a wall, though. It was a balcony that looked out at the ballroom below. There was one lit gas lamp sconce nearby and he turned it down until the flame snuffed out. Over the ballroom was one large chandelier that suspended from the ballroom's high ceiling, but it hung lower than the second floor, and a cover over the top kept the light from reaching the exposed second floor.

In other words, the balcony he took refuge in was awash with the shadows of night.

Feeling more like himself, Victor stood at the stone railing and placed his hands atop it to watch the party below. No one looked up in his direction. No one had the faintest idea someone watched from above. It took a minute, but he found Anne again just as she entered the dance floor with Ashby.

Victor scowled and refused to take his eyes off of her.

The couples below turned together in time with the music, swirls of silk, lace, and tulle. Ashby had his undivided attention on Anne, but Anne kept swiveling her head, likely keeping an eye on her daughter.

Ashby said something to Anne and she stopped searching, her focus now fully on her dance partner. This irritated Victor, as if Ashby thought he could dare request *anything* from the woman he held.

But Victor's ire flamed further when Ashby's hand, resting properly at Anne's upper back, began sliding down little by little—scoundrel impropriety.

Ashby knew exactly what he was doing. And with this minute

movement, Victor could see right through cad.

Barely resisting the urge to dive to the floor and slam a fist into the cad's face, Victor held himself in place by white-knuckling the railing. With a deep inhale through his nose, he reminded himself he was in control of his reaction. He was in control of the rising anger, of the sickening jealousy that slammed into him like an iron wrecking ball.

The raw severity of these emotions took him by complete surprise.

His heart galloped in response, though with elation or panic, he couldn't determine, and in a fit of desperation, his eyes flew to Vivian laughing with Dantes.

Victor felt nothing.

His attention then went to Evelyn on Ollie's arm: again, nothing.

Next, a woman whom he supposed was pretty enough dancing with a man he didn't know—a whole lot more of nothing.

No other woman in this room affected him in any way.

Upon this discovery, questions that had haunted him over the years started to become answered.

Whatever his affection for Anne was, it wasn't purely friendship.

He wanted her in a way he had never, ever wanted anyone before.

For another moment, Victor allowed himself to grip the railing hard as if holding on to that last thread of ignorance he'd had mere minutes ago. But then he did what he did best: he took control. Emotions like those he was feeling served no purpose. He lassoed in that jealousy, that anger, like an American cowboy retaking his runaway cattle.

It wasn't his place to be upset over another man touching Anne, a woman who had stated she was quite happy being on her own.

Victor was becoming lost in a swirl of confusion, but there was one certainty that he had: he wouldn't be happy until Anne was out of Ashby's arms and in his own.

Now feeling more determined than ever, he stayed in his place in the shadows, unmoving, watching Anne as another man, that blasted Ashby and not himself, led her in a dance. And Victor began to wonder—if Anne was the first woman for whom he had felt this affection, then it clearly meant *something*. But what was he going to do about it?

Doing nothing sounded right on the surface. Though Victor knew he held affection for Anne, he still wasn't sure what *kind* of affection it was. Anne had been the only true woman friend he had ever had. For all he knew, men who befriended women as closely as he had befriended Anne felt this same burning sensation in their hearts whenever said lady friend was around. Anne had also made it clear, to Vivian at least, that she was only interested in a brief dalliance with men this summer, not something long-lasting.

In this, Victor *should* do nothing. Yet doing nothing was an unsatisfactory conclusion.

Telling her he held affection for her would destroy their friendship, of that he was certain.

What could he do, then? What was a good middle ground between nothing and everything to test the waters out first?

Suddenly, Anne looked up in his direction. It was so unexpected, it caused Victor's heart to drop to the floor. But he held back any outward reaction. He forced himself to remain still.

Just a few days ago, he had spotted Anne watching *him* from her window while the rest of the family had played croquet. When he'd spotted her she had run, embarrassed at being caught. He knew her well enough to know this had been the reason, and he hadn't dared bring it up.

He understood now what she had felt in that moment. But he wouldn't run, and he wouldn't feel shame for watching her.

Instead, he stayed in place, daring her to make a move.

And grappling with what he had decided to do next.

✦

Chapter Seventeen

THE PEACH DRESS Anne had been so excited to wear was starting to make her itchy. She had forgotten the way fabric could rub against skin while dancing, even with her underthings. All she could do was smile through the discomfort and hope she could escape soon.

Mr. Felton Ashby was a decent dancer, she had to give him that. He moved well, made polite conversation. Admittedly, it was nice to be close to a gentleman like this again.

But she also found she couldn't immerse herself in the moment. This ball was something she had been looking forward to, and she was on the right path to getting what she wanted this summer: carefree flirtation and attention that could be left behind as a frivolous novelty in a few months.

But something kept distracting her during the dance, preventing her from fully falling into it: the strangest sensation of being watched.

As Mr. Ashby led her about the ballroom, Anne glanced around the room. Someone was watching her, of that she was certain. But who? And more importantly, *why?*

Perhaps she was worrying too much. The room was crowded. Of course someone somewhere had set their eyes upon her. She was in the line of sight of many people.

But as she thought this, the hairs on the back of her neck

stood up. It felt like a beacon of light had focused on her.

With a swallow, she looked around again. For a flash of a moment, she spotted Vivian and Dantes laughing together about something. She knew the couple well enough to guess Vivian had probably made a wry jest.

Then there was Mary talking with other young ladies as Miss Stewart and mamas hovered safely nearby. Anne knew the other young ladies were all out and Mary looked quite comfortable conversing with them all. Briefly, Anne felt a sense of pride that easing Mary into adulthood instead of throwing her into it seemed to be working out well.

Anne continued looking around. Ollie and Evelyn could not be found, and Victor was absent as well, though that wasn't surprising. It would have surprised her more is if he had still been in attendance. It would take more than one ball to reacquaint him with the aristocracy. He would have only stayed long enough to show his face, shake a few hands, and then leave.

Anne frowned.

"Is something wrong, Lady Litchfield?" Mr. Ashby asked, his gaze following hers as she watched Mary once more.

Anne startled, nearly forgetting what she was doing in the moment. She forced a pleasant smile and put her full attention on her dance partner. "Forgive me. It has been many years since I have danced and I am taking in the glamor of it all."

Mr. Ashby slid his hand down her back—a bit premature and daring, she thought. But what did she know? She'd been married off as soon as she'd been of age. Maybe this was normal for older people, who could get away with more.

And it wasn't as if he moved his hand *all* the way down.

Yes, this was probably normal. Probably.

Mr. Ashby made a comment about how well she danced, but after a quick thanks, Anne was already ignoring him again. That hair-raising feeling had returned.

Who in the blazes was watching her?

As their dancing led them past the musicians again, Anne

could see the other side of the room out of the corner of her eye and felt a pull in that direction.

She nearly jumped as she remembered the balcony that looked out above the ballroom. It was easy to overlook if you didn't know it existed.

Her heart pounded hard and once Mr. Ashby had spun her in the right direction, she looked over his shoulder and up to the balcony.

A dark figure, completely concealed by shadow from mid-shin up, was standing there. All she could see were black trousers such as one would wear with a tuxedo, but it was also entirely possible they were part of a servant's uniform as well. Could it be one of Vivian's servants watching in case of trouble? It was plausible, yet somehow, she knew that wasn't the case. All she was confident of was that they were watching her right this moment.

As she continued being led around the room, she turned her head to keep her eyes on the balcony, swallowing at the sensation the man knew she watched him back.

But he didn't move. Didn't retreat. Didn't hide.

It felt as if he, whoever he was, was daring her. But to do what?

"I was wondering," Mr. Ashby said and Anne whipped her head back around, realizing she had been staring at the balcony far too long.

She thought she had been caught. How humiliating that would have been! She knew better. Her attention should be on the one and only gentleman who'd asked her to dance tonight, not some shadowy, mysterious man.

"Yes?" Anne asked. Mr. Ashby wasn't looking at her, or at the balcony. She looked to see what held his attention and realized he was watching the gaggle of young ladies Mary was with.

"How do your children feel about the absence of a father?" he asked.

"I'm sorry," Anne said with a bit of a head shake. "I don't

understand what you're asking." Was he asking if they missed their father?

Of course they did.

Then again, it wasn't something they often talked about.

Anne had always assumed her children didn't think much about Bernard anymore. They had been sheltered from him for most of their lives, but when he had passed they'd been old enough to realize something had been amiss in his behavior. It had been a subject she had been too afraid to bring up. The children knew Anne and Bernard's marriage had been rocky, and unfortunately, there had only been so much of their horrid marriage she could hide from them, especially as they'd gotten older. She couldn't hide his absences or his lack of affection for her. She couldn't hide the gossip over their separation, informal as it may have been. And they had seen through their uncles and aunts what a happy, loving marriage looked like.

After the funeral, they'd never mentioned Bernard, never asked about him.

And she had always been too afraid to ask *why*. For so long, she'd assumed it had been because Bernard had been separated from Anne and essentially banned from seeing the children by the Duke of Chalworth. He had hardly been present in their lives. But what if there was more to it? That one single time Bernard had laid a hand on Freddy, Freddy hadn't wanted to talk about when she'd tried to bring it up to him. Could it have affected him more than he'd made it seem?

"What I mean is," Mr. Ashby said, interrupting her thoughts, "do they miss having a father figure in their life?"

Anne's eyes became huge and a sick feeling coursed through her. Suddenly, she wished to shove his hands off of her. She was absolutely not looking for anything beyond silly flirtations! "Excuse me, Mr. Ashby, but what kind of question is that? How dare you?" She hissed those last words out.

Mr. Ashby stammered, as if thrown off by her reaction. But, surely, he couldn't have been that surprised! What an audacious question!

"I-I apologize, Lady Litchfield." The song ended and they stopped moving. People began leaving the dance floor, and Mr. Ashby bowed. "I did not mean to offend you with my question. Perhaps it was a bit too forward."

Anne didn't have time for this nonsense. But she couldn't help but glance past Mr. Ashby again to look up at the balcony.

The mysterious figure still stood there. It should have disturbed her, yet she felt a strange exhilaration from it. She forced her attention back to her dance partner.

"It was too forward, and far too soon," Anne said. "Have a good rest of your evening, Mr. Ashby." She curtsied and fled before he could say anything else to her. Shaken by his questioning, she rushed off to the safety of the crowd and took another glass of champagne, her hands trembling.

As she sipped, she watched the shadowy figure above through narrowed eyes. Was this man a friend? Or a foe? She was already over male nonsense and wondered what *this* man's intention was with his incessant staring.

Without finishing her glass, she discarded it and tracked down her daughter. "I'm feeling quite tired, darling. I think I shall head to bed for the evening," she said, hoping her face looked tired.

"Really?" Mary asked with genuine surprise. "But it's only been a few hours!"

"I know. Your aunts and uncles, and Miss Stewart, will have their eye on you, though, so behave yourself."

"Of course, Mama." Mary gave her a hug. "Thank you for letting me stay. Goodnight."

Anne kissed her daughter on the cheek and then left the ballroom without another glance. She hurried up the marble staircase, her peach dress swishing with the movement. Anticipation and a bit of fear—the good, girlish kind—pumped through her.

Her heart roared in her ears as she made her way to the hallway that led to the balcony. Her breathing quickened with each step. But as she got to the balcony, she came to a halt.

No one was there.

Anne let out a huff of air. Had she been seeing things? It was quite shadowy up here. Perhaps she had only seen that.

Immediately, she cast that thought aside. No, she had most definitely seen a man up here.

But perhaps she had been wrong about what he'd been doing, and he'd been watching someone else.

Perhaps, he was currently with that woman now. It would make the most sense.

She swallowed back the silly jealousy she felt. All she'd seen had been the shadow of a man, a man whose face and body may as well have been invisible. He could have been anyone. Jealousy had no place in this. In fact, she would likely never uncover who he'd been.

Anne went to stand where the mystery man had been and placed her gloved hands upon the rail, wondering if his hands had been there as well. For a few minutes, she stood in place, her racing heart coming down from its reverie. She watched the ball below for a few minutes and studied each gentleman, wondering if he was the shadowy man.

A phantom.

Maybe he was down there right now looking up at her, some kind of game building between them.

As her eyes darted over the crowd, she came to accept no one had noticed her up here. Either he was gone or was not willing to give away his identity.

The music began again, and she let go of the railing, crestfallen to not have an answer as to who had watched her.

And then a strange feeling crawled up her back, like a finger's light caress, causing her to shiver.

With a gasp, she spun around and placed one hand over her heart.

Down the hallway, a shadow moved.

"Wait!" Anne called out. Swiftly, she lifted her skirt just enough to be able to start running toward him. But she came to a halt when she was about to pass over something lying in the middle of the floor.

It was a piece of cream-colored paper, nearly glowing white in the dim light.

Anne bent down to observe it. It hadn't been there when she'd first come up, though perhaps it had been dropped accidentally by someone and she'd simply missed it. It appeared to be nothing more than a piece of blank letter paper, but when she flipped it over, right in the middle of that side of the paper was a tiny ink drawing.

She picked it up and hurried over to a nearby gas-lit sconce to see better.

The ink drawing was a small circle, no larger than three inches in diameter. At first, she thought it was some kind of planet, but it appeared to be the night sky, with stars of varying shapes and sizes, against a dark sky background. But then, centered right in the middle of the circle was a flower, a stem, and two leaves.

A daisy.

Anne looked on both sides of the paper for more. A name, a signature, anything. But there was nothing else.

Despite this, her heart pounded as if she had uncovered something private, something precious. With a swallow, she looked back up and stared into the dark hallway. But there was no movement.

"Hello?" she called out, receiving no response.

The music and ball felt as if they were another world away. Holding the drawing against her heart, she inched down the hallway, keeping the creation safely against her.

But she made it to her bedroom door without passing another soul.

When she'd entered her bedroom, she shut the door behind her and hurried to her vanity to sit in the chair. Briefly, she stared back at herself and thought she looked haunted with the room so dark behind her. Ignoring this, she placed the drawing down on the surface of the vanity to look at it again.

A daisy surrounded by night sky. It made no sense. It wasn't growing out of the ground, either—it seemed to be floating on its own. And when she thought of daisies, she thought of sunshine. Of summer. Of daytime! Not darkness, shadows, and night.

And why just one daisy? They grew in groups. The singularness of it felt purposeful. But why, she couldn't decipher.

Gently, she traced the circle as she tried to figure out the puzzle. The Phantom had clearly left it there for her. But how had she not heard his approach?

He truly was like a ghost. Maybe he was?

Her thoughts were interrupted when she heard the faint sound of footfalls entering the bedroom next door, followed by the door closing. Her eyes flew up to meet her reflection in the mirror.

What if...?

No. Victor couldn't have been the Phantom. He had been her dearest companion for years—he didn't need to watch her from a secret place. And not only did he not draw, if he'd wanted to give her a drawing, he would have simply given one to her without any pomp. Whoever had drawn this clearly was an expert at their craft.

In the moment she recalled Evelyn, Ollie's wife, was an art conservator for a museum. If anyone could pick out clues from this drawing and perhaps uncover who'd drawn this, it would be Evelyn. She would ask the woman as soon as she could.

Then she had a funny thought. What if the Phantom hadn't left the picture? What if Mr. Ashby had followed her and put it there?

He had seemed genuinely regretful of the way their dance had ended. It made sense this could be his way of gently reaching out to her. For all she knew, he was a master artist. She would have to find out.

As she heard footfalls again, she looked at the door in the reflection of her mirror. The Phantom probably wasn't Victor. But the paper the night daisy was drawn on was distinctive. If

Victor had such paper, she would be able to find out quickly.

Anne opened a drawer to her vanity to safely store the drawing for now. Just before she put in in the drawer, she spotted her list of rules.

Never chase a gentleman.

"You didn't say anything about a phantom," she said aloud to herself while placing the picture inside and shutting the drawer.

Anne quickly observed herself in the mirror and then went to the shared door.

She unlocked and opened her door, then knocked on his.

A moment later, it opened.

Victor stood in the doorway, wearing his light-blue pajamas. He cocked an eyebrow. "Yes?" he asked.

Well, he definitely wasn't wearing black.

"May I come in?" Anne replied, hoping not to sound too eager.

Victor nodded then stepped aside.

"Why did you leave the ball?" She already knew the answer but needed a reason to be able to look around the room.

"I was bored," he replied. "Dantes introduced me to many people tonight, and I grew tired of it."

Anne looked up to him. "You own a pub, Victor. How could you grow tired of talking to people?"

Victor crossed the room to a desk that had papers and books stacked neatly. Oh, this would be rather easy. She followed him.

"That's different," he said, and then as he reached the desk chair, he added, "Mind if I sit? I've been going back and forth between some things Keer has updated me on, and the stack of papers my grandfather gave me."

"I don't mind," she said. "But how is the pub different from the ball?"

"The people." Victor lowered into the leather chair, which creaked in response. "The atmosphere, too. You've been to my pub probably thousands of times. Surely, you know what I mean.

It's people I know, people I don't need to worry about appearances around. Here, I have to put complete focus on the way I stand, the way I talk, the words I say, the way I hold my head, where I put my hands."

Anne felt a bit of pity for him. He was so far out of his element. "I'm sorry, Victor. I promise, in no time, it will feel normal to you."

"Maybe." He turned to fully immerse himself back into whatever it was he was working on. With his attention averted from her, she hastily looked around his desk to see if he had any cream-colored letter paper, but she couldn't find any. Victor reached out to the corner of his desk and lifted a notebook. The size was too big, but there was a stack of letter paper below it. He pulled one out and over to him and began to write upon it.

But it was white, not cream.

"How are things going with you being gone?" she asked.

Victor began writing on the paper, a response to his employee Mr. Keer. He didn't look up, but he still held a conversation with her. "Well, I haven't been gone long, but it appears everything is fine."

"That's good." *May as well go all in.* "Do you know how to draw, Victor?"

Victor stopped writing and looked up at her, his brow furrowed. She noted he used black ink too, but then again, who didn't own black ink? "Do I know how to *draw*?"

"Yes. You know, pictures?"

Victor stared at her with his pen hovering over paper, clearly befuddled by this question. "Have you ever known me to draw?"

She hesitated. "No. Humor me for a moment, though. Draw me something."

He lifted an eyebrow and pulled over another sheet of white letter paper. "Any special requests?"

She almost asked him to draw a daisy, but if he was the Phantom, she wasn't ready to cross over to that just yet, and asking for him to draw a daisy would be far too obvious. "How about Onyx?"

"All right." Victor hovered his pen over the paper for a moment and then began to draw a side view of a horse. The animal's body was an oval, and the legs were four thin, long rectangles. Small, parallel lines made up the mane; long, squiggly lines created the tail; and the eye was a circle with a dot inside. Finally, he ended his creation with a triangle ear.

It was horrific.

Anne covered her mouth with her hand to keep the laughter in.

Victor finished his, erm, masterpiece and handed it to Anne. Though he didn't smile, humor danced in his eyes. "Are you laughing at me?"

She pulled her hand away and cleared her throat. "Of course not." A squeak escaped. "This is... Thank you Victor. I shall cherish this forever." And she couldn't help it. She started laughing. "Forgive me," she said once recovered. "That is unkind."

"I told you I couldn't draw," he replied, unbothered by her reaction. Point taken. Victor was not the Phantom, but she would ask Evelyn's thoughts just in case. He began writing his letter to Mr. Keer again, and without looking up, said, "May I ask why you wanted me to draw something?"

Anne hesitated. She would tell Victor about the drawing someone had left for her, but she wasn't ready to do so just yet. "Oh, I was just curious is all."

"Quite an odd request, I should say."

"Yes. Do you mind if I keep it, though?"

Now *that* got his attention. He stopped what he was doing and looked up at her, his brow furrowed dramatically. He looked almost appalled. "You want to keep *that*?"

"Yes, I would. You don't mind, do you?"

He stared off at nothing for a moment. "I suppose not, as long as you promise not to frame it and put it up for everyone to see."

Amused, she promised she would not. "I suppose I should get

to bed, then."

"You're not going back to the ball?"

"Oh, no. Not tonight. I've had my fill of dancing." Anne hesitated yet again, now debating if she should share the odd questions from Mr. Ashby. Normally, she shared everything with Victor. He was wise and patient. He always knew what to say. They could debate for hours on whether or not Queen Victoria's rumored saucy diaries from her marriage to Prince Albert truly existed. Sometimes, when she was truly stumped in how to handle a situation, she would ask Victor his thoughts on an issue with the children. For example, a year ago, Freddy had seemed melancholy and when pressed, had lamented that at his boarding school, he hadn't had anyone he considered a good friend. He'd felt left out. When she'd asked Victor for advice, he'd suggested Freddy join a club for a niche interest. Not cricket, which most boys joined, but something closer to his heart. Freddy had chosen the astronomy club. There, he'd come across a young man with whom he shared a class—Ralph Ashby.

But now, she hesitated to tell Victor about Mr. Felton Ashby and the way he'd acted at the end of their dance. Something in her cautioned her against this. Why, she couldn't say. But she thought it best to listen.

As Anne rose up from her seat and began walking to the door, Victor followed. And when Anne passed the threshold into her room, she turned around and said, "I suppose this is goodnight, then, Victor."

Victor nodded once. "Goodnight, Anne." But then he did something that was so unexpected, it would take weeks for her to accept she hadn't made it up in a dream or hallucination.

"I should have told you this earlier." Victor's voice lowered to a dark, velvet tone, making the moment feel more private. "But you look beautiful tonight." Victor leaned casually against the doorframe and stared down at her with that intense stare he sometimes had. This caused sparks to dance over her skin. He had never complimented her unsolicited before—or at least, it didn't feel like *this* when he had, as if she had snuck the most scrumptious piece of whipped cream and strawberry cake. If someone had told her this moment would have happened—his compliment, how he leaned against the doorframe like a rogue while staring at her, as if she were the only person in existence, the way the air seemed to electrify around them—she would have thought the idea utterly mad.

Never in a million years would she have expected to be affected by…this. To—to her dismay—like it.

Surprised by this admission to herself, Anne stood there frozen like a fool. And amidst her stunned silence, Victor leaned down and kissed her on the cheek.

That was all it was. He didn't kiss her lips. He kept his hands to himself. He didn't tilt her chin up, he didn't run his fingertips down her back, and he didn't pull off her gloves or let her hair down.

It was a mere kiss upon her cheek. One that lingered, yes, and was soft and gentle. But it felt as if something monumental had happened.

Anne's heart pounded hard against her ribs, and she felt as light as a feather. What in the world was going on?

Still, she stood there like an idiot, not responding. What was she supposed to say? Do?

Victor stepped back and there was nothing in his face that told her his compliment or his kiss had been anything other than a friendly, parting gesture, even though nothing of this sort had ever happened before.

Fortunately, she managed to find her voice. "Goodnight, then, Victor." It came out high-pitched.

Victor gave her one regal nod. But as he shut his door, she could have sworn there was a ghost of a smile on his lips.

With haste, she shut her own door, locked it, and took several steps back as she pressed a hand to her racing heart.

It had only been a peck on the cheek. It had only been a small compliment. Yet now that she was alone with only the darkness and the rolling sound of sea, she could not rid herself of the enormous grin that grew on her face.

But instead of being happy by this reaction, Anne was horrified. This was a very bad sign, and she had enough life experience to know the threat this warm, honey feeling was.

Anne quickly hurried to her vanity and pulled open a drawer a bit harder than she'd meant to. Swiftly, she took out *A Lady's Rules to Seaside Romance*, found a pen, and underlined the last rule hard:

Never fall in love.

Chapter Eighteen

THE WEEKS FOLLOWING the ball at Summerwood, everyone was busy with unending activity. Ollie and Evelyn had the twins out of the house as much as possible; otherwise, the boys would get fussy. Anne was often away with Mary and Freddy visiting friends or going into town. The Duke of Chalworth traveled back and forth between Brighton and London, though recently, Queen Victoria had finally departed for her summer holiday, which meant Parliament was out for the next few months. Now, the duke was ever-present, which meant he and Lily were attached at the hip while Vivian and Dantes did their part by helping the duke entertain for the season.

This, to Victor's secret ire, meant he was often roped into these social gatherings. Vivian, Dantes, and the duke were set on helping Victor reacquaint himself with his future peers. It was a bit strange for the first few weeks. Some of the men who visited with their wives were former schoolmates. Victor didn't experience nearly the same severity of bullying Dantes had in boarding school, but he had experienced some. However, unlike Dantes, Victor hadn't given a single fig about that back then. He'd simply hated boarding school. After living on the streets for years, with full freedom to do as he'd wished with no adults around to tell him what to do, Victor had become fully independent. And being in a boarding school with headmasters and professors and never a single moment to oneself, it had quickly become impossible for Victor to tolerate and he'd left, never looking back.

Victor was glad the family was supportive and graciously included him in everything. He would never be able to take over the dukedom without them. But he had also hoped Anne would have been the one to help him. Alas, ever since the ball at Summerwood, Anne had all but disappeared from his daily life, even more so than her odd absence previously. And he wasn't sure what to do.

Over the years, Anne had, bit by bit, opened up to Victor about her relationship with her husband. The real relationship, that was. It all came down to this: Winthrop had taken what he'd wanted, when he'd wanted it. He hadn't cared what the ramifications would be.

Since it had taken so long for Anne to open up herself to the possibility of romance once again, even if a brief one, he knew she would be quite cautious.

That caution was why he'd given her the drawing without telling her it was from him. His artistic talent was something he had kept to himself for his entire life. Admittedly, he was shy about revealing it to anyone, especially now that Evelyn was a part of the family. He would never compare to the famed artists she knew on a personal basis, or those whose creations were at the museum where she was employed. The family often visited and were well acquainted with *real* artwork. But he wanted to share a piece of himself with Anne, and this seemed a good way to do it anonymously. Neither of them was ready for anything else just yet. That was also why he'd given her a kiss on her cheek and hadn't touched her otherwise. She was skittish, a bit like Onyx in that way, and he of course would respect that and any hesitancy she showed.

Though he never would have expected this to happen, he knew that kiss on her cheek had thrown her off. But he also knew she would have no problem speaking up if she had an issue with it or wished him to never do it again. She hadn't protested, but she had also stepped back from him a bit, as if unsure what to make of it.

And he had to respect that. He respected her, cared for her, but he didn't know what to do next, either, other than wait. It was a good sign that she hadn't told him to stop, at least.

Thankfully, he still had his horse-riding lessons with her, though they were no longer a daily event. And Freddy and Mary were always present, of course.

Not that he was complaining. He didn't like that Anne seemed to be pulling away from him, but it was nice to be around the children more.

They were all riding together on the beach this morning. The sand was cool, the air salty and fresh, the lulling waves a calming presence. Seagulls skittered away as the horses bounded past, the birds crying above with hope that the humans had food to steal.

Ahead of Victor, Anne and Mary had Onyx and Pancake. Both ladies looked smart and feminine in their riding habits. Anne wore the same dark-green habit as she had during the first disastrous lesson. She looked beautiful this morning, and it twisted his stomach in a knot.

A knot he had to ignore as he stared at her back. As he did so, Anne briefly glanced over her shoulder at him as if sensing his stare, then quickly turned back around.

The ladies were too far ahead to overhear their conversation. Mary had been agitated this morning because invites had come in for an upcoming masquerade hosted by Lord and Lady Bell, the viscount and viscountess who had a summer home not far from Summerwood, but she wasn't invited.

Mary was not shy about voicing her dislike of this. But Anne was oddly quiet about the subject.

Though Victor couldn't hear them over the trotting of Marshmallow—he had come to the conclusion Anne enjoyed pairing him with horses who had overly cute names—he could tell they were arguing, based on Mary's hands flying around and Anne's rigid back.

"I wish *we* had been invited to the masquerade," Freddy whined at Victor's side.

Victor tore his attention away from Anne with a bit of regret and looked over to Freddy with a frown. That would explain the argument. "Who, you and your sister? You want to go?"

"Of course! It's a masquerade!"

Marshmallow snorted as if he agreed with the boy. Victor, however, didn't see the appeal. How uncomfortable it must be to wear a mask and costume all evening.

"Aren't you going?" Freddy asked.

Victor tightened his grip on the reins. He had become far more comfortable in his horse-riding ability since the first day in Brighton, but he still focused too much on how he sat in the saddle and held the reins. It didn't quite feel natural just yet. "No, I don't see a reason for me to," Victor replied.

"Blast! I can't imagine an unmarried man not wanting to go. I would think you'd be jumping at the opportunity."

"Why? I don't care to find and wear a costume. Frankly, to me, it sounds like a horrific way to spend an evening."

"But the *ladies!*" Freddy responded with a boisterous voice. Victor had to keep from reacting to this. He wasn't naive or ignorant—Freddy was already past the age where he would have started noticing young ladies. But still, seeing it happen was strange. Freddy still retained some of his boyish innocence, but it was fading away. It made Victor a bit sad, in a way.

"What about the ladies?" Victor decided it best to humor the lad.

Up ahead, Anne and Mary began to trot a bit faster, so Victor and Freddy followed suit.

"Granted, I haven't seen a masquerade for myself," Freddy said as he leaned forward with the increasing speed of his stallion. "But I've heard about them. The more concealed a young lady has her face, the more *daring* she becomes. And more willing for... Well, you know."

Victor frowned deeply. He didn't like where this discussion

was going, and he gave the young man a sharp look. "What are you talking about?"

Freddy laughed with cocky exasperation. This, coupled with the black top hat perched atop his dark hair, created an unsettling flash of the lad's father. "Once everyone gets drunk, all bets are off. I've heard the stories. Lord and Lady Bell's annual masquerade is *famous* for its debauchery."

Victor ignored the discomfort this caused. "What stories have you heard?"

"Oh, you know. Courtesans, multiple partners, and the like."

Victor stared at the lad, horrified. He had visions of Anne wearing a mask, surrounded by handsy, eager men. It made him sick to his stomach, and jealousy flamed hot, even though he had no right at all to feel that way. How had Ollie and Dantes never mentioned this before? He would have to corner one of them about it later.

"Your mother goes?" Victor couldn't resist digging for information. However, he tried to keep his voice from sounding overly interested. "Every year?"

"Of course. The whole family does." As the horses' hooves pounded on the ground, Freddy's jaw became tense. "My father used to go as well. When he was alive. Obviously."

It struck Victor that Winthrop's attendance at this debauched masquerade bothered Freddy. Yet he didn't seem to mind that Anne attended.

Victor was at a loss of what to say. There was a tension in Freddy at the mention of Winthrop that was hard to ignore. But none of it gave away the lad's true thoughts on the man. Victor knew what it was like to lose a father at a young age—he knew well how the mere mention of his own father had given Victor strong emotions for many years. When he'd been a young lad himself, he'd only mentioned his father when he'd wanted to talk about him. But for the most part, Victor had been fond of him. How Freddy felt about Winthrop, Victor never could quite figure out. The lad had been relatively tight-lipped on that. And so had

Mary, now that he thought about it.

"I didn't know that," Victor said, hoping to drag out the conversation. Freddy looked over and seemed to be waiting for Victor to say something. But all he could think about was what Anne did at these masquerades. Victor decided to turn the conversation back. "Did it bother you that your father attended?"

Freddy scoffed. "Of course it bothered me. Do you think he went off with my mother? Of course not. He went with the courtesans while she stayed behind. Even I know *that*."

A mix of fury and disgust rippled through Victor. "Your father did that? You're sure?"

Freddy nodded tightly. "After he died, I confronted my grandfather about it. I had heard rumors—when you're a child, people think you don't know what they're talking about when they flap their lips about. But I heard it. Anyway, he confirmed it was true but told me to quit asking about it."

"I'm sorry." Victor meant it, too.

But Freddy responded by pushing his top hat forward slightly and made it known the discussion was over by going silent. As the ladies slowed up ahead, Victor and Freddy followed suit and trotted along the beach. Around them, the early morning, gray sky brightened with the sun as it rose higher. Waves crashed ashore with a satisfying sound. In a few hours, it would be too hot to be on the beach wearing a suit, but right now, the air, the sun, and the temperature were perfect.

"What was your father like?" Freddy asked, surprising Victor. Victor had never talked about his father to Freddy or Mary before.

Victor considered the question. "He was wild. Loud. His voice was loud, his demeanor was loud, the way he dressed was loud. Everything about him demanded attention."

"Did he have mistresses?"

The question took him aback. "To be honest, I don't know."

"Would you have mistresses if you were married?" There was a sharpness to Freddy's voice that grabbed Victor's attention.

"No."

"If you go to the masquerade, will you go off with courtesans?"

Victor looked Freddy square in the eye and noticed the lad's jaw was set tight once again. Something about the way Freddy asked these questions told Victor the young lad was quite serious about getting an honest answer, and that Victor's answers mattered to him. Did the young man look up to Victor more than he had thought, perhaps? It was clear Freddy was comparing him to Winthrop. "No," Victor said with abject certainty.

Freddy held Victor's gaze a beat longer, lifting his chin with warning reflecting in his eyes, then gave a single nod and looked away. "Do you miss him?" Freddy asked. "Or has it been too long?"

"I still miss him," Victor admitted.

"I don't miss Bernard." Freddy kept his face straight forward, but his hold on the reins tightened. Victor wasn't sure when it had happened, but there was now so much of the former marquess in the young man, it was unsettling, like a dead man walking. It didn't help there was that familiar defiance in Freddy's face that dared Victor to argue with him, or give the wrong answer to his questions. He had seen that exact face—the slight press of the mouth, the narrowing of the same eyes, the furrow of the same brows—in Winthrop when he'd made his wagers against Dantes's fights. The fights Dantes had always won.

All Victor knew was one day, Freddy, already a marquess, would be the Duke of Chalworth. And God help anyone who crossed him.

"I understand," Victor replied carefully to Freddy's admission. For all Victor knew, it was a heavy weight on the lad's shoulders and likely had taken a lot of strength to admit to. "And I think it's brave of you to admit that not only to me, but yourself."

Freddy swallowed and tore his gaze away, putting it on his mother and sister up ahead. As his face softened upon seeing them, Victor finally saw a hint of Anne in his profile. "I'm glad

Mama is not trying to get an exception for Mary go to the masquerade."

Victor felt a pang of humor in his chest. "Why, because she wouldn't get one for you?"

"No. Mary would just cause trouble."

That response threw Victor off. What had Freddy meant by that? But before Victor could ask, their horses slowed to a stop. Anne and Mary had turned around to head back to Summerwood, which had caught the attention of Victor's and Freddy's horses. Anne's cheeks had color to them. Meanwhile, Mary pouted but did her best to hide it. They had continued to argue about the masquerade, no doubt.

"That was good fun! But we should head back," Anne said in a forced bright voice. After talking with Freddy, Victor appreciated how much Anne had been dealt with on her own, and his admiration for her only deepened.

"Is everything all right?" Victor asked, concerned by the tension in her face. She was forcing a smile, but it wasn't reaching her eyes. Eyes that were filled with concern.

"Oh, everything is *just* fine," Mary said in a haughty voice, her spine needle-straight. "Mama still won't ask for an exception for me to attend Lord and Lady Bell's masquerade and frankly, I find that unfair. Why can I go to every other ball except that one?"

"Mary..." Anne let out a sigh of exasperation. "I've already explained to you. It's not an appropriate event for a young lady not yet out. Our friends don't mind you attending intimate, small balls. The masquerade is...not that."

Victor stared unblinking at Anne as she said this and couldn't help but drink her in. Her green riding habit fit snugly, and he admired the inward curve of her waist, flared by her wide hips as she perched atop Onyx. He imagined some faceless, white-faced cad in a powdered wig and eighteenth-century garb grabbing the cinch of her waist, winning a flirtatious giggle, that grin topped by a white eye mask. Jealousy reared and ran like an untamed horse, and he mentally cursed at himself.

As if hearing his thoughts, Anne lifted her eyes to his and when she realized he was watching her, she quickly looked away, her face more flushed than it had been before. She pressed her hands to her cheeks. "I think the temperature is rising along with tempers. Shall we?"

Mary made a *harrumph* sound, shouted out a command to Pancake, and she and her mare bolted back down the beach, mane and tail and habit skirt billowing with the wind. After a brief hesitation, Freddy nudged his horse after her.

"Children! Mary! Freddy!" Anne cried after them with a panicked shout. Victor could see she was preparing to gallop after them as well.

"Wait." Victor reached out and pressed a halting hand to Anne's forearm. As Onyx snorted, she stared down at it and then her eyes flew up to his, wide.

"You better not be about to tell me how to parent them." Frustration ground at her voice. Maybe Freddy had gotten his defiance from her.

"Have I ever done that, unless you explicitly asked for my opinion?" He made a point not to move his hand away, to linger his touch. Anne looked down at it again, then back up to his face, her pale eyes searching his. But once again, she didn't tell him to move or back off. This sent a jolt of hope through him.

"No, you haven't," she conceded.

"Do you trust them to ride back safely on their own?"

She huffed. "Of course I do."

"Do you want to know what I think right now? I will keep my thoughts to myself if you wish me to."

Her eyes narrowed a tad, but she eventually nodded.

"Let them go. Give Mary space to get her frustration out the way she wants to."

Anne inhaled deeply though her nose and closed her eyes as if this pained her. "Very well."

With regret, he moved his hand off of her and they began

trotting back to the house. "A minute ago, I was thinking about how much I admire you."

Anne frowned and gave him a suspicious onceover. "Admire me? Why?"

"Because you raised Mary and Freddy on your own, both before and after your husband's death. They're growing up to be good people and are well-behaved. That is no small feat."

She turned her face forward. "Frankly, I don't know how true that is anymore."

"It remains true." Victor wasn't a father, of course, but he'd been the stand-in for his brothers for a long time. "I don't know exactly what it's like, but I do know how it is to worry about people who rely on you. Always questioning yourself, if you're making the right decision, if you're raising them right or destroying them in the process. Look at my situation. I was responsible for Dantes and Ollie while living in the slums. I was not someone to admire or look up to. I've broken many laws, did many shameful things, and should have been sent to prison several times over for it. But fortunately, I wasn't. And I think all three of us turned out relatively well. I hope, anyway."

"You did," Anne replied.

"You were put into a difficult situation and I think you've come out the other side stronger for it."

Anne was quiet for a moment as their horses gently cantered along the beach. "I do worry about them. I was once a young lady like Mary, eager to become an adult, frustrated to still be treated like a child. I understand that frustration and I feel like it's easier for me to face because I've been there myself. But Freddy..." She trailed off.

"What about Freddy?"

Anne sighed. "Please don't judge me for what I'm about to say, but I worry most about him. I worry about him...becoming Bernard." She turned her face toward the watery horizon, her mouth pressed tight.

"He does look a lot like him," Victor said, recalling his earlier thoughts about the young lad's resemblance to his father.

"It's uncanny. When he came home from school this year, I walked downstairs to greet him and swore I was seeing Bernard's ghost. And if he looks just like Bernard, somewhere inside of him Bernard's demeanor lurks as well."

"Maybe," Victor replied. Freddy and Mary were now two distant dots. "Personally, I don't think he's anything like his father." Victor told her what Freddy had said moments ago, about not missing his father and how intense he'd seemed about it. He did, however, leave out the part about Freddy's supposition of Mary causing trouble and the duke confirming scandalous rumors of Winthrop to Freddy. There was only so much worry a mother could take on, and he didn't want Anne to worry more than she already did, especially over events that could not be changed.

"Has Freddy ever said anything like that to you before?" Anne asked. "Anything at all negative about Bernard?"

"No. Neither of them has ever brought him up to me before. I was surprised he did so today."

"Why did he?"

"I don't know."

As she put her worried brow back on the distant dots of her children, he couldn't help but wonder what was going on in her mind. He had sometimes wondered, too, how the trio talked about the late marquess in private. Did they often talk about him, or not at all? When Victor and his brothers had been young, they hadn't talked about their dead parents. Well, he and Dantes hadn't. Ollie would often ask questions, but he'd also had no memory of them. It had made sense he'd been curious. And even though Dantes was only two years younger than Victor, as opposed to Ollie's ten, Dantes had a very rosy and idealized memory of their parents.

Dantes remembered them being madly in love, dancing together in the house, crooning over each other, private laughter. Victor remembered those moments as well—they hadn't been created from thin air—but he also remembered the bad times. Times his father had come home drunk and their parents had argued. Their mother drinking alone herself and crying. Throwing objects at each other in fits of fury.

Then there'd been their mother's spiral when their father had died. Moving from their nice home to the rickety, drafty, tenement while their mother had been heavily pregnant. Then the difficult labor, the addiction to laudanum—and of course, the overdose.

Victor was the one who'd discovered her dead from an overdose.

Dantes spoke so highly of their parents in the rare moments they came up, Victor had decided to shoulder the truth all on his own. He didn't want to ruin Dantes's or Ollie's perception of them. Instead, he would carry the darkness for them for the rest of their lives.

He'd made that decision when he'd discovered his mother dead with numerous empty laudanum bottles beside her. The postpartum madness and the melancholy from his father's death, plus their fall from grace—it had all been too much for her.

Just before Dantes had entered the room, Victor had thrown all of the bottles but one out the window.

But it wasn't like their mother or father were only bad memories for Victor, and he didn't hate them, either. He loved them despite their flaws. They'd been very flawed people, and because of the difficulties caused by their flaws, he'd striven his entire life to evade all temptations because of it. The temptation of pride like what had led to his father's death from one of his locomotives when he should have been at home with his family. The temptation of drink, which had flamed the words and tempers of both his parents. And the temptation of women, of intimacy, which had brought three brothers into a world filled with struggle. Fortunately, this temptation was rather easy for him to avoid, as it never had appealed to him. Regardless, it had been easier to avoid these temptations than tease the risk they could bring. Temptation caused nothing but life-altering trouble.

Winthrop, meanwhile, had been a scoundrel through and through, the embodiment of sin with nothing but devils and demons on his shoulders whispering into his ear. Victor knew from Vivian and Anne that when the former marquess had been younger, though he hadn't been a saint even when he and Anne had first married, the cad had been a whole different person. But once the responsibility of children had come around, even though he'd had servants to take on much of the children's care, the man had changed into the monster Victor had known. But it wasn't as if Winthrop were the only man to change after the introduction of a baby. It seemed as if this were more common than the husband who dropped everything to care for his postpartum wife, or the husband who shrugged into the role of father as if it were as easy and sensical as putting on a jacket on a cool autumn day.

Victor heard it all the time, the way these men talked at the pub. They would laugh and laugh, drunk out of their minds, bragging that their wives were at home with the babies because that was where they were meant to be, but *their* day was so hard, they deserved to be at the pub for hours every night. Which meant the women they mocked were home alone with babies, working their own jobs while their husbands went off and faffed about however they pleased.

And these husbands weren't usually of the upper class, either. This behavior seemed to cross class lines.

Victor hardly witnessed a successful marriage. His brothers were fortunate in that regard, but there was no way it would happen a third time. A one-hundred-percent happy family success rate amongst the McNab brothers? Those odds were not possible, not with their family. He would be destined to be the miserable one. He was a betting man, though his success was with horses and not outlooks on life. But if he were to place a wager, his wager would be on him finding misery in marriage.

Something inside of him thrashed around wildly in protest, as if attempting to scream its disagreement. It was a strange sensation, one he felt on a lesser scale while looking over the future losers in the horse racing booklets. Shifting in his saddle, Victor decided to blame the strange sensation on hopefulness. He was too old, too experienced in life, to feel hope for something. Whatever it was, it was best to ignore it.

But as he rode along the beach, the warm summer breeze sweeping past, Anne riding at his side, he couldn't help but wonder if a marriage with her could be one of happiness. What would it be like if he married his closest friend? Anne knew him as well as anyone could. They shared everything together, and their families were close. He couldn't imagine them being unhappy in a lifelong partnership.

But it also seemed impossible. Neither of them had marriage as a future goal. And yet he wanted her all to himself. How in the world was that supposed to work?

It couldn't. But he did note that in letting himself think about this, the thrashing inside him had all but stopped.

Chapter Nineteen

DURING THE MORNING ride along the beach, Anne noticed Victor was out of sorts after his ride with Freddy. He appeared thoughtful and distracted, staring off into the distance, but when he looked at her there was a storm of emotion in his eyes that caused her breath to catch. Unfortunately, she couldn't quite identify what he was feeling. Was he angry? Frustrated? Something else? He was trying hard to keep it concealed, and none of those emotions made sense in the moment.

She asked him what was wrong. Perhaps it was tied to his discussion with Freddy about deceased fathers. However, he denied anything was amiss. Which only piqued her curiosity further.

Especially with the way he stared at her when anyone brought up the upcoming masquerade. That stare had been so intense, even for him, that she couldn't help but shiver under it. It was a moment that had lasted mere seconds, but hours later, Anne still felt its effect on her. No matter what she tried, she couldn't shake the feeling it had left behind.

Victor was her friend, her dearest friend in the world. There had never been any romantic feelings between them and that wasn't about to start now. And yet, if anyone else had looked at her the way Victor had in that spine-tingling moment, she would have given them an earful. It was that intimate.

It also didn't escape her that she didn't tell him to quit it, like she would have with anyone else.

This was the second time this summer Victor had thrown her into a cloud of confusion after he had done something innocuous. Weeks ago, he'd given her that gentle kiss on her cheek, yet the way her heart had pounded in response, he may as well have come up from behind and kissed her neck while grasping her waist.

It was all very confusing. Victor barely ever touched her. Yet when he did, the slightest brush of skin somehow burst her into flames.

Anne closed her eyes and fanned herself until the heat rising within her began to cool. This *must* have been due to loneliness. It wasn't that it was Victor giving her this attention—it was because *a man* was.

After a post-luncheon nap, Anne left her bedroom freshened up in a white, linen afternoon dress and was still a bit groggy when she descended the stairs to reach the main floor. Summerwood's butler, Keane, was at the front door speaking to someone. She hardly paid the scene any mind at first. However, when she passed by and her footsteps clicked on the floor, Keane called after her, "Lady Litchfield! A moment, if you may."

Anne paused and turned around, a bit curious. "Yes?"

Keane approached her, stopped, and bowed. "Are you feeling refreshed?"

Anne smiled. "Oh, yes, there really is something special about the air here."

Keane responded to her smile with his own. "I agree, and I am quite fortunate to live here year-round. These came for you during your rest. This one just now." He handed over a white envelope and grumbled about it being delivered at the improper door. "And this one a few minutes ago." He handed over a cream envelope.

Anne took the envelopes from the butler, thanked him, and opened them as she began walking down the hallway. She often received invites for tea or dinner and she assumed that was what these were. The first envelope, the one he had just received, did end up being an invite. For dinner that evening at the Ashby residence.

Anne frowned. She and the children had been to the Ashby residence a few times this summer already. Freddy and Mr. Ralph Ashby were such dear friends. But she knew Mary had her eye on Mr. Lucas Ashby, and Mr. Felton Ashby still had his eye on Anne, based on the way he followed her around whenever their families were together. He had, at least, apologized for his rude questioning at the ball at Summerwood and had been far more agreeable since.

Resigned to the fact her evening would be with the Ashbys, she then went to the cream envelope. Was it a coincidence these letters had arrived only minutes apart? That seemed unlikely. Perhaps whoever delivered the letters had forgotten about the second one and returned only minutes later with it. The face of the second letter was blank, which was strange, but she attributed it to an error. She pulled out a folded letter and immediately halted her steps.

It was another small ink drawing inside of a circle, just like the daisy from before. This time, it was a sketch of a woman, from her hip up, dancing with a gentleman, though his face was out of the circle frame. It was as if the viewer were watching from behind the gentleman's left.

The man had broad shoulders and his left arm wrapped around the woman's waist. He held her close in a lover's embrace, and the woman looked up at him, her lips parted, her focus on her dance partner attentive.

Anne gasped because she realized the sketch was of *her*. It looked exactly like her. Whoever had drawn this was exceptionally ly talented. They'd gotten so many details correct, from the shape of her ear to the earrings she often wore, to the shape of her upper lip—one side of it was slightly narrower than the other side—even the little loose hairs around her hairline that drove her mad.

But again, the artist hadn't written anything. He had no words for her, only pictures.

Did he have nothing to say? No explanation for why he was sending her drawings? Didn't he want to sign his name so she'd know who he was?

And shouldn't she have been disturbed by this? Whoever had drawn this had spent a *lot* of time studying her face.

There was a sound down the hall that caused her to look up. Her stomach flipped as Victor walked out of a room talking over his shoulder, with Ollie, Evelyn, and the twins following behind. The boys started running around the three adults and Evelyn begged them to calm down while Ollie tried speaking to his older brother over the boys' loud giggles.

Anne refolded the drawing and put it back in its envelope and made her way to the others. Victor immediately spotted her, stared at her with that intense, green gaze of his that sent sparks along her skin, then put his attention back on Ollie.

"He made it out just in time," Ollie said, though Anne had no clue who *he* was. "As he dropped from her window, Lady Greene appeared at it, covering herself only with a blanket, screeching about the ring he had lifted from her." Ollie let out a howl of laughter.

"Ollie, please." Evelyn gave him wide eyes before looking at the boys, who clearly, based on the way their heads bowed together, paid no attention to the adults. They were intently watching a ladybird that had found its way inside the house.

"What are you talking about?" Anne came to stand beside Evelyn. "Someone stole a ring from Lady Greene?" Anne wasn't particularly fond of Lady Greene. The woman had become a widow after only a few years of marriage and had spent her time since bleeding her husband's estate dry.

"We're talking about my uncle." Victor's dark, deep voice pulled her attention up to him. The voice slid over her skin like silk ribbon and it caused the hairs on the back of her neck to stand up.

"The one you don't talk to?" Anne replied, shaking off the odd feeling.

Victor held her gaze and nodded.

Ollie began talking, but Anne couldn't take her eyes off Victor. He looked handsome, refreshed after their morning ride. His black hair was back in its usual exact place as opposed to the windblown look he'd had earlier which, admittedly, Anne *also* found handsome in its own way. And his emerald eyes didn't leave hers, either. They held on to her and, somehow, seemed to darken to a moss color. Warmth rolled slow in her stomach.

"You know I'm close with our uncle," Ollie continued through Anne's and Victor's mutual staring, unaware. "And he loves ripping off nobs. They don't go after him because it would reach the newspapers. Could you imagine Lady Greene telling the police she chased after him with hardly a stitch of clothing on? The papers would go wild with that story!" Ollie began howling in laughter again.

The loud laughter broke the spell, and Anne realized she had been holding her breath. Feeling her face heat, she looked over at Ollie and hoped her racing heart didn't sound as loud as it felt.

"Ollie, *we're* nobs," Anne said.

But Ollie only shrugged. Then again, Ollie wasn't really involved much in the aristocracy. Unlike Dantes and Vivian, who embraced the nobility from which they had been outcast at one point, Ollie and Evelyn were mostly uninvolved, even though her father was a baron and his grandfather the Duke of Invermark. But Evelyn was an art conservator and Ollie had quit The Harp & Thistle to be home with their twins. Because he was one-third owner of The Harp & Thistle, he still reaped the profits, which she knew irritated Victor to no end.

"What is that?" Victor asked, looking at the envelope in Anne's hand. Quickly, she felt to make sure the cream envelope was hidden behind the white one.

"A dinner invite from the Ashbys," she replied.

He lifted an eyebrow. "And you are going?" Victor never

mentioned Mr. Ashby to her, despite the man's interest in her, which she was realizing was a bit odd. Then again, she didn't offer much up about it, either, which was also strange for her. Normally, she told him everything.

"Yes," she replied. "Of course, the children will be joining. Would you like to join us?" She hurried the question out, feeling uncharacteristically flustered.

"I would." Victor gave a small bow. Anne, now feeling even more uncertain about the evening, would have expected him to make an excuse, as he didn't seem fond of the Ashbys. And she wasn't even sure why she had invited him, either. The question had come out on its own.

"Good. That's settled, then." Anne recalled the reason she'd approached the trio in the first place. "Evelyn." Anne turned to the tall redhead beside her. "I need to speak with you. In private."

ANNE SHUT HER bedroom door as soon as Evelyn had entered the room. Evelyn looked around, quite confused as to why they were here.

"I didn't want to explain why I'm seeking your help in front of Victor and Ollie," Anne said while angling over to her vanity.

"Oh?" Evelyn followed, curiosity clear in her question.

Anne put a hand on the drawer but hesitated. She looked over her shoulder. "First, I want to make sure you understand this is a conversation that stays between you and me. You have come to me for help in the past. It is my time to come to you, if you may."

Evelyn's eyes widened slightly. "Of course. You may trust me with anything."

Anne nodded and pulled open the drawer. She first showed Evelyn the drawing of the daisy amongst the night sky. "I received this the night of the ball Vivian and Dantes hosted."

Evelyn took it. "Did someone deliver it to you?"

Anne shook her head and debated what she should tell Evelyn. She decided to tell her everything—otherwise, this would be of no help. "No. I saw someone watching me from the balcony that overlooks the ballroom."

Evelyn's mouth made an *O*. "Who was it?"

"I don't know." Anne lowered into the vanity chair while Evelyn studied the drawing. "I went up there to find out and they were gone, disappearing into thin air as if they were a phantom."

Evelyn glanced up and tilted her head. "Interesting."

"But as I headed back down the hall…" Anne pointed to the drawing. "That was lying in the middle of the floor. It hadn't been there before. He'd somehow reappeared without me knowing. And quickly disappeared."

"The Phantom left it for you," Evelyn concluded.

"Yes." Anne swallowed. "And then this arrived today." She took the daisy drawing from Evelyn, set it atop the vanity, and handed over the new drawing.

"That's you," Evelyn said immediately, not bothering to hide the surprise in her voice. "My word. Whoever your phantom is is exceptionally talented."

"It's strange, right? It's as if they have my face memorized."

Evelyn's face tensed—an odd reaction—and she responded with a nod.

"Do you think…I should be disturbed by this?"

Evelyn looked up briefly before frowning back down at the drawing. "I suppose it depends on who the sender is, doesn't it?"

Anne considered this. "Yes, I suppose you're right."

"And I suppose the sender is whoever this gentleman is holding you in a lover's embrace, his face conspicuously hidden. It's a drawing of desire, I believe."

"So, you agree that's what it is? That's what I thought too, a lover's embrace, but then I thought I was reading too much into it."

"No, whoever drew this…" Evelyn trailed off as if struck by a sudden thought.

"What is it?" Anne hurried the words out. "Whoever drew it…what?"

"They are clearly quite fond of you." Evelyn handed the drawing back and appeared to fidget as if uncomfortable. But Anne couldn't imagine why. "Do you have *any* idea who the sender might be?"

Anne set the drawing next to the other one. "I thought it might be Mr. Ashby, as he has been pursuing me. And the second drawing could have come at the same time as the Ashby dinner invite for tonight." Anne studied Evelyn's reaction to this. But her expression was carefully guarded.

Though now that she was talking this out with a friend, she concluded Mr. Ashby was rather a forward person. He had made his pursuit of her clear without resorting to mystery. Unless he found giving her mysterious drawings to be a lark? Or thought she would enjoy them? That could make sense. And Mr. Ashby could definitely have been the one to have done the drawings. With the daisy one, he could have arrived at the ball with it, waiting for a good opportunity to sneak it to her. But he couldn't have been the man hiding in the shadows.

"How would you feel about that, if Mr. Ashby were the one sending you the drawings?"

"I don't know. I've not had a great initial impression of him, to be honest. But it's possible I've been wrong in my assessment of him."

"Could there be anyone else sending them?"

Anne turned back to the open drawer and pulled out Victor's horrific drawing of Onyx. Briefly, she debated bringing Victor into this.

And yet, she couldn't quite let the unlikely possibility go, either. She really had no reason to think it would be him, yet her mind kept going that way.

Anne handed the horse drawing to Evelyn. "What do you think about this drawing?"

Evelyn smiled wide. "Rather rubbish."

"This is why I wanted your help. You're an art expert, right?"

Evelyn bobbed her head left to right. "Sort of. My expertise is in paintings, not drawings."

"I think you can still help. Could the person who drew this"—Anne pointed to the horse—"also have drawn those?" She then indicated the expert drawings on the vanity.

Evelyn tapped the horse drawing. "Who drew this?"

"I…don't wish to say."

Evelyn's red eyebrows lifted high, but she didn't comment on that. "It's hard to say. The person who drew this horse couldn't draw those." She indicated to the expert ink drawings. "But the person who drew those could have easily drawn this horse."

"I don't understand."

Evelyn set the horse drawing beside the expert drawings. "This horse drawing. If this was the sketcher's honest skill, they would never be able to draw those. But someone with the expert skill of your Phantom, he could easily draw that horrific horse to evade you."

Anne had to bite her cheek.

"I am quite curious who drew the horse." Evelyn went back in the direction Anne had been hoping to avoid. And she held Anne's gaze, unwavering, unwilling to drop the subject.

Anne opened her mouth, stammered, and then finally admitted, "Victor drew it."

"Really!" Evelyn paused. "Why did he give you a drawing of a horse?"

Anne brushed her hands over her white, linen sleeves. "I asked him to."

Evelyn studied Anne. "After you received these drawings from your Phantom? Or before?"

"After I received the drawing of the daisy. Before the one of me."

Evelyn tapped at her chin. "Forgive me, but what are you trying to discover here? Do you think Victor might be in love with you? That's why he would give these to you?"

Anne couldn't help it. She gasped loudly at this. "Evelyn!"

But Evelyn looked at her with round, innocent eyes. Suspiciously innocent. "What?"

"You can't say that out loud!"

"Why not?"

"Because that's Victor and me you're talking about!"

Evelyn was quite for a long beat. "And?"

Frustration ground at Anne. Must she verbalize all of this? "Victor is my dearest friend in the whole world. I fear even *thinking* those thoughts will destroy our friendship."

"And you…don't wish to be without his friendship?"

Anne frowned at Evelyn. Really, now! "Of course not. Let's say, hypothetically, Victor is the Phantom. He's not—but pretend for a moment that he is." She began to tap her fingers together rapidly. "And pretend for a moment that there were a mutual romantic attraction—which there isn't, but again we're pretending. Maybe it would be nice for a short time, but then what would happen?"

Evelyn waited for Anne to provide the answer.

"It would end in disaster!" Anne flung her hands out to side. "I've already been married and it was horrible. I'm never going to get stuck in such a situation again."

"Wait." Evelyn closed her eyes and shook her head. "I thought Victor was the one against marriage?"

"He was." Anne's face became hot.

"I see."

"Regardless of who is against marriage, what would happen? We have a secret liaison for the rest of our lives? That doesn't happen. Eventually, feelings will become unbalanced. One will want more than the other. Plus, I wouldn't wish to hide something like that, not with him at least."

Evelyn twisted her mouth in thought. "I can understand that."

"I don't want to lose my dearest friend because of a silly,

short-lived romance. That would be devastating to me. I won't risk it."

"Of course not. But I should add that, I *did* marry my dearest friend and it's the most wonderful way to go through life. To be passionately, madly in love with your dearest friend in the world? It's a wonderful experience. It hasn't lessened, either, and we've been married a good while now. Quite frankly, I've never been happier."

Anne clenched her teeth. This was not helping her at all.

Evelyn studied Anne's face then looked back down to the vanity. "Let me take a good look at these drawings." Evelyn picked up the drawing of the daisy with one hand and the horse drawing with the other and held them up side by side. "The paper is different. Of note, your Phantom used the same paper for both drawings. But the horse drawing is cheaper, generic, white paper. Your Phantom's paper is more expensive."

Anne nodded to show she understood.

Evelyn held the drawings close to her face. "The ink appears to be the same. It's the same color, same opacity. It doesn't bleed at all, which indicates high quality. But it's also ink. They could easily be different types or different brands while looking the same." For a long moment, Evelyn studied the drawings and Anne could see that the wheels in her mind were turning. She waited patiently to see to what conclusion Evelyn would come.

Finally, Evelyn set the drawings down and turned fully to Anne. She crossed her arms. "Does Victor know how to draw?"

"Not that I'm aware of. I've never seen him do it before."

"I haven't, either. And Ollie has never mentioned Victor having this talent." Evelyn chewed thoughtfully on her bottom lip.

"What do you think, then?"

Evelyn, her arms still crossed, sighed. "My sons could have drawn a horse better than that when they were four."

"I don't think we should be insulting Victor—"

"No, no." Evelyn dropped her arms to the side. "You misunderstand. What I'm trying to say is, Victor drew that horse terribly on purpose. Most adults could draw better than that. He *wanted* it to appear he cannot draw."

Anne felt a bit lightheaded. "You're positive on that?"

"Yes. Absolutely." Evelyn looked down at the vanity surface. "What I'm left wondering is why he drew badly on purpose, and why is he hiding this talent from everyone?"

"You think Victor is the drawer of all of these?"

"Yes, I do."

With Evelyn's conclusion, Anne was left feeling more confused than ever.

Had Victor *really* drawn these? And if so, did that mean he was also the Phantom?

She trusted Evelyn's assessment, but unlike Evelyn, she believed an adult could really draw that horrifically. It made more sense for Mr. Ashby to be the expert drawer, and Victor the Phantom. Maybe Victor had been simply watching out for her the night of the ball like the good friend he was.

Chapter Twenty

THE ASHBY FAMILY was something else.

They were rabid fanatics of charades, a game Victor couldn't stand, as it meant making a fool of himself in front of everyone when he preferred to be off to the side on his own.

Unfortunately for him, he'd accepted Anne's invite to the dinner and now was in the middle of a heated game. Even though as a widow, she didn't require a chaperone and in fact *was* the chaperone for Mary, he knew she felt better having him there with her. On the drive over, he'd tried asking about the nature of her relationship with Mr. Ashby. It was something she had been tight-lipped about, but she'd finally confirmed his suspicion that Ashby was in fact actively pursuing her. More pointedly than Victor had thought, or liked, in fact. Apparently, the cad could be rather forward about it.

But she waved him off when he tried asking *how* forward Ashby had been. Tonight, he was watching the cad's every move.

"Uncle Victor, it's your turn." Freddy nudged Victor's side. There were two teams: Victor's team, which consisted of Freddy, Mr. Ralph Ashby, Mr. Joseph Ashby, and Mr. Martin Ashby, the last two of whom Victor had had little interaction with previously. Anne's team was Mary, Mrs. Ashby, the eldest Mr. Ashby, and Mr. Lucas Ashby. The latter kept sneaking covert glances at Mary in a way Mary didn't seem to notice. It even got to the point that

Ashby leaned over to the lad to say something low, though whatever he'd said caused the young man to stop, at least.

Anne's team bowed their heads together and whispered. Ashby said, "Oh, I've a brilliant one," and wrote it on a piece of paper.

Low voices, rapid with excitement, told Victor the other team had decided on the word he was meant to act out.

Ashby stood and Victor followed the movement. They met in the empty space of floor between the two teams.

The blond idiot had a cocky grin on his face and showed Victor the word he would act out: "dragonfly."

The urge to scowl at this was fierce. Victor was going to have to flap his arms like a madman. Which, he suspected, was precisely why Ashby had chosen this word.

As Victor internally sighed at himself, he glanced over at Anne, only to find her watching him, her eyes sparkling with merriment and a flush rising on her cheeks. Anne *and* Mary had their hands up to their mouths, giggling and leaning together.

Anne looked beautiful, like a ray of sunshine with that smile of hers. Her eyes crinkled at him, full of joy.

And it was he who'd put that bright smile there. Himself! A warmth enveloped his heart.

Very well. He would act out this blasted dragonfly if it made her happy.

As Ashby returned to his team, he shooed his brother off from Mary's side and took the young man's place, pushing the round spectacles up his nose. Victor was glad the lad had been chased away from Mary. It seemed the second son also suffered from lack of tact, just like his older brother, but at least Ashby was putting a stop to the younger lad's antics.

Victor put his attention on his team and held up three fingers.

"Three syllables!" his team shouted in unison.

Pausing, he tried to figure out how to mimic a dragonfly. He stuck his arms out to the side and began to flap them up and down.

"A bird!" Freddy shouted.

"But what kind of bird?" Mr. Ralph Ashby asked.

"Oh. A parrot?"

"That's *two* syllables."

Deciding there wasn't another way to mimic a dragonfly, Victor stopped flapping and held up two fingers.

"First two syllables!" the team said.

Victor curved his fingers like monster claws and opened his mouth wide. Then he took one hand and tried to indicate fire shooting out of his mouth.

"Are you throwing up?" Mr. Joseph Ashby asked, his freckled nose wrinkled in disgust.

Victor shook his head amongst the giggling from the other team. He then stuck his arms out to the side again and began "flying" around the room, and at intervals tried to show fire spewing from his mouth. As he passed Anne, he winked at her and she gave him a bashful smile. He was a simple man and, in a silly bout of pride mixed with chest-puffing jealousy, he looked at Ashby to see if he had caught the interaction. But the cad was in conversation with Mary and hadn't noticed.

Ah, well.

Mr. Martin Ashby jumped to his feet so quickly, it nearly knocked his spectacles off his face. He fixed them and shouted quite loudly, "I know, a dragon!"

Victor stopped to nod vehemently. He hurried back over to his team and held up three fingers and pointed to his third finger.

His team responded, "Third syllable!"

He nodded once and then flapped his arms again.

"Not a bird." Mr. Ralph Ashby tapped at his cheek.

"Well, what else flies?" asked Mr. Martin Ashby.

"What about a butterfly?"

"What does a butterfly have to do with dragons?"

"Oh! Dragonfly! Dragonfly!" Freddy had jumped to his feet and held two triumphant fists in front of himself, his eyes wide with anticipation.

"Yes!" Victor shouted back. The team whooped and whistled as if they had just won a football match, and they all patted Victor hard on the back as he sat back down. Maybe this wasn't so bad, after all.

Mrs. Ashby got to her feet and was laughing along with them. "Oh, what utter fun that was! Excellent work, Mr. McNab. I thought that would take much longer!"

He nodded at her in thanks.

"I think it's time to end charades, however. We've been playing for an hour. Perhaps we mingle amongst ourselves for the rest of the evening. Felton, would you tell Gerald to fill drinks for the adults?"

Oh, thank God. Victor released a puff of air.

As Ashby went to the footman, who stood quietly near the door, Victor went over to Anne, who stood to meet him. "That was quite a lark, wasn't it?" she asked.

"Did you enjoy my dragonfly? I tried not to humiliate myself too badly."

Anne laughed and her eyes crinkled again. It warmed Victor's insides so much that, in a rare moment, he smiled, too.

Anne's laughter died and her eyes went wide. "Why, I've won a grin from you, Victor. Those are few and far between!"

Victor bowed his head in acknowledgment, though he was feeling a bit embarrassed. Was a mere smile from him really such a big deal? He couldn't help but wonder at such a discovery.

Ever since the Summerwood ball, Victor had tried to become bolder regarding his feelings for Anne. He had accepted the fact that he cared for her more than a friend and had hoped to warm her up to the idea by admiring her from afar. At first, he'd done this by sending her little drawings. As he didn't know how to explain who he was or what he felt for her by using words, and in a way that wouldn't make her run away, he hoped the drawings would do that for him.

He had sent her two drawings. Given her safe but intimate touches that went beyond friendship. A kiss on the cheek, a few lingering touches on her arm or hands while walking together down the beach or promenading on the pier. She seemed to not think much of any of those moments, yet he swore each time her cheeks had pinked ever so slightly. He took this as an encouraging sign.

For now, however, she remained ignorant to him being the man behind the little drawings.

In fact, no one in the family had any idea he possessed that talent. It was one he had been born with but had perfected over his life. It had begun as a boy by visiting the school library and thumbing through art books, copying what he'd seen as best he could. Now, he enjoyed sketching when he was alone before and after work at the pub, but he had no interest in letting anyone see his creations. He had kept them secret his entire life. Thus, neither Ollie nor Dantes would be able to give up his identity through the mystery sketches.

He had heard the family discuss on several occasions that Anne had a secret admirer she referred to as her "Phantom." Oddly, she had yet to bring it up to him on her own outside of familial discussion. The times the family had brought it up at breakfast or dinner, he had caught all of the women watching him with slight, contemplative frowns, but Anne looked the most unsure. A few times, he had even caught her shaking her head, as if telling herself there was no way Victor was the Phantom. Or admirer. Or whoever it was sending drawings. She seemed to not realize they were all one and the same.

But the spark of suspicion was there. Which was good.

However, he wasn't ready to reveal his identity just yet. Now that he had sent her the drawings, captured her attention with the cheek kiss and the lingering touches to plant the seed of *something more* in her mind, he was ready to move on to words.

Words, admittedly, were far more terrifying.

Victor leaned down to Anne's ear, his heart racing with fear. But he pushed through it. "While it may be true I am not one to often smile, every smile in these past years has been won solely by you. And between every smile, I am happy in the moments you are with me."

As he pulled back, he found her looking up at him, her mouth gently parted, her pale-blue eyes searching his face. Uncertainty reflected in them, reinforcing his theory he would have to take all of this quite slow.

"Victor…I…" But before Anne had finished her thought, that blasted Ashby interrupted. He stepped up to them without a care, his arm looped with Mary's. "Lady Litchfield, Lady Mary was telling me you are an accomplished pianist. Is that true?"

"I—yes, I play well enough." Anne's voice was strained. And now, she wouldn't look at Victor. Something had been just about to happen between them, he'd felt the shift. But the moment was gone. And he wasn't sure he would ever get it back.

Frustration ground at him, but he refused to show it and give the satisfaction to the blasted cad.

"Oh, Mama, do play for everyone," Mary begged. Victor's eyes lingered on the way Mary held on to Ashby's arm. Her fingers were digging in. Perhaps Mary liked the idea of Ashby pursuing her mother, as opposed to Victor, and was hoping to intervene. "It's too quiet now. We need to add a little more excitement to the air."

Anne swallowed. "Very well, but not for too much longer, darling. We do have to return home at some point." With a brief glance at Victor—did he detect a shared regret in that glance?— she made her way over to the piano.

As the music began, Mr. Lucas Ashby reappeared. He bowed ridiculously low to Mary. "Lady Mary, would you please join me in a dance?"

Immediately, Mary ripped her arm from Ashby's and took the younger brother's extended hand.

As Anne played, she caught her daughter and her escort dancing together, the only people doing so. But Anne likely understood if she stopped playing to reprimand her daughter, it would only garner further attention. She frowned at the couple instead. Victor was about to speak to the young woman on Anne's behalf. Though in a small setting such as this, it was technically acceptable for Mary to dance with a partner, it was clear Anne didn't like it. But, thankfully, Ashby reached them first. The young couple separated and the young lad's jaw became rigid as his oldest brother said something low to him once again. Victor watched as Ashby nudged his brother away, and then join his youngest brother and Freddy. The trio talked amongst themselves then disappeared from the room, running off to do something else.

Briefly, Victor was grateful Ashby had intervened. The fact that Mr. Lucas Ashby kept pursuing Mary despite regular intervention from both of their families did not give the young lad a good look.

But then Ashby turned to Mary and bowed. Mary's eyes went wide as yet another gentleman asked her to dance.

Anne started banging loudly on the piano keys as she shot daggers from her eyes at her daughter—if she wasn't keen on Mr. Lucas Ashby dancing with Mary, she would be quite against the eldest brother doing so—but Mary was far too much in awe of being asked to dance by an older gentleman. Victor knew the cad was only trying to woo Anne by charming her daughter, but did Mary know that?

Victor looked over to Anne and lifted his eyebrows in a way that asked if he should intervene. Anne shook her head and kept playing. It ended up being the right decision because only a minute later, the dancing ended and Ashby departed from the young lady with a cold bow.

Mary was left behind, her mouth agape.

THE CARRIAGE RIDE home later that evening was soaked in a heavy silence. Freddy fell asleep two minutes into the drive and leaned against Victor. On the seat across from them, Mary and Anne sat beside each other, but the tension was so thick, it could have been cut with a knife.

Victor knew Anne worried about her children and she had a particularly tight hold when it came to her daughter. He understood, to a degree. Girls and women were at risk when it came to boys and men. And Anne knew this better than anyone. He understood, with her experience, why she would want to be so strict with Mary.

Both Anne and Mary were staring out their respective windows, refusing to acknowledge each other.

If Victor had been a chatty man, he would have been able to ease the tension with some kind of conversation.

Instead, he sat in silence with them and watched Anne.

The drive would only be about twenty minutes, and whatever explosive argument was building between Anne and Mary, he hoped he wouldn't have to get in the middle of it.

Unfortunately, that explosion happened only a minute later.

"I didn't do anything wrong!" Mary shouted, unprompted.

Anne and Victor both jolted at the sudden noise. Freddy let out a snore.

Anne's mouth pinched as she considered her response. As she ran her hands swiftly over her skirts, she looked up at Victor. However, her eyes were shuttered.

He had no idea what she was thinking or feeling.

"You and I," Anne finally said to her daughter, "have discussed, on numerous occasions, that you are not to dance with anyone until you come out."

"It wasn't that serious, Mama. It was a dinner party, which is a perfectly fine place for me to dance! It wasn't like I was dancing at a ball!"

"It doesn't matter if society thinks it acceptable. My rules are my rules! Your behavior this entire evening was ridiculous."

Mary released a rather overdramatic gasp.

"Mary." Anne rubbed the bridge of her nose. "Over the entire hour-long dinner, you sat beside Mr. Lucas, shamelessly flirting with him and leaning toward him so he could look down your dress. I've been on this planet far longer than you. You may think I'm old and out of touch, but the truth of the matter is I know *all* the tricks. You can't get anything past me and you'd best realize that now."

Mary crossed her arms and slouched. "It was only meant to be a bit of fun, Mama," she said with a pout. "There's nothing wrong with flirting with a cute young man. You even said *you* wanted to do that this summer!"

Anne replied with her own overdramatic gasp. "Mary! How dare you?"

"What's going on?" Freddy asked sleepily. He pushed himself up and seemed startled to realize he had leaned on Victor. But as Mary and Anne continued sniping at each other, he looked over at them. "Oh. They're arguing again."

As they argued about men and flirting—the entire conversation lost on Victor—Victor instead put his attention on Freddy. "Do they often do this?"

Freddy yawned. "Not really, just ever since we got here. Mary keeps throwing herself at Lucas Ashby and Mama doesn't like it."

"I do not *throw myself* at him!" Mary whined.

"Yes, you do," Freddy bit back. "It's a bit desperate, really."

Mary leaned forward and slapped Freddy's arm.

"Ow!" He rubbed the spot, making a big show of it.

"I'm not desperate. And anyway, I'm not interested in Mr. Lucas Ashby anymore. I don't like how he danced—he was rubbish at it." She said this with a haughty tone and lifted her nose.

"Thank goodness," Anne replied, putting her attention back out the window into the darkness. "I don't wish to hear anything further about him, then."

"Fine," Mary quipped.

"Fine," Anne replied. And then she let out a sigh. She met

Victor's eye and shook her head just enough for him to see it. In a show of support, he lifted one corner of his mouth ever so slightly.

The remainder of the drive was, thankfully, free of argument. When they arrived at Summerwood, Vivian and Dantes were still up.

"We just put Lily to bed for the third time tonight. How was the Ashbys' dinner?" Vivian led them into the drawing room in her usual willowy elegance. Mary and Freddy were about to follow, but Anne made them stop. "To bed with you two," she said. The children let out groans of disappointment but didn't argue. Anne's eyes followed them up the stairs and once she seemed satisfied they were obeying her wishes, she entered the drawing room as well. Victor followed and went over to his brother, who poured out whiskeys for the two of them.

"Mary and Freddy looked tired. It must have been a good evening." Vivian took a seat in a wingback chair.

"It was, for the most part. Mary was being quite difficult tonight, though, which is unusual for her. I don't know what to do about it."

"Why, what was the matter?"

Anne sighed and sat at the end of a sofa near Vivian. Meanwhile, Victor and Dantes sipped their drinks in silence, relishing in the cool, sea breeze wafting in through the open windows.

"Oh, young gentleman drama. We went to the dinner with her nearly bouncing off the walls in anticipation of seeing Mr. Lucas Ashby, to leaving with her deciding he wasn't worth her time."

Vivian laughed. "I remember being that young. I wouldn't fret about it too much."

As the women giggled about their own silly behavior from youth, Dantes and Victor settled in. For a bit, they discussed their evenings and then something on a nearby table caught Dantes's eye.

"Oh, I mustn't forget." Dantes went to grab the object, then returned. He handed the item over to Victor. A card of some sort.

"What is it?" Victor asked.

"Your invite to Lord and Lady Bell's masquerade. They also sent their apologies for not sending you one earlier. They didn't have you on their annual list, but you have since been added."

Victor frowned. "That was nice of them, but I won't be going."

Dantes knew better than to argue with Victor. "Suit yourself, then. You'll be missing out on the fun, though. It's only in a few days."

"I don't even have a costume." Costumes had to be ordered in advance, and if the masquerade was only days away, he wouldn't have any time. Not that he wanted to go, anyway.

"Hm. Good point. Never mind, then."

Victor glanced at Anne and, convinced she paid him no attention, turned to his brother and lowered his voice. "Is it true, what I hear about it?"

Dantes raised his eyebrows. "What do you hear?"

Victor hesitated. "Courtesans. People going off with strangers. Multiple partners, and the like."

Dantes pulled back a bit, as if surprised, then glanced over at Anne. Understanding seemed to cross his face. He took a sip of his whiskey, topping it off with a satisfied sound. "You'll have to go to find out for yourself."

And before Victor could argue back, Dantes hurried on to share a funny story about Lily and the twins discovering a few rogue chickens that had wandered over from a neighboring farm. Victor was only pretending to listen, though.

He was vehemently against going to the masquerade.

The debauched masquerade in which Anne would be participating.

Forget the jealousy that tried to rear, the masquerade would be the *perfect* place to approach Anne as her secret admirer. If he could find a costume.

But would she be receptive to it? He hoped.

Chapter Twenty-One

June 1889

EVERYONE IN THE carriage groaned with that special frustration long travel instilled.

Anne, the children, their governess, and the three McNab brothers had traveled to Brighton from London as Mr. Dantes McNab had to get to Vivian before she married someone else. Then, once they arrived, the worst storm Anne had ever seen unleashed upon the seaside town. The rain was so bad, the children and governess decided to wait it out at the station while Anne and the three McNabs went on ahead. Vivian was expecting Anne's arrival but was *not* expecting the brothers. Unfortunately for the four, just as the carriage turned up the long drive to Summerwood, one of the wheels sunk into the mud.

During their multi-hour trip, Anne had spent most of the time thinking about Bernard, knowing she would face him here. It would be their first time seeing each other since their separation months earlier. She recalled the many nights over the years where he hadn't come home and left her unable to sleep, wondering where he was, or wondering what could possibly been more enticing to him than coming home to his wife and small children.

She recalled the stacks and stacks of bills she'd found shoved into the back of a drawer at his desk, unpaid and ignored. When she'd given birth for the second time, Bernard had left the house and disappeared for many hours, returning late and reeking of alcohol. To this day, she still didn't know where he had gone.

That night, when she'd been left alone in pain, trying to nurse a wailing baby who'd refused to latch, had been the moment she'd known their marriage would never be one of love. She had been duped into hell.

There was one thing she had control over, to some degree.

She vowed to never let him touch her again.

At first, she thought he would put up more of a fight. For a time, he did try to whine and guilt. Surprisingly, he didn't force it.

But he had found the attention he wanted elsewhere, instead.

That had been five years ago. Five years ago, their marriage had died. And a few months ago, it had all but ended in the only way it could: by separating. Neither of them wanted to be in this marriage, but there was nothing they could do about it, either.

Anne would never be free until one of them died.

Feeling hopeless, Anne pulled her focus away from Bernard and onto her gloved hands. Something odd had happened today, and she kept trying not to think about it.

During their trip from London to Brighton, Anne, the children, and governess, along with the eldest Mr. McNab had become separated from his younger brothers. She'd ended up sharing a train compartment with Mr. McNab.

She knew Mr. McNab, of course, and had met him a few times before thanks to Vivian and Mr. Dantes McNab's budding romance. He was quiet but seemed nice despite the fact that he always looked rather dour. Secretly, Anne thought Mr. McNab was the most dashing gentleman she had ever set her eyes upon. There was something about that dark dourness to him that fascinated her. And those green eyes—oh, those green eyes! They haunted her in her sleep, and she swore she could feel it when he looked at her.

Not that she would ever admit any of this aloud, of course. That wouldn't help her situation *at all*.

She'd been feeling rather down about seeing Bernard again

and may have had a bit too much to drink during the train ride. Not one to usually imbibe, the governess Miss Stewart had thankfully distracted the children by taking them to the dining car, leaving Anne and Victor alone for a majority of the train ride.

Mr. McNab had taken pity on her pathetic self and listened as she'd drunkenly told him some of the stories of Bernard. He hadn't said more than maybe three words the entire train ride, probably spending the entire trip thinking about how stupid she was. Because she *was* stupid. She had gotten herself wrapped up in the charms of a scoundrel and married him. Now look at her life. If only she had known better as a girl!

Sober once again, Anne was now feeling a bit foolish at opening herself up to the pub owner. Surprisingly, he'd seemed genuinely interested in listening to her as a good friend would, even though she knew he'd probably thought her foolish. But every time she was around him, she felt more and more comfortable with him. Now she felt she could slouch if she wanted to or say a curse word without judgment. It was, admittedly, nice to let her guard down a bit around someone. To tell someone about Bernard who already knew how awful Bernard was and knew she wasn't embellishing her stories. She felt like herself around him. There were other friends she felt comfortable around, yes, but none to the level of comfort she felt with Mr. McNab.

Which was mad. He was a he! But she had no interest in flicking his friendship away. She liked him—as a friend only—and her husband would simply have to deal with it if he ever voiced an issue with it. He had done far worse, thousands of times over.

But knowing Bernard, he would never notice.

The four sat in silence in the carriage as the rain loudly pelted the roof. The driver was long gone. The moment their wheel sunk into the mud he'd jumped off and run to take cover under Summerwood's covered porch.

As she looked out the window to judge how soaked she would get walking to the home—finally deciding she would be soaked to the bone—Anne spotted Bernard jogging up toward their carriage to offer help, clearly not realizing who was inside.

Something inside of her cracked.

Without saying a word, she jumped out of the carriage, causing the McNab brothers to shout in alarm, and began running through the downpour toward Bernard, her fists clenched tightly, anger pounding through her veins.

Bernard's eyes went wide upon seeing the white-hot fury in his wife, and he spun around and started sprinting across the sprawling lawn back to the house.

Anne shouted after him. "Get back here, you blasted coward!" She was furious at everything he'd put her through. All the pain he had caused over the last decade, all of the lies and deceit, the distrust…Anne had finally reached her limit. And this had led to her chasing Bernard through a downpour, thunder and lightning cracking above. But she didn't care at all. It felt brilliant!

Bernard slipped and fell into the mud with a splat, staring up as she loomed over him, drenched to the bone. Her chest heaved with exhaustion.

"I hate you, you bloody bastard!" Anne shouted as years of pent-up tears streamed down her face, camouflaged by the rain. "Why did you treat me like that? Why did you run around on me? Why did you drink so much, gamble so much? Why didn't you pay our bills? Why? Why the devil did you marry me if you can't stand the sight of me?"

But Bernard didn't answer any of her questions, and he likely never would. Instead, he rolled in the mud to his side, jumped back up to his feet, and began sprinting toward the house once again. Anne's chest heaved desperately, but she began running again too, lifting her lead-heavy, soaking-wet skirts. But he was too fast, and she was too slow from the heavy clothes, and then she slipped and fell in the mud, too, with a loud splat herself.

But unlike Bernard, she stayed there, bawling with anger into her hands. Anne didn't bother getting up. She couldn't get any more soaked at this point, couldn't fall any further. She had finally reached rock bottom, quite literally in the mud. Could she ever recover from this?

"Lady Litchfield." That deep, comforting voice was right beside her. Her hands fell away from her face and she was startled to find Mr. McNab crouching next to her, his face over hers, the rain making his black hair stick in strings to his face.

"I'm so…" She sobbed. "I'm so tired!"

He didn't say anything, but he stared at her with intensity, evidently waiting for her to continue.

"Why did he do all of that to me? Why did he sneak around behind my back, get drunk and scare me? Why, Mr. McNab?" They were impossible questions to answer, but she wanted to ask. She wanted to know what Mr. McNab thought. For some reason, it was important to her.

"Because he's stupid, my lady. He's a stupid, arrogant, greedy, sinful, foolish, idiotic man. A bloody bastard of the highest order. And he always will be."

The tears began to fall again, but she surprised herself by laughing a bit through them.

"Forget him," Mr. McNab said, still serious. "Forget him. Please."

She searched his kind, green eyes. Her heart began to race even faster, realizing how close he was in the moment. She had never met anyone like Mr. McNab before. And in such a raw moment, he didn't judge her at her lowest point, didn't think her a joke of a woman. She felt a pull to him. "I haven't loved Bernard in a long time."

Mr. McNab simply stared into her eyes as he held out his hand. Anne took it, and he helped her sit up. They held each other's hand for a brief moment before letting go.

"It's going to be hard." She didn't know what, exactly, she meant by that. And yet, he nodded, as if understanding perfectly.

"I know," Mr. McNab replied.

The rain continued to pour. "It could be a long time." Anne swallowed. Something about this moment—it felt like she was baring her heart to him.

But she was, wasn't she? She cared for this man—oh, it was stupid to keep denying it! And he cared for her. But there was nothing either of them could do about it. And, maybe, there never would be a chance to.

"I don't know how long." Anne's voice cracked. "But it could be a long time."

"That's all right."

"What if it's years? Decades?"

For a bit, they simply stared at each other. The rain and fog was so thick, it hid them from the world. They couldn't see anyone outside of their little corner of the world, and no one could see inside it, either.

He didn't need to speak because his eyes told her everything. This man, one of few words, bared his soul to her through that life-changing gaze. She saw what he felt for her, what he would always feel for her.

Finally, Mr. McNab spoke. "I will wait for you for as long as it takes."

July 1899

ANNE JOLTED AWAKE and had to catch her breath. Had she had another fever dream? Her hand flew to her forehead. No. She was fine. She wasn't sick this time.

She thought she had remembered most of that day, but apparently, there was a lot she had genuinely forgotten about. Most importantly, those last words Victor had uttered. That final promise to her. It hadn't been wordless, like she had always recalled. He had stated it. Quite clearly. But she had buried it so far down into the abyss of her memory, it had lain there, nearly forgotten.

As Anne swallowed to again attempt to catch her breath, the

door opened.

Dutton entered, looking cheery. "Ah, good morning, Lady Litchfield."

"What year is it?" Anne hastened the words out.

Dutton flung the curtains open and the stream of light caused Anne to squint momentarily.

"Very funny, my lady. Usually, you have some coffee first before you start jesting with me."

"I'm serious."

Dutton turned around at this and frowned at Anne. She hurried over and pressed the back of her hand to Anne's forehead. "Are you ill again?"

"I just had a very vivid dream and…and I'm quite shaken from it." Anne shivered. It had been so realistic, she'd actually felt Victor's hand holding hers. And felt Victor lifting her from the mud, and Victor's closeness. His voice had sounded real, his presence had felt real.

Covertly, she looked at the place in the bed beside her, as if only his presence there could explain it.

Of course, he wasn't there. Why would he be?

Dutton crossed her arms and was trying not to look too concerned, but Anne knew her behavior was quite strange right now, and of course her lady's maid would be worried.

Anne took a deep breath. "Forgive me. It was a dream, but it was also an old memory. One I had forgotten about."

"Interesting. So, it was a dream, but the dream had actually happened?"

"Yes." Anne swallowed. Forgetting all of that had been her protecting herself, that was clear. But why was her mind now trying to force this all back to her?

"What was the dream, or the memory, I should say?" Dutton asked, unaware of Anne's internal panic.

"It doesn't matter."

Dutton twisted her mouth in thought. "It isn't my place to argue with you, so I won't. As much as I may want to."

Anne couldn't help but smile at this.

"However, I will say. It is quite unusual for a dream to be a real memory. I would have to say your mind wanted you to think about it for some reason."

Anne looked down at her lap.

"Something for you to mull over, I suppose. Anyway, do you recall what today is?"

Anne's mind was still foggy from sleep. She turned her eyes up to Dutton.

"It's the masquerade!" Dutton spread her arms wide with an explosive voice. She loved getting Anne ready for masquerades.

This caused Anne to perk up. "Oh! I must start getting ready now." She flew out of bed and over to her vanity. Getting ready for Lord and Lady Bell's masquerade was always an all-day event. First, she would breakfast, then bathe, then she and Vivian and Evelyn would spend hours on their hair and makeup, getting dressed, getting excited, and then they would leave.

It didn't sound like much, but it somehow always took up the entire day.

A knock on her door caused her pause.

"Yes?" Anne shouted out over her shoulder.

"That wasn't your bedroom door, my lady," Dutton said in a low voice. "That was the door you share with Mr. McNab."

Anne felt her face go hot. She was still in her pajamas.

But it was also only Victor. Who cared if he saw her first thing? He wasn't a lover or anything like that.

"Let him in," she decided.

Dutton pulled back. "My lady, are you sure?"

"Yes, it's fine."

Dutton gave a hesitant nod before going over to the door. Anne watched the scene in the mirror at her vanity. Needing something to distract herself from her nerves, she opened her drawer, pulled out the hairbrush, and started brushing her hair without Dutton's usual assistance. As she did this, she glanced at the open drawer.

A Lady's Rules for Seaside Romance was right on top. *Never fall in love* had been underlined and circled by her multiple times. Recently, she had found herself needing the reminder of this right before bed each night.

That blasted dream had exposed why.

All of this was ridiculous. Victor was *only a friend*. Despite that silly afternoon ten years ago. She slammed the drawer shut.

"Forgive me. I didn't realize you were just waking." Victor appeared behind her, freshly dressed and washed for the day already.

Her heart galloped like Onyx in one of his erratic moments. She had to force a blank face and shutter her brain off from the list of rules and the dream—or had it been a nightmare?—she had just woken from. "It's quite all right, Victor. Did you sleep well last night?"

"Yes, I have found I sleep quite well here."

She smiled at him in the mirror. "It's the sea air. Isn't it exquisite?"

He nodded, silent, those green eyes intense.

She cleared her throat. "You are still set on staying home tonight?"

"Yes. I don't understand the appeal of masquerades, to be honest with you."

She gave him a single nod, as this didn't surprise her at all. Frankly, she couldn't imagine Victor dressed up in a costume.

"You said you're going as a swan?" he asked.

She held his gaze in the mirror and her irritating heart started quickening again under his scrutiny. Blast it all *and* that silly dream, too! "Dutton," she said over her shoulder, "will you bring my costume out? I'd like to show Victor."

"Yes, my lady." Dutton disappeared from view and for a moment, Anne and Victor returned to staring at each other in the mirror. Finally, she forced herself to look away and went back to brushing her hair to give herself something to do other than stare at him like a madwoman.

"May I?" Victor asked, causing her to pause.

This time, she turned around to look at him directly. "May you what?"

He didn't respond, and instead lifted the hairbrush out of her hand, his fingers gently brushing against hers. He held her gaze, but all she could do was raise her eyebrows at him. He wanted to brush her hair?

Completely thrown off by this, all she could do was turn to face the mirror again and let him.

While she tried to comprehend what was happening, Victor started to brush her hair. Gently, slowly. He swept the soft bristles over the blonde locks and down her back, and he seemed to be engrossed in it. His face held little expression as he did it, but his eyes followed the movement of the brush as it swept through her long hair.

Anne studied him the entire time. He had, of course, never seen her first thing in the morning before. He had never seen her hair undone.

After a few more slow and gentle strokes Victor set the brush to the side, looking at her in the reflection of the mirror once again. Anne assumed he was done. However, he surprised her greatly as he began to run his fingers through her hair. But this time, he didn't break their eye contact as he combed through.

This admittedly quite inappropriate and intimate moment would have been exceptionally bizarre if he were anyone else. But instead of her body wanting to pull away from him as it should have, she tingled with pleasure at his touch, and sparks ran up and down her spine.

She was sure she would purr like a cat if she opened her mouth.

"You know, I've never *brushed* a woman before," he said, holding her gaze in the mirror.

On the surface, it seemed like an offhand comment to make conversation. But the way he'd said it caused her pause. His eyes looked brighter than usual, and the way his gaze held on to hers told her that he was sharing something important. There was hidden meaning behind it, she was sure of it.

She chuckled nervously. "Why does it seem like you're giving me a clue to something?"

Amusement danced in his eyes. But he didn't say another word.

Anne's heart seemed to still. "Victor, what are you saying?" It came out a whisper. Was he telling her that he…

No, that was impossible.

Dutton swept past the reflection of the mirror, ending the moment. "Here we are," the lady's maid said in a singsong voice. Farther back in the room, Dutton began laying out garments over the top of the bedspread.

While Dutton paid them no attention, Victor stopped combing Anne's hair with his fingers. Her breathing had quickened, Anne suddenly realized. Victor then crouched beside her chair, lifted her left hand, and kissed the back of it. His lips felt soft and warm against her skin, and his beard scratched her in a delightful way. Her heart leapt.

"I should go see this costume of yours," he said in a deep whisper. Mischief danced in his green eyes.

"All right," she whispered back, almost in a daze. It felt like she had been hypnotized and was just waking up from it.

She had to shake herself out of it, whatever *it* was. As soon as Victor's back was to her, she lightly slapped her cheeks. "Get a hold of yourself," she chided to her reflection. What was the matter with her? And what in the blazes had just happened?

Victor called out from the other side of the room. "Incredible work! Let's see. You have a white, feather eye mask; white, feather wings; and a white dress with some feathers on it as well. This must have taken months to create," he said with genuine awe in his voice.

"It's too bad you aren't going," Anne called back over her shoulder, hoping desperately that she sounded normal and not as shaken up as she truly was. She quickly fanned herself and rose out of her seat, her legs faltering for the first steps.

"Don't worry," he replied when she reached his side. "I've got to catch up on some work-related things. You won't even notice my absence." He lifted the eye mask up and placed it over her eyes, and he tilted his head, as if in study. She blinked through the mask. Why did it feel as if he were memorizing what she looked like?

Chapter Twenty-Two

S OMETHING ANNE HAD learned since the death of her husband was sometimes, the past didn't stay in the past, even if it was where it belonged.

This had been a struggle of hers, particularly with Lord and Lady Bell's masquerade. It was a fun event, one Anne looked forward to every summer, but there was always a sick, nervous feeling that lingered throughout the evening.

And it was because of her late husband's past behavior.

It had a simple explanation. Bernard used to disappear for long stretches of time at the masquerade. She wasn't stupid, though. She'd known what he'd been doing. And while she and the rest of the family had been enjoying themselves and socializing, she would spend most of her time looking around the crowd for her scoundrel husband, hopeful he had simply become caught up in conversation with someone.

He'd always returned to her side disheveled, and denied it whenever she'd pointed it out.

Those days were long over, though, and she would never put herself through that again.

Anne shook her hands at her side, straightened her back, and entered the parlor in full costume. She wore a low-cut, white, silk dress with white feathers that almost looked like a boa draped around the neckline and the hem of the dress. The back of her skirt was full of feathers as well. Upon her head was a *papier-mâché* swan, too, perched atop her blonde head as if swimming across water. It had a tail, flush wings, and a long neck and head that stood proud above her face. Luckily, it wasn't heavy, but it felt precarious. She also wore a white eye mask and long, white gloves.

Mary, Freddy, the Duke of Chalworth, and Victor were all seated together amongst sofas and chairs. Lily and the twins were already asleep, of course. Mulling around the room was Vivian, who was dressed as a honeybee with a striped yellow-and-black dress and fake wings. Dantes, who, like Victor, wasn't big on costumes, wore the same costume he used every year—a medieval highlander with a McNab tartan kilt. Evelyn was a bat and Ollie was a pirate. Everyone had eye masks on as well.

"Mama, you look stunning!" Mary jumped up from her seat upon her mother's appearance in the room. Apparently, Anne was the last to arrive. "Why, you will be the *belle of the ball*, as they say!"

Anne forced a smile at her daughter. It wasn't that she wasn't charmed by compliment. Anne had been bracing for another explosive argument since she'd woken up, just waiting for Mary's final desperate attempt to receive permission to attend the masquerade.

Mary had been very upset these last several weeks about not being allowed to attend the masquerade ball. But today of all days, Mary hadn't once asked to go.

In fact, she had spent most of the day sending letters. Mary had sent one in the morning, two in the afternoon, and one only half an hour earlier. Amused, Anne had questioned the young lady about the sudden increase in correspondence and Mary had explained she was simply keeping up with her friends in town. Anne was quite relieved that, finally, the young woman had become distracted by something that didn't involve eligible gentlemen.

Mary looked to be in good spirits right now as well.

Perhaps this was all a sign that Mary was maturing and learning how to better handle disappointment. "Thank you, Mary," Anne replied, feeling a bit of pride. "You two will be in bed at midnight, correct?" She sent pointed looks through her mask at Mary and then Freddy. "That's only two hours from now."

"Yes, Mama," Mary and Freddy said in unison.

"You appear to be in good company tonight, at least!" She turned a smile to the duke and to Victor, at whom she had been too nervous to look at since she'd walked into the room. But now that she had an excuse to, she glanced at Victor and found him appraising her costume, studying it quite intently as he slouched slightly in his seat. A lazy gaze trailed up until their eyes met, causing something within her to jolt. He didn't look away, embarrassed to have been caught. Instead, his eyes darkened.

Shivering, *she* looked away.

The duke, with his white hair and round cheeks, smiled at her. "Mr. McNab and I have been in deep discussion about ducal duties. I thought tonight would be a good chance for us to get into the details of it all. He has several properties and did you know many of the tenants are sheep herders? They have wool up to their ears, and Americans apparently can't get enough of real Scottish highlander wool. You should see what those New York department stores are paying to have highlander wool garments in their stores." The duke leaned toward Victor. "Didn't you say something about that fellow Andrew Carnegie, also?"

Anne looked over to Victor and realized he hadn't taken his eyes off of her. Her cheeks flushed—she could feel it. "Carnegie is a Scotsman and wanted Scottish wool for his workers' uniforms. The wool comes from our tenants." Victor paused, his stare at Anne lingered, but then he looked over to the duke. Anne could practically feel his gaze ripping away from her. "These tenants have become quite wealthy because of Americans. It's almost funny, as I've been putting off digging into the finances of it all, afraid to find farms which no longer keep up with production, or farms with tenants who have left for better-paying factory jobs.

While there will be some of that, I had no idea how lucrative wool has been. It's been a boon for the dukedom. Fergus has kept this a well-hidden secret."

"Oh! Well, then, congratulations are in order!" Anne said, knowing Victor has been worrying about the dukedom all summer. Though it would still be a heavy responsibility, at least it wasn't failing financially.

Victor looked back at her, causing another jolt in her heart. Thankfully, Vivian clapped, interrupting the moment, and announced they would be departing. Anne promised to see her children in the morning and gave Freddy and Mary a hug and kiss on the cheek. Freddy rolled his eyes at her but allowed it. Mary, however, stiffened under Anne's affection. Anne brushed it off and remained thankful they hadn't come to the explosive argument she had been expecting all day.

Anne followed everyone else out of the room and as they exited the front door for the awaiting carriage, Victor called after her.

Anne turned and smiled up at him. "Yes?"

"What, exactly, happens at this masquerade?" he asked in a low voice. And was that a hint of panic?

The corners of Anne's mouth turned down. "What do you mean? It's a ball, but with costumes."

Victor hesitated as he seemed to be deciding what to say next. "I confess, Freddy told me it is a debauched party and all kinds of…mischief occur."

Panic coursed through her. Why would Freddy know anything about debauchery? "What did he say happens?"

Victor hesitated again. "Courtesans." He lowered his voice. "Multiple partners."

Anne's eyes went wide. "He told you that? Oh, dear, where did he hear such a thing? I don't know where he heard that. I mean, it's a masquerade, so people do get a bit silly and some get into mischief they wouldn't normally. It does have a reputation, but it's not nearly as scandalous as rumors make it sound. And most people do not partake in the worst of it."

Victor nodded and his shoulders seemed to ease.

"Why?" She nearly made a joke about him being jealous but thankfully snapped her mouth shut first.

"I was simply curious is all," he replied in a low voice.

Anne didn't believe his reasoning for a moment. Was he trying to find out if *she* would partake in debauchery? Did he not know her at all, or did he think he had any claim to her? All this did was make her defiant. "I have every right to partake in whatever I like if I so wish," she said in a too-stern voice. But it was mostly said for her benefit, she realized. In some way, she wanted Victor to know she went to the masquerade simply for the drinks, food, and socialization. Not to disappear with anonymous men, like Bernard used to do with anonymous women.

Yet what she did in her free time with men—as if there were any—was none of his business.

Even though, deep down, she wanted him to know there wasn't anyone who'd captured her attention. Even Mr. Ashby had grown stale. Nothing seemed to be coming of that, her Phantom had not reappeared, she had received no other drawings. Any hope for a seaside romance seemed to be falling flat.

Victor stared down at her with a thoughtful look, as if he somehow knew what she was thinking, and surprised her. "Yes, you're right. Be safe, then, Anne. I will see you tomorrow." He bowed, turned around, and returned to the parlor without looking back.

She stared at the empty space he'd left behind, stunned. Had he just dismissed her?

"Anne!" Vivian's voice carried through the open front door. Outside on the drive sat a glossy, black carriage. "Are you coming or not?"

"Yes! Sorry!" She decided to forget Victor, spun around, and hurried into the carriage.

WHILE LADY MARY paced around the room, presumably irritated that she had not figured out a way to attend the masquerade, Victor stared at the clock on the table beside him. It was now only a few minutes until midnight. The duke was talking about sailing, a pastime he enjoyed, but Victor had discovered early in the season he could not stomach it. As the duke and Freddy talked about a recent sail in which a family of dolphins followed them, Victor took one last opportunity to figure out what to do about the masquerade. He had spent days trying to find a costume so he could sneak over as the Phantom. He had contacted several stores in town, offering high sums for a quick costume, but unfortunately, with the impossible time constraints, they didn't want their names attached to a hastily made and shoddy costume, no matter what sum he offered.

The clock rang for midnight.

"Oh, would you look at the time!" The Duke of Chalworth jumped up with unexpected spryness. He stretched his arms up and yawned. "Mary, Freddy, time for bed."

Mary halted in her pacing. "Oh, yes, I am quite ready for bed," she said.

Freddy looked between his sister and the duke with a deeply furrowed brow. "But—"

"But nothing." The duke began to rush them out by gently nudging their backs toward the door. They were both much taller than him, making the scene humorous. "Your mother wanted you in bed at midnight. Made sure to remind me of that multiple times," the duke explained.

"But you let us stay up late *every* year they go to the masquerade!" Freddy argued over his shoulder. "I thought we would stay up and have sweets like last year!"

"Not this year."

"Don't be so difficult Freddy," Mary quipped. "Mama said *bed at midnight*, and we must follow the rules."

From his seat, Victor raised an eyebrow up to her. She noticed but simply closed her eyes at him and spun around to give him her back before walking away with her brother.

"Goodnight, Mary! Goodnight, Freddy!" The plump, white-haired gentleman cupped his hand around his mouth as he called after them. Then he quickly shut the door.

Victor rose and began heading over to the duke. He opened his mouth to ask if the duke would be headed to bed as well when the man shushed him.

Victor's eyebrows raised, but he kept quiet.

The duke stilled for a long moment—it appeared he was listening to ensure Mary and Freddy had followed his direction—then slowly and quietly opened the door.

Chalworth stuck his head through the opening and was apparently satisfied by what he had or hadn't found because he then motioned to Victor and whispered, "Come with me."

Now quite curious, Victor followed the duke. They went up the stairway, down the long hallway, and into Chalworth's private quarters.

The duke shut the door behind them, hurried over to his bed with a face filled with glee, and went down on his hands and knees to reach for something under the bed.

"Your Grace!" Victor said, a bit horrified. "Please, let me get that for you."

However, the duke didn't stop what he was doing and instead pulled out a large box from under the bed. He rose up to his feet—slower this time—leaned back against the bed, and crossed his arms.

"Open it." The duke indicated to the box on the floor.

It wasn't enormous, a square of about three feet by three feet. Victor lifted the paperboard lid and found tissue paper beneath it. As he set the lid to the side, the duke continued talking.

"Before you lift that tissue paper up, I have something to say," Chalworth said.

Victor gave the duke a questioning look.

"My daughter and her husband didn't get their heads on straight until I got involved."

Victor looked off to the side, trying to figure out what the man meant. His gaze returned when he had given in to being perplexed. "I have no idea what you're talking about."

"I know." The duke's eyes glittered with mischief. "When Vivian started to realize she was developing some feelings for Dantes, she wouldn't do anything about it. She was convinced it was *only* a friendship."

There was a long pause and Victor realized the duke was expecting a response. "All right?"

"At the time, I didn't know *who* had captured her attention, but I knew someone had and it was serious. She was constantly distracted, which she had never been before. So, I put a friend of mine's attention on her. I knew my daughter well enough to know she would have danced around the issue for her entire life if she had been able to. As you know, she didn't have the time to do so."

Victor remembered she'd had to get married within a certain timeframe to keep the inheritance her grandmother had given her. "No, she didn't."

"As soon as I inserted myself, everything came together." He paused. "Well, eventually. Either way, I knew when it was time to nudge her in the right direction. So I did."

Victor stared, waiting for more. "And you are telling me this…why?"

The duke pushed away from the bed and took the few steps over to Victor, who remained crouched by the box. "Because I see it happening again. See this as my nudge to you." The duke held an inviting palm out to the box and Victor began pulling back the tissue paper.

He stilled. Beneath the paper was a large, wide-brimmed, dark-blue tricorn hat with one large, white, fluffy ostrich feather and long, black, curly wig attached. What in the blazes? Victor set the strange hat to side. Below the hat was a blue tabard, similar to a tunic, with a white embroidered cross on the front and back. He looked up at the duke with furrowed brow.

"Keep digging," Chalworth said.

Victor lifted the tunic out and below it was the final item: a full-face white mask.

"A musketeer!" The duke clapped with excitement. "Luckily for you, you can wear any trousers and shoes you like, as I don't think we're the same size in that regard." The duke was significantly shorter than Victor. And rounder. "Though to be most historically accurate, you would need those old-style boots that go up to your knee and fold over, but I doubt you have those handy."

"A musketeer," Victor repeated. "And musketeers wore full face masks?"

Color rose high on the duke's cheeks. "No, but a mask is required for Lord and Lady Bell's masquerade. I always preferred to have my face fully covered."

"Ah." Victor set the mask to the side and was already thinking about which of his linen shirts could go with it. "Why are you lending this to me?"

"So you can go to the masquerade, of course!"

"But I don't want to go," Victor lied. However, it was what he had been telling everyone.

The duke chuckled. "Mr. McNab, very little gets past me." He raised his white eyebrows. "Very. Little. Like I said, this is your nudge to get moving."

Victor began placing the items back in the box. He tried not to show it but was feeling relieved that this problem had been solved, though he was a bit put out that the duke had had to figure it out for him.

"And what do you believe you are nudging me toward, Your Grace?" Victor stood with the box and put the lid back on.

The duke knit his hands behind his back, opened his mouth, and paused. "All I'll say is, you are taking much longer than

Vivian, and I have lost patience. Now, I'm intervening, even though you don't have a timeline to follow like she did."

Victor clenched his jaw but thought it best not to respond.

Chalworth began leading Victor to the doorway.

"What *exactly* have you concluded, Your Grace?" Victor asked this in an unamused voice. Yes, he was grateful to have a costume. But he didn't like the fact that someone to whom he wasn't even related was meddling in his personal business. The *most* personal business, at that. He had promised Anne he would wait as long as it took. And that fact remained.

The duke twisted his mouth in thought but began talking. "I've seen you watching my son's wife from afar for a very long time."

Fear jolted through him. Victor tried to keep his face frozen, but he felt his nostrils flare just a bit. And he saw the duke catch this. "Nothing has happened—on that, I swear."

"Yes, I know. That's the problem." They came to a halt at the doorway and the duke looked him over. "My grandchildren mean the world to me. Freddy is a marquess already and next in line to the dukedom. However, no matter how old the children are, they need a father in their life and they look up to you more than any other man. In my opinion, it's even better that someday you'll be a duke yourself."

Victor felt the corners of his mouth tug down.

"I know you well enough to know you're a good man. I love my son, but I have come to love Anne like a daughter as well. Bernard is gone. I want to see her happy with someone who loves her."

Victor's shoulders tensed. "I never said I l—"

"Do you love my grandchildren?" The duke crossed his arms and that jovial air that was always around the stout man melted away and a darkness surrounded him. His eyes narrowed and his jaw clenched. Victor blinked—he knew that darkness well himself and was surprised to find it in someone so different from him. "And think hard about your response, Mr. McNab, for I will remember it for the rest of my life. I may also remind you again that Freddy and Mary both look up to you and love you themselves."

Victor swallowed. "They do?"

People other than his brothers loved him? *Him?* He had never really thought about this before. Despite his parents' imperfections, he did know he'd been loved by them. But it was never something he'd really thought about as an adult. And he had never been loved by a woman before. Love simply had never been a big part of his life.

Though he was beginning to feel less certain about that.

The duke nodded. "Now. What say you?"

"I… Of course I do." Victor felt embarrassed at exposing such a hidden piece of him.

Chalworth looked him over and nodded once. "One day, you'll have to be able to say that word, of course. But for now, I'm satisfied. Now, I know you're the lad who's been admiring Anne from afar. The one she calls 'the Phantom.' Correct?"

Victor's grip tightened around the box. "Yes."

"Good. Tonight is your only chance to approach her fully concealed. And that is something I think she would appreciate." He tapped his temple upon seeing Victor's raised eyebrows.

How had the duke known of Victor's belief that approaching Anne as slow as a snail was the best way?

"Like I said, I know far more than you give me credit for." The duke then nudged Victor out the door like he had done to his grandchildren earlier. "Go now, Mr. McNab. I may be too old for Lord and Lady Bell's masquerade nowadays, but you aren't. However, you don't have an eternity waiting for you, either."

The door slammed shut before Victor could say anything, but the duke was right. Love didn't wait forever for anyone, and he was ready to get the rest of his life started.

Chapter Twenty-Three

THE INVITATION GAVE Victor entrance to the masquerade of the enormous country home—it was made of stone and had been built in the seventeenth century—and he eventually found himself in an enormous ballroom. There were stone pillars around the edge of the room, three enormous crystal chandeliers that hung overhead, and a long wall of French doors, which led out to the gardens. The room was mostly being used for dancing, with a full orchestra and some masked wallflowers fanning themselves around the edge. Victor looked around with haste, hoping to avoid his brothers and their wives. He was fully concealed from head to toe but didn't want to take any risk. And, of course, he wished to find Anne as soon as possible.

As he slid through the room, he noted the costumes around him. Though there were many Venetian-style masks and costumes, there were also historical people and literary characters. There were kings and queens, spirits, animals, and countless others he couldn't identify.

Victor slid past Georgian ladies and gents with white-powdered wigs and watched the couples swirling around the dance floor. Dantes and Vivian appeared, about to fly by. Victor ducked behind a tall, powdered wig, accidentally bumping into the woman wearing it.

"Oh!" She turned around quickly. She had on a small, blue

eye mask and a pale-blue dress with hips several feet wide. How had she gotten through doors?

"Forgive me," Victor said with a small bow, quickly checking to ensure he was not in sight of Dantes and Vivian.

The woman gave him a slow look over and began fanning herself quickly with her white, lacy fan. "You are quite forgiven, *mon seigneur.*" She added a sultry laugh at the end and reached up to his arm, running her hand slowly along his bicep. Then she looked back up through her lashes, giving him a wry smile. "Heading out to the garden?"

Victor cleared his throat and stepped back. "Yes."

"That's where all the fun happens. May I join you?" The masked woman took a step toward him to close the space once more.

"No." This situation was making him rather uncomfortable, and a bit guilty, too. He was here for one reason and one reason only, thus he dismissed the woman with another bow. "Good evening," he said, turning away and hastening out the door.

Outside, relieved to have escaped, Victor took in his surroundings. The night air smelled like a fresh meadow and was cool as it breezed behind his full mask. Guests mulled around with glasses of crisp wine and bubbly champagne. The stone patio he found himself on was quite large, with numerous footmen about. Stairs led down to the grassy green lawn and an extensive garden beyond that. Lanterns hung above both the patio and the lawn below, strung between decorated posts to provide a low, golden light to the party.

He also noted part of the garden was not lit and under a blanket of darkness.

But he looked everywhere and could not find a swan.

Two gentlemen nearby, one a cowboy and the other a pope, partook in light conversation based on the tones of their voices. Victor went over to them. "Forgive my intrusion, but have either of you seen a swan in attendance?"

The two men looked at each other. The cowboy replied first.

"Yes, though I believe I've seen more than one."

"I think there are three, perhaps?" the pope said.

Hiding his frustration, Victor thanked them and resumed his search.

What would he do, though, when he *did* find Anne? How would he approach her, how would he talk to her without giving his true identity away?

He went to the stone balustrades and rested his hands upon the rough surface. Below, more people mulled about the garden. A violinist and a cellist provided light music for the atmosphere. Overlapping the string instruments were the murmurs of conversation, with light laughter here and there.

To his right, just out of the corner of his vision, there was a flash of white.

He turned his head and spotted Ollie the pirate walking down the stairs beside a man dressed as a sailor. Behind the men trailed a bat—Evelyn—and a swan.

Anne.

Victor's heart skipped a few beats. He could not move as he watched her glide down the stone stairs, the picture of elegance and grace. But who was the man to whom Ollie was speaking, the sailor? Was it Ashby?

Victor watched them until their feet met the grassy grounds and then he began to follow at a safe distance, his eyes stuck to Anne like a ship's anchor to the sea floor.

The group lifted champagnes from a passing tray and continued strolling through the garden, Victor following noiselessly, paying no attention to the people he passed. As they got farther into the garden, the air around them thickened and noise became muffled by the foliage of trees and plants growing everywhere.

The group entered an opening between tall, trimmed hedges. In complete silence, Victor followed and stopped at the hedge, where he was able to find a spot to look through. The group stood before a stone statue in the middle of a space completely enclosed by the tall, trimmed hedges.

"Ah, a cherub!" That was Evelyn's voice. "In classic Italian art, cherubs represent innocence. They rose in popularity during the Baroque period…" As she continued, Ollie, Anne, and the unknown gentleman listened with interest for her every word.

Anne moved closer to the sailor—the suspected Ashby—and Ashby leaned over to say something to her briefly, though Victor couldn't make out what was said. Anne nodded but did not react otherwise.

Victor moved to a space between the hedges where a gap was big enough to see better. He became completely still and silent, controlling his breathing to be as slow and quiet as possible. The enclosed area held nothing other than the statue, stone ground with a variety of flowers around the edge, and a stone bench on one side. Victor didn't have to think too deeply about what this spot of the garden was intended for.

Victor watched Anne and couldn't help but study every movement she made. The way she kept adjusting the eye mask as if slightly uncomfortable, then how she moved to push a tuft of light hair back behind her ear. The way her earrings dangled and reflected the dim moonlight. The long column of her neck, where he would have sensed her heartbeat, if only he'd been close enough. It was where she'd dabbed her perfume, the honeysuckle scent she preferred for evening. If he were close enough, he would wrap his arms around her waist, lower his face to her neck to inhale her, to kiss her, and he would never let go.

As wicked thoughts began to churn up in his mind, Anne's shoulders tensed. And she began looking around as if she had heard something and was trying to locate the source of the sound.

And then she looked directly at him.

Victor took a sharp inhale and jerked to the side to be fully concealed by the hedge. He shut his eyes tightly and held his breath, but the roaring of his heart in his ears made it hard to focus.

He had to act fast. He had to assume she had seen him.

Victor could slip around the corner of this line of hedges, but if she came to investigate, that would be the most obvious place for her to look.

But about twenty feet off the walking path behind him was a willow tree beside a pond, its long branches arching and hanging low to the ground and calm water, almost like a chandelier.

With haste, Victor made his way into the willow tree and was pleased to discover it was quite dark inside. From here, he could watch Anne leave the cherub's enclosure. This time, she would not be able to see him.

Sure enough, not even a minute later, the group reappeared. Ollie and Evelyn emerged first, then Ashby, with Anne following. Upon her exit, she looked around quite rapidly, as if searching.

She *had* seen him.

As he had guessed, she went around the corner of the hedge to investigate, the white, feathery skirt billowing in the night breeze. Ashby took a few steps in that direction and asked, "My lady, what is it you seek?"

Anne reappeared and though he couldn't see her expression too well with the costume, he could *feel* her restlessness.

Ashby seemed to recognize it as well. While Ollie and Evelyn held hands and waited for them, Ashby held his arm out to Anne, an invitation to walk together.

Victor's face became hot with jealousy. He clenched his teeth hard to keep from ripping the cad away from her.

"My lady, shall we all head back for more refreshments?" Ashby asked.

Anne began to reach her gloved hand out to him, hesitated, then dropped her arm. "You all go on ahead. I'll catch up in a moment."

The trio exchanged a look, and Ashby chuckled. "You cannot be here by yourself."

"Mr. Martin, I appreciate your concern. However, I am a widow, not a young debutante. And *you* are Mrs. McNab's employer, not someone who can dictate what I do." It wasn't Ashby! Victor nearly *whooped* with delight.

"But—"

"Thank you, sir, again, for your concern. I will be walking about on my own for a few minutes."

The trio stood in place, as if unsure what to do.

Finally, Ollie jumped in. "No use telling her what to do, Mr. Martin. I know Lady Litchfield well enough for that." Ollie placed Evelyn's hand on his forearm. "Twenty minutes, though, and if you don't return, I'm sending out a search party. We'll be waiting at the stairs for you."

Anne nodded wordlessly.

She watched them leave, her shoulders stiff, and as soon as they were gone, Anne began looking around frantically. Her head swung around like a spinning top, her body turning in the opposite direction, as if she were trying to go two directions at once. She went back around the hedge corner, reappeared, and hurried down the walking path. There was a small copse of trees with ornamental grass and rose bushes. Victor had to suppress a snort when she lifted her feathery, white skirt to step into the garden to investigate the area, swearing loudly when she got caught on the roses. Her swan hat began to slide down as she worked to untangle herself.

"Bother that," she said to herself once safely returned to the path, and she pushed the hat back on straight with a huff.

As she did this, she looked over the expanse of garden around her.

This was his moment. Taking a deep breath, Victor stepped through the willow branches out into the open, into the moonlight. When she saw him, she stilled.

Come to me, he thought to himself.

His heart pounded hard as she began moving.

Determined in her footsteps, she walked straight up to him, stopped, and angled her head back to look up at him. "It's you," she said. "The one who watched me at the ball."

He nearly replied but stopped himself. She would recognize his voice. Instead, he stared down at her, unblinking, concealed by his mask and costume and the night.

"Oh, that's how it's going to be then, is it?" Anne stepped past him and began walking toward the pond.

And he followed. Of course he followed. He would follow her for as long as she let him.

She went to the edge of the pond, the willow tree now behind them, and Victor stopped beside her. The pond was still, but the half-moon above twinkled upon the water.

"You're the one also sending me drawings." She paused, as if uncertain about this. "Aren't you?"

Victor bowed his head to her.

"Why?"

But he couldn't respond to this question. It wasn't time, just yet.

"And it was me you drew." Her eyes turned up to him again. A warmth engulfed his heart, causing an ache in his chest. He had to resist the urge to reach out and touch her.

Instead, he nodded again.

"I should be more bothered by it than I am." She turned back out to the water. "A man who melts into the shadows. A phantom following me, sending me drawings? And yet..."

He waited. Oh, how desperately he wanted to hear the rest of that sentence.

But she didn't finish it.

She sighed. "I want to know why you follow me. My friends call you my secret admirer. Would you say that is an apt description?"

He bowed his head.

Her eyebrows lifted high. "Do you know I'm a widow?"

Again, he nodded.

"And do you also know I have children?"

He hesitated. How much of what he knew should he give away? Tonight, he didn't want her to figure out who he was.

Anne turned to face him fully and crossed her arms. "Does it bother you that I have children? That I am a mother?"

He would have to respond to this verbally. He knew this question was important, and he wanted her to know he meant his answer. Mary and Freddy were her entire world and if she even suspected the tiniest bit that her having children gave him second thoughts—they didn't—she would leave right now and never look back.

Whispering in a raspy voice to conceal it, he replied, "No. I know you have two. A daughter. A son."

Her shoulders softened. "Yes." She stared off, as if lost in thought. "So, you admire me."

"Greatly."

She blinked and looked back up to him. "Do we know each other outside of you following me anonymously?"

Not wanting to lie to her, he didn't respond.

"Hmm." She frowned and went silent.

But he couldn't stop watching her as she looked out over the pond again. Around them, crickets sang and frogs chirped, the nostalgic sounds of summer nights. Being this close to her, without the wall of friendship coming between them, without having to pretend he didn't want her, that he didn't love her, nothing existed outside of them.

Love. The thought shocked him to his core. Did he love her?

He took in a sharp inhale. Anne tore a look up to him. "What is it?"

Of course, he didn't tell her. He was still reeling from the shocking realization.

She turned to face him again and looked him over. "I've been quite amiable about you following me, Phantom. In theory, it's concerning. A man following a woman, watching her from a distance? It should be disconcerting. And yet I find myself drawn to you instead. Am I mad?" She chuckled a bit at the end. "Or am I a hopeless romantic?"

His heart began to race faster.

"How long have you been admiring me? Weeks? Months? I only noticed you recently. And you've only tried making contact recently as well. Maybe, you saw me at the Duke of Chalworth's Christmas dinner party."

"Years," he whispered.

Her widened eyes and mouth gave away the true shock she felt. "*Years?*"

He nodded.

"But I never noticed you before."

He hesitated. "You weren't ready before." He wasn't sure she was even ready now. But he had to give it a chance at some point.

Anne's eyes bored into him, but she quickly looked away. "What do you want from me, Phantom? It's rather unfair of you to hide your face from me. Will you remove your mask? I want to see who you are."

He shook his head.

"I must say it's rather bold of you to make yourself known to me at Lord and Lady Bell's masquerade. Surely, you are aware of its reputation?" She looked him over slowly before her eyes met his again.

He didn't respond.

Anne gave him a coy smile and lifted one eyebrow. "Perhaps that is precisely why you did it. Do you wish to take me, Phantom?" she asked this question in a lowered voice. A bedroom voice. A voice she would never have used if she'd known who he was.

Women had never had much of an effect on Victor, and with no desire to tempt fate, he had never paid them any more mind than he did men. But in this moment with Anne, his identity unknown to her, amongst a warm, summer night, the smokiness in her voice, her nearness, all without anyone around? Maybe he didn't care for men *or* women. Maybe all he would ever want was Anne.

And here with the privacy of the pond and willow tree, no one would know if he gave in to temptation.

Victor was becoming unwound.

"Well?" She wasn't willing to let the question go unanswered.

She took a step closer and traced her finger around the embroidered cross on his costume. The touch, no matter how light it was, branded him beneath.

Swallowing deeply, he leaned down close enough that his mask brushed against her temple, his enormous hat hiding them further from the world. He stayed that way for a moment, listening to her breath quicken. Finally, he whispered in a deep voice. "There is no woman more desirable, no woman more tempting—nothing else in this world that equals the need, the want, I have of you in this moment. Yes, I wish to take you, Lady Litchfield. But I cannot."

Chapter Twenty-Four

ANNE'S EYES WERE closed as the Phantom whispered in her ear in that sultry voice. A voice of silk wrapping around and caressing her. Throughout this interaction with the Phantom, she had of course tried to figure out who he was. If she had to choose an identity, she would guess he was either Mr. Ashby or Victor. They were both as tall as the Phantom, with similar enough builds that this baggy costume made it possible to be either of the men. One would think the eyes would have given it away, but she couldn't tell if the Phantom wore spectacles like Mr. Ashby, or if his eyes were green like Victor. And would spectacles even fit beneath the mask? Perhaps he could go without spectacles for a short time. A conundrum to be sure. Unfortunately, his tricorn hat shadowed his eyes enough that she couldn't see enough detail outside of the fact that he had both eyes in place.

Another point: Victor would never act this way toward her, so bold and fiery. Nor could she imagine him willingly dress up as a musketeer. But she wasn't convinced it was Mr. Ashby, either. Earlier, she had tried to identify Mr. Ashby at the masquerade but had only been able to find his mother.

Then again, the first time she'd seen the Phantom, she had been dancing with Mr. Ashby. That should easily have ruled him out. However, the family knew about the Phantom and had openly talked about him before. It was entirely possible Mr.

Ashby had been told about it or overheard someone speak of it—maybe even Freddy had told the man about it. And Mr. Ashby could have used that to his advantage and taken over the secret identity, knowing it intrigued her. But also, why would he go through all that trouble?

Well, to take advantage of her, of course. Surely, Mr. Ashby would jump on the opportunity to take her. Most men would have. Would Victor? That, she couldn't say with confidence. Another point of interest, the Phantom hadn't said he *wouldn't* take her. It was that he *couldn't*.

She thought back to her rules. *Never chase a gentleman.* Well, the Phantom was quite clearly the one doing the chasing. She'd had no opportunity to interact with him before. *Never flirt first.* Another rule that applied nicely. With his mask nearly against hers, she would have been able to tell if he had bad breath, which he didn't. He had good hygiene, so that was another rule that passed. Every single one of their interactions up until now had taken less than ten minutes, another rule.

There were a few more rules she had to ensure applied to him before she allowed herself to completely succumb to him.

As she thought about them, the masked Phantom, who remained standing close, lifted a gloved finger and ran the back of it over her cheek. Slowly, his finger brushed down over her jaw, down her neck, pausing at her collarbone, then slid lightly back up. Anne dared a glance up to his masked face. His hat shadowed his eyes. If only she could see them…

Her breath caught from his touch. "Phantom, I have three questions to ask you."

He didn't respond, which she took to mean he was waiting.

"Do you enjoy discussion about politics?"

His finger stilled. "No."

She let out a breath. "Do you enjoy laughter?"

He restarted his caress. "I am not one known for my humor, but I suppose I enjoy it on rare occasion."

She couldn't help but smile up to him up. She was forgetting something. What were the other questions? Oh, yes. "Then my last question. How old are you?"

He stilled again. She sensed she may have touched a nerve. "Why?" he whispered.

"I—" She debated if she should tell him about her rules and decided there was no harm in doing so. "When I first arrived at Brighton this year, I decided I wished for a seaside romance. As you know, I am a widow. I did not have a good marriage but did learn much from it."

"What did you learn?"

She turned her face toward his mask, the blasted mask she was going to convince him to remove. "Between my marriage, and the years of being alone that followed, I learned what rules I would put in place to protect myself."

He slowly nodded. "Very well," he whispered. "You wish to know my age. Why?"

"Any gentleman of my choosing must be within ten years of my own age."

"What is your age, then?"

"I am forty."

"Then I am within your desired ten-year age range," he whispered in the obvious attempt to conceal his voice. And unfortunately, it worked. She still wasn't *exactly* sure who this was.

But, whoever he was, he fit the rules she had created to find her seaside romance. All she had to do was ensure she didn't fall in love, which should be easy enough. She couldn't fall in love with a masked man.

At least, she hoped.

"Very well." Anne hurried away from that, though. "Now, I am to convince you to remove your mask. And then perhaps you could kiss me, Phantom. And quite passionately."

The Phantom straightened upon hearing this. And though she half-expected him to scoff at the suggestion, instead, he looked around, his gaze falling upon the willow tree behind them.

He looked back down at her. With the wig and tricorn hat framed by moonlight, she really did think he could be a ghost for a quick moment.

He didn't say a word, but his hand reached out to hers. His leather-gloved hand was hot against her own glove, but again, there was that layer between them. His mask, the gloves, blast it all!

The Phantom led her to the willow tree and pushed aside branches for her to walk through. He followed her in, and the branches fell closed.

Inside the canopy, it almost felt like being in a room—a very private room. Anne looked up and around at the long branches and leaves hanging and was amazed by the transformation of their surroundings.

Her eyes fixed upon the mysterious masked Phantom. He was watching her study their surroundings, and upon having her attention once more, he began leading her deeper in. They took a few steps, and he paused and turned to her, as if waiting for her to pull back. But she didn't, and soon, they were completely concealed by darkness. Though she could just make out the silhouette of his large form, she could see nothing else.

Anne took a chance and stepped up to him to run one of her hands slowly up his chest. The simple touch caused him to take a sharp inhale, and she could feel his heartbeat quicken beneath the hardness of his body. The effect she had on him stoked the low embers within. In a strange way, it made her feel powerful, not helpless like Bernard had. Here was this man, one so enamored by her that he, apparently for years, had admired her from the shadows. He created beautiful drawings for her, concealed his identity to get closer to her. He followed her, not the other way around. And he was large and strong and could easily overtake her, yet she was the one in control. If she wanted to stop, she felt comfortable enough doing so. He never seemed to take a step ahead of her, instead somehow following one step behind. Even though he was the one who'd approached her.

She was in full control of whatever happened between them. And the thought was freeing.

For some reason, though, his identity was an issue. But she wasn't going to dwell on why that was. Not right now.

Feeling daring by her newfound power, Anne felt for the Phantom's tricorn hat and wig and lifted them off, letting it drop to the ground with a thud. He didn't protest. As she lifted her hand again, she wondered what she should do. She wouldn't be able to see him if she removed his mask. But she would be able to feel his face.

When she reached up to his mask, however, his hand flew up and covered hers, preventing her from moving further.

Blast it all, she thought to herself, disappointment coursing through her.

But then he whispered in that raspy voice, "Allow me."

Her heart galloped as she pulled her hand away. The low thump that followed meant he now stood before her unmasked, his identity revealed. If only there were light to show her!

On a swallow, she removed her gloves, lifted one hand with hesitation, then gently touched her fingertips to his face. He wasn't made of air. He wasn't a ghost. Hot man, made of flesh and blood, met her fingers. She felt his cheekbone and a beard and her heart picked up its pace upon this discovery. Her fingers swept over the Phantom's nose, his forehead, then she gently felt for spectacles. Oh, she hoped Mr. Ashby would be one to wear them beneath a mask and make this easy.

What if it turned out this *was* Mr. Ashby? What would she do then?

The thought was distressing. She was drawn to this man, to her Phantom. There was something about him that made her heart race, pulled her to him, made her want to feel him and touch him. Not run away, like men usually made her want to do. Somehow, she knew the Phantom meant her no harm. But for whatever odd reason, he refused to reveal who he was.

Unfortunately for him, she was determined to find out.

And if it turned out he was Mr. Ashby, well, she would have some trouble coming to terms with that. Because she did not want Mr. Ashby in her life in such an intimate way.

Ready to get the answer to her question once and for all, Anne swept her fingertips over the Phantom's temple and across his eyes.

No spectacles. It didn't matter that there was a chance Mr. Ashby might not wear spectacles beneath a mask—somehow, she *knew* it wasn't him. Anne's heart fluttered and her breathing quickened as her hand brushed back down to the rough hairs of his beard, suppressing a sharp inhale that would have given away the depth of her surprise. As her heart raced faster and faster at her discovery, she felt around his face a bit more, as if she couldn't quite believe it.

She didn't need a shred of light to reveal who stood before her. When she felt the Phantom's lips, she knew without a doubt who he really was.

How long had she studied this face? How many times had stared at these lips, secretly wondering what they felt like?

The Phantom and her secret admirer were one and the same. And *he* was Victor.

Which meant tonight, Anne could satisfy her curiosity. She could finally find out what it would be like to kiss him, to be in his arms. And then afterward, she would pretend it had never happened. He wanted to hide his identity from her? Perhaps that was wise.

"Who are you?" she asked to make it seem as if she didn't know.

The Phantom remained quiet for a long beat. Anne was nearly ready to turn and leave when he pressed a large hand to her back and lowered his face to hers. Her eyes closed as his closeness warmed her exposed skin around her eye mask. The bridge of his nose brushed across her temple and over to her ear. Gently, his lips swept along the shell of her ear, the tingling sensation causing an unfurling within, like a flower opening up for the first time. "I am of the shadows," he responded in a private voice. "Your Phantom, your endless admirer."

She reached up to cup his cheek to feel the roughness of his face once more. It was soft, but also somehow rough at the same time. She sighed, contented.

As if encouraged by her reaction, the Phantom swept his lips down to her neck, gently trailing a hot line with the tip of his tongue. Anne's eyebrows lifted high in the dark—she had *not* been expecting that from Victor. Desiring more, she angled her head to the side in invitation, and he eagerly took it, pressing a soft and slow kiss to her neck. Despite his meandering pace, she could sense his hunger, his desire, barely restrained in the way his hand flexed on her back.

But why wasn't he taking what he wanted? She was willing. Very willing. He had said he couldn't, but surely, she misunderstood what he'd meant by that?

Hoping to encourage him, Anne let out a small moan. And he responded with a growl.

Oh, my. Growling during intimacy had never happened to her before. But it was the most magnificent sound she had ever heard.

Her mind liquified by his closeness as heat blazed off of him and scorched her despite the already warm, summer night. Soon, she would be nothing but a puddle, she was certain of it.

But she wasn't happy with innocent caresses. She must have more, especially as this would be the only time anything would happen between them. Having Victor all to herself in the dark, their passion held secret in the branches of this willow tree, it made her greedy. It had been so long…

Would he be prim and proper? Or would the darkness that always seemed to shadow him break him out of his restraints?

Hoping to encourage him further, she gave him a deep, throaty laugh as she twisted her fingers into his tunic.

The tension between them seemed to snap and finally— *finally*—they could hold back no more and crashed together. Her arms circled back around his neck as his wrapped around her waist. As mouths pressed hard together, he pulled her tight and close to the firmness of his body, the muscles in his arms, his torso, even his legs flexing with their erratic movements. He fumbled around in the dark, more so than her, but once she'd angled her head the right way, their mouths fit together as perfect as a puzzle. His tongue swept over hers, eager, searching. He tasted like mint, and she briefly envisioned him nervously brushing his teeth before leaving for the masquerade, knowing what he would do once he found her. She couldn't help but smile against him at the thought, and this caused him to pull away for a breath. Victor then nibbled at her bottom lip and she gasped. He was full of surprises—never would she have expected *any* of this playfulness from him.

And it was doing a number to her mind and her heart.

Anne fisted the front of his tunic and pulled him farther into the darkness of the willow tree. She stopped when she backed against the trunk of the large tree, and Victor's breathing became desperately labored.

"Are you done with me already?" She traced a finger over his lower lip and made sure to ask in a velvet voice.

He swore under his breath and she allowed herself to smile widely under the cover of darkness. For she heard his voice quite clearly then and there was no mistaking it for anyone else.

Anne pulled him back down to her and the desperation from their first kiss moments ago—*their first kiss*, the thought made her stomach flip—had cooled. Victor took her face in his hands, tilted her face further up, and kissed her much slower this time. He brushed his lips over hers, their breaths mingling together in the humid, night air as his front pushed against her, her back pressing hard against the rough tree bark behind her.

This was heat. This was passion. *This* is what mutual desire felt like. A hunger she had had for so long was so close to being satisfied.

But there was something else going on too that caused her

pause. The fire of desire that burned between them—it didn't feel new. It felt strangely familiar, a dim but low glow just waiting for the oxygen it needed to explode into an inferno.

And tonight, it received that oxygen and the inferno burned in her heart.

Anne accepted Victor's low, slow kiss but wondered what that roaring, hot feeling in her heart was.

It didn't matter, though, did it?

Victor obviously didn't want their passion realized outside of tonight, and quite frankly, neither did she. Whatever flamed between them this evening would *never* go beyond the willow tree. There were too many walls to knock down between them. It would be an impossible, heartbreaking feat.

Reaching up to caress the muscular arms, she felt the round hardness of them flex in response to her searching touch. For some reason, he seemed rather content with following her lead and the fire in her heart sparked at the thought. If they were going to move forward, she would simply have to take them there.

Quite happy to do so while Victor's large hands held her hips, Anne reached under and up his tunic to begin unbuttoning his shirt. Victor's breathing became loud and labored and it swept down over her neck, but he didn't protest. She unbuttoned halfway down his shirt and, unable to hold back any longer, allowed her hands to roam over hot skin. His grip on her hips tightened with possession as she explored his body in the darkness, his hot breath sweeping over her faster and faster. But here, she received another unexpected surprise. Thick, rough hair covered his chest and trailed down his torso.

Victor was quite hairy, which was a rather unexpected discovery for Anne, and it surprised her how much she liked it. But she needed to feel *all* of it.

"Forgive me, I—" His voice waivered, as if nervous, and he let her go. Was he embarrassed by his body?

"Shh." Anne ran her fingers through the hair, over the hard

pectorals and the rigid planes of his stomach. As her fingers trailed slow, lower and lower, he took in a sharp breath. However, something about that inhale did not sound like he was pleased.

So she moved back up. "I want to see you," she said, hoping to coax him out of his shell. "I want to see this." She luxuriated in the hair upon his body. Victor again pressed his mouth hard to hers and kissed her with wild passion, pulling her close, rendering her hands unable to move. When she needed to breathe she pulled away, and she removed her hands from his front. "And I want to see this." She put one hand to his face.

"No," he whispered.

"Please." It almost came out as a plea. Why didn't he want her to know who he was? And why did *she* want to see so bad? She was perfectly happy with this anonymous passion beneath the willow tree. She didn't want it to go beyond this.

Or so she had thought. But what would happen if Victor *did* reveal himself? Could this continue?

Did she want it to?

It didn't matter because he didn't respond. For a moment, she thought he was going to let go of her and leave. Instead, he threw her off completely by going down to his knees and burying his face into her stomach while wrapping his arms tightly around her.

What in the world?

Shocked, and unsure what to do, Anne ran her fingers through his hair and waited. When he didn't do anything further, she lowered to the ground, too.

He responded by gripping her waist with his hands. He could lift her with ease—he had done it before. He could, quite literally, do whatever he wanted with her right now.

Her heart, her body, screamed with desperation. *Do it. I don't want anyone else.* She didn't want Mr. Ashby. She didn't want another man. All she wanted, all she had *ever* wanted, was Victor.

"Take me," she said in a low voice. His breathing began to quicken and she pressed soft kisses to his rough cheek, to his jaw, to his neck. She gently sucked his skin there and felt his ribs expanding quickly, his hands tightening their hold on her. She repeated her request. "Take me. Please."

He moved quickly. Next thing she knew, her costume was crushed beneath her and her swan hat had tumbled off. Victor hovered over her, his hands planted on the ground on either side of her shoulders. His breathing was loud, erratic. She could feel him staring down at her, though neither of them could see much. But she could also sense that he was having an internal battle with himself.

Was being with her really such a battle, though?

"I don't know who you are and I don't care," she lied, hoping to reassure him. "All I want is you, Phantom. I look for you everywhere I go, hoping to find you in the shadows again. I want you to follow me. I want you to watch me. I want you to touch me anywhere and everywhere and devour me. I am at your mercy to do with as you wish. And I am very willing in that regard. You can feel for yourself if you don't believe me."

He swore loudly again. "Lady Litchfield, you haunt me in my wicked dreams. You have no idea what you are daring me to do." Before she could respond, he slammed his mouth down to hers. Their tongues were at war with each other—hot, fast, desperate, that heated, erratic stumbling fire tumbling between them. She gripped his hair with one hand and pulled up the hem of her skirt with the other.

But when he realized what she was doing he stilled, and the heat around them suddenly chilled.

She had gone too far.

"No." He choked the word out and, quick as lightning, was back up on his feet. "Forgive me." Victor was fully talking in his normal voice now, not the raspy whisper he had been using to conceal himself. Did he even realize that? "Christ, what in the blazes am I doing?"

Anne, now panicking, hurried up to her feet, too. "Not enough." She tried to add a laugh.

But he didn't respond in kind.

"Please—" She reached out to him. He didn't step away, and in fact pulled her close, burying his face in her hair.

Victor, oh, Victor! Don't shy away now! "What's the matter? Why are you stopping?"

"I told you." He was back to his whispered voice. "I cannot do that."

Anne frowned to herself. Why wouldn't a man be able to take her? "Why not? Are you maimed?"

He made a strained, choking noise. "No."

"Then why can't you? I'm willing, if that hasn't been clear. If you're worried about pregnancy, all you need to do is ensure you pull out at the appropriate moment."

However, he didn't respond to that. For a long and confusing moment, they stood in the silent embrace, their breathing fast, hard.

But then he took her hand. He lifted it and placed her open palm over his heart, to feel how wild his heart was beating—for her.

He didn't utter another word, still didn't explain why he couldn't lie with her, but in this moment showed her everything he needed to.

Understanding started to dawn on her. Victor's feelings for her were far more potent than she ever would have imagined. Unlike her, he was attracted to her beyond physical desires. Was he…in love with her? Was that what he was trying to show her? Anne gasped and, terrified, locked away such thoughts. And in response, he stepped away, walking around to presumably find his costume. Then there was a brief bit of light as he parted the willow branches and disappeared.

He'd left her behind without saying goodbye.

Anne's hand flew to her mouth to barely suppress the sob that had escaped.

AT THE END of the night, once they had returned to Summerwood, and once Anne was out of her costume and in her nightgown, she stood at the door between her room and Victor's room.

Anne's hand rested upon the cold wood as she stared at the brass doorknob, emotion in her thrashing around violently. Victor's intentions with her were as clear as mud. He didn't want to use her, as he had the opportunity to do so. But he wanted nothing to do with her, either, at least in the way a man wanted a woman and a woman wanted a man. And he wanted nothing to do with her outside of their tryst beneath the willow tree. He'd only wanted those few minutes of kissing, and nothing more.

But why?

And why didn't he want her now, here, in their own bedrooms? He could simply knock upon her door, admit to everything, apologize, and they could climb into bed. No one had to know. Had he perhaps come to decide their feelings for each other were imbalanced?

It didn't matter, anyway, because there was no knock from him. And though she made to knock on his door several times, she never did manage to do it.

Instead, she went back to her vanity and pulled out her list of rules.

With her pen in hand, she underlined and circled and boxed and drew angry, jagged arrows pointing to the very last rule:

Never fall in love.

Chapter Twenty-Five

EVENINGS OFFERED A respite from the summer heat. It didn't get nearly as hot here in Brighton as it did in London, but it still made sleep difficult sometimes. Which was precisely why Victor had all of his windows open. And why he had pulled a chair to one window, to sit in front of it. With his third whiskey. Inhaling the cool sea air, to cool off from the summer heat.

Yes. That was it. The summer heat.

Victor threw back the remaining sharp liquid and set the glass down heavier than he'd meant to. He sunk further into the seat, letting his head fall back against the chair with a *thud*.

Tonight, Anne had called him "the Phantom." But she was the one doing the haunting.

Victor closed his eyes and visions of Anne spun around him. That first time he'd laid eyes on her crying in Vivian's receiving room, he had been stunned to his core by her. Then there was the time they'd shared a train car to Brighton and she'd gotten tipsy as she'd told him her entire life story. Every word she'd said to him had been a gift he'd held on to. Then there was the way she'd run after her scoundrel husband and slipped in the mud. The promise that he would wait for her for as long as it took. Years, decades—it didn't matter.

And he remembered all of the little moments in between. Brief, loud conversations over the heads of patrons at the pub.

Dinners at her home. Offering her a hand to help her step out of a carriage. To step into a carriage. Family carriage rides around Hyde Park. Easter egg hunts with the children, which became a whole family affair when Ollie's boys had been born, then Dantes's daughter. Years of Christmas dinners, New Year's Eve parties, and every other holiday, it seemed.

Every moment, big and small, he'd locked safely away in his memory like a precious gem.

Although she claimed to have no memory of their promises made in the rain, or the declaration he'd made. Maybe he had gone mad with his wanting of her, and it was a figment of his imagination.

Because it *was* mad, this deep obsession he had for Anne. He'd spent every free moment he could with her. Watched her, year after year, recover from her marriage and the sudden shock of widowhood. Watched her raise her children as a single mother, and break through the shell of her former self. The meek, pliant creature she used to be when he'd first met her had blossomed into the strong woman he now loved and admired endlessly. He would never know what his own mother, what Anne had gone through as widows with young children. But he could appreciate the special difficulty of raising young children in the midst of mourning and grief. The constant worry their unbreakable melancholy would turn them into ruffians or ruin their lives, or any other number of worries a caretaker shouldered in silence.

Victor reached out to his glass and made to take another sip before remembering it was empty. He let the glass fall out of his hand and drop to the carpet below him to roll away somewhere.

Anne.

Anne, Anne, Anne.

Beautiful, tempting, luscious, breathtaking Anne.

How in the blazes was he supposed to recover from the masquerade? He had never known desire, had never know this feral, animalistic urge to consume a woman before. If he had even the faintest idea of what lust, passion, and love had felt like, he *never* would have messed with it.

Despite his lack of experience in the ways of women, he had heard far more than he'd ever wanted to from the lads at the pub. For decades, he'd been forced to listen to scoundrel men's stories about taking women, the details about what happened behind closed doors. Or in carriages. Dressing rooms at the theater. Alleyways. On the floor, on the chair, on the table. He knew far too many details about how it happened and what it entailed. It had all sounded ridiculous to him, as if these people had had a brain fever at the moment.

He'd never understood the appeal. Until tonight.

Those little moans and sighs she'd made as he'd kissed her. The smell of her hair, of her skin. The way she'd pressed against him, begging him for more, the taste of champagne upon her tongue a temptation and a promise of its own.

Christ, she'd begged him to bed her. *Begged.*

And he'd refused.

Victor leaned forward and pulled at his hair. He may have known what happened, he may have known how it worked, but he had never gone to bed with a woman before.

No one had ever tempted him enough to, but also, he was terrified of even one night resulting in a child. After raising Dantes and Ollie in the streets of Whitechapel, running off to start his own life, then seeing his mates from the docks struggling to support families on meager wages…he'd wanted nothing to do with that.

It didn't matter that he had money now. It didn't matter that he would have more in the future. He would always worry it could be taken away, somehow all lost, and his young children would be left to fend for themselves in the streets like he had been.

It would sound like nonsense to anyone who hadn't experienced what he had. But it was an all-consuming fear he would also never be able to get over. Simply, he couldn't stomach the worry that would come with having children of his own.

But how could he tell Anne that? She would just try reassuring him again that there were ways to prevent pregnancy. Except… nothing other than celibacy was risk-free. If she became pregnant, he would have to do honorable thing and marry her, which he knew she would not want. Would *he* even want that? He was unsure.

He knew one thing, if he did give into Anne's temptation despite his fears, he would be forced to admit to her that he had never lain with a woman. A man his age! She would think him daft, or laugh in his face. Surely.

In an idiotic moment, what felt like ages ago, he had tried to tell her about this while he'd brushed her hair. Too ashamed to outright say it, he'd hinted at it by telling her he'd never brushed a woman's hair before. Which, looking back, was idiotic. Of course he'd never brushed someone's hair before. Not surprisingly, she'd simply looked confused, scaring him off from being more explicit about what he'd meant. Now, he was too afraid to bring it up.

Him, afraid! Pathetic.

Victor let out an audible sigh. Celibacy had never been a problem. Until now.

Now, he had held Anne. Tasted her kisses. Felt her hot skin against his lips, her waist and hips in his grip. Heard her sultry bedroom voice, her sighs and moans.

And she had no idea the Phantom was *him*.

Victor had to fight back the urge to roar out at the thought.

He could feel himself unraveling. And nothing could stop it.

What in the blazes was he going to do?

Victor jumped to his feet and stared at the door that led to her bedroom. He was half-tempted to embrace his drunkenness, bang on that door, and admit he was the Phantom. He took a few steps toward the door but stopped himself. What, exactly, would he say?

Even if he had the perfect words, it would never end well. She thought of him as her dearest friend in the world. So he would, what, say, "Anne, I'm the Phantom. I'm in lust with you. I'm in love with you. I've no experience with women and don't know what I'm doing. What do you say?"

No. Any woman, from young maidens to experienced widows, with half a mind would run away cackling.

Victor let out a sigh and went back to his chair to focus on the sea air that cooled him.

Eventually, he fell into a restless sleep. Vivid, dark dreams of Anne consumed him. Just as the sky was turning light, the faintest dusty pink lifting on the horizon, he awoke with a start. He felt horrid but couldn't stand another minute dreaming about Anne. He was also mostly sobered up, and though he had a terrible headache, at least he didn't feel as if he would vomit.

But he had to get out of his bedroom. Victor washed up and dressed, walked past the dining room, and went straight for the stables.

Recently, he had gained the confidence to ride on his own for long lengths of time. He now understood why riding appealed to nobs—the solitude, the freedom one felt from riding was unmatched by any other activity. Upon seeing him, the stablehands saddled up Pancake—of whom Victor had grown to be fond—and off Victor went.

Together, mare and man galloped across the open, green fields of Brighton as the morning sun climbed higher, peeking over the horizon and then rising for the day. Hungry seagulls cried overhead as salty waves crashed into the shore.

He started to feel better, and after a time, he stopped to let Pancake rest and nibble on grass.

And that was when he heard her.

Off in the distance, Anne shouted his name, the sound carried by the wind. She was a mere dot at the moment, but she was coming toward him.

He had not been expecting to see her so soon after last night and had hoped to ride to clear his head and his heart. Moments later, she came to a stop beside him upon Onyx. The pretty, black stallion nickered and shook his mane, as if showing off to Pancake. Anne was wearing her dark-green riding habit that Victor loved her in. Her face was flushed from the ride, but her smile was wide and bright. "Good morning, Victor!"

He nodded, dour. Kissing mysterious men apparently put her in a brilliant mood.

"What a lovely morning. Dew upon the grass, salty air in the lungs. Did you sleep well last night?"

Victor looked out at the sea's horizon, forcing back the passionate memories. "Not particularly."

"Oh. I'm sorry to hear that."

He looked back at her and nodded. Pancake slowly moved to another patch of grass and lowered her head again to graze.

Onyx and Anne followed.

"How was the masquerade?" Victor tightened his grip on the reins, hoping nothing in his face would give anything away.

"Oh, you know." Anne laughed, but it sounded quite forced. Victor frowned at her and she paled a bit. "It was pretty typical. For Lord and Lady Bell's masquerade, that is."

Victor stared at her, waiting for her to say more. Would she tell him about the secret tryst beneath the willow tree? Or would she hide that from him?

Anne's mouth opened and she paused, as if weighing what to say. "And, erm." She scratched the side of her nose. "My secret admirer was there."

His idiotic heart skipped a beat. "Did he finally reveal himself to you?"

She stammered, then laughed nervously. "Sort of. He, well, he kissed me."

Victor raised an eyebrow. This seemed like the way he would react if he weren't deeply involved in this. "And who is he?"

"He didn't reveal that. Yet." She held his gaze as he said this.

This was possibly the most uncomfortable conversation he'd ever had. "And he's going to in the future?"

"I certainly hope so! I mean, he *did* kiss me last night. Quite passionately, I might add." She looked down with a coy smile as if remembering the night before. "It was very nice, and I thought about him all night."

Ah, Christ.

"Why would he do that only once, never to reveal his identity? Wouldn't he want to see me again?" Anne looked up at him through her lashes.

Victor could feel his face harden, even though he was trying his best to remain expressionless. After last night, he would not return to her as the Phantom, of that he was certain. It was impossible to. Now that he realized he loved her, that he wanted her in the most basest of ways, he *needed* to keep that part hidden away.

Anne frowned deeply. "What are you so upset about?"

"Upset? Nothing. I'm not upset." He turned Pancake back in the direction of Summerwood. "I should head back." The mare began to trot.

Anne and Onyx kept up beside them. "I would very much like my secret admirer to return," she said. "I think it's quite strange he hides his identity. I suppose I could understand it at first, but now that he's kissed me, doesn't he want to kiss me again? As his real self?"

Victor cleared his throat. "I haven't the faintest idea."

"I mean, it was clear he desired me. Of course, I wanted him just as ferociously."

Victor resisted a groan.

"Though he made a curious comment last night. He said he cannot take me. Not that he wouldn't, that he *couldn't*. Isn't that curious? Why wouldn't a man be able to bed a woman?"

Victor had to bite the inside of his cheek. Hard. In fact, he was pretty sure he drew blood.

She continued, unaware of his strife. "But he was quite *energetic*, which is why I'm confused. I did ask him if he was maimed and he said he wasn't."

Victor made a choking noise and covered it up by clearing his throat.

"I bet he's fun in reality. I mean, his real self, not his masked self. I'll just have to convince him, I think." She smiled, evidently pleased with her decision.

"Blast it all, Anne." This was becoming far too much. "What happens then?" Victor slowed Pancake to a stop. Anne's determination needed to be quelled. "You don't wish to marry again. This secret admirer of yours—what if he isn't satisfied with summer trysts beneath trees? What will you do then?"

Anne's eyebrows went sky high. He was showing too much emotion and interest in this. Too late now. "I didn't say anything about a tryst under—wait, you think he wants to *marry* me?" The horror in her voice was clear.

The way she'd said the word *marry* sent a severe jolt of humiliation through him. What mess had he gotten himself into? "Never mind," Victor said, scowling darkly. And with that, he flew into a gallop, leaving her behind.

BACK AT THE stables, Victor quickly left Pancake with the stablehands. He had hoped to get at least a minute or two's head start from Anne to get back into the house, but, of course, she was right behind him. He scowled at her as he walked by her climbing down from Onyx.

"Victor!" Anne shouted after him. "What in the blazes is going on?"

"Nothing." He kept walking, his strides longer than normal.

Infuriatingly, she jogged to keep up. "I don't understand why you're so invested in this. It has nothing to do with you, right?" When he didn't respond she repeated herself. "Right, Victor?"

"Right," he replied sharply.

As they approached one of Summerwood's back doors, Anne sprinted ahead and stood with her back against it, her arms crossed, a determined chin lifted as she watched him with a dare in her eyes.

Victor sighed loudly and ran a hand through his black hair. "What are you doing?"

"I will move out of the way when you answer one question. Only one question. That's it."

He rubbed his palms over his beard as frustration pounded through his veins. "Fine. What is this all-important question, Anne?"

She lifted her chin higher. "Are *you* my secret admirer?"

Victor felt his face go hot and his head go light. Had she figured it out or was she simply trying to eliminate him? If she *had* figured it out, when had that happened? Had it been just now, or had it been last night? Christ, had she known it was him when she'd been pawing through his shirt?

The heat in his face worsened.

"Well? Are you going to answer me?"

He could lie. He could easily deny it was him. But that would only make it worse. The entire reason for last night had been for them to come together without her knowing it was him. To ease out of friendship into…whatever it was that was happening between them. For her to see, feel, that they could be more than friends. But the most unfortunate outcome of the entire saga was he had come to realize he loved her. Deeply.

And he knew while Anne may have accepted lust between the two of them, she would *never* accept love. Nor would she reciprocate it.

The thought, admittedly, hurt his heart.

Now he wasn't sure what he wanted. It was a bit frightening—he didn't like losing himself this way. But at least now he knew they had two wildly different desires. It would be one thing for him to reveal his secret of inexperience to her if they were marrying, which wouldn't happen. But he couldn't tell her about that for a short-lived summer liaison, which was what *she* wanted.

Victor looked down at her as he scrambled, deciding what to say. And she looked up at him with narrowed eyes. She wanted to know the truth.

But she wasn't going to get it. Ever.

Victor stepped closer to her and set his hands on her waist, causing her to inhale sharply. And then he lifted her up and set her to the side.

"Hey!" she shouted quite loudly. And he went through the doors with ease. Somewhere behind him, Anne swore. "Victor, stop!"

But his attention was immediately taken away from Anne when he saw the scene in the house. Down the hall, in the foyer, Mrs. Ashby was shouting and her hands were flailing about. She was talking to Vivian, who was trying to calm her down.

"Mrs. Ashby," Vivian tried saying over the woman's erratic wailing. "I don't know where she is!"

Victor halted in his tracks and turned around to look at Anne. Anne had paled. Something was wrong. She looked up at him and said in a low voice, "This isn't over." And then she rushed past him.

Anne approached Mrs. Ashby, who was speaking in strange shrieks Victor couldn't understand. As he got closer, he realized Ollie and Evelyn were standing in the doorway of the parlor, watching the scene. His Grace was just outside the doorway next to them, his arms crossed and worry set upon his brow. Dantes appeared, running down the stairs rapidly, carrying something. Dantes's eyes snapped to Victor and though no words were said, Victor knew something quite bad had occurred.

Immediately, Victor went to his brother's side as Anne, Vivian, and Mrs. Ashby spoke.

"I don't understand," Anne said, shaking her head. "That doesn't make any sense! Where's Freddy? Freddy!" Anne shouted loud and scurried about the foyer, screaming her son's name.

Something had happened to Freddy? A wave of fear struck Victor and his heart plummeted. It had been a long time since he had felt ice slide through his veins like this. Not since the days he'd cared for Dantes and Ollie in Whitechapel.

A strong hand gripped his shoulder. Dantes. Victor, dazed, looked over at his younger brother. Dantes's jaw was clenched, but just as he was about to say something, Freddy appeared with Miss Stewart trailing. The governess was red-faced and wide eyed, as if she were about to cry.

Victor nearly collapsed from the relief. Unfortunately, it was short-lived.

"I looked everywhere," Freddy choked out. His face was red, too, and there were wet streaks down his cheek. "She isn't here. She's gone."

Miss Stewart looked as if she were shivering. "I'm so sorry! I'm so sorry, Lady Litchfield!"

"I found this." Dantes dropped his hand from Victor's shoulder and brought the object he was carrying over to Anne, who bowed over it with Mrs. Ashby.

"That's similar to the note I found," Mrs. Ashby said with a shaking voice.

Anne didn't respond. Instead, she lifted her head and looked around, searching desperately for something. Finally, she turned and found Victor, her wide eyes set on him. "Victor." She released a sob and went over to him, holding out the note. Her hand flew to her mouth as he read it.

Dearest Mama,

I know you will be cross with me when you first read this, but I want to assure you I am quite happy and excited. By the time you read this note, I will be well on my way to Gretna Green. I'm getting married! Soon, I will be Lady Mary Ashby and what a dream it will be! He is so handsome, Mama, so lovely, and I know he will take good care of me, don't you fret. I am not a little girl anymore, and I knew you never would have agreed to me marrying so soon, which is why I must elope. I know I was supposed to debut next year, but what if one falls in love before then? I'm making the right decision, and one day, you'll forgive me.

Your loving daughter,
Mary

Victor blinked several times hoping to clear the words away, but the note remained. Fear pumped through his veins. Mary wasn't his daughter, but in this moment, he felt like an angry, protective father. Calmly, he handed the note back to Anne and she burst into tears. "What do we do?" Anne sobbed out the words. "I don't know what to do. I don't know what to do!" And she immediately went to Victor and buried her face against his shoulder.

He felt a surge within him. Protectiveness, love. Right now, he didn't give a single fig if his love for her would never be reciprocated. He wrapped his arms around her and held her tightly. Shushing her, he spoke low into her ear while rubbing his hand over her back. "We will figure it out, I promise," he reassured her as his mind whirred on what to do. What time had Mary left? What time had that bloody cad Lucas Ashby left *his* home? Over the past few weeks, the blasted idiot wouldn't leave Mary alone. Victor hadn't liked it, but he'd felt it hadn't been his place to intervene.

Now, he was regretting that.

Victor took in a deep breath and looked around the foyer. Some were looking at him, and others were looking at Anne. No one appeared like they knew what to do. Freddy held a deep frown on his face. His shoulders were drawn up tightly and his head dropped.

"Freddy," Victor said and Freddy's head lifted up. When the lad met his eye, Victor lifted one arm. Freddy immediately came to him, allowing Victor to put an arm around his shoulder while Freddy put an arm around his mother. The trio found solace in each other. In a way, he held Anne and Freddy up.

Victor was not part of Anne and Freddy's family. Yes, he was Uncle Victor, and he was close to them, but he was not one of them.

This also meant he had to be the strong one, despite the fear and worry—even anger—he felt himself.

"Mrs. Ashby, do you know what time Lucas left your house?"

Victor met eyes with the Ashbys' mother. "We need to know how much time they have on us."

Mrs. Ashby sniffed and dabbed at her eyes with a handkerchief. "Lucas?"

Why was she wasting time? "Yes. Lucas. Your son who ran off with Lady Mary?"

The older woman stammered and looked around at everyone. "It wasn't Lucas who left with Lady Mary, Mr. McNab. It was Felton."

Chapter Twenty-Six

ANNE'S BLOOD RAN cold upon hearing that name.

Mr. *Felton* Ashby had run away to elope with her daughter? The thirty-two-year-old man who had spent months wooing *Anne? He* had run away with her seventeen-year-old daughter?

Anne lifted her head to look up at Victor. He stared down at her with his piercing, green gaze, doing his best to keep his face level, but he never could cover up the emotion in his eyes. He was *furious*. And she was oddly comforted by the fact that his anger mirrored hers.

She rested her head upon him again and closed her eyes. It had hit her that she had gone to Victor for comfort. She'd felt so lost, so distraught, so confused upon reading Mary's note that she'd immediately gone to him because she'd had to. And she hadn't even thought about it, either. It had been her natural reaction to seek him out.

All she wanted right now was Victor to hold her as she worried herself sick over her daughter.

And he did, even after the row they'd just had.

He was her support, her rock, her comfort. He had even offered his solace to Freddy, who needed it just as badly as Anne.

Warmth sprung within her heart and she choked on another sob.

Anne took several deep, shaky breaths, then wiped at her

eyes. Mary, her baby, had run away to get married in Gretna Green to elope with a horrible man! She could only imagine what his motive was. Prestige? Money? Perhaps Mary's very young age?

Anne pulled away from Victor with a bit of regret and turned to Mrs. Ashby, finally regaining the ability to talk. "What do you mean, my daughter ran away with your *eldest* son?"

Mrs. Ashby began wringing her hands as everyone watched and waited for her response. "Don't ask me. I had no idea! I thought she and Lucas liked each other. I had no idea Felton had designs on her. He never said a word to me about it!"

"But—"

A large, warm hand gently rested on her shoulder. Victor. "What time did you discover Ashby was missing?" Victor asked.

Mrs. Ashby swallowed. "This morning. He also left a note. I immediately came here."

"Did you have any idea he would do something like this?"

"No." She paused and shook her head. "No, Felton is the responsible one. I have no idea what got into him. A seventeen-year-old? Even if the daughter of a marquess... It isn't unheard of, but... Well, I'm quite surprised, to say the least."

Anne's thoughts were a jumble. She couldn't allow this to happen. "I need to stop it from happening," Anne said with finality. But she felt frozen in place. She looked up at Victor again and could feel how colorless she probably looked. Her heart was racing with fear and she was so confused.

Victor stiffened and looked around the room. "Mrs. Ashby, return home in case your son or Lady Mary returns. Send word if they do."

"I will," Mrs. Ashby replied with a nod.

"Dantes," Victor turned to his younger brother. "I need your help finding out the quickest way to get to Gretna Green from Brighton."

"On it." Dantes hurried off.

"Ollie." Victor turned to Ollie. And he paused. Ollie, the

youngest of the McNab brothers, and the most carefree of them all. Their stark difference in personalities had always put tension between them. But Ollie had grown up, hadn't he? Victor could rely on Ollie for this. "I need you to visit the hotels in Brighton and make sure they aren't holed up in one of them. If they are, drag them back here."

"You want me to do that?" Ollie asked, surprise ringing clear in his voice.

Victor narrowed his eyes. "Unless you can't handle it?"

Ollie grinned widely and kissed Evelyn on the cheek. "I'll be back right quick," he said to her before dashing out the front door.

Victor looked down at Anne. "Dantes will be able to tell you which trains will get you to Gretna Green quickest. Hopefully, you will get there before Mary does something idiotic."

Anne frowned. "You're coming with me, aren't you?"

"I—" Victor wasn't even sure what to say. Go with her?

"Please." Anne lowered her voice as Freddy looked between the two of them. "I need you to come with me. I can't do this without you."

He frowned. "But—"

She placed a hand on his forearm. "I need you, Victor."

He swallowed but nodded.

She gave him a brief flash of a smile before turning to her son. "Freddy, I need you to stay here with your grandfather in case your sister returns. And then you're both to nail her windows closed and lock her in her room."

The duke came up to the young man and gave him a brief squeeze on his shoulder, while giving Anne a reassuring nod. Freddy chuckled as he wiped the back of his hand over his eyes. "We can do that."

Anne then finally turned to Miss Stewart, who rushed forward with more tear-filled apologies. Anne put up a halting hand. "Miss Stewart, please, I would not expect you to have known my daughter had snuck out of the house in the middle of the night.

Could you please find Dutton and let her know she and I are to leave posthaste? And why?"

Miss Stewart wrung her hands as she visibly shook. "Dutton went into town, remember? Lady Mary had a bee in her bonnet yesterday about some boots she had seen in a window. And as Dutton already had errands to run for you this week, she offered to go this morning to see if they had the boots in her size."

Anne sighed. "She thought of everything to delay me, didn't she? No matter. I can throw together a bag and travel just fine without her help." Anne was just about to suggest the governess join her when she began having a fit.

"Oh, Lady Litchfield, I wish I could have predicted this! There must have been signs she was planning this behind our backs! How could I not have seen? How could I have missed it?" She looked as if she were about to let out a wail but instead turned quite pale and crumpled to the floor.

The Duke of Chalworth immediately ambled over to her and put two fingers to her neck, checking for a pulse. "She's not dead," he proclaimed after a moment.

"Of course she's not dead—she fainted!" Vivian set her fists on her hips.

As father and daughter went back and forth, Anne began to think of more important matters.

It was sheer luck that they only had to switch trains once in London. From Brighton, they managed to make the express train to London, and from London, they only had to wait about half an hour for their next train on the London & Northwestern Railway, which took them all the way up past the Scottish border, past the city of Carlisle, and to their final destination: Gretna Junction.

They were expected to be at their destination three hours from now. It was an entire day of travel on train, and Anne hated travel. But the trip so far had been a hazy blur. She didn't talk much to Victor, and he seemed to sense she had nothing to say and didn't interact with her more than required.

He was present. And it was everything she needed in the moment.

But she had now had hours to take in the news that Mary had run away with Mr. Ashby. No one knew what time they'd left. They could already be married by now.

"What did I miss?" Anne finally asked, her eyes still out the window, though she didn't see the lush countryside.

"Sorry, I don't know what you mean," Victor said after a moment.

Anne looked over to him and she was surprised at how disheveled he looked. "Why am I so surprised she did this? Does that mean I don't know her, don't know my own daughter? I mean, this isn't a small mistake. This is life-altering. Elopement is an enormous humiliation to bring upon one's family. And with Mr. Ashby, of all people! What does he want from a seventeen-year-old?"

Victor clenched his jaw and looked at his lap.

"Don't answer that." Anne rubbed the bridge of her nose. "But it still makes no sense. I thought he was pursuing me." She stilled. "Do you think that was a ruse?"

Victor looked up. "You think Ashby used you to get close to Mary?" He looked off to the side. "I suppose that could be possible. It would explain a lot. It could also be he's a fortune hunter and didn't much care which one of you went off with him."

Anne frowned at this thought. With a sigh, she asked, "Am I that terrible of a mother?"

Victor frowned deeply at this. "Absolutely not."

"Then what did I do that made her into a young lady who would do something this idiotic?" Anne, feeling despair rising again, looked at the empty seat across from them. It was just the two of them in the private compartment. And she was only now realizing Victor had chosen to sit beside her, not across from her. She swallowed.

"I don't know. Maybe you did something. Maybe you didn't do something. Mary has always been spirited."

There was a heavy pause that made Anne think Victor was

going to say more but had stopped himself. She looked up at him and his jaw was tense again. "What is it?"

But he shook his head.

She turned her body to face him better. "I need to know whatever is on your mind. *Please.*"

"I don't think my opinion much matters. And I worry it will upset you, which I do not want to do."

But Anne was desperate to know. She placed a hand on his upper arm. "Tell me."

He glanced down at her hand quickly. "I think you've been so worried about Freddy taking after his father that it didn't occur to you that Mary could be the one to do that."

Anne's hand fell away and her mouth dropped open. The words stung. But it was the truth, wasn't it? Her worries in her children had been backward. All this time, she'd assumed, because Freddy was a man like Bernard that he would turn into Bernard. But Freddy was nothing like his father. Mary, however, had resemblance to him. She wasn't bashful about anything, and very little could shock her. For the last few years, she had been very interested in young men, to the point that Anne should have taken this as the warning sign it had been.

Not that she would have been able to change her daughter's delight in the opposite sex, but Anne should have been more open with Mary about the risks of men. All this time, she had tried protecting her daughter through ignorance, too afraid to expose the young woman to reality. Yes, she had told Mary how men could be risky to women. But she should have given real examples. She should have been more open about what she had experienced, the way men could manipulate and play on a woman's weakness. The way Bernard had done so to her.

But having too tight of a hold around the young lady had led to risk, not safety.

Anne sunk back into her seat. "You're right."

"Really?" Victor couldn't mask the surprise in his voice if he had tried.

"Yes. As much as I hate to admit it, but denying it helps no one." Anne sighed and watched the fields and trees and stone fences fly by. Despite the fact almost an entire day had passed, it was still full daylight this time of year, and this far north. "If only I knew what to do once we arrived. Where will we look? Goodness, there must be dozens of places they could be."

Victor surprised Anne by putting his hand over hers, resting upon the seat. Her heart raced at his touch, and it lifted the heaviness upon her ever so slightly. She was glad he was there with her. She couldn't have done this alone. She also couldn't have done this with anyone else, including Dutton. Not even this moment right now, but the past several years. Victor had always been there for her, always there for the children, no matter what. And he'd never complained about it. He was so important in her life, and she'd taken his presence for granted.

She wouldn't take it for granted any longer.

What that meant, exactly, she wasn't sure, but now was not the time to unravel it. Instead, she turned her hand and fit her fingers between his.

HOURS LATER, THEY arrived at Gretna Junction. The black steam engine whistled out loud as they disembarked. Anne shielded her eyes from the sun with a flat palm and looked around the small platform and the crowd amongst it. There were a few benches along the small, white building that was the train station. Perhaps Mary sat upon one waiting for Anne. That would make their trip much easier.

Alas, Mary was not there.

Anne needed to have some sort of plan to at least settle her nerves. But neither she nor Victor had ever been to Gretna Green before. They had no idea how many inns, how many churches, how many blacksmiths there were. While blacksmiths were popular officiants for Gretna Green elopements, technically, Scottish law allowed couples to marry anywhere they wished. All they needed was to be at least sixteen years old and have two witnesses. Mary and Mr. Ashby could be getting married right now out in the middle of some field, for all Anne knew.

"I need a plan. Any plan," she said.

"We will knock on every single door if necessary," Victor replied.

Carrying both of their small travel bags, Victor hovered at Anne's side like a black cloud and she immediately reached out to grab his free arm. "You're all that's holding me up right now." Anne let out a nervous laugh. But it was true. She was shaking with fear and was feeling unsteady on her feet.

"I'm glad to be the one to do it," Victor replied with his dark voice, looking down at her, his green eyes sharp. It sent a bright surge through Anne's heart. His eyes tore away to search the platform. He jutted his chin in a specific direction. "Look, there's the stationmaster. Let's start with him." Victor then led her over to a man in a stationmaster's uniform, who stood off to the side to watch the disembarkation. As they approached the gentleman, it occurred to Anne how young everyone on the platform was. Lots of very young *couples*, most of whom appeared to be around twenty years old. She couldn't help but wonder what their lives would be like in a few years. The motherly urge to scold them and tell them to head back home was strong.

But she bit her tongue, instead, knowing that they would not care what she said and would have to live with the choices they made of their own volition.

"Excuse me," Victor said to the stationmaster and they came to a halt before the man. Anne tightened her grip on Victor. What if he wouldn't help them? What if he didn't know anything? Furthermore, why would he? The man probably saw hundreds of people every day.

"Good day, sir." The stationmaster bowed his head at Victor. He seemed a friendly sort, with lines at his eyes and rosy, round cheeks. The gray mustache added a grandfatherly joviality to the man. "You look like you're in need of assistance. Are you here to elope?"

"No." Victor shifted.

"Um, we are looking for—for my daughter," Anne squeaked out.

The stationmaster stared, as if waiting for her to say more. But Anne felt tongue tied.

"Her name is Mary," Victor jumped in, relieving more of the heavy weight upon Anne's shoulders. He looked down at Anne in a study. "Lady Mary. She has black hair and is taller than her mother here." Victor put his hand about four inches over Anne's head. "About this tall, I'd say."

"So, she takes after you?" the stationmaster asked, confusion in his voice.

Victor spun his head around to the stationmaster. "No, I'm not her father." When the stationmaster opened his mouth to respond, Victor continued quickly. "Mary arrived with a man named Felton Ashby. He has blond hair and a blond beard, and he wears round spectacles. He's also..." Victor paused and glanced at Anne. He swallowed before he continued. "He's also about the same size as myself. She is seventeen and he is, erm..."

"Thirty-two," Anne added, the disgust in her voice apparent.

The stationmaster nodded in understanding and pinched his chin. "Unfortunately, I do not recall anyone who fits either description. But as you can see..." He indicated the crowd with an open palm. "I see plenty of people daily who could easily fit those descriptions. It doesn't mean they aren't here, just that nothing about them stood out to me."

Anne was feeling hopeless. The stationmaster was the one person they knew would have most likely crossed paths with Mary. Once Mary had left the platform, there was no telling where she'd headed next.

"We are eager to locate Mary before she does something she will one day regret. Where would an eloping couple most likely go?"

The stationmaster scratched the side of face. "Well, there's the town blacksmith—he's the one most people like to go to. You know, the whole wedding-over-an-anvil tradition. *Old Smithy*, the anvil is called. But they could really go anywhere."

"That's what I'm afraid of," Anne said with a sigh. "Victor, where did Ollie and Evelyn go when they came here?"

"I think the blacksmith."

"Why don't we start there, then?"

After getting directions to the blacksmith, they thanked the stationmaster for his help and hurriedly made their way. They found a small, white cottage that made up the blacksmith's shop. With haste, they entered and soon found the wedding room. Old Smithy—the name painted on the side of the large, metal anvil— sat in the middle of the room on a pedestal, with two identical, plump elderly women sat in chairs against the wall, crocheting. A young couple—not Mary or Mr. Ashby—stood on either side of the anvil. The blacksmith, a portly fellow with a black jacket over his linen work shirt, stood in the middle.

"Are you old enough to get married?" the blacksmith asked. The elderly women continued their craft without looking up.

"Yes," the couple replied in unison.

"Are you related to each other?"

"No."

"Have either of you been a resident of Scotland for at least twenty-one days? That's a requirement since the 1850s and not enough people know about it."

The couple looked at each other with wide eyes and the young lady's lip quivered.

"Just say *yes* or *no*," the blacksmith said helpfully.

"Y-Yes?" the groom sputtered out. The twin elderly women stopped their task and exchanged a look. One snorted, the other rolled her eyes. But the women—Anne surmised they were the witnesses required by law—didn't intervene.

"Then you are married." The blacksmith slammed a hammer down onto the anvil, the loud ding causing Anne to yelp and jump. The blacksmith then took coin from the groom. "Congratulations. Next!"

There was another couple about to head in. "Just one moment," Anne said to them and she hurried past, ignoring their protests. The elderly women exchanged excited whispers, but the only word Anne could understand was *eager*.

Victor followed her inside, keeping silent.

"You stand here, lass." The blacksmith directed Anne to the left side of the anvil.

"Sir, please—"

"You over here, laddie." The blacksmith put Victor to the right of the anvil then looked up at him, blinked, and glanced at Anne. "Why, you're the oldest couple I've had elope here in a long time!"

Anne gasped, offended by this. "We are not old!"

The blacksmith lifted his hands in surrender. "All right, all right. Shall we begin, then?"

"But—"

"Are you old enough to marry?" The blacksmith then laughed quite loud. "We can skip that one. Are you related to each other?"

With eyes round as saucers, Anne looked at Victor. They were in the middle of a wedding ceremony, *their* wedding ceremony! But he wasn't saying anything, or doing anything. Had he gone mad? Instead, he was staring at her, his jaw clenched tight. She had to get this cleared up posthaste. "No, we're not related! Sir, I must say—"

"Have either of you been a resident of Scotland for at least twenty-one days? That's a requirement since the 1850s and not enough people know about it."

"No, we haven't!" Anne was now fully panicked. Good God, what was happening?

"*I* have," Victor said.

Anne inhaled sharply. "Victor, you are *not* helping right now." What in the blazes was he doing? He should have been putting a stop to this madness, not encouraging it!

"Excellent! Then you are married." The blacksmith picked up his hammer and raised it above his head.

"Stop!" Anne took a few steps back from the anvil. "Mr. Blacksmith, sir, we are not here to get married. Victor, have you lost your mind?" She nearly hissed at him, her heart pounding against her ribs.

But a horrifying thought hit her. Had they *really* just gotten married?

Oh, blast it all!

Victor blinked as if coming out of some sort of trance. "Wait." His eyes flew up to hers and then widened. Their travel bags tumbled to the floor. "Wait!"

The blacksmith looked quickly between them. "So, do I ding the anvil? Or no?"

"No!" Both Anne and Victor shouted together. Somewhere off to the side, the two witnesses let out small gasps.

The blacksmith lowered the hammer hesitantly and then set it to the side. "Hmm."

Anne took in a deep breath and told the blacksmith their purpose for being there. She described Mary and Mr. Ashby, but the blacksmith, unfortunately, didn't know if the couple had come through or not. But he also seemed quite distracted. "Sir, did you hear anything I just said?" Anne sputtered.

The blacksmith rubbed his palm over his cheek. "Something about your daughter." He took in a deep inhale. "Look. I've never had a ceremony interrupted like that before."

Anne shook her head. "What are you talking about?"

The portly man laughed nervously. "I went through all the required questions and words for a wedding. But I didn't ding the anvil." He scratched at his chin. "Were either of you married before this moment?"

"Well, I'm a widow."

"Recent?"

"No."

"Interesting." The blacksmith went over to a window, where

a few books were stacked. He picked one up and begun thumbing through.

Anne and Victor exchanged a look. Something was happening, and she didn't like the sinking feeling in her stomach.

Thankfully, though, Victor took charge of this moment.

Finally.

Victor cleared his throat. "Forgive me, but what is *interesting*?"

The blacksmith was mumbling to himself as he looked through the book and stopped at some page. And all he said was "Hmm. Interesting." There was that word again.

"Victor," Anne said in a warning voice. They couldn't have been married—that had to have been impossible. Neither of them wanted to be married to the other.

Right? It was her biggest nightmare, to be married again. And so unexpectedly, to add!

The mere thought, coupled with the chaos, was starting to make her feel dizzy.

"So." The blacksmith turned back to them with the open book. "This is a quite awkward."

"What. Just. Happened?" Victor's darkness had decided to return. Finally.

The blacksmith paled. "It's funny really." He laughed. "You two, ah, might be married."

Anne gasped and faltered back.

"But..." The blacksmith raised his pointer finger. "You also might not be."

"How do you not know if we are or not?" she snapped back.

"Well..." He thumbed through the book again. "I can't determine if the anvil ding is required or not. It's the sound that indicates the anvil ceremony is completed, you see."

"But it's not required for other ceremonies," Anne said.

The blacksmith hesitated. "That is true, but it is a requirement for the anvil ceremony. I don't know if there's some strange law that means it must be a part of it for the type of ceremony only. Anyway, don't you want to know that for certain either way? I know I would." He chuckled. Rather inappropriate for the moment.

"As the expert, what is your professional opinion?" Victor asked through clenched teeth.

"I'm only a blacksmith, sir." The blacksmith said this with round, innocent eyes. "Honestly, I've never had this happen before. I really, truly, don't know. But if I had to make a wager on it, I would wager you're married. But I could lose that wager, too."

Anne took a deep inhale through her nose at this wishy-washy man, turned around, and stormed out of the building.

Chapter Twenty-Seven

AﬀFTER GIVING THE blacksmith a death glare—and paying the man, as the last thing Victor needed was an argument over that—Victor went after Anne, though he was unsure what he would do once he'd reached her.

They couldn't *really* be married, though.

No. Certainly not.

He opened the old, wooden door and stepped out into the evening sun, which cast a deep-yellow glow and long shadows over the small town of Gretna Green. He knew well it wouldn't get fully dark until at least eleven o'clock. After looking about and searching beyond the people meandering about, he finally found her at the far end of the building sitting on a bench.

He sat beside her and asked, "Where should we check next?"

Immediately, she spun her head in his direction and he was certain she was going to murder him.

"Very well, wrong question, then." He cleared his throat. "Sorry about, ah, what happened back there."

Anne jumped up to her feet and loomed down at him. "You're *sorry* about what *happened back there*? As if you had accidentally ordered a too-expensive bottle of wine at a restaurant? Or had caused me to lose my place in a book? You're *sorry* about what *happened*?"

Victor stammered. "I—yes."

Anne threw her hands out to her side. "You didn't stop him. You didn't say anything! You just stood there, slack-jawed. Staring at me! And then—then! You confirmed you had lived in Scotland before! After I said we hadn't!"

He frowned. "I wasn't *slack-jawed*."

She ignored that comment. "You can't seriously tell me you didn't realize what was happening."

He stammered again, like a cad, while rubbing the back of his neck. The truth was, he had, after a few moments, realized what had been happening and he'd been so surprised that they had gotten themselves caught up in their own wedding ceremony, and then, the idea hadn't sounded too terrible, and... Well, he'd decided to see what she would do.

Now, of course, his head was back on straight and he knew how idiotic that had been. He cleared his throat and turned up a palm. "Is it really that bad, though?"

She inhaled sharply through her nose, her eyes widening with it. Victor resisted the urge to wince. "*That bad*? What do you mean by *that*, Victor?"

"We already spend so much of our free time together." He paused, grimaced, and opened one eye, risking a look up at her. She was still looming over him like the grim reaper himself. "Would it truly be that bad if we were married? All things considered?"

"Are you mad?" she shouted this out so loudly that everyone around paused what they were doing and looked over to see what was going on. Anne blanched, grabbed Victor's arm, pulled him off of the bench, and marched him around the corner of the blacksmith's building to escape prying eyes.

She crossed her arms and looked up at him. "We have no business being married, Victor. We are friends. Quite good friends, yes. But we are not husband and wife. Not..." She made a choking noise. "Lovers."

For a moment, Victor considered admitting he was the Phantom. If they didn't have the potential to be lovers, if that wasn't something possible between them, then why had the kiss beneath the willow tree been so desperate and heated? He may not have been experienced when it came to women, but he knew far more about intimacy than he'd ever wanted to before this. And he knew what they shared together was *not* common.

But again, this was not the time to be discussing this. Perhaps, if Anne stewed in the idea, she would come around.

Telling her he was the Phantom would be his next step. This possible marriage changed everything, and it was only fair that she would know.

Victor cleared his throat. "I have a solicitor I can contact. He should be able to tell us if we are married or not."

"Thank you." Anne's shoulders fell. This seemed to satisfy her for the time being. "The more pressing issue, though, is finding Mary. We have been delayed for far too long." Anne's jaw set, and she stared off as if thinking. "I think we should check inns next. I don't think they would have known to go anywhere other than the blacksmith."

Victor nodded. "That's a good idea. A town this small shouldn't have too many inns, either."

It turned out there were several in town—who would have guessed? After checking the fourth inn, they began walking toward the fifth when they passed the train station. Victor paused and looked at it. "We should see what time the last train leaves."

"Good idea," Anne said.

They found the stationmaster again and discovered they had minutes until the last train to London of the day. They would never make it. And unfortunately, they had also discovered it was quite difficult finding vacancies at inns this time of year. All they could do was trudge on and hope for the best.

When they reached their eighth, or maybe it was the tenth, inn Victor started to truly worry about Anne. She was walking slower, her feet dragging behind her, and her shoulders were starting to slump. As with all the other inns, they went inside to inquire about any bookings with Mary and Ashby.

The innkeeper, in a crisp, white shirt and neat tweed flatcap, confirmed they had no guests that matched Mary's and Ashby's descriptions.

"Do you have any vacancies?" Victor asked as he looked down at Anne. "It's been a long day for us."

"Unfortunately, I do not," the innkeeper said with a genuine frown of pity. "Perhaps another inn does."

And so, they continued trudging around Gretna Green as the sky became darker and darker.

"What if we don't find her?" Anne asked as they left another inn with no news, her voice sounding weak and exhausted. "Do we leave without her?"

Victor couldn't fathom the thought. He was going to turn this blasted town upside down to find Mary if he had to. "No. We look as long as we need to. And when you get tired, I will continue looking. I won't rest until I find something."

"I won't, either," Anne replied, but her voice gave away the true depth of her exhaustion.

"Please." Victor put a hand on her shoulder. He looked over at the inn they had just left. "Go and sit down, eat something. I will keep looking."

"But—"

"Anne, sometimes you need to let others help you."

She seemed to mull over this for a moment before giving him a weak nod and took their travel bags to bring inside. "You find me the *second* you learn anything."

"I promise."

"What are we going to do about sleep? Where will we go?"

"I don't know. We will figure it out."

She gave him a small nod and he watched her go inside the inn.

With renewed determination, Victor continued the exhaustive search, glad he was able to convince Anne to take time to rest. The next inn, the innkeeper was actually two people, a husband and wife duo called Mr. and Mrs. Baker.

"Sorry," the short, red-haired fellow said after licking his finger to flip through their reservations book. "No one of that name here."

"What did they look like?" Mrs. Baker asked. She had crossed her arms and skewed her face up to Victor, pinched with interest. Victor described Mary and Ashby.

"Don't recall anyone like that," Mr. Baker said.

But Mrs. Baker didn't respond. Instead, she pinched her chin and stared off with thought. "You said they're how old again?"

"Lady Mary is seventeen and Ashby is thirty-two."

"I recall a couple coming in here earlier today. He looked far older than her, at least to my forty-year-old eyes."

Mr. Baker jumped in. "Seventeen and thirty-two is hardly unique."

"True, but it's not common, either. Not with the sort that comes through these parts. Most of the young couples that come through are middle class or working class and about the same age. An age difference like that when the lass is so young mostly happens with the upper class and is rare enough to stand out." Mrs. Baker frowned down at the reservations book while looking through it. "Now that I'm thinking about it, though, it might have been them. I didn't pay enough attention to be certain, but she did have black hair and he had light hair. I can't recall if he wore spectacles, though."

Victor felt the first surge of hope all day. It was a mere flicker, and he knew not to get too confident. But it was the most he had. "Where did they go?"

But Mrs. Baker shrugged. "Couldn't tell you." She paused and furrowed her brows. "But I do remember something."

"Yes?" Victor said a bit too eagerly.

Now the woman looked him square in the eye. "They were frustrated with each other. The way they stood and talked? Again, I don't remember too much, but I do recall her turning her nose up at him and she said, 'Of course you don't have the coin.'"

Upon this, Mr. Baker slammed an open palm down to the

table, causing his wife to yelp and Victor to flinch. "I remember now! I remember that comment! They said they were on their way to see the blacksmith but wanted to reserve a room first. When the lad asked what a room goes for, I told him, even though we had nothing available, and he balked at the price. That's when the lass made that comment. I told them that sometimes the Green Inn has openings when everything else is booked, as it's the oldest inn in town and a bit rough around the edges because of it. Best thing I can say is maybe they went there."

That glimmer of hope turned into a full glow. "Where's the Green Inn?"

"Just around the corner there!" Mr. Baker thumbed over his shoulder to the wall behind him. Victor thanked the couple profusely and rushed out of the inn.

When he went around, he saw the place almost immediately. Unlike all the white buildings in town, this inn was aptly painted green, though it desperately needed a fresh coat.

Once inside, the innkeeper knew exactly who Victor was searching for.

"Och, aye." The ruddy-faced man slammed a fist down to the table he sat behind. Unlike at the previous inn, this place had a noisy dining room. The patrons were loud, but there was also a fiddler playing a plucky tune. "Won't forget those two for the rest of my life."

"Where are they?"

"I haven't seen the lad for hours now. I didn't like him much—he was a bit pushy. Kept trying to reserve a room, even though I wouldn't let them have one until after they married. I'm not running a house of sin, you know!"

"Of course not." Victor was trying not to hurry the conversation along, but he was growing impatient. "So, what happened?"

"The lass said, *'Do you have enough coin for* this *place or shall I expect to sleep outside tonight?'* And then he goes, *'Well, you're the one with money. I thought you would have brought coin,'* and she says,

'*You want* me *to pay for* you?' The lad then says to me, '*Christ, man, just let us have a room.*'"

The chatty innkeeper raised his eyebrows at Victor with a knowing look.

That did sound like Mary. "And?" Victor needed to hurry along this conversation.

"I've lived here my whole life, laddie." The man lowered his voice a bit. "The pushiness, the desperate look in his eye. Too many of the couples that come through town are men promising marriage to women in order to woo them into the bed. Every single time, the lad leaves after he succeeds, the promise of marriage unfulfilled." He *tsked* and shook his head with pity. "That's why I won't take reservations until after the ceremony. I want no part of that!"

"But you gave them a room." Victor leaned down to the innkeeper, gripped the front of his shirt, and growled.

The innkeeper shoved Victor's hands off. "Och, no! I knew what he was doing. He wanted her money, a tumble in the sheets, and then he'd leave her without a thought. And I was right. When I suspected what he was up to I told him to leave, I did. The lad promised the lady he would be right back. I told her to sit tight in the dining room and order whatever she wished. Naturally, her beau never returned. But I had a feeling someone would come looking for her. And I was right. Here you are!"

Victor couldn't believe his ears. Ashby's intentions—he would deal with that later. But Mary was here? It felt as if the boulder pressing down on his back had been lifted. He had to find her and make sure she was all right, that she was safe and truly unharmed. The innkeeper had only seen them in that short moment—had Ashby done anything before then? The thought struck cold fear in his heart.

Victor thanked the man and rushed into the dining room. His eyes darted around. Based on the older ages of the people in here, as opposed to the twenty-year-olds he'd seen milling around the blacksmith's, this was where the locals preferred to congregate.

At first, he couldn't find her and was worried she had left. But then, he found her and could hardly believe his eyes—there was Mary, seated alone at the bar, swaying as she intently focused on a glass full of ale that she was holding at eye level.

With one eye closed, and black hair quite messy.

She was drunk.

Victor let out a breath and hurried over to her. "Mary," he said, purposely dropping her title to protect her. He realized he was choking up. The back of his throat was tight with the emotion and relief that flooded him. Until this moment, he hadn't allowed himself to comprehend how terrified he was for her. But here she was, in the flesh. Appearing rather unconcerned, and quite drunk.

Mary turned her head in his direction and her body swayed with the movement. Upon seeing Victor, her eyes opened wide and her grip on the glass loosened. Victor quickly grabbed it and set it down before she dropped it and spilled.

"Uncle Victor?" she said quietly, though it sounded more like *Ungle Vigder*.

The barkeep—a tiny wisp of a woman with gray hair and a sharp face that said she would take no sass, immediately hurried over.

"No bothering the lassie." She whipped a rag loudly against the bartop. "Or you'll have to deal with me."

"It's all right, Bertha," Mary said. So, she was drunk *and* on using Christian names with the barwoman. What a day she must have had. "This is my father."

Victor immediately shot her a glare and she responded by giggling, the giggle then cut off by a hiccup. Granted, it didn't happen often, but this wasn't the first time someone had mistaken him for Mary's father. But he also wasn't about to correct her, as it would make leaving more difficult. Bertha did not seem one to let things go lightly.

"Your mother is absolutely sick with worry." Victor stared down at Mary, trying not to let himself get too angry. Now that she was safe, the anger that had been pushed down finally started to rise. She was safe, but… "What in the blazes possessed you to run off like that? And with *Felton Ashby*, of all people?"

She pouted and hiccupped at the same time, causing her body to jolt. But she didn't answer.

Victor sighed. "Come on. Let's go."

Mary slid off her barstool and a travel bag tumbled to the floor without her notice. Victor grabbed it. "Goodbye, Bertha. You're my dearest friend, you know."

"Stay away from the lads a bit," Bertha said, shaking her head.

As Mary started to stumble away, Victor hurriedly asked Bertha, "What does she owe you?"

Bertha waved him off.

Victor shoved his hand into his pocket, grabbed whatever he could, and slammed it down to the bartop. Bertha's eyebrows shot up. "Then take this as my thanks for keeping an eye on her, then."

"Aye." Bertha began counting out the coin and let out a low whistle.

Victor caught up to Mary and led her outside. Mary could barely walk but spotted a bench about twenty feet away and collapsed into it.

"Have you had anything to eat?" Victor asked, trying to think of ways to sober her up.

Mary flung a floppy hand in his direction. "Yes, but I have no idea what it was. Bertha practically shoved food down my throat."

"Good." Victor set her bag on the bench beside her and lowered himself to sit as well. "What happened, Mary?"

Mary's easy-going drunkenness immediately disappeared and she tensed. "He abandoned me."

"Yes, I know. But I meant before that. Why did you do this?"

Mary crossed her arms and slouched in the seat. For a flash of a moment, Victor saw Winthrop in her profile. "Felton wooed me for a few weeks. I thought he really cared about me. I used to think I liked his younger brother, but then Felton kept inserting himself into everything. He was more confident, knew how to act, knew how to talk. His brother was nothing compared to him. Felton was a real gentleman, or so I thought." She paused for a moment. "The other night while we were at their house, he asked me to marry him during charades. But he didn't want me to tell Mama. Which I should have seen as a problem, but I was too swept up in the moment. Here was this older man, and he thought little me was someone worth marrying! Someone worth spending his life with! I was flattered, and I thought he meant it. And then he had convinced me Mama would never support us getting married."

"Which is true."

She nodded. "Yes. I knew there was nothing I could say or do that would convince her to agree to it. And Felton kept saying, *'Oh, but, Lady Mary, it's* your *life! Don't you think* you *should do what you wish with your own life?'* Things like that. Yesterday, he sent me a letter asking me to elope. We spent the day writing back and forth, planning it all out. Then we left." She shifted in her seat. "You know, after Freddy and I were sent to bed?"

Victor nodded.

Though her face was pale with exhaustion and too much drink, there was a ghost of a smile on her lips. "By the way, I saw you sneak out, too."

Victor tensed.

"You were dressed as a musketeer. Where did that outfit come from?" She gave a small laugh.

"Your grandfather gave it to me. Where did you see me?"

"I must have left right before you. I heard someone coming and hid around the corner of the house. I saw you hurry out of the house to grandfather's awaiting carriage, dressed in that costume. Why didn't you just go with everyone else?"

"Let's stay on topic," Victor said hurriedly. "So, you left after midnight."

"We met at the train station and discovered, unlike in London, there weren't any night trains. So, we slept there and took the first train out. When we arrived, I was all set to go right to the blacksmith. I was so…" She made a choking sound. Victor looked away to give her some semblance of privacy. "I was so excited. How ridiculous am I?"

"You're not ridiculous."

She let out a shuddering breath, then continued. "He didn't want to go right away, though. He wanted to get a room first, to make sure we didn't lose out on a place to stay. It made sense, but at the same time…"

"Something about it bothered you," he finished for her when she didn't continue.

Mary looked over at him with worry set on her brow. "Yes."

"That's a very important feeling that you experienced. I learned far too young to listen to it. But it has never led me astray or into more danger. Promise me—now that you know that feeling, that warning feeling—you must listen to it from now on. Every single time you feel it, even if your mind tries to brush it off."

Mary looked him in the eye and nodded. "I will."

Victor eased back into his seat. "Then what happened?"

"He just kept…pushing it. It was a bit obsessive and annoying, but I followed along, anyway. We began to realize how difficult it would be to get a room at an inn. Everything was already booked up. I was upset, but Felton was absolutely furious. He wasn't showing it just yet, but I could see it festering. I could tell he was doing everything he could to dampen the rage. But despite keeping quiet at the time, I could see the vein starting to bulge on his forehead. The flushing of his neck. The tight fists that he wouldn't release. It reminded me so much of—" She stopped and paled.

"Of what?"

"Of, um, of Papa." She looked down at her hands. "Papa used to get furious with Mama, but he would remain calm when we were around—for the most part. But the room always felt different when he was like that. He wasn't yet yelling at her, but you could feel it simmering. As I got older, I could see the little signs of rage, like I saw in Felton. I thought it was normal, though, for men to be like that. Until, well, you I suppose."

Victor swallowed. "Me?"

She looked over at him with a small smile. "You hardly ever get mad at Mama and when you do, it's mild annoyance. It's nothing near the level Papa would get. You wouldn't shove her to the ground, for example."

Terror rang in his heart. "I would *never*."

"But he used to play with us," Mary said with a whisper. She rubbed her nose with the back of her hand. "I have good memories with him. I remember his hugs. I didn't realize how bad he was."

Victor could sense the internal battle Mary was having with herself over her father. An ache began to form in his heart. He had to remind himself that Winthrop was gone, had been gone for a long time, and could no longer hurt Anne. Or the children. But Winthrop would always remain their father.

"I remember my parents' fights," Victor said slowly. "I would hear them yell at each other, my mother cry over it, my father leave the house in anger or frustration. But those same people who held those negative feelings loved me, hugged me, played with me. Like your father did with you."

Mary's jaw set tight and she stared at the ground. "Until that time he hurt Freddy."

Caution snaked through Victor, and as he didn't know what to say to this, he kept quiet.

"Papa once slapped Freddy. The only time he hurt one of us. And after that, he was sent away and we only saw him a few times after with Grandpapa. Freddy and I were terrified of Papa by that point. Anyway..." Mary continued on a swallow. "Felton reminded me of Papa. And now I know that's not normal for a man." Mary sniffed. "Then Felton started talking about my money. Another thing that made me suspicious. Where was his money? Then, we left one inn and he… Well, I don't want to tell you this part."

The hairs on the back of Victor's neck raised. "Mary, if he did anything untoward, you need to tell me." He tried to keep his voice calm, but knew he wasn't wholly successful. But he couldn't help it. Mary was as close to a daughter as he would ever have and he would murder Ashby if he'd laid his hands on her in any way.

Mary looked away. "He led me into this rather desolate place." She took in a sharp inhale. "He kissed me, even though I told him to leave me alone." She paused. "It didn't go beyond that because I kneed him between the legs. To be honest, I wasn't sure it would have gone further, but I wasn't going to take my chances."

"Good lass," Victor breathed out. He rubbed his hands over his face.

"You're not going to tell Mama that part, are you?"

"I can't keep anything from her, Mary. You're her daughter."

She studied him for a moment with those innocent, dark eyes but ultimately gave in and nodded. "We then went to the place where you found me, but by then, I already knew what was going on. He wanted my money and…well, *me*, but not for marriage. I don't know if he ever even truly wanted that, but I suppose I'll never know. I'm glad I even knew what he was doing when he got all handsy! Mama made it a point to make sure Freddy and I knew all about intimacy and what it *really* meant to be an adult. If she hadn't told us about that, I probably wouldn't have realized what he'd been doing until it had been far too late. And maybe not even then."

With vividness, Victor imagined all of the different ways he could kill Ashby and get away with it. "Dukes don't go to prison," he mused aloud.

Mary looked at him with a furrowed brow. "No, they don't. Why, do you think Grandpapa will do something?"

"No. I mean me." He looked over at her and smiled.

She smiled wide. "You made a joke, Uncle Victor."

He couldn't help but let out a huff of a laugh. "Yes, I suppose I did."

"Unfortunately for you, I don't think the queen would be keen on you murdering someone and would not save you from prison for that." Mary paused and turned her whole body in Victor's direction. "So, you *do* know how to laugh. I suppose that one laugh is good enough for me."

What a curious comment. "For what?"

"Oh, nothing," she replied in a singsong voice. "Can I ask you something while I'm sozzled? I heard someone at the inn say that."

"Erm—"

"Will you and Mama ever get married? Or are you going to spend your entire life pretending you're not mad for each other? And then one day, one of you will die and the other will die right after from heartbreak?" She ended this with a romantic sigh.

Victor coughed.

"It's just…you're not *really* my uncle. And you're always around. I thought maybe something was there that you were keeping secret, I suppose."

Humiliated, Victor began to rub his forehead. "No, and honestly, I would not get your hopes up about that."

Mary's shoulders slumped. "Why not?"

Did she really feel disappointment about that? It didn't matter. "Your mother and I are good friends, Mary. That's all."

"I don't believe you."

"Why not?"

Mary twisted her mouth in thought. "You know, whenever you leave our house, she always watches you out the window."

This surprised him greatly. "She does?"

"Yes. And she doesn't do that for anyone else. I once pointed that out to her and she got quite flustered and denied it."

Victor mulled this over. "Do you think your mother holds affections for me?" Christ, he sounded daft. Hopefully, once Mary fully sobered, she would have no recollection of this conversation. Or at least, very little of it.

Mary hiccupped. "Do you mean do I think Mama is in love with you? Of course she is. I don't care how much she denies it. I'm surprised you question it—it's *so* obvious. I've been trying to push her toward you, but she's rather stubborn about it."

Victor noted Mary's slurring had lessened, along with her swaying. There was no time to wait for full sobriety, but at least she wasn't as bad as she had been when he'd first found her. Anne would have exploded if she had seen Mary in such a state. "Forget all of that," he said, pushing the brief hope away. Even if it were true that Anne loved him, she would never admit to it. "Right now, we need to get you back with your mother."

Chapter Twenty-Eight

A S SOON AS Victor left to track down Mary and Mr. Ashby, Anne waited inside the inn at which he had left her and tried to force herself to eat a bit. Neither she nor Victor had eaten much, other than a small lunch on the train, yet she could only manage a few bites.

And then she waited.

And waited.

It was horrible, the waiting. Several times, she debated going after him. But where would she find him? And what if he came back and she had left?

It was difficult, but she forced herself to stay put, even though she questioned herself constantly. She wasn't accustomed to such unwavering support. Everything, even when Bernard had been alive, had always rested on her shoulders.

Setting her chin in her hand, Anne stared down at the mass of food in front of her, not really noting what it was. She had never trusted Bernard, not even when they'd first married and he'd been on his best behavior. She'd always had the sense that he'd been up to something. At dinners, he would ignore her and pay attention to other women in attendance. It hadn't sat right with her, she'd ask him about it, he would come up with a reasonable explanation. Or he would make an offhand comment that he had a certain amount of coin on him, but then later she would discover half of it had disappeared. He would offer no explanation of where it had gone and instead, he would blame her for misremembering the amount. His explanations to her questions never sat right with her, and sometimes she'd sworn she'd been going mad. But Victor? She trusted *him* completely and without a single doubt.

It was an incredible feeling to know someone was there on whom she could rely during a difficult time. Her body and mind were nearly ready to give out from exhaustion, but Victor had taken over without a thought.

It wasn't much later after this thought that Victor appeared again, and this time with Mary in tow. Anne immediately stood up from her small table, and in her fear and worry, found the strongest emotion bubbling up was anger.

Now that Mary was here and safe, Anne could feel her face getting hot. She wanted to take Mary by her shoulders and shake some sense into her. She wanted to ask what in the world she was *thinking* by eloping in Gretna Green?

But Mary wouldn't look her in the eye and kept her gaze on the floor. And she was swaying.

Was Mary drunk?

Anne took in a deep breath and opened her mouth to give her daughter a piece of her mind.

But Victor intervened first. "It's been a long day," he said, holding Anne's gaze. "And we still don't know how we're going to overnight."

"Is she married?" Anne asked, dreading the answer.

"No. And Ashby's gone."

Anne let out a breath and clamped her mouth shut. Maybe anger wasn't the best way to approach Mary, at least at the moment. Anne closed her eyes, willing back the anger and humiliation that boiled within her. She took in a deep, calming breath. Then another. "Mary." She forced her eyes open. "Are you all right?"

Mary nodded, though her eyes remained anchored to the floor.

"Let's go. We'll talk later."

Mary's wide eyes lifted to her mother, then went to Victor, as if the young woman couldn't believe Anne had resisted tearing off her head.

After paying for Anne's henpecked meal, Victor grabbed all of the travel bags and they decided to head to the station to find out what time the next train would be leaving. It turned out to be six o'clock, which was still hours away. As they had nowhere to go and the pubs would close soon, the trio decided to return to the bench on which Victor had sat with Mary earlier. Mary lay sprawled across the bench, her head resting on one of the bags. Anne sat on the bench at her feet, and Victor sat on the ground next to Anne's end of the bench. Between short bouts of restless sleep, Anne was sure Mary was the only one getting a measurable amount of rest.

At some point, Anne gave into the fact that sleep would likely evade her, at least for a while. When she realized Victor was as awake as she was, she moved to sit on the ground beside him.

She leaned her head back against the building behind them, reeling from the day's saga. "Tell me everything." Anne let her head drop to the side to see Victor better. "And don't protect me from any detail."

And so, he told her. It took a good half an hour to go through the whole story and then answer the myriad questions she had.

The biggest question that remained, however, was: where was Felton Ashby?

"I will find him, of that, I'm confident." Victor rubbed a cheek with his palm. He was so serious, his jaw set so tight, Anne believed and trusted him wholeheartedly.

"And you will kill him too?" She made sure to say this just bright enough so he knew she was joking, but also not really.

He grinned at her, a rare sight indeed, and it made her heart soar, a brief light in the darkness. Victor's smiles and laughs were far and few between, and she basked in them when they occurred. "Unfortunately, there will be no killing," Victor said.

"But I will deal with him and this entire scandal, of that, I have no doubt."

"You promised to find Mary and did. I completely believe you will deal with him as well." Anne leaned forward briefly to eye her daughter sprawled across the bench, one arm hanging down to the ground. Mary was either asleep from exhaustion or passed out drunk—Anne couldn't say which and frankly, she didn't want to know. Bernard had spent his entire adulthood getting drunk and acting foolish. And now, his daughter was doing the same thing.

When it got out that Mary had gone to elope in Gretna Green, with a fortune hunter at that, and that the marriage hadn't taken place—even if Mary was still chaste—the family would be scandalized for generations to come. Not even the Duke of Chalworth could cover this one up. Mary wouldn't be able to make her debut next year. And perhaps not ever.

Anne had to shove this out of her mind for now. Even she could only manage to worry so much at one time.

Though it was now well into evening, the summer night air remained warm and comforting. In the silence of the now-sleepy town and the gentle swaying of the trees around them, Anne soon found her head bobbing as she tried to fight off sleep.

"Anne."

Something within Anne leapt at hearing Victor say her name in that low, deep voice. The moment reminded her of that summer storm so many years ago, when he'd pulled her out of the mud. His voice had wrapped around her name like a caress. The promise he'd made to her that he would wait for her forever if necessary, the one she had tried to forget these past few years— there was no denying anymore that it had happened. And it was now a possibility, if she wanted it.

But still the thought of tying herself to another man terrified her, and Mr. Ashby's behavior had reinforced that. Mr. Ashby had initially come off as sweet as honey, and if he had been a bit more polished and strategic, Anne might have been convinced to succumb to a brief summer liaison with the man. Never in a million years would she ever have expected him to go after her *daughter* at the same time!

Truly nauseating.

But then there was Victor.

Victor was her dearest friend, and if she'd ever had had the smallest doubt of his feelings for her, this mess had proven how much he cared for her. Not just her, either, but her children too. The fact he'd comforted both herself and Freddy upon Mary's disappearance, gone with her to chase down Mary, then taken over without a thought when it all had become too much for Anne, it really showed what kind of man he was. Yes, he was kind. Yes, he cared about her and most importantly, he cared about Mary and Freddy. He would balk at this, but he was as protective of them as if he were their father. A *good* father.

And coupling all of this with the way he'd kissed her at the masquerade, she was pretty confident it meant one thing: he loved her.

But did she love him in that way?

Victor was important to her. And if there were ever a time he was gone from her life, she wasn't sure she would be able to handle it. It would be as if a piece of her had been taken away.

Anne closed her eyes again at the thought, at the gentle, warm breeze, and emotions began to rise.

Maybe she loved Victor, too, as a woman loved a man. But assuming they weren't already married—she refused to even entertain the ridiculous idea and clung desperately to the fact that the anvil had not been dinged—could she want to marry him someday far into the future?

If they ever did *really* get married, what would happen when something went wrong? Victor may have been wonderful, but he was also human.

How would he be when he did become a duke? How would it change him? Would he grieve for his grandfather, the life he'd never had, and ease the melancholy with liquor? Would the stress of his responsibilities turn him into another monster? Bernard had been pleasant enough when he'd courted her. But when they had married and life had happened, his scoundrel habits had worsened and turned her life into a nightmare she hadn't been able to escape until he'd died.

If down the road she chose to marry Victor and he succumbed to his worries, his stressors, she would never be able to leave. Never be able to escape. If he drank too much and shouted at her, she couldn't leave. If he gambled all their money away, she couldn't leave. If he laid a hand on her, or worse?

She wouldn't be able to leave. Unless he died young, and what were the chances that would happen twice?

There was a war in her heart. Love for Victor, and fear of vulnerability to men.

Despite not meaning to cry, silent tears began to slide down her cheeks. She wiped them away, hoping Victor wouldn't notice.

"Anne," Victor's deep voice said again.

Anne looked over to him. He appeared as weary as she felt. His normally neat, black hair reflected the repeated rush of frustrated hands from a nightmare of a day. And his eyes were weary, reflecting the same exhaustion she felt.

"Yes?" Anne finally said.

Victor lifted his arm in invitation. "Come here," he said in a low voice.

Anne hesitated, surprised he would invite her into such closeness. But had he not kissed her upon the cheek and held her hand? And though he had been in disguise, had he not given her the most passionate kiss she had ever experienced in her life? Oh, to be in his embrace and rest her weary head against him! It would reflect heaven.

But that battle in her heart was still at war. *Do it. Don't do it. Do it. No, don't—you will only get hurt.*

"Please," he whispered the word.

But Anne was too tired for the battle of heart versus mind. She threw herself into the temptation and snuggled against his side.

At the feeling of his hot, hard body beneath hers, his strong arm wrapped around her, Mary safe and sound and asleep nearby, the tears slid down again.

Victor wiped them away with a thumb. "Why are you crying?"

Because I know you love me, and now I know I love you, but I'm too scared and broken to give anything a chance.

"The whole day," she replied with a small, forced laugh.

"We got Mary back, as I promised we would," he said as he lightly rubbed his hand up and down her arm.

"I know," she said, trying to still her voice. "Thank you, Victor."

"Of course."

The battle continued, but in the moment, love was winning out. Anne lifted her face to look up at him. "No, I mean, thank you. For everything. Not just today. All of it."

Victor's hand stilled and he gave her the brush of a crooked smile. "Of course. Though to be honest, I don't know what you mean, exactly."

"I, um…" Anne shifted and sat up straighter. She wasn't quite sure what she was doing. What if she told Victor about her fears? Would he understand? Would she lose his friendship?

Blast it all. She couldn't keep wondering and waiting.

"Victor," Anne said, still not sure what she was going to do. He waited with patience, so close to her in the moment. She loved the way he felt against her, and she felt so safe with him. But would it always be that way? "Something is happening between us, isn't it?"

"Yes." His green eyes flashed with surprise, but it was all he replied with. And maybe, it was all there was to say.

Anne quickly glanced at Mary to ensure the young woman was still asleep. And then Anne put her full attention on Victor. She lifted her hand to his rough cheek and held his gaze. He watched her, waiting, his green eyes ablaze with wanting.

The desire, the love she found in his eyes took her breath

away. And she tilted her mouth up to his and kissed him.

Her heart raced and it felt like everything moved slowly. But the moment her lips connected with his, all the worry of the day melted away, as if he were her remedy. Victor shifted to wrap both arms around her to pull her closer, slid his fingers up into her hair, and he turned his head to fit their mouths better together.

The moment ignited the way it had beneath the willow tree—that same fiery passion tempted her, pulled her.

Anne moved away, her breathing rapid. "Oh," she whispered.

Victor nuzzled against her hair and pressed a soft kiss against it.

"I think—I think we have something to discuss," Anne said as her heart pounded hard.

"I have been waiting a long time to hear you say that, my love," Victor whispered in her ear. "Far longer than I think I may even know."

My love. It caused her breath to catch.

"Right now, though, I think you should get some sleep. We've a long ride to London in the morning and it could be a while for the next train to Brighton. If we need to, we can stop at my home. You and I can discuss everything there."

Anne intertwined a hand with his, darted another quick glance over to Mary, and then looked back up to him. "Yes, I think that's a brilliant plan. I should probably go to Mary's side in case she wakes up. But just so you know, I do wish we were in London, in your bedroom instead." She couldn't help but giggle when his face flushed a deep red.

Chapter Twenty-Nine

ANNE SHUT THE door to Victor's guest room, in which Mary was sleeping. They had spent half the day on the train and had been able to change into fresh clothes and wash up on the train. But Mary had not been feeling well most of the trip, and the swaying of the train had prevented her from sleeping well. As it would be a few hours until the next train to Brighton, with them finally arriving at the seaside town well after the dinner hour, they were passing the time here at Victor's.

The moment Mary's head had hit the pillow in Victor's guest room, she'd fallen right into a deep sleep. Anne hadn't slept very well, either, but she also knew sleep wouldn't come until they had returned to Brighton and all of this mess was behind them. Not just the mess with Mary's near-elopement, but everything with Victor as well.

With Mary settled and no longer in need of Anne, Anne stepped out of the bedroom, peered down the hall, and fiddled with her skirt. When they had arrived, Victor had taken her aside to inform her he had sent a telegram to his solicitor during their trip. Apparently, during a rare moment on the train in which she had been asleep, they had stopped at a large station with a telegram office right on the platform. At that time, Victor had been able to send a telegram to his solicitor about the marriage conundrum. Right now, he was downstairs, awaiting a response.

It was strange. Anne wished for the news the marriage ceremony had been invalid. And yet, another part of her anticipated going downstairs to see Victor again, that warm, glowing feeling churning in her stomach knowing they would be discussing what, exactly, was happening between them.

Fear and love remained at war inside her mind and heart.

As Anne descended the stairs, willing her racing heart to calm, she wondered what she should say to Victor. Should she admit to loving him? Share her fears, and if so, would he understand? Or would he think her silly, or worse, get frustrated?

When Anne entered the parlor, she found Victor standing in front of a mirror, leaning in close to inspect his hairline. His fingers slid through his black hair, but then his entire body froze, as if he had found something. Victor's face flushed in the reflection and he swore quite loudly.

"What's the matter?" Anne asked.

Victor spun around quickly to face her and stared wide-eyed, as if embarrassed to have been caught doing…whatever it was he was doing. He cleared his throat and forced his face and stance to level out. "I believe recent events have led to my first gray hair."

"I see." Meanwhile, she'd found her first gray years ago. However, she decided it best to keep this thought to herself.

He shifted on his feet. "How is Mary?"

Anne stopped halfway across the floor and began to fiddle her hands together. "She's asleep," Anne said with a smile.

"I'm glad," he replied.

They stared at each other for a moment, as if each were unsure how to cross over.

As she was the one who'd brought up having a discussion, she forced herself to put one foot in front of the other and crossed the rest of the room to him, her heart beating faster and faster with each step.

"Now we talk," she said brightly, feeling self-conscious. She cleared her throat and smoothed her fiddling hands down over her skirt. "This summer has felt different to me. Maybe it's because you're actually with us? I don't know. But I'm glad you've been around." She paused in thought. "It has…forced me to reconcile with some things."

Victor shoved his hands into his trouser pockets and cleared his throat. "Such as?"

Anne twirled a hand in the air. "Well, we are friends, are we not?"

Victor gave a single nod.

"In fact, we are great friends. And have been for many years." She looked up at him. They had been friends long enough that she could see a difference in his appearance. The faint lines he'd once had around his eyes were deeper. In fact, his face overall had aged. But her own had changed, too, of course. Yet Victor remained as handsome as ever. He was still strong and fit, and his black hair and dourness still appealed greatly to her. She would probably feel this way decades from now, even when he grayed beyond one single hair, or lost his hair altogether.

"Remember the first day of your horse riding lessons?" she continued. "Afterward, you brought up that last time you'd been in Brighton. You know, when I chased Bernard in the rain and fell in the mud. And I denied remembering that moment when you helped me."

Victor's green eyes intensified, but he remained silent.

She looked down at her hands. "I didn't forget it. Well, not fully. I hid it away from myself for a while. But I remember it all again."

"Why did you try to forget?"

She smiled up at him but could feel hot tears stinging behind her eyes. "I was scared after Bernard died. Frankly, I'm still scared."

Victor didn't respond for a long moment, as if letting the words settle in. "We made a promise to each other that day," he finally said. "We both realized we felt greatly for each other."

"Yes." Anne closed her eyes for a moment. "Yes, we did."

"I don't think either of us, however, really realized what that meant."

Eyes still closed, she shook her head.

"And then, I told you I would wait for you as long as it took."

Anne inhaled sharply and her eyes flew open, her heart galloping at hearing these words from him once more.

There was the slightest softening of his face. "But please, I beg of you. Put me out of my misery, and let that moment be now." Victor stepped forward to close the gap between them, his face becoming etched with pain. "I will wait until the end of time, but it is torturous. I love you, Anne. I love you and life is short, and I do not wish to go much longer without you."

Anne let out a sob as Victor closed the final space between them and pulled her against him. She buried her face against his chest, gripped the front of his shirt, inhaled his scent. He smelled like *him*. It wasn't a strong soap, or expensive cologne—it was simply him and she inhaled it with greed. Victor had always been a source of comfort for her, but she could no longer fight off how much she desired him in every way.

But that fear was always lurking—even now, an ever-present shadow amongst such a beautiful moment. Victor loved her. And instead of telling him how she felt, the fear of it overshadowed everything.

Anne sniffed and pulled her head back to look up while he slowly rubbed her back, leaving tingling heat beneath his touch. "But I'm so scared. I'm a broken woman, Victor. I'm a bag of shattered glass that will never fully be put back together."

Victor cradled her face in his hands. His large hands were rough with the calluses of a lifetime of hard work. "What are you afraid of?"

She searched his intense, green eyes and found nothing there but love and patience. Wasn't that what she wanted? "I'm scared something will happen in your life that will cause you to turn away from me, to change. I'm scared one day, you'll be a different person than you are now. I'm scared one day, you'll succumb to liquor, or some other ruinous temptation, that so many men suffer from. I'm scared I'll be trapped again, like I was with Bernard. I'm scared and I don't know how to escape it."

The corners of Victor's mouth turned down, and she braced herself for a scoff.

But no scoff came. "What if we *are* married, Anne? What if we receive a note from the solicitor confirming it? What then?"

Anne took in a shaky breath. "Is that what you want in the end, to be married to me?"

For a long while, Victor was quiet, gently sweeping his thumb over her cheek as he watched the movement, as if contemplating how to respond. "Yes, I suppose I do. I never thought I would want that in my life, but then I met you. I love you, Anne. I want to be with you, and I want to experience life with you. I think the question that should be asked is, why *wouldn't* I want to be married to you?"

"But what would I do if you turn into a scoundrel?" She spoke desperately, not considering how these words would affect him. "What if you became another Bernard?"

Victor's face darkened as he pulled his hands away from her face. "I would never treat you the way that blasted idiot treated you."

Panic started to rise. How could he be so certain? "I wouldn't be able leave you, though, if you did. You do realize that? The scandal that arose when I left Bernard was horrific on my nerves. And even if we separated, what would keep you from following me, coming after me? No one could stop you. And no one knows what the future holds. *No one.*"

"Why are you already talking about leaving me?" Victor's voice cracked. "I just told you I love you, Anne, multiple times. And you haven't responded in kind. How am I supposed to interpret that?"

Anne stilled upon this realization. To herself, she had admitted her love for him. But could she tell him she felt that way?

She tried to form the words but couldn't. Was it worth the risk?

Victor got down to his knees and gripped her hands in his as he tilted his face up. "Anne. Please."

He was begging her, begging her to love him, too.

And she did. But she couldn't bring herself to say it. She just could not accept the risk love put upon her. However, this did remind her of her rules for seaside romance. Did all of the rules apply to Victor?

"Do you ever get drunk, Victor?"

His eyebrows furrowed, but he remained kneeled at her feet. "Have you ever known me to be drunk?"

Her lips pressed in a tight line. She did not. "When *was* the last time you were drunk?"

"I..." He looked off to the side. "In truth, it was the other night, but that was a fluke. Otherwise, I never—"

"I see." An excuse. She had heard many of them in her life. "Do you think you would be more prone to smiling and laughing if we were married?"

Victor stammered. "You-You think I should laugh more? Anne, while you may win a laugh or smile from me on occasion, I have never been and will never be a jovial man."

She inhaled through her nose. That was true, and she supposed she couldn't count that one against him. "What about gambling? I know you used to place wagers on fights when Dantes was a pugilist. But do you have a secret gambling habit?"

Victor paled at this. "Why all the questions?"

A sick feeling began to rise up her throat. "Are you unable to answer? I don't think it would surprise you to learn these questions are rooted in my experience with Bernard."

Victor shut his eyes tightly and took in a deep breath. "I...I often place wagers on horse races. But you must understand—"

"You often place wagers on horses?" Anne frowned deeply at this. "That was Bernard's favorite way of wasting our money! Curious that you've *never* mentioned this to me before."

"Yes, but—"

"Were you keeping it a secret?"

"No!"

"How long have you been doing that? Is it a newly acquired interest of yours?" She hoped with all hope that it was. For she could simply not tolerate a man who wasted money on wagers, and she would simply beg him to not make it a favorite pastime of his if it were new. On one hand, he didn't owe her anything. He didn't owe telling her he was a horse racing addict, or owe it to her to give it up. But on the other hand, they were so open with each other about everything. All in all, it was quite concerning that he was being evasive during this key moment between them.

Victor bowed his head as if feeling defeated. "I've been doing it for nearly twenty years."

She couldn't help it. She gasped and her hand flew up to her heart.

His mouth pressed into a tight line as he considered what to say. "It isn't what it sounds like. You must trust me on that."

"You are everything to me," she said on a sob, her heart shattering as the words came out. "But I cannot say what you wish me to. Not after all of that."

Victor's grip on her hands tightened, as if she were pulling away and he refused to let her go. "Blast it all, Anne. Why not?"

She wanted to fall to the floor with him. She wanted to be in his embrace. She wanted to hold him, to love him, to kiss him whenever she wished, to stay up all night with him. That was what she wanted right now. But thinking about forever, intertwined legally? It didn't lift warmth within her as it should have. It terrified her.

Anne lowered herself down to be level with him. She attempted a smile, but it was too shaky. "What if we take a few steps back? I went into this summer seeking out a brief, silly liaison. I wanted companionship, nothing permanent that could put me at risk. We could be lovers, Victor, but that's all I'm willing to do. If we are married—well, I won't be a good wife for you. I cannot commit myself to the role. You must understand that."

Victor's face, his eyes, immediately shuttered. That raw desperation as he'd begged on his knees for her to love him, it wiped from his face.

The sudden and severe change made her feel sick, as if this went against nature itself.

Victor rose to his feet and looked down at her still on the ground. "That's what you want from me? A *brief liaison*? I cannot agree to such an arrangement."

Anne clambered up to her feet. "Why not? Do I not appeal to you?"

"*Of course* you appeal to me," he said in a sharp voice. "But while you have your own fears, I have mine as well."

Anne frowned. What could he possibly be afraid of? "What is your fear?"

"Children." The word came down like a gavel.

"Victor, there are ways to prevent that—"

"No. You don't seem to understand. There is no way to completely prevent it from happening. I went through hell keeping my brothers safe when we were younger. I cannot handle the nerves of being responsible for my own flesh and blood. I may be in a better place now, but the fear of losing everything, of going without, will haunt me until my last breath."

Anne shook her head. "Then what did you do before?"

Victor clenched his jaw but didn't respond.

Anne lifted an eyebrow. "Victor, what have you done before with other women if you're so worried about it? We could always do that, whatever it was."

His jaw still set tightly, he looked over at the empty fireplace and his eyes seemed to glimmer with shame.

Suddenly, it hit Anne. Her mouth fell open before she quickly regained control of it. "You've never been with a woman. You're inexperienced."

He rubbed a hand over his black beard and went over to the fireplace, his back toward her. He pressed a hand to the mantel and leaned into it. "Do not ever say that to me again."

It shouldn't have, she knew it shouldn't have, but for some reason, this unexpected revelation only made her fall in love with him more. She didn't think it was embarrassing, or bad, or anything to be ashamed of, like he seemed to think. "Victor—"

His voice darkened. "If it's passion you seek, you should find it someone else."

Sick despair began to rise. "But—"

"Your Phantom, your secret admirer—go chase after him instead." Victor turned his face so she couldn't see it. "You said you shared passion with *him*. Go seek him out, then."

Anne growled—growled!—with frustration. "That was *you*, you big idiot!"

Victor spun around, his face stark white and his eyes as wide as saucers.

She stormed up to him. Now she was mad. *"You're* the Phantom. *You're* my secret admirer. Not someone else!"

Victor inhaled sharply through his nose. "I don't know what you're talking about."

She scoffed. "So that's how it's going to be? You follow me around all summer, you tempt me beneath the willow tree, kiss me as if you were about to take me to bed, then skip off because I don't like gambling?"

"How?" Victor asked in a whisper. He pulled away from the mantel. "How did you know it was me?"

Anne rolled her eyes. "Wearing a mask and costume can only hide your identity for so long, Victor. I know you far too well for that."

He swallowed. "How long have you known?"

"I briefly suspected you in the beginning but brushed it off. Throughout the summer, my suspicion would come and go, but I was never fully sure until we were under the willow tree."

Victor's face reddened and he looked away.

"I knew it was you when we did that," she said gently. It was clear this was an uncomfortable subject for him. "I kissed you knowing it was you, Victor. I lay on the ground with you, knowing it was you."

He didn't respond.

"You drew those beautiful pictures for me. I didn't even know you could draw."

"No one knows," he replied, still unable to look her in the eye.

"But you're so incredibly talented. Why not?"

He shrugged one shoulder. "It started out as something to do in my spare time. And then as I got better at it, I didn't want anyone to see what I had created. It was only for me, I suppose. Until I shared it with you."

"Oh, Victor." Anne sighed and took a cautious step toward him.

But he moved away.

Despite the fact that it was a small movement, it felt as if the ground beneath them had shifted. They had come together tonight to discuss what, exactly, was happening between them. And she had to make sure he fully understood she would not take on the role of his wife if they were, in fact, married. But this moment was supposed to move them forward to something, not pull them apart, as it seemed to be doing.

And with the way he had put walls up around him, it felt more like she was speaking to a stranger.

"Don't you want to share more with me?" she asked. "You felt that passion between us that night—I know you did. I felt it, too. It was as if we were on fire. I've never wanted, *needed*, so badly in my life before. Don't you want to be with me?"

Victor straightened away from the mantel and cleared his throat. "We are seeking two different things, Anne. You wish for a few tumbles in the sheets, which is something I cannot offer you. I wish us to love each other until our dying days, to spend our life together whether or not we've already married, but you cannot offer that to me. I suppose, then, there is no use in furthering this discussion, as it only complicates the matter and hurts feelings. You could be my wife on paper, but you will never truly be that to me."

The man was maddening! What, so he was just going to shut her out, then? "So, you want to be married me, but you'd never go to bed with me, your wife? Is that what you're saying? That's the most ridiculous thing I've ever heard you say." She didn't care to hear what his response would be to this, so instead of waiting for one, she stormed out of the room.

Chapter Thirty

T HERE WAS THE matter of one Mr. Felton Ashby that had to be dealt with and Victor suspected he knew where the cad was hiding.

Unable to sleep last night on the bench, or even this morning on the train, Victor had instead spent those hours trying to figure out where the idiot would have been. At first, he wondered if Ashby had hidden somewhere in Gretna Green, apparently with little coin. However, the man was far too pampered to allow himself to get stuck in a small, rural Scottish village and Victor suspected the man would have had no problem scamming his way onto one of the trains.

Victor supposed Felton had gone back to Brighton, but considering both his and Mary's families were there, there was no chance of that. Perhaps he would instead have been hiding in a London hotel, but if he hadn't had enough coin for an inn in a small village in Scotland, then he certainly wouldn't have had the coin for a hotel in London. The man was too prim to settle for anything cheap and seedy in the East End. It was possible he could be at one of the gentlemen's clubs, but few nobs remained in London this time of year. Anyone still here would be quite interested in why anyone else remained and would pester Ashby about it too much. There was a fleeting chance he was at Bron's gaming hell, but Bron didn't seem to know him well and wouldn't stick his neck out for a near stranger. Especially one Victor was going after.

That left only one possibility: the Ashby townhome. While this seemed like the obvious choice, it wasn't a clear winner, either. The townhome would be closed up for the summer, the furniture covered and bedding removed.

Once Victor had figured out that, he determined all the ways he could beat Ashby into a pulp. *That* helped his horrendous mood.

Victor left after his row with Anne. He couldn't face her after humiliating himself so terribly. She wanted a liaison—he wanted a lifetime. She would run off if they were married, never be around him again. She had made that clear enough. No use in getting emotional over it.

It took a visit to the postmaster, but, a little over an hour after leaving his house, Victor found the Ashbys' London residence. Fortunately, they still had some time before the Brighton train— enough so he could take as long as he wished with Felton.

Victor rang and waited.

He shoved his hands into his trouser pockets and forced a loose stance despite the roiling emotions in his head and heart. Anne may not have loved him, but he would always love her. And he would always love her children.

Unfortunately, they couldn't remain friends after what had happened, especially if they were married. Remain friends with his wife, who refused to be in the same house as him? He wasn't that pathetic.

He *was* foolish. Friendship couldn't weather unrequited love! Now too much had happened between them and too many emotions were entangled to pull apart. But there was one last task that remained before he would leave Anne and her children in his past.

Dealing with the blasted idiot Ashby.

Ashby's behavior made no sense. If Ashby were a halfway decent man, he could have landed Anne and had all the tumbles he'd ever want for the rest of his life. All the coin he could ever want. He was too focused on satisfying his wants immediately. If he had exhibited even a small bit of patience and played his hand correctly, he could have had it all. And forever. By being idiotic and greedy, Ashby had lost something that could have been amazing.

The idiot had been so close to having the life Victor wanted.

Victor paused in his thoughts. *Was* that the life Victor wanted? Anne had questioned him about it. How could he love her, be married to her, but deny any affection between them?

How could he not want that with her? He didn't want it with anyone else—and never would. But Anne was different to him, wasn't she?

She was right. It didn't make sense.

But it didn't matter, he supposed. It wasn't a conundrum that would ever need to be solved.

He should have been relieved by this. There would remain no risk of a child, no obsessive worry about losing everything and them ending up like he had. Yet he curiously wasn't relieved in the least.

A rough-looking housekeeper answered the door, appearing as if she were still in her cups from the night before. Her mousy-brown hair was a nest of a mess, her gray uniform wrinkled and crooked. And she positively reeked of sour liquor. Perhaps this was the best the Ashbys could afford. "Yes?" she asked as she tried to straighten out her appearance.

"Ashby," was all Victor could manage to get out. Just hearing that name stirred up the emotions in him even further. "Felton."

"He's not here," the housekeeper said. But she looked away as she said this.

Instead of leaving as polite society dictated he should have, Victor barreled past the woman. If Ashby were here, it would be just him and the house staff. As the housekeeper scolded him and tried to drag him back out the door—she couldn't even get him to falter on his feet—Victor cupped a hand around his mouth.

"Ashby! You are a dead man!"

Upstairs, it sounded like someone had fallen out of bed and run across the floor.

Victor began to climb the stairs two steps at a time while the housekeeper followed him. "Sir!" she shouted. "Sir, please, you can't go up there!"

But he ignored her. The first door he found, he flung open. Nothing was inside, other than covered furniture and threadbare beds.

Same for the second room. And the third.

The fourth room, however, had a bed with unmade bedding, as if someone had slept in it last night.

Victor stepped inside and looked around the room. There was no one in here. A window was open, though, and Victor crossed the room to peer out of it.

And then he heard the chaos behind him.

Victor turned around right as Ashby emerged from his hiding place—beneath the bed—and promptly ran out into the hallway, a loud crash of breaking glass following.

Naturally, Victor went after him, leaping over a fallen and shattered vase.

The house shook as if there were a stampede of elephants in its halls. A half-naked Ashby fled down the stairs, as if running for his life—and in a sense, he was—while Victor hunted him down.

Ashby ended up at the back door—but it was locked. The cad jiggled the handle, looked back over his shoulder, and squealed upon seeing Victor.

As Victor approached, Ashby apparently thought he could dodge past the angry man. He nearly succeeded, but Victor quickly caught the cad and threw him against the wall, causing the younger man's spectacles to become crooked.

Ashby, panting hard, put his hands up in surrender.

"I think we need to have a little chat, don't you?" Victor growled and got so close to Ashby's face, their noses nearly touched.

Ashby whimpered. "W-W-What did you have in mind?"

Victor grinned but knew well how terrifying it looked. Ashby gulped. "Let's talk about Lady Mary, hmm?"

Ashby straightened his spectacles. "I'm sorry. Could you remind me who that is again?"

One of the only good outcomes from living in Whitechapel as a young lad was that Victor had learned how to size other men up almost immediately. It had been crucial for survival. Otherwise, you could have been dead or maimed before uttering, "God save the queen!"

And though he'd had Ashby pegged immediately upon meeting him and knew the cad was a coward despite his size, it wasn't until now that Victor realized how much he had let this idiot get to him. Victor's jealousy over the attention Ashby had given Anne had made the cad seem more powerful than he really had been.

Victor was a McNab. He was bigger, stronger, better. He would someday be a duke. He had more money, and even superior looks, if he were being honest with himself.

Ashby was *nothing* compared to Victor.

Victor wouldn't hit the man. Not because he didn't want to, but because he knew it wouldn't need to come to that. The best outcome for all of this, for everyone involved, didn't require flying fists. He was sure Ashby would be well in agreement. Though Victor would still need to be threatening to make a point.

Victor wound a huge fist back and Ashby covered his face. "All right! All right." When nothing happened, he peeked between his fingers.

"Do we need to have a long discussion about how you terrorized the people I love more than my own life?"

Ashby began shaking like a scared pup. "No. Just go on with it and hit me."

Victor kept his fist wound back. "Did you lay a hand on Lady Mary?"

"No!"

"Ashby, I swear to Christ—"

"I didn't! On my own life, I promise I didn't. She…She kicked me in the bollocks when I tried. A man doesn't come back from that."

Victor had to resist a snort. "And that's when you left?"

Ashby's eyes darted to the fist, still at the ready. "It's about when I gave up. I realized it was pointless and stupid."

"So you left her behind."

Ashby was quiet for a moment but then dropped his hands from his face. "It's when I realized I had made a rather bad mistake and needed to quit while I was ahead. What was I going to do, take her back to Brighton with me?"

Victor lowered his fist but continued to block Ashby. "You do realize it's not over, though, right? Lady Litchfield may not do anything, but I have no problem making up for that ten times over."

Ashby let out a nervous laugh. "What do you mean? Lady Mary remains unmarried, unspoiled by men. Everything is fine!"

"No," Victor growled out. "Everything is *not* fine. This scandal will ruin her life and my family's lives when it gets out."

"Your family?" Ashby's face twisted in confusion.

He had misspoken. Why in the blazes would he refer to Anne and the children as his family? Christ, he *really* needed sleep. "Lady Mary will not be able to debut next year. Despite her station, she will likely not find any gentleman willing to marry her after this mess you caused. She ran away to elope in Gretna Green, Ashby, and didn't end up marrying! That isn't a silly trip to the carnival—it's practically a death sentence with the repercussions it will have over her entire life."

Ashby straightened his back and put his hand over his heart. "I won't tell a soul."

"That's a load, and you know it." Victor was getting to the best part. Ashby's mother knew the ramifications of her son's idiotic escapade. This all could simply be an unspoken embarrassment kept secret between the two families. But Ashby was a boaster. And there was no chance he would keep it to himself, even if he did at first. He would absolutely go around and lie that he had sullied Lady Mary then left her behind. It wasn't a risk Victor was willing to take. "Here's what you're going to do."

"Yes?" Ashby whispered.

"You are going to go pack your bags and head to America."

Ashby's eyes went wide. "I beg your pardon!"

"You heard me." Victor growled again, relishing in the flicker of fear in the cad's eyes. "You are going to get on the first ship that will take you across the pond. Multiple ships head that way each day. Go to the docks, buy a ticket, send me the bill and I'll pay you back if that gets you over there. But you're leaving English soil forever, and you'll die on American land."

Ashby laughed cockily. "You can't make me do that."

"Do you know who my grandfather is, Ashby?"

The cad furrowed his brow as if searching his memory. "No?"

"The Duke of Invermark. His only son, my father, is dead. I am next in line and he is currently on his death bed." That last bit was a lie but also could be argued to be true in a sense. "Once the title passes on to me, I can do anything. I could keep you locked up in my cellar like a prisoner if I so wished. Once I release you, you could go and tell whomever you want to about it. I would simply deny it. No one would believe you over me."

Ashby swallowed and went pale. "B-But I've never heard anyone call you 'Lord Victor'?"

"I don't give a fig about titles. You are, of course, welcome to go research the claim yourself—however, the clock is ticking and I don't have time to spare. If you leave today, we will never speak to or see each other again. But if what you did to Lady Mary ever gets out, I will hunt you down, even if I must go to the Wild West, even if you're on the other side of the world, and I will make sure you regret it."

Ashby looked off to the side as if contemplating the position he was in and then cleared his throat. "Right. Very well, then. I suppose I should pack up."

"And write a letter to your mother."

Ashby grimaced. "Of course."

"Admitting full fault, denying you touched her in any way, and asking it never be discussed again."

Ashby didn't respond for a moment, but when Victor bared his teeth, the cad yelped and immediately agreed.

With that business taken care of, and once convinced Ashby would genuinely comply—it did take a bit of coin to convince him, unfortunately—Victor left to return to his home to prepare for the departure to Brighton. He would not be staying there for the remainder of the summer, however, and had to break the news to Anne and Mary. Upon stepping through the front door, he could hear loud conversation of the women somewhere in the house. He stopped to listen, to get a feel of how they were faring this morning. But when he heard laughter, his chest filled with warmth. It was odd to walk into his home to find it filled with loud conversation and laughter. Normally, he was greeted with silence, aside from the odd shuffle or knock from a servant. But it was strangely…pleasant.

Immediately, he remembered the reality of his situation: he was moments away from putting Anne in his past. It would put a wedge between him and the rest of the family, especially if their marriage did end up legitimate, but he wouldn't be able to see Anne again, even in half measures. All holidays, alone. All dinners, alone. There would be no more antics for him to read in Freddy's letters home. No more girlish giggling between Mary and her mother. No more *Anne*. His confidant, his truest friend— blast it all, the woman he loved would be gone. Her smile, her voice, her honeysuckle scent, those pale-blue eyes he could pick out in pub crowd from across the room… It would all be gone.

Anne would become another ghost from his past.

The lightness he had just felt was quickly replaced by the clouds that always seemed to shadow him. As Victor followed the laughter, his heart began to race with nerves at seeing Anne again after their emotional argument earlier.

He found the pair in the dining room, and they appeared to have recently finished eating.

Both Anne and Mary froze upon his appearance. Would Anne have told Mary what had happened?

Feeling awkward, he stood in the doorway and cleared his throat. "Felton Ashby will no longer be a problem."

Mary perked up. "Did you kill him and throw him into the Thames?"

Victor's mouth quirked. "Unfortunately, no. But I have convinced him that the best course of action is that he leave for America today and never return. That our family would not tolerate ever seeing him again if he dared show his face here again."

"*Our* family?" Anne said with an arched, blonde eyebrow.

Victor stammered. He had done it again. "Said for clarity only."

Anne and Mary looked at each other. "So that's it? It's over?" Anne asked.

"It's over."

Mary put a hand to her mouth. "I'm not going to be the scandal of the decade? I can still debut next year?"

He bowed his head. "Yes."

Mary stilled for the slightest of moments but promptly flew out of her seat, over to Victor, and placed a kiss on his cheek. "Thank you, Uncle Victor." She smiled up at him with misty eyes. "I don't know what else to say, as that hardly conveys how thankful I truly am."

"You don't need to say anything else." Really, he didn't need Mary emotional now, too.

Mary looked over her shoulder at Anne. "Good idea. I'll leave you two to talk, then." With one loud giggle, Mary hurried out of the room before anyone could protest.

So, she *did* have some idea of what had happened. Lovely.

Victor, now feeling even more uncomfortable, looked at

Anne and then her plate. "I hope the food was to your liking?"

"It was," she said, sounding a bit guarded. "Did you enjoy it as well?"

"I haven't eaten yet."

Normally, Anne would have had something to say about this but this time kept any comments to herself. "Thank you. For what you did with Mr. Ashby."

"I had to do something." *Before saying goodbye.*

She shook her head. "But you didn't."

"I did, but let's not argue over it." An empty place setting remained—his—but he remained standing, too nervous to sit. He shifted on his feet. "The important thing is Mary has learned her lesson, I believe, and Ashby will never be an issue again. It's in his mother and brothers' interests as well to not let the scandal get out, if Mrs. Ashby wants her other sons to marry well."

"What, exactly, did you say to him to get him to leave for America?" Anne cocked her head.

Victor slowly inhaled through his nose. "A little of this, a little of that. Flexed some muscle, made some threats."

Anne gave him a small smile. "Good work. I'm assuming you had to pay him off as well?"

Victor looked down. "Unfortunately, I think that was his biggest motivator. That and finding out I would be the Duke of Invermark someday."

"I will pay you back. It's the least I can do."

"No. And I will not budge on that."

Anne studied him for a moment before looking down at her plate. "Look, Victor, about earlier."

"There's nothing to say. You and I want two different things, and there's nothing more to it."

Anne pressed her lips together tightly. She knew he was right.

"I'm very sorry for the argument, though. And I wish you saw it my way of course. But you don't."

"I'm sorry."

Victor's throat became tight. Hearing this from her, it was

like the gavel falling. She'd said it so easily.

Anne lifted her head. "May I ask you something?"

"Of course."

"Why the whole 'secret admirer' bit? Why did you hide your feelings for me and not just come out with it? The uncomfortable air between us, I think, would have been avoided if we'd started off with an honest conversation."

Victor was quiet a moment as he considered the question. "Both Mary and Vivian told me you were hoping to find companionship this summer."

Anne pulled back a bit. "They did?"

"Yes. I figured, since you were open to that, perhaps it would be a good time to finally approach you about…us, I suppose. This would be the summer to finally determine if we could have a future together. You would have panicked if I were straightforward about my affection for you. In fact, I had to be straightforward with myself first. It took time for me to accept I had affections for you, and much longer for me to accept that I…I love you."

He swallowed and continued when she didn't say anything. "And if I struggled with it, I knew you would have been completely against the idea right away and denied me immediately without even a second of consideration. Maybe I didn't go about it the right way. I don't know. If I went to you first as a secret admirer, as 'the Phantom,' as you called me, perhaps you would develop an affection for me as myself without knowing my face."

Was that really the best way to explain it? He shut his eyes tightly. "It sounds mad, I know, but I showed my true self to you as the Phantom. I will always be in the shadows, Anne, like I was as the Phantom. I am utter rubbish with words, so I talked to you through those drawings."

Anne looked down, as if feeling ashamed.

"Next step, I came to you in person at the masquerade with my face covered, and we felt that draw to each other. We—" He cut it off, as he was veering back to their earlier argument. He rubbed a hand over his jaw to re-center himself. "All I wanted to find out this summer was if you could love me, too, if you could fall for the most honest form of *me* without our friendship getting in the way."

Anne lifted her head to stare at the empty chair across from her and was quiet a long while. Torturously long. Contemplating something, he supposed. "You put that much thought into it? Into me? You strategized over months."

"Years." He whispered the correction.

She looked at him with wide, blue eyes. "Years," she repeated. And she rose from her chair to stand behind it but didn't get any closer to him. "Oh, Victor, how could I have not seen?"

He gave her a small smile but hardly felt any happiness. "I told you the truth that day, all those years ago, that I would wait for you." The smile faded. "Maybe I approached you too soon. Maybe it never could be. But what's done is done." Tension pulled in his face. "Are you ready to leave soon?"

Anne blinked several times. "Leave? Oh. Yes. Brighton. Mary and I don't really have much, so we're ready when you are."

"Anne…"

"Yes, Victor?"

With force, he said what he'd never wanted to hear himself say. "Upon our return, I'll be grabbing my belongings and coming back to London. I cannot be there anymore. Unfortunately, I do not have faith our friendship will survive this. I still have not heard back from my solicitor, so if you don't mind, we will have to work out the details of our marriage at a later date if it turns out the ceremony was legitimate." He was desperately sure it wasn't, but best to plan ahead anyway.

She let out a small gasp and took a step toward him. "But, Victor—"

Unable to stomach any of this further, he put a hand up. "Please. I simply cannot do it. I cannot continue on as if everything is the same. As much as it pains me, I cannot have you in my life any longer."

Anne's hand flew up to her mouth and her eyes started to well.

And with it, his heart shattered.

"Victor, I—" Her voice cracked. But before she could continue, the housekeeper, a cheery middle-aged woman with round cheeks, entered the room. Anne turned away and presumably swiped at her eyes while no one could see.

"Mr. McNab." His housekeeper looked up at him with a small smile, blissfully unaware of the doom settling over the room. "Two envelopes were dropped off for you."

Victor frowned deeply. Though he was expecting to hear from his solicitor, who else would send him correspondence here? Almost everyone knew he was on holiday. Even Keer, who had been sending his weekly uneventful updates to Brighton, didn't know Victor was in town for a short time.

Still reeling from the end of his friendship with Anne, Victor reached out and grabbed the white envelopes. The first one was from his solicitor, as expected. As the housekeeper left the room, he stared down at the face of the envelope.

Were Victor and Anne husband and wife or not? It seemed almost impossible, and he knew he shouldn't have felt this, but there was a glimmer of hope that maybe they were. Maybe Anne could still be in his life.

This was a stupid thought, as she was clear that she didn't want to the ceremony to have been legitimate. But a man could dream, couldn't he?

"Do you want me to open it?" Anne asked in a gentle voice.

"No." Though he kept a calm air about him, his hands were shaking as he ripped open the envelope. "It's from the solicitor."

As he pulled out the piece of paper that could potentially upend the rest of his life, he tossed the empty envelope and the other unopened envelope over to the table.

Victor read through the solicitor's response and promptly dropped it to the floor.

Chapter Thirty-One

ANNE WATCHED VICTOR fumble with the letter.

There was a sick, roiling feeling in her stomach. She was moments away from knowing if she had the unfortunate luck of being in a second marriage, one she would have to separate from immediately. How humiliating, especially since Victor admitted he wanted to marry her if they weren't already! But maybe, maybe they weren't actually married and she was worrying about nothing?

Oh, who was she kidding? They *had* gone through the ceremony. There was no chance the ding had to be a part of it. What other marriage ceremony required a ding? None of them did, but they were all legitimate ways to marry.

While waiting for the confirmation to be read to her, Anne couldn't help but compare Victor to Bernard with such a future looming over her. Marriage to Bernard had been a prison. A gilded prison. Yes, she and her parents had managed to snag a marquess, a future duke, for her. It had elevated her station, and it had brought her Mary and Freddy. And of course, Bernard's sister and father, whom Anne adored. But it had been a prison for her as well. Years of mental anguish, constantly wondering where he'd been, or where he *really* had been if he'd told her where he would be. He would come home hours, days, after his expected time and that had sent her into fits. Never had he explained where he had been, laughing at her if she'd asked. All she'd had had been her imagination, and that imagination would run wild until she'd vomited, pulled out her hair, or locked herself in her room to scream until she'd passed out.

It had been years of hell.

But Victor was nothing like Bernard. *Nothing.*

Aside from both being tall and both having dark hair, the two men couldn't have been any more different.

She didn't flinch when Victor reached out to her. She didn't cry after he touched her, and unlike with Bernard, she actually *wanted* more of Victor's touch.

Victor had, to her great surprise, never lain with a woman, whereas Bernard would lay with whomever was convenient in the moment. Anne would be the only woman Victor would ever love, ever touch, in his entire life if she allowed it. That seemed to embarrass him, yet it only endeared her to him more. Logically, she knew he would never stray from her. But his lack of experience was solid proof he wasn't a scoundrel, something she so desperately needed.

That wasn't all that made him different from Bernard, though.

The days she didn't see Victor, she missed him and couldn't wait to see him again. She wasn't choked by the sense of doom like she had been with Bernard. The days she saw Victor were full of sunshine and she went to bed those nights smiling. Victor listened to her when she talked—he didn't brush her words aside or ignore her. He never laughed at her. He wouldn't dare, wouldn't even consider it, even if he had been a man who laughed often.

Victor knew what it was like to have to be responsible. He had a business, and he had to watch over his brothers. He'd raised them for a few years, but she knew well enough that even when they'd all gone their own ways in life, Victor had never stopped worrying about them.

Just like she would never stop worrying about Mary and

Freddy, whom Victor practically treated like his own.

Victor was a good man. Why was she so afraid to be married to him?

If all went well, Mary would have her own husband in a few years. Freddy would not be home like Mary has been until he was done with university. And then, he would marry and have a family of his own. Their home would become his, and Anne would feel like an intruder if she remained there.

What would her life look like once her children had begun their own lives?

She had no idea what that would be like. But she could visualize Victor. He would be there with her, if she wanted him to be.

No, Victor and Bernard were nothing alike.

Because Victor loved her, whereas Bernard hadn't.

And Anne loved Victor.

And maybe marriage could be terrifying if the husband was a scoundrel. But if he weren't, it could be wonderful, right?

What did she want her life to look like when her children began their own lives? She wouldn't intrude on Freddy, even if he offered her space to stay put, as she could imagine his future wife would not be happy with that, but did she really want to be alone until the day she died?

No.

She wanted Victor.

Anne took a sharp inhale at the realization that yes, she loved Victor. And yes, she wanted to spend the rest of her life with him. Was it terrifying? Of course, and there was nothing she could do to change that. But at the same time, Victor wasn't a scoundrel. She had always trusted him. Why should that change? And if for some reason he *did* turn into a nightmare of a husband, which would have already happened with the trauma he'd experienced in his life, she would simply go live somewhere without him. He would be the Duke of Invermark someday, after all, and there would be plenty of property she could live in if it came to that. It would create gossip, but she had already planned to separate from him if it turned out their marriage ceremony was legitimate.

What was holding her back, then? Even having a plan to escape, though it would likely never be needed, helped her immensely.

Though his surprise gambling was a sticking point, and something they would need to have an honest conversation about, she knew for a fact that Victor was not in dire finances, which meant gambling didn't affect him the way it had affected Bernard.

Though there would always be difficulties in life, she would have those with or without a husband at her side. And while it was true she didn't want some unknown husband beside her, she did want Victor there. Maybe his ending of their friendship had been the slap in the face she'd needed. She simply could not comprehend living without him in her life. It was impossible. She couldn't go through the rest of her life without him. She needed him. She wanted him.

For too long, she'd taken advantage of the fact that he was always there. All this time, all these years, they had loved each other deeply. But her trauma from her previous marriage had colored her vision too dark for too long and she hadn't seen it until now. Victor had patiently waited for her all this time. The least she could do was take a chance on him, take a leap of faith.

Yes. Yes, she *did* want to be married to Victor.

Upon this realization, she had to bite the inside of her cheek to keep from smiling or spewing a string of nonsense that would go against everything she had previously said about her thoughts of marriage.

Anne returned to the present moment and calmly watched Victor read through the note. The poor man looked exhausted. His black beard had grown out more than he liked, his black hair was messy, and even though he had changed into fresh clothes earlier, they were already rumpled. The lines around his eyes were now coupled with dark circles.

Poor thing. She would have to do something to relieve his stress once they returned to Brighton. Being the only one to show him how love translated in the bedroom sent a shiver up her spine. He didn't know it yet, but their evening was already planned out. It would be long and sensual and Victor wouldn't even know what hit him.

Oh, she couldn't wait.

Victor dropped the letter and stared at her with that intense, green gaze.

It caught her breath. "What did he say?" she asked.

Victor stared at her for a few more seconds, blinked, and then picked up the letter. He didn't say a word, shoved the letter at her, and looked off into the distance.

Anne took it and read.

Mr. McNab,

Quite a curious experience you and Lady Litchfield have been through. I can confirm that the blacksmith's ding does not determine if you are married or not. What does determine it above all is her consent in the marriage. A marriage, whether in England or Scotland, can only be made between two willing parties. Since she was not willing, you are not married.

Sincerely,
Peabody Hickinbottom
Solicitor at your service

Anne was stunned—and it felt as if the world around her was starting to collapse.

But this was what she had wanted. It was what she'd asked for.

Anne looked up at Victor, not caring if he could see her thoughts, see the horror in her face.

"There. I know you are satisfied with this conclusion," Victor said. He wouldn't look at her. But the pain etched in his face was obvious.

"Victor, please." She stepped toward him and placed a gentle hand on his arm.

He ripped it away and took a few steps back.

She clasped her hands together. "I know that wasn't what you wished to hear, but maybe—"

"I don't care," Victor said. "I don't care for your platitudes right now. I don't care for your words of comfort. I'm glad you are relieved. I would never wish you to be married to me against your will. But for Christ's sake, can I not be upset for one blasted minute?" He hissed the last words through his teeth.

Her heart broke at his distress. All she wanted was to comfort him, to make him feel better. But she had caused this.

Why, oh why, had she had to have her face shoved into a marriage, then pulled back out right before she'd drowned, simply to discover that actually, she did want Victor now and forever?

"Victor—"

"No." He turned his back to her and then, seemingly remembering he had one other letter, picked it up. He opened it, read it, and started laughing.

But it wasn't a pleasant laugh. It was almost maniacal. The blood drained from Anne's face.

Victor wiped a tear of laughter from his eye. "Fergus has died." He laughed again. "He's dead. My grandfather is dead. My grandmother didn't know I went to Brighton—that's why she wrote me here. Just so happened he died peacefully in his sleep three days ago." He laughed more. "He's already buried! He didn't want us there for the funeral!" Victor flung his hands out wide to his sides.

Anne stood in place feeling very small. It seemed as if everything that Victor had shouldered throughout his life had finally caused him to snap. He looked and sounded utterly mad.

Victor let out a long sigh and then started laughing again. Hard. He had to bend over and put his hands on his knees. "Do you—Do you know what this means?" He looked over at her and tears of laughter were spilling down his cheeks.

She could only manage to shake her head.

"It means I'm the Duke of Invermark." He let out a howl of laughter. "Me, right now! Fergus's biggest disappointment—well, aside from my father."

"He's already buried?" How wretched that he hadn't wanted his heir, or any of his grandsons, to attend his funeral. She hadn't liked the man very much the few times she'd crossed paths with him, and wasn't really that surprised he had done this. But now was not the time to be sharing those thoughts.

In fact, she didn't know *what* to do. Now the subject of marriage was all but forgotten with this news. They weren't married, and he had just been dealt a devastating blow. How could she now tell Victor, *You know, I actually changed my mind and think we should get married?*

It would look like she had greedily changed her mind at the opportunity to become a duchess if she expressed a sudden change of heart right after Victor had learned he was a freshly minted duke. And who knew, now that his dreaded future was here, he might change his mind about having an heir and would need to marry someone who could provide children. Because she wouldn't go through that again.

"That." Victor pointed at the two letters now on the table. "All of that. It's a lark. Don't you think?"

"No, I really don't."

He grinned widely and laughed again. "Well, I suppose you'll be leaving, then. Marjory has requested a visit from me, so I guess I should go."

"Will you come back to Brighton after that?" Anne asked this, but she already knew the answer.

"How could I?" He laughed again. "But isn't it brilliant that everything my grandfather gave me in regard to the estate is in Brighton? More luck for me!"

Anne swallowed. "We will be sure to send everything back since you cannot fetch it."

Victor waved her off. The laughter, the mad humor, immediately fell away from him like he had tumbled over the edge of a cliff. Victor gripped the back of a chair, leaned into it, and dropped his head.

He stood that way for a long moment and Anne carefully, cautiously, stepped over to him. She placed a gentle hand on his arm. "Victor." She didn't know what else to say.

Victor took in a deep, shuddering breath and tilted his head over to her. His eyes were red, and it looked like he was crying.

He collapsed to his knees and wrapped his arms around her waist, buried his face into her stomach, like he had done before. And he sobbed.

She ran her fingers through his hair, hoping to comfort him. "I know you weren't expecting this, but I promise everything will be fine." She hesitated. Was this a good time to bring up that she had changed her mind about getting married? It didn't seem like it, but at the same time, she needed to tell him. And soon. But would he take her seriously? That was the question.

Victor quieted and took in one last deep breath, pressed his face against her one more time, then clambered up to his feet. He sniffed. "No, I don't think it will." His head flew up to look at something behind her and he paled. "Mary."

Anne spun around and found her daughter at the dining room door, hugging herself.

"Mary!" Anne tried to sound cheerful. "How long have you been standing there?"

The young woman looked so small and frightened in the moment. "About ten minutes."

She had seen the whole thing.

Victor rubbed a hand over his mouth and put his attention back down to Anne. His usual calmness seemed to be returning, though his face remained tense with grief. "Take my carriage to the train station. I'll find my own way to visit Marjory."

"Look, Victor—"

"No." He closed his eyes and shook his head. "Please, just get away from me."

Anne swallowed back her argument. There was nothing

more to say. They weren't married and may never be now.

And it was physically painful. It felt as if her insides were being split apart. She wanted to run after him, pound on his chest, and tell him he was stupid and wrong and she did love him and did want to marry him.

But that would only make everything worse, not better.

She couldn't make it better. He wouldn't believe her if she tried.

Victor walked away from her and paused at Mary. To Anne's surprise, Mary was crying too. "Uncle Victor…" she said in a soft voice.

"I'm sorry," he replied. He left the room.

It took a moment for Anne to gather herself. Out in the hallway, Victor was nowhere to be seen. And there was nothing they could do but leave him behind.

ON THEIR RIDE to the train station, Mary kept quiet. She wouldn't look Anne in the eye and seemed to want nothing to do with her, staring out the carriage window as if the view were endlessly fascinating.

"Mary, what's wrong?"

Mary didn't respond at first, but finally, she spun her head to Anne. "You are so stupid!"

Anne gasped loudly. "How *dare* you speak to me that way?"

"You are!" Mary cried out. Tears began to slide down her cheeks. "You're so worried about me falling for some cad—"

Anne was not having this. "Which you did!"

"You act as if being male equates to being evil, to the point you are incapable of recognizing a good and decent man when he's staring you in the face! You just chased one off. Like I said, *stupid!*"

Anne's mouth hung open.

Mary choked out a sob. "And now, Uncle Victor's gone forever and wants nothing to do with us, because of *you*! What am I going to do now? What is Freddy going to do? *We* didn't want him to leave!"

"I'm sorry," Anne said, her already soul-crushing despair even worse.

"Do you ever consider *us*?"

"I consider you for *everything*! You come before me, always!"

Mary slumped back into her seat with a pout, but the angry air that seemed to surround them felt as if it were easing. "I'm sorry. I just… We always thought you two would get married one day. Not just me and Freddy, but *everyone*! It never even occurred to me that you might not. He was always there, Mama. Always."

Anne sighed. "We haven't been seeing eye to eye on that."

Mary straightened, as if feeling hopeful. "What does that mean?"

Anne studied her daughter. She had always shielded Mary from the difficulties of life as best she could, a protective measure after being married to Bernard, she would guess. But what had that done? It had ended up with Mary trying to elope in Gretna Green.

"It means," Anne said, choosing her words carefully, "he and I have discussed it before. But at the time, I didn't like the idea of marriage. A second one, I mean."

"Why not?"

Anne took in a slow inhale. "Your father and I did not marry for love, and our marriage reflected that." She closed her eyes. "I don't wish to speak ill of him to you, so I will leave it at that."

Mary tilted her head and scoffed. "Mama, we were *there*. Maybe we didn't see everything, but we, or at least I, saw enough. Papa hated you."

The rawness of those words, coming from the daughter she'd tried so hard to protect, stabbed her straight into the heart.

Mary must have realized this because she covered her mouth.

"I'm sorry. I shouldn't have said that so bluntly."

"No." Anne swallowed. "No, you're right. He did hate me. I got in the way of everything he wanted." She gave her daughter a small smile. "Any man who puts you aside for any reason—be it excluding you from a conversation or an important decision, not standing up for you to family or friends, or simply ignoring your worries or difficult feelings—is not a man you want in your life."

Mary nodded and her face was so stern, Anne thought the young woman might actually have been taking note of this.

"Uncle Victor isn't like that, though." Mary paused. "Right?"

"No. He isn't. And when I realized that, I thought maybe being married to him wouldn't be so bad. And then the letter from the solicitor came to clarify everything."

Mary shook her head. "What are you talking about, 'clarify everything'? Clarify what?"

Anne stilled and frowned at herself. "Did I not tell you what happened in Gretna Green?"

"You mean beside chasing after me?" Mary had the good sense to look sheepish.

There had been so much chaos over the last twenty-four hours, Anne realized she had yet to tell Mary about getting caught up in a wedding ceremony with Victor. She told her daughter the story briefly.

"Wait." Mary's back straightened and her eyes went wider and wider as the story sunk in. *"You're married?"*

Anne vehemently shook her head. "No. The solicitor said that if I didn't consent, then the marriage was null and void."

"I was going to say, you're so against elopement, but then you and Uncle Victor go off and elope in Gretna Green yourself!"

Anne pressed her mouth together tightly. Her daughter had a point and she didn't like it much, either. "Maybe don't refer to him as 'Uncle Victor' anymore under the circumstances."

Mary's eyebrows lifted as she nodded, but then she tilted her head in a study of Anne. "Are you sure the solicitor said *if?*"

"Yes." Anne frowned. "Why?"

"And you are totally sure that Victor wanted to be married to you? He said this out loud?"

Anne's eyebrows followed her frown. What was Mary trying to say? "Yes, he said it a few times, in fact. At least, until he got that letter about his grandfather's passing and told me to go away, basically. You saw his reaction." Anne had worried about how Victor would react to the duke's future death and now that she had witnessed it, she'd been right to worry. He had gone mad from it. But what did surprise her was how much she wanted to be with Victor now. She wanted to help him and comfort him, not stay away in fear, like she had expected she would.

Mary pressed her nose to the window. "Do you happen to know where this solicitor is located?"

"I believe the envelope said King Street. Why?"

Mary began to rapidly knock on the ceiling of the carriage, as if there were an emergency. The carriage immediately pulled off to the side and the driver flung the door open, revealing the tall, skinny man with gray eyes. "Is everything all right?"

"We need to go to King Street. Immediately," Mary said.

The driver looked at Anne. "What's this about? I thought you were going to the train station?"

Anne stammered as it washed over her what Mary was trying to do. The solicitor said *if* in the letter. If. That meant…

"She's right." Anne gripped her seat as her nerves screamed with impatience. "We need to go to King Street instead."

Mary squealed and bounced in her seat as the driver mumbled to himself and shut the door.

It felt like forever before the carriage rounded St. James Square to finally turn down King Street. King Street was a small street of three blocks—they should have no problem finding their destination.

Anne and Mary peered out either side of the window, studying the signs that flew by. "I don't remember the exact address. All I remember was his name was quite strange and Peabody was part of it." Anne's breathing fogged up part of the window and she wiped it off with the side of a fist.

"'Odd name with Peabody in it,'" Mary repeated as she searched out her own window.

The first block resulted in nothing. Anne hoped they hadn't accidentally missed it and would have to round back. The second block was the same, no luck.

Then, just as they started passing by the third block, Anne spotted it. Hanging above a door and over the sidewalk was a wooden sign hand painted with "Peabody Hickinbottom, Solicitor at Your Service."

Anne knocked on the ceiling to let the driver know they had found their destination. Within seconds, he was helping them disembark, informing them he would wait for them around the corner on St. James's Street.

"There it is." Anne pointed to the sign above. "Let's go."

Mary giggled at the name and followed her mother inside the old, Georgian-style building.

The room was small, with two wooden chairs against the wall near the window—a little waiting area. There was also a small desk beside a closed door, a young man with a loosened bowtie and collar seated at it with his nose deep in some kind of tome. The office was nearly boiling from the summer heat.

The young man looked up upon their entrance. "Do you have an appointment?" he asked.

"No." Anne introduced herself and briefly explained her purpose in being there. "I really just need a minute of Mr. Hickenbottom's time, nothing more."

The man gave a tight-lipped nod. "One moment," he said as he stood up and went to the door by his desk. He knocked lightly on it and poked his head in the room. Anne could hear the murmuring of voices, but not what they said.

After a moment, the young man pulled his head out of the door and opened it fully in invitation.

Anne hurried forward, Mary trailing behind.

The back room was a much larger office than the front room,

with floor-to-ceiling windows on the left side and dark, oak-wood paneling around the walls. Behind the solicitor's desk were bookshelves filled with what Anne assumed were law-related books and papers.

The solicitor was a small man with gray hair and a gray mustache. He flew to his feet and hurried over to Anne. "Lady Litchfield." A bit too exuberant, he shook her hand harder than necessary. "This is, quite honestly, a great surprise. Would you like to sit?" He indicated to a chair.

"No, thank you. I really wish to make this brief. Mr. McNab received your letter this morning and in it, you said if I was not a willing party in the marriage in Gretna Green, then the marriage didn't happen."

"That's correct."

Her heart raced with anticipation. "What if I came here to tell you I do consent to it?"

The man's mouth opened with surprise. "Oh, well, then that makes it quite simple. If you are telling me that you did, in fact, consent to the marriage, then congratulations are in order, I believe."

Anne's racing heart turned into a gallop. She still had a chance to back out. She also had the chance to move forward. Anne had one chance to make a decision that would forever alter the rest of her life. The decision *she* wanted. She could choose what would happen next. Not her parents, not Bernard, not Victor, not society, not the solicitor, nor the man at the anvil hurrying through a ceremony to get to the next couple and their coin.

"Mama," Mary whispered at her side. "What do you say? Are you willing to be married to Un—I mean, Mr. McNab?"

Anne opened her mouth to respond. But before she could, Mr. Hickenbottom's door opened again.

And in walked Victor himself.

Chapter Thirty-Two

A s Mr. Hickenbottom's clerk shut the door behind him, Victor stilled upon seeing Anne and Mary standing in his solicitor's office, with Mr. Hickenbottom himself.

"What in the blazes are you doing here?" he asked with utter shock. Anne and Mary should have been well along on their way to Brighton by now. Instead, Mary held clasped hands at her cheek and kept darting glances between himself and her mother.

Anne, meanwhile, kept fidgeting her hands together.

Admittedly, he was feeling quite fidgety himself. He was so tired. So worn. He had just come from a brief visit with his grandmother and his grandfather's solicitor. It had all been very business-like. Marjory hadn't had much to say except that she had already moved into the London dower residence and didn't want him to or expect him to visit. She'd had no apologies to share with him, no words of regret over their treatment of him as a boy. No explanation of why his grandfather hadn't wanted anyone—not even his peers—to know of his death until he'd been buried. The man had hated fuss, so Victor had decided to blame it on that.

Between her wails, Marjory and the solicitor had simply laid out what properties Victor had to manage now that he was the Duke of Invermark, and had given him the contact information for those currently managing the properties. Then he'd left. And, not knowing what to do with himself, he'd come here to tell his own solicitor what had transpired.

But, really, why was Anne here meeting with *his* solicitor?

Mr. Hickenbottom gave Anne a brief smile and hurried over to shake Victor's hand. "Mr. McNab! Another pleasant surprise. Are you here for the same reason your wife is?"

Victor narrowed his eyes at the man. "What did you just say?"

Anne let out a nervous laugh. "Victor, what are you doing here?"

"My grandfather is *dead*. That's what I'm doing here." His unexpected grief over his grandfather's death, plus mourning the loss of Anne in his life, had made him snippier than he normally wished to be. It physically hurt to be seeing her so soon after he'd told her they could never be in each other's lives again. His heart ached from it.

It felt as if something had been ripped from his body when she'd left, and he was quite certain she'd taken his heart with her. Upon this thought, he finally met her eyes with his own. He stared, though he didn't blink, and the emotions roiling inside him seemed to intensify with her presence.

Anne stared up at him with her gentle, pale eyes. Her cheeks were rosy, and her lips perfectly pink. This was why he couldn't be around her any longer. Even amongst the storm that surrounded him, he wanted to claim her, he wanted that mouth of hers in the most loving, and most sinful, of ways.

Upon the news of the former duke's death, Mr. Hickenbottom let out a very loud gasp, breaking Victor's spell, then hurriedly bowed to Victor. "Your Grace."

Victor groaned and rubbed the bridge of his nose. He hated the sound of that. But there was nothing he could do about it, either. It was his life, his reality, his present and future. "I've just visited with my grandmother and my grandfather's solicitor. I wanted to stop by and figure out… I don't even know, what this means for my business, I suppose. You've been my solicitor for a long time now."

Mr. Hickenbottom gave a polite nod.

"Do we continue working together?" Victor felt completely lost. "Frankly, I've been left in the dust by my grandparents and I'm picking up the pieces."

"I understand," Mr. Hickenbottom said with a slight bow. "Like you said, I've been your solicitor for a long time. I know your business inside and out. Does this other fellow know your business?"

Victor frowned. "No."

Mr. Hickenbottom closed his eyes and placed a hand over his heart. "Then it's settled. I remain your solicitor."

Victor looked the man over. "Can I do that? Have you represent everything related to The Harp & Thistle as normal, and the other one deal with everything related to the ducal estate?"

Mr. Hickenbottom pulled back. "Of course! Many people of your station have even more than two solicitors for various reasons. You can have as many as you need or wish."

Victor found his eyes trailing back to Anne and stared at her. Blast it all, she was beautiful. He could spend hours, days, simply studying and drawing her. He wondered what she would think about being drawn in the nude. He would enjoy studying the hidden parts of her he had never been fortunate enough to see before.

He rubbed his hands over his face. What in the blazes was wrong with him? He'd told her to leave his life. Why was he thinking about *drawing her nude*? He needed help. Maybe he would see a physician next. Clearly, he had some kind of brain disease.

Mr. Hickenbottom clapped his hands together. "The reason your wife is here is because—"

"Why do you keep calling her that?" Victor's voice ground in frustration. Anne wasn't his wife, and she never would be—she had made that quite clear! And the solicitor had seemed to understand that in his response this morning. Why the change?

"That's why I'm here, Victor," Anne said gently. She took a few steps toward him and placed a hesitant hand to his arm. He didn't pull away, though he knew he should have. He couldn't help it, though. He was weak in every possible way when it came to Anne. "In Mr. Hickenbottom's letter this morning," she continued, "he said the marriage was null if I didn't consent to it. So I came to tell him I *did* consent to it. I was a willing party."

Victor's eyes anchored to hers. Joy shone from her gaze. "What are you saying?" he asked, not believing his ears for a moment.

"I'm saying, we are, in fact, married." She smiled widely, her beautiful eyes smiling with it.

"We're married?" Victor said, still not believing it. "You're my wife?"

"Yes, and you are my husband."

Victor faltered back.

Mary's voice sounded. "Mama, is he going to be all right?"

"Yes, darling, he's simply in shock. It will wear off."

Victor had begun to pace the room. But it felt like he was floating. It wasn't a bad feeling, as if he were about to be ill.

He was…elated.

After the news sunk in just enough for him to believe it, he returned to his senses. His wife was right there, what in the blazes was he doing? There she was, the only woman he had ever loved, the only woman he had ever wanted. Anne. Lady Litchfield. Now, the Duchess of Invermark.

It had a nice ring to it.

"But you were so steadfast against this," he whispered. "Why did you change your mind?"

She met his whisper. "I kept telling myself I was afraid of marriage because it would be like being married to Bernard again. But you aren't like Bernard and never will be. It took losing you to get me to admit that to myself."

Victor closed the distance between them, wrapped his arms around his wife's waist, and pulled her close, winning a gasp in response. Smiling, he angled his head down to hers and kissed her with joy, with relief, with maddening love. She was the light in his life, the sunshine that broke through the clouds. Just her being *his wife* made everything seem better somehow.

Anne ran her fingers through his hair and kissed him back, giggled, then pulled away. "Victor," she whispered. "We have an audience."

"Right." He cleared his throat and stepped back. "Sorry."

Mary giggled and then hurried over to her mother and the two began whispering excitedly together.

While they did that, Victor went over to his solicitor. First things first—his wife and new marriage. "I'll be heading back to Brighton. I'm not sure when I'll be back just yet."

"Very well, Your Grace."

"Keer will still be your contact unless you need me specifically for some reason."

Mr. Hickenbottom glanced at Anne then leaned forward. "Go be with your new wife, Your Grace. Everything will still be here whenever you come back."

IT HAD BEEN more than twelve hours since Victor had learned Anne had consented to being married to him. Upon their return to Summerwood, they shared the news of what had happened. Not just the chaos Mary had caused, but also the death of Fergus. Most surprising to all, though, was Victor and Anne had married, plus *how* they'd been married.

The family's reactions were understandably varied. It was a lot at once and some people, like Ollie and Freddy, were angry. Ollie shoved Victor and said, "You made a big fuss over not being at my wedding and here you are getting married at Gretna Green too? Without me there, either?" And even though Ollie hadn't been particularly fond of their grandparents, they had been a key part of his life. He was struggling with not being told about the death, and not being invited to the funeral.

Dantes acted as if he didn't care about any of it, but Victor knew he did. He also knew there was no use in talking to the gruff man about it. Vivian would do that and would be a far better listener. Thank God for wives.

The Duke of Chalworth was surprised, if anything, and told Victor to prepare to double down on ducal lessons because that was what they would be doing all day every day for the rest of the summer. Victor pretended to act like this was a big sacrifice, but he was infinitely grateful for the Duke of Chalworth. Especially as the older man felt that it was, in fact, possible to run a dukedom and a pub.

"It's merely like having one additional property, on top of the several others. You'll simply have to rely on Dantes and Keer more, like you rely on property and estate managers," the duke helpfully said.

Perhaps Keer was due for an even better promotion.

Like the elder duke, Vivian and Evelyn were surprised as well, but Victor didn't witness their full reaction to the news, as they were with Anne and Mary most of the day, while the men reeled together in the parlor.

The hardest part to Victor was breaking the news to Freddy. Anne had talked to him privately for a good hour and the poor lad had emerged so confused. He'd yelled and cried but hugged them with happiness too. He'd then gone to the stables, where Victor had followed and the two had spent a portion of the afternoon racing along the beach. It seemed to help immensely, as the boy had finally smiled when he'd won his fourth, and the final, race.

"One day, I'll be a duke too," Freddy had said while walking back to the house from the stables. "Will you help me then like my grandfather is helping you?"

"Of course." Victor tried to ignore the pride that swelled in his heart.

"What do I call you now?" Freddy stopped, forcing Victor to stop walking as well. "Who are you to me?"

Victor shoved his hands in his pockets. He recalled the heart-to-heart conversation he and Freddy had had earlier in the summer. Though they had experienced two very different childhoods, they'd both shared the loss of a parent, of a father. "What do you want me to be?"

Freddy considered this. "I don't know. You're not my father."

Victor stayed quiet, letting the boy talk through it.

"But you're not just a friend, either. You are my mother's new husband. But you were there a lot while I was growing up, too. If I'd been younger, I would have called you 'Pops,' but I think I am too old to do that now. I guess, I will simply call you 'Victor' when I don't have to call you 'Your Grace.'" Freddy made a face. "That sounds so odd."

Victor chuckled. "I'm having a hard time getting used to it."

Freddy smiled up at him, but the smile fell away and his dark-blue eyes, so much like his father's, hardened. "I don't ever want to see my mother cry because of you."

"I'm sure she will get mad at me from time to time, but I will do everything I can to ensure I never make her cry."

Freddy's jaw was tight and he nodded once. "Good."

And that was that.

Now, it was far into night. Victor was standing at the door separating his bedroom from Anne's, his heart pounding hard. He opened the unlocked door, knowing the most stunning woman he had ever known was on the other side waiting for him.

Anne sat at her vanity, wearing a silk house coat, her long, blonde hair trailing down her back. And she was looking down at something.

Victor went over to her and after hesitating like he would have just days ago—this marriage business would take some getting used to—he began to rub her back. "What is that?" he asked, looking down at a list laid out on the vanity.

Anne looked up at him and smiled. "Oh, you'll think it quite silly." She handed the piece of paper to him.

It was a list titled *A Lady's Rules for Seaside Romance.*

Victor furrowed his brow as he read through it. He then chuckled to himself as he realized it was her list of requirements in a man. They made sense, and he could see those that had been inspired by her first husband.

He reached the one about gambling and pointed to it. "For your information, I almost never lose."

She looked up at him with one cocked eyebrow. "You almost never lose? Are you sure you don't mean you almost never win? That's what the odds usually are."

"Apparently not when you're related to a seal."

Anne pulled back. "What?"

He chuckled, remembering his grandfather's claim they had magical blood. "Never mind. I have the records to prove it, whenever you are inclined to see them. I win money far more often than I lose it, the opposite of Winthrop."

"Hmm," Anne responded, but she seemed to believe him. "Perhaps you can still reconsider it because I still don't like gambling, even if you do win more than lose."

He tried not to grin. "If you feel that strongly about it, then so be it, although I have a friend who might not be so pleased with that. In fact, I should introduce you. I think he would be happy to meet you finally." Victor put his attention back on the list and got to the last rule. *Never fall in love.* This rule was underlined multiple times, boxed, and circled—and there were angry, jagged arrows pointing at it. He raised his eyebrows at her.

She blushed prettily. "These are rules I made for myself to find a decent companion for the summer. As you can see, I was quite stubborn about not falling in love, not realizing I already had."

Victor crouched by her side. He looked up to her and could see the nervousness in her pale-blue eyes. He probably reflected a similar hesitant look himself. There was no doubt they loved each other. But they both had reasons to be frightened. She only knew marriage by the way Winthrop had treated her. And he was terrified of being responsible for another person. And now there would be risk of pregnancies, something they both were hesitant about. "We haven't had much of a chance to talk, just the two of us, about what this marriage entails."

Anne swallowed and averted her gaze to her hands. "No, we haven't."

What was the best way to go about this? Victor's eye's landed on the paper. "Do you have a pen I could use?"

Anne gave a small nod and reached into one of drawers to reveal a fountain pen. She handed it over to him.

Victor turned over Anne's rules to the blank back. "I have one question for you first. The subject of children." He couldn't look her in the eye as he said this. Fear coursed through him.

Anne cleared her throat. "There are ways to prevent it, but like you said, nothing is guaranteed. There will always be that risk."

"Is that…something you want?" He dared a look up at her.

And her eyes became enormous. "Do I want more children? Heavens no! My God, Victor—I mean…" She hurried along. "If that's something you want, then I suppose we could discuss it. You'll need an heir, but—"

"No," he whispered. "No, it is not something I want in this lifetime. Dantes, any sons he may have, Ollie and his eldest— what I mean is, there are enough males in the family that we don't need to concern ourselves with that if we don't wish to. And I'm perfectly happy with that, too."

Anne's shoulders fell. "Thank heavens. Oh, Victor, I'm not a mother who enjoyed pregnancy, and childbirth is horrific. I'm getting to be too old for it, and I don't ever want to go through that again if I don't have to."

"You don't have to."

Anne put her hand over her heart. "Thank you. I've been worrying about that all day. But what if something happens?"

"Then we worry about it then." He placed a hand over hers.

"And only then. But we will face it, together. That, I can promise you."

Anne nodded again, tears welling in her eyes. After pressing a soft hand to his rough cheek, she leaned down and kissed him. Oh, the way sparks exploded all over his body! And he realized, this was the first time he and his wife had been able to kiss each other the way they wanted to. Victor straightened himself higher on his knees and wrapped his arms around her waist. She wore nothing beneath her silk robe. Underneath it, she was soft, supple—he had never felt need like this before in his life.

He turned his head to fit their mouths together better and swept his tongue over hers, moving it languidly, the way he imagined their bodies would move together soon. But first, he had to do something.

He pulled back and they were both panting. And after hesitating first, he ran a hand up her leg, over her hip, the dip of her waist, and the round side of her breast. The feel of her, of Anne— his wife—her body in his hand was nearly sending him over the edge.

"Were you telling me the truth that you've never been with a woman before?" Her voice was husky.

Victor nearly groaned with embarrassment. "Yes. Utterly humiliating."

"Why?" she nearly shouted back. "I wouldn't love you any less either way, but after everything Bernard put me through? I don't know. It makes me happy in a way, I guess. Special. As if that part of you was always meant for me."

"You *are* special. And I'm glad it makes you happy." Victor realized that, at least for the time being, Anne would secretly be comparing their marriage to her marriage with Winthrop. There was nothing Victor would be able to do about that. But, he did have an idea that might allay her fears at least a bit.

He put his attention back on the fountain pen and began to write on the blank side of paper.

A Gentleman's Promises for Marriage:
Never chase other women.
Kiss you often and well.
Always be hygienic.
Politics are a lark, anyway.
Laugh more, or attempt to.
No more horse races, or any other gambling.
Never become a drunk.
Never lay an angry hand on you.
Treat Mary and Freddy as if my own.
Love you until the end of time.

Victor signed his name at the bottom. "These are my promises to you, Anne, my love. And we can always add more, if you ever feel the need to."

ANNE FOUGHT BACK the hot sting of tears in her eyes as she read the list of promises he'd given to her. Point by point, they upheld the rules she had made. He even added a few of his own that he knew would make her feel more confident in him. She placed a hand over her heart. "I don't know what to say other than *thank you*. And *I love you*. But those words don't do justice to how much this means to me."

Victor gave her a crooked smile, and, oh, how handsome he looked! How had she ended up with such a loving, beautiful husband? She reached out to run her fingers through his black hair, then down over the black beard. His green eyes watched her with that intensity they always held, and it caused a fire to spark inside of her. As she held his gaze, she touched his face, his hair. The hardness of his shoulders, the planes and valleys of his torso. Her fingers unbuttoned the shirt he wore and he allowed her to part it and run her fingers through the thick mass of hair upon his body. His skin was hot, and his hard muscles flexed beneath her touch.

Victor's eyelids became heavy. His eyes became shadowed with lust-filled darkness.

She rose to her feet and knew the way the silk of her house-coat shone and slid over her body with the movement. Victor watched it all with a clenched jaw. "Anne..." He trailed off.

"Come now, husband." Anne took his hand in hers, causing him to stand. Slowly, she walked backward toward the bed, pulling him along with her. She smiled up at him coyly. "I have much to teach you tonight, and we shouldn't delay any further."

Victor's eyes darkened into wickedness and there was a bit of wildness to them that caused her breath to catch.

"In that case..." He picked her up into his arms, causing her to giggle. "Let's move a bit quicker than that." As he crossed the room with her cradled safely against him, she stared up at him, still in shock that this was now her life. Victor was her husband, he would never leave her life, and he would love her until the end of time.

When they'd reached the bed, Victor tossed her upon it and jumped in after her, causing them both to laugh louder than they had in a very long time.

Epilogue

London, April 1901

ANNE AND VICTOR waited at the back of the church with the rest of the family. All of the guests had already arrived—it felt as if there were a thousand people in attendance—and all who remained back here were those closest to Anne.

Although Freddy was already up near the altar with the rest of the groomsmen.

Vivian stood beside Dantes, who held their sweet girl, Lily. The little girl's eyes were growing heavy as she rested her head against her father's shoulder. Lily was growing like a weed and had the McNab green eyes and the dark, wavy hair of the Winthrops. But she would not be able to rest on this important day, for soon she would be throwing out white rose petals down the aisle.

Evelyn and Ollie, and their twins, Theodore and Simon, were off to the side for a private moment. The twins were now ten and even more full of mischief, if that were possible. Only moments ago, Ollie had realized the boys had stuffed frogs in their pockets to release during the ceremony. Presumably they'd thought they could follow Lily and her flower petals. Ollie had, thankfully, released the innocent animals outside and he and Evelyn were giving the boys a stern reminder that a wedding was *not* a place for frogs. The boys bowed their heads, as expected of them, but from where Anne stood, she could see them exchange mischievous smiles out of view of their parents.

The Duke of Chalworth, meanwhile, was with Victor and talked low to the younger duke. Anne couldn't hear what was said but suspected the elder gentleman was giving Victor tips on walking down the aisle without fainting. At least, that was the wisdom she would impart to a man about to walk a bride down the aisle to hand over to her soon-to-be husband.

Anne, her heart pounding hard on this special day, turned to Mary, who was quite literally the most beautiful bride Anne had ever seen in her life. Naturally, the young woman had chosen a dress from the House of Worth. Mary had had two requirements: it had to be bobbin lace from head to toe, and it had to have a longer train than anyone else getting married that year.

The fashion house had been happy to oblige for one of their best clients. Now, Mary stood before Anne in the handmade, cream, lace gown. The body of the dress beneath the lace was cream silk, but the full-length sleeves had no lining and were just a bit sheer over Mary's arms. The train was currently rolled up safely to be unfurled in only a few minutes by the bridesmaids, and the white veil hung long and down along the ground as well.

"Mary, you look utterly beautiful today," Anne said, her eyes misty. And knowing this day was special to her daughter, she had to say something kind about her father. After Anne and Victor's marriage, the family had made a point to open up about their feelings of Bernard. And while Freddy had nothing good to say about his late father, Mary had come to admit that even though she knew how her father could be, a part of her still missed him.

"Bernard would be so proud of you today if he were here to see what a lovely woman you've grown to be," Anne said to the young bride.

Mary gave a small smile and looked down at the ground. "Do you think?"

"Oh, yes, I know. And I'm sure he's watching right now."

Mary nodded and glanced at Victor, still talking with the elder duke. She lowered her voice. "Victor is terrified."

Anne had to cover her mouth to keep from laughing. "I know. He was up late last night practicing walking a straight line without tripping."

Mary rolled her eyes. "He's not going to trip."

"That's what I keep telling him," Anne replied. The two women exchanged a small giggle.

"I'm glad Victor likes Jack," Mary continued. "I think Jack being an American actually endeared him a bit more to Victor."

"I think so, too," Anne said in agreement. Over the past year, a multitude of men had set their eyes upon Mary. Thankfully, the near-elopement had never gotten out, and Mr. Ashby happily remained in America, or so his mother said. Anne and Mrs. Ashby had become friends after the incident, as their sons remained the best of friends. The attention Mary received from her debut, though, nearly rivaled the attention Vivian had received when she'd become London's richest heiress years ago.

Naturally, Victor had hated it.

The unending visits. The continuous balls. Making sure Mary followed the rules, which felt like a constant task. Mary had fallen for Jack nearly from the beginning. He had come to England with the hopes of marrying a woman of influence to elevate himself amongst wealthy Americans and he'd just happened to fall hard and quick for Mary. Several men had ended up asking for Mary's hand. Victor had sat with each of them for two hours in private, asking them questions that, he had explained to Anne, seemed innocent but would reveal if the man was a gentleman or a scoundrel.

Jack McCaig was the only one of whom Victor had approved, and Victor believed it was because of Jack's roots. Jack was an American, thus he wasn't from a family with aristocratic blood. Arrogance and pretentiousness did not fit the man's demeanor— in fact, he seemed to be perpetually in nervous awe of everything around him, especially Mary. His family had Irish heritage but had been across the pond for a few generations. They lived in a state called Montana and were quite wealthy, wealthier than most of the nobs, as Jack had helpfully pointed out to Victor. Apparently, the McCaigs had one of the biggest, most lucrative ranches found in the western half of America. But it was true—the man's family was American rich, not English rich. Unlike English nobs, the man could buy the moon if he so desired.

"So, you'll be here in England for six months, and then Montana after that?" Anne asked.

Mary nodded. "We'll go back and forth. Don't worry, Mama, you'll still see me plenty. You'll be so busy as a duchess when I'm gone, though, you will hardly notice."

"Oh, I'll notice," Anne said. "But I'm glad you've found Jack. I don't think there was a better man created for you."

Mary gave her a huge, sparkling smile. "No, I don't think there is, either. Do you think I'll like living out West, Mama?"

Anne fussed over Mary's dress to buy her time to respond. "I think it will be a very big adjustment. But they have endless open space, and as many horses as you could ever want. It will be very different from what you are used to, but I think your free spirit will feel right at home."

At these words, Mary hugged Anne tightly and sniffed. "Thank you."

Vivian appeared at Anne's side. "Anne, it's time."

Anne nodded and gave her daughter one last kiss on her cheek as Lady Mary Winthrop. For in just a few minutes, she would be Lady Mary McCaig.

The family, save for Victor and Mary, went in and took their seats in the pews at the front. Anne gave a small wave to Freddy, who stood with Jack and smiled back.

Jack, suntanned and handsome in his dark wedding suit, had his eyes planted on the door closed at the back of the church. Anne was sure nothing could pull him away from looking for his bride.

The quartet began playing and the doors at the back opened. The guests gasped as Mary appeared and began to walk down the aisle. Mary smiled widely, her eyes on Jack up ahead, his eyes on hers. Victor walked tall and proud with Mary on his arm. He looked at nothing else except straight ahead. But when he passed Anne, he met her eye for a brief moment. He gave her a quick, teary smile. As they reached the front, he handed Mary over to Jack, then sat with Anne.

Neither of them said anything. But Victor took her hand in his and didn't let go the entire ceremony.

Hours later, after the party of a century, Anne and Victor lay in bed together. Anne was snuggled up against him and his arm was wrapped protectively around her.

"She'll be happy with Jack," Anne said, her head resting upon Victor's bare chest.

"Yes, she will." Victor's voice rumbled in his chest.

"They will always be happy."

"I think so."

Anne closed her eyes and took solace in the hot feeling of Victor's body against her cheek. She could hear his heart beating and let the lull of it calm the last remaining nerves from the big day.

"Everyone is happy now," Victor said after a moment. "And I think that's all I've ever wanted."

Anne lifted her head up to see her husband's face. "Yes, everyone is happy. Even you."

"Very happy. Out of my mind with it, I should say." He gave her a crooked smile before kissing her. As he began to move his mouth down her neck and over her collarbone, and she knew exactly where the trail of his mouth would end, she let out a contented sigh.

Yes.

She was as happy as a woman could possibly be.

About the Author

Born and raised in Chicago to an artist family, Arden Conroy grew up attending museums and played piano and cello for fifteen years. When she isn't writing or reading, Arden enjoys historical fashion, art history, and historical dramas and comedies. She has lived all over the United States from the Hudson Valley, NY to Tulsa, OK. Currently, she resides between Chicago and Pennsylvania with her husband and two children.

Website – www.ardenconroy.com
Facebook – facebook.com/profile.php?id=100083677291622

www.ingramcontent.com/pod-product-compliance
Lightning Source LLC
Chambersburg PA
CBHW071229300726
48975CB00002B/347